LISTEN TO YOUR HEART

Watching Aaron walk across the yard, Colette realized with a pang that her attachment to him had grown far too strong. It was one thing to favor a man's company, quite another to feel your heartbeat quicken whenever he was near.

This is not good, she thought to herself. She should put the brakes on. Tamp down the emotion. A woman her age couldn't be acting like a teenaged girl on rumspringa, her heart running wild.

But as she headed to the shed, she didn't want to let go of the joy that sparked within her at the thought of Aaron being nearby. Was it so wrong to enjoy that feeling? What was the harm in savoring the sweet emotions that Gott placed in her heart?

Books by Rosalind Lauer

AN AMISH HOMECOMING

AN AMISH BRIDE

THE LOVE OF A GOOD AMISH WOMAN

AN AMISH CHRISTMAS STAR
(with Shelley Shepard Gray and Charlotte Hubbard)

Published by Kensington Publishing Corp.

The Love of a Good Amish Woman

ROSALIND LAUER

ZEBRA BOOKS
KENSINGTON PUBLISHING CORP.
www.kensingbbooks.com

First Printing: January 2023
ISBN-13: 978-1-4201-5213-5
ISBN-13: 978-1-4201-5216-6 (eBook)

10 9 8 7 6 5 4 3 2 1

Printed in the United States of America

Chapter 1

As Miriam sliced into a plump, red tomato from the garden, she let the hum of the busy kitchen wash over her like a beautiful song. On this golden August evening when the warm air smelled of honeysuckle and freshly mowed grass, some of Miriam's family and friends had assembled at their farm home to celebrate two birthdays. Few things delighted Miriam more than having the people she loved gathered around her dinner table.

Happy voices filled the house and yard. The heat of the day and the earlier baking seemed to be trapped in a soggy cloud of humidity, right here in this kitchen, and yet a half-dozen females were gathered in the warm space. Funny how a kitchen was always a magnet to girls and women.

Miriam fanned the disks of dark red tomato over a platter and started slicing another as conversation flowed around her. These dark red gems were ripening in the garden faster than the family could eat them, inspiring Miriam to add a side dish. Tomato sandwiches! Who didn't love fresh baked bread, mayonnaise, and a sweet, juicy tomato?

Everyone else was outside, enjoying the breeze of the evening. The children had already occupied the picnic tables in a first seating, as there were so many to feed tonight. Not just Miriam and Alvin and their seven offspring, but also daughter Essie's husband, Harlan Yoder, his mother, Collette, and sister Suzie. There were the Englisch girls, Miriam's teenaged nieces, who'd lost their mother far too young and had arrived here from Philadelphia a year ago. And no family celebration was complete without Alvin's mother, Esther, and the family of Alvin's brother Lloyd and sister-in-law Greta, who ran another branch of the Lapp Dairy just down the road a piece.

The "surprise" addition to the guest list had been Aaron Troyer, the bishop of their church, along with his teenaged daughters, Tess and Amy.

"So the bishop is coming to the birthday dinner?" Alvin had asked earlier in the week as Miriam sat at the kitchen table making a list of the groceries she would need to feed two dozen or so people.

"Yah, along with his daughters," Miriam had answered. Understanding her husband's hesitation before he said another word, she'd added, "I know, it's a bit intimidating to have the bishop so near at hand, but if you can respectfully put aside his role as our leader, he's simply a man who needs our help. We need to step up, Alvie. We always have plenty of food and good will to spare. Last week at church I heard that his mother is going for surgery soon. Nothing too serious, but she'll need to be off her feet for a few weeks, and you know Dinah has been cooking and cleaning in Aaron's house since Dorcas passed. More than two years now. It's a lot for an older woman to manage."

"I'd say a home is a lot for any woman to manage," he'd said, reaching back to fish an oatmeal cookie out of the jar on the counter.

"That's true. It's so good you see that." How she loved her Alvin! So quick to imagine what it might be like to walk in someone else's shoes. "Anyway, heaven knows when Dinah will be back on her feet. Apparently, she's been pressuring Aaron to get a housekeeper, but he's reluctant to hire someone. And I get that, with the girls at such tender ages. What if they didn't get along? It might cook up a stew of misery. So the church women, we're getting organized to pitch in and feed the family when we can. A casserole here, along with the occasional dinner invitation. It's the least we can do."

"It is, indeed." As she'd been speaking, Alvin had remained a captive audience, leaning against the kitchen counter as he polished off the cookie. "I'll be happy to have the Troyer family at our table."

"Ach, Alvie, I knew you'd be on board. Think of what that family's gone through since Dorcas died. The girls lost their mother, and Aaron had to go on with his church duties without his wife at his side. It breaks my heart at the sorrow they endured."

"Such a big heart you have." He brushed the crumbs from his hands and placed a hand on her shoulder, his fingertips stroking the back of her neck. Even after two decades of marriage, she still felt a tingling sensation at his touch, that sweet mixture of passion and comfort that they brought each other.

"'And do not forget to do good and share with others,'" Miriam said, covering Alvin's hand with hers. "That's in the Bible. The book of Hebrews, I think." She'd never been the student of Gott's word that her mother desired, but somehow, Gott's message lived in her heart.

"A good lesson to us all." He'd placed a soulful kiss on her forehead as Peter and Paul had bounded into the kitchen in search of something to drink.

"We're going to grill those ribs that your brother gave us, and Essie and I will bake," she had said, looking back at her list. "Essie loves mixed berry pie, and Collette's favorite is German chocolate cake. We've got to cater to our birthday girls!"

"Sounds delicious," he said, moving aside so that the boys could get plastic tumblers from the shelf. "I'm happy to open our home to the bishop's family, but something tells me there's more to this. A bit of matchmaking up your sleeve?"

"Oh, you." She waved him off. "Who's got the time for all that?"

"You, my dear wife. You're a bundle of energy."

She let her fingers flicker at him again, smiling down at her list because she didn't have the nerve to look him in the eye and confess.

He'd been right. He'd hit the nail kerplunk on the head.

Miriam had a plan, an idea that made her giddy with joy. How she loved bringing people together! Not to meddle in anyone's business, but to make sure that other folks had a clear path to having love in their lives. And when she had an opportunity to play matchmaker, nothing could stand in her way.

Now Miriam arranged the last slices of tomato on the platter and swiped the back of her hand over the perspiration on her brow.

Over at the table, daughter Essie was giving her young sister-in-law, Suzie, a lesson on the slicing of fresh-baked bread. Since Essie's marriage to Harlan Yoder last December, Essie had taken Harlan's only sister under her wing, teaching her some homemaking skills and chatting her up to boost the shy girl's conversation skills. Like a tender sprout reaching toward the sky, sixteen-year-old Suzie was gaining strength and a more solid footing after a difficult spell. The buggy accident many months ago had nearly crippled Suzie's mother and left Suzie with a long scar on her face. Poor thing, so self-conscious. Honestly, Miriam barely noticed the thin, pink crease on Suzie's face, but she understood that some scars reached deep inside, marking wounds of the soul. Thankfully, Suzie had some support. It was truly a blessing that Essie and Harlan's marriage had placed Essie in the Yoder family at a time when Suzie needed a young woman she could confide in.

What a difference from this time last year! Back then, their celebration of Essie's eighteenth birthday had been interrupted when Miriam's brother-in-law had arrived from Philadelphia with a surprising request—that she and Alvin care for his three teenaged daughters who were acting out beyond his control.

So much had changed in one year. Megan, Serena, and Grace Sullivan had adjusted to life on an Amish farm, and in the process, the Englisch girls had worked their way into everyone's hearts. Truly a blessing that Gott had brought them here. At the end of the summer, Megan would be heading off to college. College! Sending a young person off to study was a wonder that Miriam had never expected to experience as an Amish woman, but in the Englisch world many young people continued their education into later years.

Over at the sink, twelve-year-old Lizzie refilled the water pitcher as she talked with Grace and Sadie, the lovely young woman who would soon be Miriam's daughter-in-law. Their topic? The wedding, of course. Not everyone enjoyed a wedding day, with the long ceremony of exchanging sacred vows, and the even longer day of festivities. 'Twas a lot of work, even for the hardy. But what woman didn't love to talk of weddings and marriage and love? It was a joyous topic at frolics and sewing bees. Nothing warmed a girl's heart more than the prospect of a couple finding love, joy, and a happy home together.

"And do you have any brothers to invite?" Grace asked Sadie.

"No, it's just us three girls," answered Sadie.

"Don't worry about that," said Lizzie. "When you marry Sam, you'll get Paul and Peter as brothers. You know what they're like."

"They're the ones who are usually running around in a cloud of dust," said Grace Sullivan, the youngest of the Englisch girls who'd moved in last year. "Those guys have one speed—and that's go."

Sadie laughed. "They're busy bees, all right."

Miriam nodded to herself as she considered Sadie's level response. Having spent much of her childhood at this farm, Sadie knew all about the twins. She'd helped Essie mind them when they were toddlers. But Sadie was humble enough not to boast to Grace. Smart girl—and considerate. She would make the perfect wife for Sam.

"All right, girls. I'm definitely ready for some delicious dinner," Miriam said as she wiped her hands on a towel. "Come out as soon as you're ready." Holding the platter high, she led the way out, sighing as the gentle breeze whispered relief over her damp skin. Still chattering, the other girls followed, bearing trays and pitchers.

Outside, it was a relief to step from the warm wooden porch and feel the coolness of the grass on her bare feet. Miriam wriggled her toes, thanking Gott for the pleasure of summer. Nearly everyone at the gathering was barefoot, as was the custom this time of year in Lancaster County. Only Miriam's Englisch nieces tended to wear sandals or flip-flops, which they needed since the soles of their feet hadn't been toughened up by a lifetime on the farm.

The women had cleared off the dining tables from the first sitting, as most of the children had already scattered off to play on the lawn. The sliced bread and tomatoes were delivered to the table beside a platter of smoky barbecued ribs that Greta and Esther had just removed from the grill. The smoky scent made Miriam's mouth water.

"Batch number two! Come and get it," Miriam called, standing back as folks assembled in a casual line and began to fill their plates. Miriam stood back, hands on her hips, as she eyed the feast, complete with pickled beets, celery, and radishes from the garden, Mammi Esther's potato salad, and deviled eggs from Greta. Delicious summer blessings.

"You can't catch me!" Pete called to his twin brother as he ran across the lawn faster than a jackrabbit and bounded toward the tables.

"Easy, Pete," Miriam warned as he brushed past her.

Following in close pursuit, Paul circled Miriam and launched a water balloon, which missed his brother but burst open as it landed on the patio near Alvin's feet.

"Boys . . ." Alvin's voice was stern but patient. "I admit, that was cool and refreshing, but keep it on the lawn while people are eating."

Just then Mammi Esther came up behind Pete and clamped her arms around him. It made Miriam grin, seeing the diminutive older woman clinging to the thirteen-year-old boy whose recent growth spurt made him a head taller than his grandmother.

"My boy," she said quietly, her mouth near his ear. "Do you have another water balloon?"

"Yah, Mammi."

"Let me see."

He reached into his half-open shirt and held up a roly-poly lime-green balloon filled with water.

"Let me show you what happens when you let your game spill over to the family meal." Esther deftly pulled a straight pin from the edge of her apron, held it up to show everyone, and popped the tip into the balloon in Peter's hands.

"Mammi, no!" Peter exclaimed as the balloon burst and water squirted over his shirt and hands.

Laughter resounded through the yard as Peter belly-ached a bit, and then joined in the laughs. "You're supposed to be on my side," he told his grandmother.

"I'm always on your side," she said, ruffling the brown hair that hung over his forehead. "That's why I take the time to teach you a thing or two. Now, what do you say?"

"Sorry, Mammi. We'll keep the games over on the lawn." He reached into his shirt and removed a yellow water balloon. "At least I have a few left for when I find Paul."

"Over there, by the trees," Miriam said, shooing her son away. "We'll call you when it's time for dessert."

Peter took off running as the second seating found places at the tables. The younger adults—couples and teens alike—congregated at the table closer to the flower garden, while Miriam's peer group chose the table near the back porch. Miriam was glad to see the older teens going out of their way to make Aaron's daughters feel at home. Once seated at the tables, everyone bowed their heads for the silent prayer to thank Gott for this wonderful meal. The silence was cut by a sudden cry—a pathetic little bleat that resembled a startled lamb. Over in her playpen, Greta and Lloyd's youngest was howling, as if right on cue to interrupt her mother's meal. Miriam smiled at the beautiful noise. Nothing made a woman feel needed quite like a baby's cry!

Miriam motioned to Greta to stay put and went to the baby. "What's the matter? What is it, little pumpkin?" She cradled little Nora in one arm and pushed her downy hair off her forehead. "Did you think you were forgotten? We could never forget you. Auntie Miriam has you now."

The infant squirmed, staring at Miriam with a pouty face. "Come. Sit at the table with the grown-ups. It's a special occasion."

The baby nuzzled her face into Miriam's shoulder, warming her heart. With her youngest child about to start school next month, Miriam had spent a few years without an infant in the house, and sometimes she did miss having a baby on her hip. She returned to her place at the table and, cradling Nora with one arm, proceeded to eat a spare rib with the other hand.

"I'll take her," Greta offered.

"Nay, I'm savoring a bit of baby time," Miriam insisted. "Besides, eating with only hand may be the new diet trick I've been seeking."

That brought a few chuckles from the women at the table, while the men wisely focused on eating.

As folks ate and chatted, Lizzie filled glasses from the water pitcher, and then took a seat in an empty spot near her grandmother, Esther. Twelve-year-old Lizzie had chosen to eat with the older folk today, and Miriam was pleased by her daughter's consideration and maturity. The girl had a special fondness for her grandmother, Alvin's mother, and it was clear from Esther Lapp's tenderness toward the girl that the feeling was mutual.

When talk turned back to the wedding plans of Sam and Sadie, Miriam decided to share her recent news. "I just got a letter from my mother in Michigan," she announced. "She and Dat will be here for Sam and Sadie's wedding in the fall."

"Is that right?" Alvin looked up from his tomato sandwich. "Lois and David are going to make the trip from Michigan?"

"Yay!" Lizzie exclaimed. "We haven't seen them for so long!"

Despite her own reservations about seeing her mother, Miriam had known that Lizzie would be thrilled. "Your grandmother was a little shocked to receive a 'save the date' announcement," she added. "Mem wrote that she hoped it was all right with the church leaders."

A few heads turned toward Bishop Aaron, who paused with a forkful of potato salad held aloft over his plate. "There's been no objection to those early notices," he said. "The traditional way of keeping a wedding secret until the announcement had its purpose. But with wedding season being so busy, an early announcement seems to be the only way that families can manage to coordinate their calendars and travel to the big event. And it's good to bring the family together, isn't it?"

Murmurs of agreement came from most everyone at the table.

"I understand Lois's surprise," said Mammi Esther. "In my day, when a couple planned to marry, it was a closely held secret until the announcement was made in church." She sighed. "Times have changed."

"Do you think the old way was better?" asked Lizzie. "Sadie and Sam could have kept it a secret."

Miriam looked over at Sam, who rolled his eyes at the idea that he and his bride-to-be could have kept the news under wraps any longer. After circumstances had kept them apart for months, Sadie and Sam wanted first and foremost to be together.

"That's a good question, Lizzie." Esther shrugged. "You get used to tradition, but sometimes there's a good reason to change."

"We do love our traditions," Miriam agreed. "Porch sitting on a lazy Sunday afternoon. Frolics and quilting bees. Birthday gatherings like this . . ."

"Christmas morning," Lizzie said with the delight of a girl who still has one foot in childhood.

Miriam smiled at her daughter. "I'm grateful for traditions that bring us together. But sometimes, I think it's good to look at things from the other side of the fence and be open to making a change."

"Just what I was saying," Esther agreed. "We're never too old to try new things."

New things . . .

Was that the topic Miriam needed to transition to her suggestion for Collette and the bishop? Somehow, there seemed to be too many people around to go there. No, not now. She simply couldn't spring the plan with all these folks in the conversation.

Miriam cast a subtle glance down the table to where Bishop Aaron was seated across from Collette Yoder, who'd recently joined the Lapp family. *My fellow mother-in-law,* Miriam thought. Over the past year, in the wake of Collette's injury in a buggy crash, Miriam had gotten to know her new friend on a different level. The poor woman had suffered an injury and months of rehabilitation, she'd been uprooted from her home, and she'd learned of her estranged husband's death, all in a matter of months. Through it all, through thick and thin, as they say, Miriam had tried to be a good friend to Collette. What an inspiration it had been to see Collette work her way back to good health.

The baby gurgled and raised a small fist to capture one of the strings of Miriam's kapp. "Well, look at you. Got a handful?" Miriam teased.

"I'll take her, Mem." Suddenly Essie was at her side, leaning down to take the baby. "I'm finished, and you haven't touched your sandwich."

"Denki," Miriam said, smiling up at her eldest daughter.

"Come here, sweetheart!" Essie said, her caramel eyes alight with love as she took her little cousin into her arms.

For a brief moment, Miriam saw herself more than twenty years ago, a young Amish woman so in love with her husband and ready to start a family. As Essie cradled the baby, Miriam noticed something different about her daughter. Was that a new fullness in her face? Was there possibly, oh, please Gott, a baby on the way?

The wondrous notion left Miriam speechless as she watched Essie move off with the baby. She was so wrapped up in thought, she didn't notice Lizzie and Grace hurry over.

"Mem, Grace and I are so excited about the news!" Lizzie exclaimed. "I was trying to explain Mammi Lois to Grace, and we figured out that she's Grace's grandmother, too, right?"

"Yes, she is. Lois and David are your mother's parents." Why hadn't Miriam made this connection on her own? "This will be your first chance to meet your Amish grandparents."

"Yay for that." Grace's eyes were wide and glowing. "I've always wanted to meet them. Finally, someone who can tell me more about my mom." Of the three Sullivan girls, Grace was the most curious about her mother's background. She was always asking about Sarah's childhood years growing up in an Amish home.

"I'm sure our mem has stories of Sarah," Miriam said, forcing herself to smile at her niece. Although Miriam had shared many childhood memories of her older sister with Grace, sometimes the act of digging around in the past made her heart ache. She chalked it up to tender feelings for her sister Sarah, who had died of cancer a few years ago, but the truth was a bit more complicated. There had been some tumultuous episodes at home when teenaged Sarah told her parents she was leaving Joyful River to "see the real world." Miriam felt it was her duty to protect her niece from those difficult memories, but of course, she would never tell a lie.

"I'm so psyched to meet them," Grace said. "Especially my grandma. I can't wait to hear her stories about Mom."

Trouble ahead. Miriam wasn't quite sure how to navigate the situation, but she had a month or so to figure out a plan. "I think your Amish grandmother is making a point of attending the wedding so that she can meet you and your sisters," Miriam told Grace. That much was true.

"When did you say Mammi and Dawdi are coming?" Lizzie asked.

"Sometime in September. Remember, the wedding is the last Wednesday in September, and they'll want to arrive at least a few days before that." Miriam took a bite of her sandwich, hoping to veer away from the topic. As she chewed, she noticed that most everyone else had finished eating and plates were being cleared. "Time to get back to my hostess duties," she told the girls, picking up her plates.

"We'll help," Grace offered.

"Can we put the candles on the cake?" Lizzie asked. "That's one of my favorite things."

"That would be a huge help," Miriam said. "Come. It's time for one of my favorite things—dessert!"

Chapter 2

Seeking to fetch the dessert dish she'd prepared from the fridge of the Dawdi House, Collette Yoder had left the celebration and ventured down the short path to the small cottage that had been her home for many months now. The fresh air and quiet were a balm for her nerves, which could get a bit frazzled after spending time around so many people—and a certain person. What a contrast the big, sprawling Lapp family was to Collette's own compact family. For so many years, it had been just her and the two children.

She walked down the lane with careful, measured steps—as she'd practiced during hours of physical therapy—until the two-bedroom cottage came into view. On Amish farms the Dawdi House was normally reserved for the elderly couple that had retired from the family business. Here at the Lapp farm, Mervin Lapp had passed years ago, and his wife, Esther, now felt more comfortable living down the road with her son Lloyd and his young family. Esther had offered the use of the place to Collette during the end of her recuperation, when she'd been unable to manage stairs but eager to reunite with her family. Since then, the cozy little house had been a godsend for Collette and her children. There'd been a slight worry of crowding when Essie had moved in after her marriage to Harlan, but it had been a blessing having Harlan's bride in the little house. After a few months of close interactions and conversation, Collette looked upon Essie as a second daughter.

As Collette opened the cottage door and stepped in, she felt the comfort of the small space that was her home. These walls had provided a cozy, safe place for their family to live, but she knew it couldn't last much longer. Sooner than later, Harlan and Essie would need this space for their growing family. Time to think of other living arrangements for herself and Suzie.

Collette removed the strawberry dessert from the fridge and nudged the door closed with her left foot. Such a feat for a woman who'd been in a wheelchair not long ago! She chuckled softly, enjoying the achievement. In the past year she'd learned that you had to find joy in these moments when they came along.

Time to head back to the dinner gathering. After years spent as a single parent, conversation, stories and laughter were a welcome social treat. It would all have been so gay and easy if it wasn't for the powerful, wise man sitting nearby, commanding her attention and making it hard to take a deep breath.

Bishop Aaron.

He was a tall man with broad shoulders that gave him a big presence, one that commanded respect from men and women alike. A handsome man, with thick salt-and-pepper hair and beard, and eyes as blue and glimmering as the river in summer. Even a prudent woman like Collette could see how it would be easy to fall for a man like Aaron Troyer. It was even easier to lose your heart when he showered kindness upon you.

"Call me Aaron," he'd said months ago when he'd visited

her in the care facility as part of his duties as a church leader.

"I'm not sure I can do that," Collette had said, pulling a knitted quilt to cover herself in the hospital bed. Although she'd been clothed, her hair pinned up and covered with a prayer kapp, it seemed wrong to meet with a man, especially a church leader, while in bed. "We were much more formal in the Swartzentruber settlement where I grew up."

"In New York. Is that right?"

She'd felt pleased that he'd cared enough to learn something about her. "That was my home. Where I met my husband."

The glimmer in his eyes as he'd nodded had been nothing short of heavenly, and she'd felt sure that Gott had indeed chosen this wonderful man to do His will in the town of Joyful River. And what an enormous blessing that Gott's will had brought Aaron to her meager bedside.

Although she had thought the visits would trail off, that the glow she felt in his presence would fade, Aaron had remained a steady supporter.

And the spark of attraction crackled every time he was near. She suspected that the feeling was one-sided, and simply thanked Gott for adding a bit of excitement to her life now and again. In any case, she wasn't ready for a relationship in her life. With one child still under her wing, she was saving money for a place of their own. Although she'd needed to leave her job at the pretzel factory, which had kept her on her feet all day, she'd recently found parttime work as a housekeeper for Len and Linda Hostetler's family, and for all those blessings she was grateful.

Gratitude.

Collette Yoder felt it in the waning sunlight, the smell of warm clover and honeysuckle as she walked the expanse of lawn on her way back from the Dawdi House, the gurgle of laughter from the group gathered 'round the wooden picnic table like old friends. Gratitude was set deep in her bones, but moments like this amplified it, like ripples traveling the surface of a pond.

Her greatest blessings came from what had seemed like the most devastating tragedy of her life—the buggy accident last fall that had left her bedridden with a broken leg. During those darkest hours, she had learned to work through the pain. But it had been the loss of income, the loss of her home, and the loss of stability for her family, that had made her feel like a broken woman.

Fear had weighed heavily on her in those days, clouding her vision of the future. How could she go on? How to take care of Harlan and Suzie and herself? The church charity fund sustained them for a while, but she could not lean on community generosity indefinitely. She'd seen no choice but to abandon the community she loved, tear her children away from Joyful River, and travel back to New York to beg care from her mother and brothers. She could only imagine the ordeal she'd have to go through to ask forgiveness and acceptance in the conservative Swartzentruber Amish community.

So many years ago, Jed had led her away from their stern ways, and with good reason. The strict rules of the conservative Amish community had made for a bleak childhood. Her childhood memories were marked by cold winter days, hunger pangs, and hard work around the house from sunup to sundown. As a child, she had believed there was nothing to look forward to in her life. Their community had been suspicious of medical care from the Englisch, and so Collette and her siblings had suffered through a range of childhood maladies. One winter, her little sister Hester did not make it through the night. Scarlet fever, they said, though no doctor ever treated the poor little girl. Collette had tried to tell herself Hester was the lucky one; she no longer had to rake the muck, feed the chickens, and wash clothes in icy cold water against the washboard that scraped her frozen fingers. For years, a bitterness festered inside her over the way her parents had let Hester die without helping her.

"We need to get away from here. There are better places," Jed had insisted as they came in from working the alfalfa fields one hot summer evening. "One day, we'll escape."

Indeed, they had gotten away. And so many years later the notion of returning had made her wince for her sake and for the future of her children. Life in New York would be bleak, but what choice did she have?

Planning had been underway. They would leave as soon as her doctors permitted her to travel. Then, one afternoon, everything had changed. Harlan and Essie had found a place for them to live. "There's a way we can stay, Mem," Harlan had said, a light in his eyes. "So many people are working to make it happen."

Indeed, the good folks of Joyful River had answered her needs in every way. Many church members had joined in to help Collette and her family, but none had offered as much as the Lapps. In the months since Collette, Harlan, and Suzie had moved onto the Lapp property, Miriam had given Collette all the space that she needed, while providing daily meals during the early days. To this day, Collette couldn't help but smile when she saw a Tupperware container labelled "Miriam Lapp" in Sharpie marker. So many soups and casseroles that had brightened her cold winter days.

Yah, she was grateful for the love and support of her community, grateful to Gott in heaven for blessing her in her time of need. She braced the chilled platter against one arm as she stepped around a stone jutting out of the grass.

Since the accident, she'd learned to identify possible tripping hazards, as it wouldn't do to reinjure her leg. Suzie had offered to fetch the Jell-O mold—a delicious strawberry, sour cream, and Cool Whip concoction that they'd put together earlier—but Collette had wanted the brief respite to clear her head.

It wasn't easy being in such close proximity to a man who made her pulse race, and she worried that folks around them might notice her response.

As she emerged from the shady cover of a canopy of trees, Miriam called to her from one of the outdoor tables, which had been reset with desserts and a fresh stack of paper plates. Collette found a spot for the Jello-O mold, which glimmered ruby red as it wobbled into place.

"That looks delicious! You're back in the nick of time." Miriam smiled up at her. "The children are eager to light the candles and sing happy birthday."

"It's been a long time since I've blown out candles." Girlish delight bubbled up inside her at the prospect. "But I won't hold up the important part—eating cake!"

"And it's bound to be a good one. German chocolate. I told Essie it wasn't necessary to bake in this heat, but she insisted." Miriam turned toward the lawn and waved at the children, who were engaged in various activities, from a game of tag to a Frisbee toss. "Time for happy birthday!" she hollered. "Where's my Essie? There you are!"

Miriam scooted two lawn chairs over to the head of the table and insisted that Collette and Essie sit side by side as the others gathered 'round. Matches sparked to life in Esther's capable hands, and the older woman nimbly reached in to light the candles on Collette's cake and Essie's berry pie.

Essie and Miriam had gone to so much trouble. Everyone here had done so many turns of good will toward Collette and her family over the past year. Dozens of small points of light dotted the air before Collette's eyes as the candles were lit.

Collette searched the faces for her little family. Just beyond the halo of light, she spied her daughter, Suzie, that sad but hopeful look caught in her blue eyes as she held one hand cupping her cheek to cover the scar. Off to the other side stood her oldest, Harlan. With hands on hips, he looked like the strapping man he'd become. It was no surprise that his gaze was locked on Essie, the strong young woman who was quickly mastering the challenges of being an Amish wife.

As folks began to sing the birthday song, Collette reached over and clasped her daughter-in-law's hands. "I'm so glad to be your birthday buddy," she confided in a whisper.

Essie smiled and squeezed her hand tenderly.

This is happiness, Collette thought. Floating in a cloud of joy, surrounded by people who wished her the best. Who knew she could find such contentment at the age of thirty-nine? It was true that you appreciated a sunrise more after a stormy night.

Collette helped serve the desserts, cutting the chocolate cake into small slivers. "Such a beautiful cake," she said. "We need to be sure everyone can have a taste."

With the pies, cookies, and Jell-O dish, there was plenty of everything to go around, and Miriam circled 'round a few times, making sure everyone got their fill. Collette was talking with Greta Lapp, who was carefully trying to eat pie over the infant in her lap, when Greta's husband, Lloyd, interrupted them.

"Greta, is there any more of that Jell-O left?" Lloyd asked. "The bishop and I wanted to try it."

"I'll go see," Collette offered. At the dessert table she found that her Jell-O creation was more than half-gone.

She doled two reasonable portions onto paper plates, found plastic spoons, and brought them back to the men.

"Here you go." Collette handed the plates to the men. "Suzie and I made it this morning, and it's got strawberries, sour cream, and whipped cream in the layers."

"It reminds me of a dish my grandmother used to make," said Aaron. Something glimmered in his blue eyes as he smiled up at her. A certain peace, that inner spark of inspiration and rock-solid faith that made Aaron Troyer stand out from all the other men in their community. That spark in the bishop's eyes touched Collette in a personal way, making her feel as if the light there shined for her and her alone.

Was it silly to think that? Those same eyes gazed upon everyone else in their church community—the children and the old folks and the young people in between. A fact was a fact. And yet, she allowed herself this indulgence, thinking that Aaron saw something special when he looked at her.

Savoring a spoonful, Lloyd declared it delicious.

Collette nodded, preparing to back away. Already she'd exchanged more than the usual conversation with the men, who usually sat off on their own during these gatherings, their beards wagging as they talked away.

"It brings me back to summers when I was a boy," Aaron said. "As soon as my mother is back on her feet, she'll be asking for your recipe."

"How is Dinah?" she asked.

"She'll be glad to have this surgery over and done. The doctors delayed it a few times due to swelling, but at last, she's staying off her feet."

"Give her my best," she said. As she turned and walked away, her pulse seemed to beat so loud in her ears that she was sure folks could hear it over in Plumdale. That man put her senses on alert like a rabbit hearing a rustle in the woods, and no amount of trying seemed to keep her nerves calm. She tried to tell herself it was a matter of respect, that she held their bishop in high esteem and feared doing something to offend him.

But that spark of serenity in his blue eyes told her time and again that this was not a man to fear. She poured herself a cup of water and returned to her seat beside Greta, taking her turn at holding the baby and lolling the rest of the evening away with these good Amish women.

Chapter 3

The Amish sure loved a party.

In the past year that she'd lived on this Amish farm, Grace Sullivan had seen countless get-togethers. Picnics with dozens of people. Dinners with "just family" that included more than twenty people. Frolics and bees that brought in buggies of Amish women to sew quilts or cook down giant vats of berries or tomatoes or green beans to store in jars. And who could forget Essie and Harlan's wedding when hundreds of people had gathered on this farm for the big celebration.

Having grown up in Philadelphia, Grace had seen plenty of crowds. Though being one of the few non-Amish people in a group of fifty did make her feel like an oddball at times.

But tonight was cool. She knew everyone here, and though her sisters were off chatting and playing Frisbee with the Amish kids their age, Grace was comfortable hanging on the fringes of the party with her friend Suzie, Harlan's sister, who lived on the property in the little cottage everyone called the Dawdi House. Though Grace had two friends at school—studious, quiet girls who seemed content to eat lunch with Grace and text occasionally—she was getting used to spending most of her time with Amish

kids her age, her cousins and their friends who had grown
up here in Joyful River.

Grace moved around the edge of the patio to avoid
passing the tables of grown-ups, who chattered on through
the after-dinner lull. She landed at the dessert table, grabbed
three plates of German chocolate cake—which took some
juggling—and then headed back to where Suzie sat with
cousin Lizzie.

Grace wasn't sure why, but twelve-year-old Lizzie
looked up to her. Maybe it was because Grace was a serious
student, and bookish, smart Lizzie admired that in her.
When Grace was here on the farm, it seemed that Lizzie
was always nearby, her shadow. Most people might find
that annoying, but Grace found it comforting. A sidekick is
a good thing when you're afraid to be alone.

"Denki!" The girls thanked Grace when she delivered
the slices of cake. The three of them were situated in a
patch of grass that backed up to a white fence. As they ate
and chatted, Grace noticed the way Suzie sat, her body
angled so that her left side faced the fence. That was her
way of keeping the scar on her face out of view.

The red line on her cheek—the result of a cut that had
required stitches and special glue to close the wound—
wasn't too pronounced, but it really bothered Suzie.

"I can feel people staring at it," she'd told Grace the one
time they'd talked about it.

And Grace had understood. Every day she felt people
staring at her nose ring or her colorful tinted hair. It was a
weird feeling for sure, but Grace tried to use her piercing
and hair tint as a shield, a sort of body armor. She figured
that those distractions kept people from trying to stare deep
inside her, trying to see things she wasn't ready to share.
So she understood Suzie.

"I can't wait for Sam and Sadie's wedding next month,"

Lizzie said as she set her empty plate aside. "Weddings are more fun than Christmas!"

"If you like having hundreds of folks descend on your house," said Suzie. She exchanged a pointed look with Grace, who shared her discomfort with the large crowds that an Amish wedding attracted.

All three girls remembered Harlan and Essie's big wedding last December. Grace hadn't attended the actual ceremony, which was more of an Amish insider thing in a language she didn't speak. But the celebration afterward had been an all-day affair that included two big meals with plenty of desserts and snacks, games and sports. Even ice skating. Sure, there'd been some fun moments. But the day's events had stretched on like an endless rope of taffy.

"But the good news is that Mammi Lois is coming from Michigan," Grace said. "I finally get to meet my grandmother."

"That will be nice," Suzie said sweetly.

"Are you close to your grandmother?" Grace asked Suzie. It seemed to Grace that Amish folk had extended family all over these hills and valleys.

"Not so much," Suzie admitted. "Really, not at all. My dat and mem grew up among the Swartzentrubers in New York."

Grace squinted. "What's that?"

"It's an Amish community, but very strict," explained Suzie. "I've never been there, but Mem says it was a hard life. Everything was black and gray, she says, but talking about it makes her sad, so I don't ask questions anymore. I think her family was very poor, so food was scarce and the winters were cold. My parents didn't dare go back, so I don't know my grandparents or cousins."

"That's sad," Grace said.

"You don't miss what you never had." Suzie shrugged.

"I always had a good family with Mem and Harlan. Three peas in a pod."

"Like the three of us!" Lizzie exclaimed, slipping her arms over their shoulders for a hug.

Unable to resist her young cousin's enthusiasm, Grace smiled and hugged her back.

"You guys are the best," Grace said, and was rewarded by the light in Suzie's eyes.

"But Grace has a special reason why she wants to meet Mammi Lois. Right, Grace?" Lizzie prodded.

"Yup. I'm hoping she can tell me more about my mother." The search for Sarah Stuckey, an Amish girl who had left Lancaster County as a teenager, had become an obsession for Grace. "When my mom died, I realized there was a lot I didn't know about her. Like, what was she like as a girl, and why did she leave Joyful River?"

Grace had been barely a teenager when her mother died, and she couldn't shake the feeling that she'd barely gotten a chance to know her mother. She'd started asking around, questioning anyone who had known her mother. Unfortunately, there weren't many people who had deep knowledge of a teenaged girl who had left the Amish community some twenty years ago.

"But my mem told you all about her," Lizzie said. "And they were sisters. She knew her well."

"I know but . . ." Grace let her voice trail off, not wanting to admit the truth. "Aunt Miriam tried to answer my questions, but I think she's kind of uncomfortable talking about her sister."

"I think Mem misses her," Lizzie said, and both Amish girls nodded sympathetically.

Grace shrugged, not wanting to disagree by pointing out the obvious. Her mother, Sarah, had left the Amish, which, as far as Grace could tell, was not something people approved of. No one wanted to talk about someone who'd abandoned them. Not that anyone had said that, but a distinctive awkwardness crackled in the air when she mentioned her mother's name to Amish old folks.

But it would be different with her grandmother. Grace imagined that the older woman would hold a treasure trove of information about her daughter Sarah.

She couldn't wait to hear some stories about her mom. Stories that would help her feel a connection that she worried was fading as time went on.

As they were talking, an Amish girl emerged from the group of teens on the lawn and started walking their way with a tentative look.

"Tess!" Suzie waved her over with a bright smile. "Come, talk with us!"

"Who's Tess?" asked Grace as the girl headed their way.

"One of the bishop's daughters," Lizzie said.

Grace nodded, recognizing the girl as one of the added guests for tonight's dinner.

With a round face and thick lips that seemed to be in a pout, Tess moved confidently, though her big blue eyes revealed the hesitance that plagued so many girls in their early teens.

"Why don't you come play volleyball with us?" Tess asked, pausing over them with folded arms. "We need more girls on our team."

"Maybe later," Suzie said, raising an arm to Tess. "Come, sit with us."

Tess joined them on the grass and immediately squinted at Grace. "You're one of the girls from Philly."

"Grace Sullivan."

"Miriam's nieces," Tess said, staring at Grace as if she were a rare breed of horse.

"Yup." Grace shifted in the grass, then met the girl's gaze, standing her ground. "What's wrong?"

"Your hair is such a strange color," Tess said, fizzling away the tension. "I've never seen hair like that."

Grace lifted her chin and steeled herself. "It's dyed."

"Green like a field of clover," Tess declared. "I love it."

In that moment, Grace instantly liked this girl.

"The dye comes in a package," Lizzie said. "I helped her do it. It goes on like a dark green pudding. But it doesn't smell like pudding." Grinning, she held her nose. "It's sour and stinky."

"The smell washes away," Grace said, tossing a dandelion head at her cousin.

Tess leaned down to touch Grace's hair, stroking in a gentle way that made Grace's scalp tingle. "Did it hurt?"

"Nope. But you need to keep the dye away from your eyes and skin," Grace explained.

"How long has it been green?" Tess asked.

"Just since June. I like to change it every few months."

"It was pink when she moved here last summer," Lizzie explained. "Pink as strawberry ice cream!"

Grace smiled, enjoying Lizzie's enthusiasm on the topic.

"Colorful hair, and a gold ring in your nose." Tess nodded. "I've never met anyone like you. Amazing Grace, like the song."

The girls chuckled at the joke.

"And her mother had pink hair, too!" Lizzie exclaimed.

"She did." Grace nodded, thinking back to that first time they had both colored their hair together, bright pink, for breast cancer awareness. "It was actually my mom's idea, something we did together," Grace said. "We both had boring hair. Not brown and not blond. So my mom took me to a salon and said that we needed to have more exciting hair. We both walked out with hot pink hair."

"My mother would never do that," Suzie attested.

Tess shook her head. "Never. When your father is a bishop, you can't step out of line."

Grace nodded. "I get that. But do you ever want to do something a little different? Something that breaks the rules? Take a step out of the box?"

Suzie, Lizzie, and Tess exchanged a confused look, then said "No" in unison.

"But I love your green hair," Tess insisted. "It suits you well."

"Thanks." Grace nodded, trying to absorb the conversation. These girls were really happy with the status quo, or at least they thought they were. She picked another clover, wondering if she'd ever be that content.

Maybe. But every person had to find their own path. And Grace was convinced that there would be lots of twists and turns in her journey.

She was too much of a rebel to accept a nice, straight path.

And that, she concluded, was the little bit of the restless spirt of Sarah Stuckey inside her.

Chapter 4

At the end of the gathering, when Collette went across the yard to thank Miriam for the wonderful meal, she spoke slowly, acutely aware that Aaron was seated on the nearby garden bench, talking with Alvin Lapp.

"It was a fun evening, wasn't it?" Miriam said. "I do love bringing folks together, and there's nothing like the summer for an outdoor dinner. Did you like the cake?"

"It was . . . delicious," Collette said, trying not to stare as the two men rose from the bench. From this close, she was reminded of Aaron's height—so tall—with a solid build. She'd had her eyes on him every other week at church, but during those gatherings she forced herself to keep her mind chaste and focus on the sermon and prayers.

"I'll gather the girls and head out," Aaron told Miriam. "But I'm grateful you included us tonight. Good food and better company. Denki." He looked from Miriam to Collette as he said this last piece.

His words melted something inside Collette, but she told herself that he was just being kind. Nothing personal. Besides, they'd barely talked tonight, unlike the times when he'd visited her during the healing months, when they'd spent long afternoons discussing everything from the weather to the difficulties of raising children alone.

"Good night, then," Aaron said.

"No, wait!" Miriam's hands went up, as if she were trying to stop a charging bull. "If you two have a minute, I had an idea I wanted to run by you."

You two? Collette squinted. Did that include her? Not quite sure, she waited.

The bishop turned his straw hat in his hands. "There's always time under Gott's heaven. What's on your mind, Miriam?"

"That would be my first question," Alvin said, raking his hair out of his eyes with a look of concern. "What's up, my dear?"

"Don't worry, Alvie." Touching her husband's shoulder, Miriam confided in Collette and Aaron. "Sometimes my plans make him nervous. But I'm always trying to think of ways to help folks, and I think you two could very well help each other."

Collette couldn't summon a response at the notion of helping the bishop. It was too strange and wonderful and unbelievable.

But Aaron mustered the question. "How so?"

"I've been thinking about your mother and her much-needed surgery. Dinah is worried about you and the girls having no one to look after you."

Aaron's eyebrows drew together as he shook his head. "She does worry, but I told her we'll manage. I'm grateful for the hospitality of folks like yourselves, but it's time for the girls to learn how to run a house. They need to know how to cook and clean on their own."

"Such important skills for our girls to learn," Miriam agreed. "But these things take some time, and you can hardly expect Amy and Tess to keep the household going without any instruction. That's why I thought of Collette. She's been raising two of her own, she's a fine cook, and she's quite handy with needle and thread—a skill that I've never quite mastered."

"It's too much to ask of anyone to fill in for Dinah," Aaron said. "Collette, I know you have a job working for Len and Linda Hostetler."

"That's just two days a week," Miriam said. "Which leaves three full days that Collette could do housekeeping for you. Not as a charity, though I'm sure you'll be getting plenty of meals from the womenfolk. This would be a part-time job for Collette. A perfect arrangement, as she's been looking for work to replace her job at the pretzel factory."

Aaron pressed his hat to his chest and turned to Collette. "Is that so?" he asked her. "Are you looking for more work?"

"Yah, it's true," Collette admitted, forcing the words that seemed to be stuck in her throat. Even if she'd shared Miriam's gift for gab, she couldn't have summarized her situation much better. Collette needed the work. She needed money for food and future rent. And the bishop needed help around the house.

Such a simple equation. At least it seemed simple until she factored in the way her heart swelled whenever Aaron Troyer was nearby.

"Maybe we could work something out for three days a week," Aaron said, his attention making Collette feel as if she were the only person in the Lapps' yard. "Not for you to be a maud and wait on the girls. You could teach them how to run a home. They'll be grown soon, and they need to learn how to manage. From our conversations I know you understand how it is, raising young people on your own."

"I do." It warmed her heart to know that he remembered their talks, that he'd tucked the details away in his memory. "And your girls wouldn't be any trouble at all. Having been blessed with both, I have to say girls are easier than boys."

"Your help would be a blessing, at least while Mem is off her feet. It would help her rest easier, knowing we're well taken care of." He pinched the brim of his hat, his forehead wrinkling as he added, "That is, if you would be agreeable to the situation."

Looking beyond him, Collette saw Miriam watching in wide-eyed joy, her head bobbing in the affirmative, as if she were coaching a teenaged sister on how to court a young man. Miriam's enthusiasm and good intentions were a kind gesture—truly touching—but Miriam couldn't have realized the burdens that came to any man who would dare to engage too deeply with a woman like Collette Yoder. Worse than an old maid, Collette bore the taint of abandonment by her husband.

The hint of inadequacy.

Many folks believed that any woman who had been difficult enough to drive her husband away was best left alone.

But Collette knew her friend Miriam saw her as a plain woman with a good heart. "I'd be happy to do it," Collette said. She would prove her friend right. And in the process, maybe she'd manage to teach Aaron's girls a thing or two about cooking and sewing.

"Very good. I'll let my mother and the girls know. You can start next week. What days will we see you?"

"Monday, Wednesday, and Friday, if that's good for you?"

He nodded. "How about you start Wednesday? That would give me some time to set things right with the girls."

"Wednesday it is," she said.

He fixed his straw hat on his head, and then headed across the yard to fetch his daughters.

"I'll help you hitch up the buggies," Alvin said, walking alongside Aaron.

Collette squared her shoulders as she watched Aaron go.

Suddenly she felt lighter and taller, pleased to have a full week of work ahead.

"That went well," Miriam said from Collette's side.

When Collette saw that she was grinning from ear to ear, she couldn't help but chuckle.

"What's so funny?" Miriam asked.

"You. Your schemes. How did you know I needed more work?"

"A little birdy may have mentioned it," Miriam said.

"Harlan." Collette had told her son not to worry, but did he listen?

"Harlan thinks it's too soon for you to be back on your feet full-time, but I assured him that working in someone's home won't be as trying as the factory."

"I'll be sure to find a chair when I tire. I can certainly snap peas or do mending while sitting down. I'm grateful for the work, but the matchmaking is a bit much."

"You noticed?"

"I did, and honestly, I'm too old for such a thing. Love and romance are prizes for the young ones. An old woman like me is content to have her family safe and healthy with a roof over their heads."

"Collette, you can't be saying that you're old, especially since we're around the same age. Still on the sunny side of forty."

"You're right. Every year is a blessing, and I'm truly grateful, though deep in my bones, sometimes I feel ancient. Like an old mule put out to pasture."

Miriam laughed, pressing a hand to her mouth to try to keep the volume down. "I'm sorry, but you don't look anything like an old mule. Age is all relative, isn't it? Sometimes struggles make a person feel older than they are. Worry and heartache can make us weary and we get all twisted up like a pretzel."

"I know that feeling," Collette admitted. "Having made pretzels for years."

Both women chuckled at that.

"Your pretzel days are over, Collette. Over the past few months I've watched you grow younger. Your steps are lighter, your head held high. It's wondrous to see Gott's healing." Miriam winked, then bent over the table to blow out another citronella candle. "Though I know those exercises you did in physical therapy had a bit to do with it."

"I do feel so much better," Collette agreed. "Not long ago, when I was learning to walk again, each step was a challenge. It began to feel like I'd never get out of that wheelchair. Looking back, I see how blessed I am that Gott carried me along, with the help of good folk like you."

"You've come so far." Miriam touched her shoulder. "It's an answered prayer, you being back on your feet. I'll keep praying that Gott will make your heart light, too."

"You're a good friend, Miriam." Collette covered her friend's hand as they shared a moment of contentment. "I can't thank you enough for all your help. But really, my life is full. I have everything I need."

"Do you?" Miriam asked, her round face lit with a gentle smile.

The probing question took Collette by surprise. With a roof over her head, plenty to eat, and her little family intact, Collette's life was wonderful good.

"Everyone should have someone to love."

Collette thought to argue, but in the gathering darkness the night and the fireflies and the song of crickets seemed to close in around them, making Miriam's point. Yah, it could be lonely, being on your own. By filling her days with chores and family and her work as a housekeeper, the hours flew by. But the nights . . . the nights sometimes stretched on for an eternity.

"You know, it makes me think of that Bible story," Miriam said. "The time when Jesus tells this woman that he's come to help the lost sheep of Israel, and that doesn't include her. But she doesn't back down and she persists in asking for help for her daughter. Do you know that story? I'm not sure why it popped into my head, but I'm thinking that we need to persist in seeking Gott's help. We need to seek Gott and ask that He heal us and make us whole. And part of living a whole, fruitful life is sharing it with a husband."

Collette pressed a hand to her chest, as if she needed to make sure her heart was still beating inside there. Miriam did tend to gab, but on this point she made sense; it was worth seeking Gott's help to answer a need, to fill the hole in one's heart. But this was not a topic Collette had ever discussed. With anyone.

"I love a good Bible story," Collette said, "and you've found one that hits home. But really, I've never prayed for anything so . . . so personal. As a girl, I was taught that Gott has more important matters than the concerns of normal folk."

"Mmm. But Gott is powerful and mighty, and He loves His people. I have faith that He can answer all prayers, large and small."

All prayers, large and small. Collette nodded, tucking the insight under her wing to explore later. "Thank you for the wonderful dinner. I don't remember the last time I celebrated a birthday."

"You know you're always welcome here. Now don't forget your platter. Your Jell-O was a huge hit."

A favorite of the bishop, Collette recalled with a soft smile. Perhaps his recollection of the dessert from his childhood had been just a memory; for Collette, it seemed to be yet another common experience, another path that they shared. No one else had to know how much she'd savored Aaron's satisfaction in the dessert she'd made. She was reaching for the empty dish from the table when a shout came from one of the twin boys, ending the quiet night.

"Mem! Is there any cake left?"

"Bottomless pits, these boys," Miriam murmured with a smile, gesturing Paul over to come fetch one of the last slices.

Chapter 5

That night, when the guests were gone, the kitchen tidied up, and the children off to bed, Miriam led the way up the stairs. The bedtime ritual of turning off battery lanterns or kerosene lamps and locking doors held a certain pleasure for Miriam and Alvin as they took inventory of their children, their home, and their blessings. By the time they made it to their bedroom, Miriam was yawning and unpinning her kapp.

"Was that a bit of matchmaking with the bishop?" Alvin asked as he closed their bedroom door behind them.

"You know I love to bring people together, and the bishop, under that heavy cloak of responsibility, is a lonely man who lost his wife years ago." Miriam removed her dress and hung it on a hook, glad to be free of it in this warm weather. Her summer nightgown was long, but made of a light fabric. "He needs the love of a good Amish woman."

"We're talking about Aaron? Our bishop?" Alvin asked as he lowered the shade and pushed the window open to allow the cooler night air to circulate through the room. "I don't know that he's lonely at all. He's never mentioned it to me. And what makes you think Collette would be the type of wife Gott intends for our bishop?"

"There are some things a woman just knows." Miriam sat on the edge of the bed, brushing her uncoiled hair away from her face.

"Do you think it's right to meddle in the bishop's affairs?" Thumbs tucked under his suspenders, Alvin paced across the room.

"Aaron and his girls need someone to help out at home, and Collette needs work. Right now it's as simple as two people helping each other out."

"Not if *you* have your way." He squinted, pointing a finger at her. "Admit it, my love. You are trying to play matchmaker."

She pressed her lips together to suppress a giggle. "Oh, Alvie, you know the old saying. 'It's better to hold out a helping hand than to point a finger.'"

He paused, stared at his pointed finger, and then raised both hands in the air. "I give up." He lowered his suspenders and shrugged out of his shirt. "It's two different worlds that men and women live in. I don't understand it, but I'm too old to question it."

"You understand more than most," she insisted. "I'm telling you, this time I feel truly inspired. While I was talking to Collette I remembered a Bible story that supported my point. A Bible lesson popped into my head, and you know I've never been a good student of the Bible."

"Is that so?" Alvin rolled up the window shade to allow more of the night breeze into the room. "That's quite a blessing."

"No one was more surprised than I was." She put her hairbrush on the dresser and sat on her side of the bed. "It was as if a breeze was blowing through me, spreading Gott's word. I know that sounds kind of pompous, and it wasn't that way at all. It's just that I felt like Gott's messenger, and I liked the joy and surprise of it all."

"Gott works in surprising ways," Alvin agreed.

"It was nice." She folded the quilt down to the foot of the bed; they probably wouldn't need it tonight as the air held the soft velvet warmth of an August night. Leaning back against her pillow, she pulled the sheet to her chin and considered the evening. Nearly a perfect night. So many happy faces, growing children, teens crossing the path to adulthood. Their oldest son, Sam, was a baptized member of the church, and soon to be a husband. Daughter Essie and her husband, Harlan, were saving up for a house of their own, and if Miriam's instincts were right, they had a baby on the way. Collette Yoder was coming into her own after her full recovery, and Miriam was sure her new job at the bishop's house would lead to wonderful things.

Only one development worried Miriam.

Her mother's visit.

"It's been so long," she said aloud. When was the last time?

Miriam hadn't seen her mother for years.

Not even when Sarah had passed.

Miriam's throat tightened at the memory of Sarah's funeral two years ago last May. Sarah Stuckey Sullivan had made it to forty-two when cancer took her away. When they got the news, Mem and Dat had been unable to make it to Philadelphia in time for the funeral. That rainy day. Puddles of water had reflected the gray buildings of the city, and rain had dripped steadily from leaves outside Sarah's kitchen window, as if the angels were sobbing uncontrollably. Although Miriam had tried to be supportive and sympathetic toward Sully, her sister's husband, and their daughters, in her heart she had been railing against her mother.

What sort of mother missed her own daughter's funeral?

Miriam couldn't imagine it. Not that it was her place to

judge, but there was no forgetting the raw pain of that time. *Mem, oh, Mem, you should have been there for Sarah, for her daughters, for me, her grieving sister.*

"She'll probably be grumpy when she gets here," Miriam said, imagining her mother reeling off a list of disappointments in the kitchen downstairs. The coffee was too strong. The pie crust underdone. The kitchen too warm. The open window too cold.

"What's that?" Alvin asked as he hung his pants on a hook.

"My mother," Miriam said, catching his gaze. "I'm glad she's coming, but it makes me nervous, too. You know how she is. Nothing I do is ever quite good enough for her, and I'm worried that she'll turn a harsh eye on our children when she's here."

"Hmm. She might do that, but our children can take it. We've always told them that if they're making good choices, there's nothing to be shy about."

"Still. It worries me."

He raked his reddish brown hair from his eyes and stared off thoughtfully. "This is something you can't control, so worry will only make it worse. Pray for the serenity to let it go."

She let out a raspy sigh. "And what about Grace? Sweet, wounded Grace. That girl's finally coming around, finally starting to trust again. She's looking forward to meeting her grandmother." She turned to punch the pillow behind her into shape. "My mem will eat a tender girl like Grace for breakfast."

Alvin took two steps toward the bed and paused, hands on his hips. "The Amish settlement in Michigan must be a strange place. Either that or your mother's choice of breakfast cereal has changed?"

She sucked in a breath, and then let it out on a laugh.

"Oh . . . you." With a grin she hoisted the pillow and tossed it at him.

He caught it in the air with a huge smile. "I think you're exaggerating."

"Maybe a little. But of the three Englisch nieces, Grace has struggled the most to understand plain folk. For all her bravado, I think she's a little scared of Englisch folk, too. I'd hate for her to go back into her shell over something my mother does or says."

"Then you will talk to your mem in advance. Warn her to be cautious. And kind."

"I'll try. You know I will. But Mem does not like to take instruction from her offspring." Miriam's mother was from the old school of child-rearing in which offspring—no matter their age—followed their parents' orders and were considered to be disrespectful if they questioned their elders. That tradition had kept order in their household—until someone like Sarah rebelled. "I want my mem to visit—you know I do—but sometimes when I'm near her, I feel like I'm nine years old and my opinion doesn't matter."

"You matter, my dear wife. Maybe it will be different with your mem this time."

"I hope so."

He turned off the lantern, and she felt the bed jiggle as he climbed in. She turned to him and placed a loving hand on his shoulder. He rolled toward her and pulled her into his arms.

How blessed she was to have a partner in this life who put up with her quirks and loved their family and friends with fervent loyalty! In Alvin's arms, she could be over the moon with happiness.

"I know my matchmaking bugs you, Alvie."

"Bringing people together is a wonderful thing." His voice was hushed and tender in the darkness. "As long as they don't mind the push. Just remember, you're not playing with puppets."

"I don't mean to be pushy." Her hand found his beard in the darkness and she stroked the soft hair. "I just want everyone to have someone to love."

His palm moved down her arm, sending a current of sensation shivering through her body. "Everyone should be as happy as we are," he whispered.

"Everyone," she agreed.

Chapter 6

When Wednesday dawned, Collette was glad that Harlan had offered to drop her off at the Troyer house on his way to work at the Amish furniture factory. As Beebee, their beloved mule, pulled them along, her son talked of his new assignment crafting fancy window frames for an Englisch home over in Plumdale. With the sun rising in the open blue sky, the earth was warming fast, but the airflow created by the moving buggy kept Collette comfortably cool.

"Zed's been teaching me," Harlan said. Zed Kramer was a senior carpenter at the furniture factory. "You start with a window surrounded by raw pieces of drywall. Jagged edges everywhere. And by the time I'm done, there are layers of wood trim around the window. The finished product looks right good."

"So now you can build the window sills and frames on your own?"

"From start to finish. It makes me feel good, making something out of pieces of wood."

"It's good to use the skills Gott gave you," she said, sharing in his contentment. "You know, your father was good at carpentry. He enjoyed working with wood and building things."

Harlan stroked his seven months' growth of beard

thoughtfully. "You hardly ever talk about Dat, and I don't remember much."

For years Collette had found it difficult to think about Jed, the father of her children, who had abandoned his family a decade ago. "During the years of not knowing if he'd come back to us, the nights spent worrying about him, I couldn't bear to talk about him. I didn't want to make you and Suzie any more anxious than you were."

"You did a good job of hiding your worries, Mem."

"Over the years, it eased a bit. I was sad to learn he had passed, Gott rest his soul, but the news did help close a chapter in our lives. I like to think that it was Gott's way of telling me I no longer had to worry." Collette had given up on ever hearing from Jed again when an Englisch detective had informed them that Jed Yoder had passed away. "Now, I think my heart is healed enough to talk about your father, to share some of the stories from better days, when he was a young man making his way in the world. He could be such a thoughtful man. I think it would be a good thing for you and Suzie to learn more about him."

"I'd like that. I wish I'd paid more attention when he was with us."

"You were just a boy."

Harlan nodded. "Eleven when he left. I do remember him building things in the buggy barn. I think I was allowed to stay and watch as long as I kept quiet and still."

"That sounds like your father. The strict codes of the community we were raised in were engrained on our minds. Your dat was hard on you. I probably was a bit hard, too."

"But you raised us well," Harlan said, a warm gleam in his eyes.

She chuckled. "Let's not get ahead of ourselves. The quest for Gott's goodness and grace is an everyday challenge."

"But so far, so good, right?"

"Oh, you! Such a charmer. You know, Jed and I were even younger than you and Essie when we fled Upstate New York and came here to Lancaster County."

He whistled. "Essie just turned nineteen. How young were you?"

"Sixteen."

"So young?"

"And so desperate to get away." She smoothed the skirt of her sky-blue dress as she thought back to the society she had fled. "I wasn't allowed to wear a pretty blue like this dress. Black was the color of every dress, all the time. But that was just a small part of our bleak lifestyle. Our Swartzentrube community was very poor, and we were not allowed to rely on food from grocery stores. We didn't have running water in the house, and hot water was a special treat for a weekly bath, if you were allowed that. I worked from sunup to sundown, and in the hours in between, school was a break. It was a hard life." She stared out at the land as they rolled past. The crimped green leaves of corn stalks reaching toward the sky. The silver silo and red barn of Iddo Dienner's farm. The rolling hills tipped in gold light by the rising sun. Despite the sorrows she'd endured over the past few years, she had always felt a sense of wonder at the beauty Gott had created here in Joyful River.

"So you don't regret leaving?" he asked.

"I only regret having to leave my brothers and sisters behind." She shook her head. "Thinking back, it reminds me to be grateful for the life I have here."

As they reached the outskirts of town, she directed Harlan toward the small farm the bishop managed with assistance from another farmer. She told Harlan she would find her own way home if Harlan would give her a ride here in the mornings. "Monday, Wednesday, and Friday, if it all works out."

"I'm sure you'll be a lifesaver," he said, pulling up in front of the two-story white house with an older brown barn off in the distance. "Who couldn't use a woman who cooks, gardens, and sews?"

"I suspect it's not my skills in question, but the attitudes of two teenaged girls," she answered, gathering up the skirt of her dress to climb down from the buggy.

"You'll show them what's what, Mem."

She shook her head, grateful for his confidence in her. "I'll see you at dinner."

Harlan waited in the buggy, watching her approach the house as if she might change her mind and run back to him. From the rapid flutter of nerves in her chest, she was sorely tempted, but she realized the feeling wasn't so much anxiety over working as a housekeeper as awkwardness over being close to Aaron all day. It was a hard truth, but she wasn't going to let her feelings for a man ruin a job she sorely needed. She turned to give her son a quick wave, then felt relief as she heard him call to Beebee and head off.

If she could mind her emotions around Aaron, this job would be a piece of cake after keeping house for Linda Hostetler and her crew. As she approached the house, she wondered which door to approach. Normally a hired person would go around the side to the kitchen door, but this being her first day, she didn't want to enter without knocking and startle anyone.

The front door would be the place to start. As she approached the wooden porch, she noticed the weeds sprouting along the walkway. When Dorcas was alive, there must have been beautiful border flowers here. Yellow and orange marigolds, or red and white impatiens blooming in plentiful bunches. Such a shame, these weeds.

She bent down and plucked them as she walked along. No time to start like the present.

By the time she reached the porch, she had a handful of stray green sprouts. She dropped them onto the ground, intending to come back to the gardening later, even wondering about the possibility of purchasing some annuals to create a bit of a border for the bishop's walkway. Summer flowers would be so much more welcoming for visitors!

Halfway up the steps, she noticed a leviathan weed dominating the space beside the stairs. Nearly five feet tall, the weed was an eyesore, growing right beside the front porch, the place of greeting, the face of any house.

She hurried down the porch steps and reached forward to grasp the fat stalk and give it a tug.

Firmly rooted in the ground, the green giant didn't move. She tugged again, without success.

Stubborn thing.

This would require two hands.

Gritting her teeth, she planted her feet, tightened her grip, and tugged with all her might.

The weed held tough, then suddenly let loose, sending her falling back in a spray of flying dirt.

"Oof!" she cried as clumps of soil went sailing through the air. The mighty weed flailed in the air over her as momentum sent her stumbling back. Her backside met the ground with a hard thump.

For a second she lay on the ground and assessed the damage. No pain, at least. Nothing harmed but her self-confidence.

"Collette? Good grief, are you all right? Tell me you didn't reinjure yourself."

Embarrassment heated her already-hot cheeks when she looked up to see the bishop looming over her.

"I'm fine, I think. I was just pulling weeds, but then one got the better of me."

"I was in the kitchen, and I thought I heard a buggy pull

up. I came out the side door, just in time to see you take a spill."

As he spoke she closed her eyes, wishing he hadn't seen that, but accepting that she couldn't undo reality. When she looked back at him again, his eyes held such a raw compassion that she couldn't deny his kindness.

Aaron leaned down, his handsome face so cool and composed in the sphere of her klutziness. "Let me help you up."

She took his extended hand and allowed him to help her back to her feet. His hand gripped hers for a moment, a good thing as her knees felt a bit unsteady.

"Are you okay?" he asked.

She looked down as she shifted from one foot to another, testing the leg that had been injured last year. "No pain," she announced, "unless you count embarrassment."

"Garden work is nothing to be embarrassed about."

"It was foolish of me not to wait until I found a spade. Sometimes I just get impatient." She rubbed her hands together, and then brushed off the back of her dress. She knew that bits of dirt had sprayed over her kapp and face, but she would have to address that later.

He gave an easy nod. "Why put off 'til later what you can knock off right now? I'm always overdoing it, pushing to accomplish one more thing until I find myself burning the midnight oil."

She appreciated his kindness, his attempt to ease her humiliation. "Well, no harm done," she assured him.

"Come inside and you can sit for a moment to get your bearings, if you like." He directed her around to the side door as he spoke.

"I'll be fine," she assured him, following him around the house to the side door that faced the buggy barn and a wide gravel drive. The kitchen seemed neglected and sad, like an old grandfather clock that no one had bothered to wind for a few weeks. Dishes cluttered the sink, and crumbs had settled on the linoleum in the corners and nooks and under the cupboards. She pushed back her sleeves, thinking to get to work immediately, but Aaron motioned her through to the front room.

Collette followed, heartened by the pleasant space. Early-morning light spilled in through the windows, bathing the floor and furniture in a buttery shade of gold. This was a room that had seen fellowship, a place where folks could feel welcome. Something about the room spoke of home, of hope and consolation and comfort. All the hesitations and worries that had tugged at her over the weekend now flew off in a flock, leaving her with the sense that Gott had brought her to this place for a reason.

"I've got to get over to the hospital. Jerry Kraybill's having a pacemaker put in, and Netta was a ball of worry last time I talked with her. And then there's some corn to bring in at Iddo Dienner's this afternoon. I won't be back till four or five. If you can stay until I return, I'll give you a ride home."

"That'll be fine," she said, taking in the calendar on the wall with a pretty picture of fjords in Norway. A breathtaking view of water, trees and sky—though she noted that the calendar was still back on the month of May. "I'll leave a dinner for you and the girls."

"Before I go, let's sit and talk things through a bit. Can I get you a cup of coffee?" he offered as she took a seat on the small sofa. "The pot is still warm."

"On the stove? I'll find it later. Or would you like some now?" She sprang back to her feet. "I'd be happy to get it."

"I'll fetch it."

"Oh, no, let me," she insisted. "That's why I'm here."

He held out a hand, firmly stopping her. "Are we not both the servants of Gott? I'll fetch it. Milk and sugar?"

"Just milk."

As she waited, smoothing down the skirt of her dress, she took a deep breath to make sure she wasn't dreaming. In the months that she had worked at the Hostetler household, she couldn't imagine Linda or her husband, Len, serving her a cup of coffee or tea. It simply wasn't done, especially by the likes of Linda Hostetler, who considered the hired help in her home or shop to be inferior and not worthy of small acts of kindness. Only a few minutes in, and it was already a very unusual first day at work. Still, her silly weed-pulling tumble had broken the ice and eased the nervousness she'd felt about being near the bishop in his home.

When he returned with two coffees, they talked about the chores he needed done in the house, the hours she would work, and the salary he insisted he was happy to pay. As he tried to break down the chores, he frowned over the dust on the table beside him and the smudged linoleum floor.

"Now that I look around, this place really is in a sorry state. As I mentioned the other night, my main concern is my daughters and their tendency to let others take care of them," he said, resting the mug on his thigh. "My oldest, Laura, learned well from her mother. But since Dorcas passed, Tess and Amy have been coddled by their grandmother. Oh, they can do a bit of baking and cleaning, but when it comes to the essentials that a good Amish woman masters—cooking meals and keeping a tidy house—I'm afraid they're lost."

"It's hard on a child, losing a parent," she agreed, thinking back to the years where she had needed to care for Harlan and Suzie and keep a roof over their heads. Sometimes those tired, bleak years blurred together.

"I haven't forgotten that you've been raising your children on your own. How long has it been since your husband left?"

"Ten years, at least." Somewhere in the hectic push to be a mother and provide food and shelter for her family, Collette had stopped counting the days since Jed had left.

"I didn't mean to bring up a painful subject, but good on you for raising two on your own."

"I had help. The job at Smitty's Pretzel Factory paid our room and board. And our church community has always lent a hand when I needed it."

"Those helping hands keep us going, don't they? As a widower myself, I've had many casseroles come my way since Dorcas passed. I'm grateful, though I have to admit, if I ever encounter another Yumasetti casserole, it will be too soon."

The twinkle in his eyes made her smile. "Every Amish cook has her own way of making that one."

"And I think I've tried them all!"

She chuckled. The casserole always included ground beef, noodles, and cream of mushroom soup, but from there the variations were endless. "I'll make a note not to prepare Yumasetti for your supper."

"I'd appreciate that. And I'm grateful for you spelling my mother in this house. I had hoped that Laura could come to us from Bird-in-Hand, but with children of her own and a shop to run, she has a very busy life there. When Miriam suggested you help us out, it was like an answered prayer." He took a final sip of coffee and rose. "Just don't let the girls get the better of you."

"Girls I can handle," she said, standing and heading to

the kitchen. "It's those giant weeds out front that I'll be watching out for."

His eyes went wide as her joke landed, and he let out a rich, rumbling laugh that warmed her heart. In that moment, she wondered why she had held her tongue all these years when a silly comment like that had come to mind. Serious minded—that had been her demeanor. Well, after all these years, she was finding her voice at last.

Collette started with a rag and broom. Leaving the upstairs to tackle later, she went from room to room, knocking down cobwebs and swiping tables and chairs with her damp cloth. Very dusty. She knocked the worst of it down, then swept up and collected it all in the dustpan. There was something satisfying about chasing dust bunnies out from under the wooden legs of chairs and accumulating a pile of dirt and dust—the sign of her efforts. It didn't take long to sweep the downstairs, which consisted of the kitchen, dining area, living space, and a small office where Aaron had a desk set up with a calendar, stacks of books and magazines, and accounting ledgers for the farm.

She filled a bucket with Mr. Clean and warm water and set to work mopping. The scents of lemon and ammonia pinched her nose a bit, but who didn't love seeing the shine of a clean white linoleum floor? Within an hour or so, the downstairs was spick-and-span.

She was about to set upon the dirty dishes when she paused, noting the silence in the house and the light breeze that filtered in through the window over the sink from the sun-swept fields in the distance.

Seizing the moment, she stepped outside and took in the expansive view of Gott's creation: the garden, with scents of honeysuckle and rows of plants bearing melons, squash, and tomatoes. The garden fence was heavy with a carpet of sweet honeysuckle, nectar to buzzing bees. Tall oak trees bordered the yard, reaching into the sky with thick bonnets of leaves that shaded parts of the lawn.

Beyond the broad yard, the fields stretched on into the afternoon heat. Corn and alfalfa and wheat, the thin golden stalks shimmering in the breeze, reached up toward the heavens.

Such a sight could fill the heart, and then some, with the wonder of this good earth. Plain folk tried to live their lives close to the land, connected to Gott's creations, and for Collette nothing fed the soul quite like the change of seasons on a farm. As a child in rural New York, she'd been too cold, too hungry, and too tired to appreciate her rustic home. Now, after living in a small apartment in the town of Joyful River for many years, she relished the color, light, and air on a farm.

"Ever so grateful," she said aloud to no one but Gott.

She picked a few handfuls of blueberries, then cradled them in her apron as she went back into the house to tackle the kitchen.

It only took a few minutes to put the kitchen aright. She dumped the water in the bucket and refilled it with a fresh burst of Mr. Clean. With her cleaning tools in hand, she climbed the stairs, where she suspected that Aaron's daughters were still sleeping. Such a life! It wasn't something that happened often in Collette's home, as her children had taken on jobs even while they were in school. Which was a question she had about Tess and Amy. If they were both too old for schooling, when were they going to set to work? Surely they'd want something constructive to fill their time. Most Amish youth spent their days working either at home or at a job.

At the top of the stairs she paused to prop the mop

against the wall and look around. One open door was the bathroom, and another was clearly Aaron's room, with a double bed and men's clothes hanging from the hooks on the wall. The bed quilt was a traditional design, with tulips, hearts, and birds—a pattern some folks called love birds. Probably Aaron and Dorcas's wedding quilt, it was worn and a bit tattered with some of the stitching giving way. But it seemed too personal to delve into a project like that. Collette closed the door and went on to the next room.

Another open door led to a bedroom with a set of bunk beds and a feeling of emptiness. From the dark quilts and fishing gear lining the wall, she guessed that it had been a boy's room. Probably occupied by the son who had left home during rumspringa. How long ago had that been? She wondered if Aaron ever heard from the boy. It must have been hard, losing a son to the Englisch world.

She turned around to the other two closed doors and took a breath. Now was as good a time as any.

"Rise and shine!" she called. She knocked on one door, then pushed it open to summon the sleeping beauty in the bed. "It's time to wake up and greet Gott's new morning. Before morning is completely gone."

The girl moaned and thrashed. "I'm still tired." She faced away from the door, only the back of her honey braided hair visible above the quilt.

"Well, you can sleep some more at the end of the day," Collette said, moving on.

Behind the second door, the young woman pushed back the sheet and sat up with a doleful look. "You must be Collette."

"I am."

"I'm Amy." This was the older one, still the soft cheeks and round eyes of a girl, but certainly past the threshold of womanhood. The look in her eyes was a mixture of annoyance and curiosity as she scratched her head and ran a hand down over her long, wheat-colored hair. "You should know that Tess and I like to sleep in."

"And miss the morning? What about all the things you have to do?"

Amy raked her hair back and paused. "Like what?"

The list was endless, but Collette would get to that later. "For starters, breakfast."

Even with Collette's summons, the girls moved slowly. It was at least a half hour, the time it took to clean the bishop's room from floor to ceiling, until they appeared like sleepy children in the hallway.

"I'm so hungry," Tess bellowed as she followed her sister down the stairs.

Children, Collette thought. Amy and Tess were seventeen and fourteen, and yet they often acted like children. She propped her mop outside the bathroom and went down to the kitchen.

"Can we have eggs and pancakes?" Amy smoothed down her nightgown and took a seat at the kitchen table. "We haven't had a good breakfast since Mammi was here."

Collette washed her hands, then opened the refrigerator to peruse the contents. At least there were a dozen eggs and a few sticks of butter. "I'll make breakfast this morning, and tomorrow I'll show you how to do it yourself. That way you won't go hungry when your grandmother isn't around."

"I don't like cooking," Tess said in a gloomy voice. She wound a wavy wisp of her amber hair around one finger— hair that hung over her shoulders. Collette had been surprised when the girls appeared downstairs in their nightclothes with their hair unbound. She couldn't remember the last time she'd left her bedroom in the morning without at least pinning her hair and kapp. Apparently things were quite lax around here.

Amy picked at the bowl of blueberries Collette had brought in from the garden. "Mammi always promises to teach us to cook, but then she shoos us out of the kitchen."

"Cooking is rewarding when you know how to make tasty food," Collette said.

Tess shook her head. "I've tried it before. It's a lot of work."

"The real work is the cleanup," Amy said. "All those dishes. When Mammi was here, she made us help wash the dinner dishes, and it took forever."

"That's funny," Collette said. "I washed a sink full of dishes when I got here, and it only took a few minutes."

"You must be very good at it," Amy said.

"With a little practice, you'll master it quickly." Collette smiled as she turned toward the counter and cracked eggs into a bowl. *Oh, these two were going to want her gone before the week was out.*

"While I make breakfast, you two need to skedaddle upstairs and get dressed," she said without looking back. "You don't want to be caught in your nightgown if someone stops by."

Tess let out a sigh. "Can't it wait?"

"You'll have plenty of time while I make the pancakes. Go on, now."

Sagging in annoyance, the girls got up from the table and headed toward the stairs. "And you might as well make your beds while you're up there," Collette called after them. "It'll only take a minute."

A low moan emerged from the hallway as the girls disappeared.

Expertly whipping the eggs with a fork, Collette smiled.

Imagine a young girl expecting never to wash a dish in her life. Ha!

She was not going to be popular around here, but she wouldn't back off. Not until she taught these girls how to fend for themselves and their families. And one day, they'd be grateful to have learned life's most important lessons: cooking, sewing, and cleaning!

Chapter 7

As Thumper trotted along the road in the golden light of morning, Aaron Troyer found himself chuckling—laughing aloud like a crazy man.

Laughing at himself, the man who saw his own plans thwarted by Gott.

He had planned to tell Collette Yoder that he wouldn't be needing her after all. He had estimated that his mother would be in rehabilitation for a few short weeks, and that he and the girls would make do during that time. As Collette was easy to talk to, he had known she would understand, and bow out gracefully.

Of course, the truth was that he did need the help, and Collette was one of the most amiable women in their tight-knit community. She wasn't the problem. The bone of contention was the meddling of women in the congregation, setting him up with widows and inappropriate old maids who invariably showered his home with casseroles and cookies and cakes.

He wanted no part of that.

So he'd planned to send Collette home this morning, and his resolve had been set until he saw her engage in that tug-of-war in the garden.

Her determination. Her grit. Her sense of purpose.

These were things lacking in the Troyer household. To be honest, those qualities were lacking in himself right now.

Since Dorcas had passed, Aaron had lost the focus and the edge that had once guided his days. Sure, he pushed onward, attending to church matters and praying to Gott over the important decisions. But after all these years, running the district was akin to coasting downhill on a scooter; he had to pay attention, but one way or the other, he was going to get to the bottom of the hill without too much trouble.

Most days his focus was on managing the flock and the fields. Honest work, though by the end of the day, he had nothing left for his family at home. The girls didn't seem to care that he rarely looked them in the eye or struck up a conversation with them. With their grandmother around, they didn't really need him. So be it. They were good girls most of the time, unlike their wayward brother. Mose . . . a thorn in his side. Much as he tried to give that matter up to Gott, it stuck in his craw. But with the boy gone, the matter was out of his hands.

Anyway, he had plenty on his plate, and he had started the day with no intention of adding one more heaping scoop of pressure with a new maud in the house.

Until he saw Collette Yoder tangle with that weed.

The weed had won, and yet, in Collette, he had recognized the strength and determination that his household needed. She was an answer to his prayers. She would provide help in the house, a voice that might reach the girls, and perhaps a decoy to ward off solicitous widows for the time being. If nothing else, Collette would at least be one more adult voice in the house, where he was close to giving up that his daughters would shed their childish ways and begin practicing the skills of good Amish women.

And so his plans had changed in a split second—a quick

change so uncharacteristic of Aaron Troyer—and Collette was ensconced in the house for her first day at work. Something about the situation made him smile. He didn't know why, but best not to look a gift horse in the mouth. "Thanks be to Gott," he murmured as his horse and buggy approached the hospital.

Life was full of surprises, sometimes for the best.

"Chocolate chip muffins," Netta Kraybill said, passing a basket of heavenly smelling baked goods under Aaron's nose. "Henrietta baked them just this morning. Won't you have one, Bishop?"

The aroma reminded Aaron that he had skipped breakfast, wanting to get out of the house early and keep Jerry Kraybill's family company in the hospital waiting room, and now the coffee he'd sipped earlier seemed to have soured in his belly. While he usually tried to limit baked goods from well-meaning church members, for he would be fat as a cow if he always said yes, he needed to allow himself the occasional break.

"Who could say no to that?" Aaron took a muffin from the basket and nudged Doug Kraybill, Jerry's brother, who sat beside him in the waiting room. "You'd better get one while it's still warm."

"Denki, Netta." Doug chose a muffin and immediately started unpeeling the paper wrapper.

Chewing a morsel, Aaron watched silently as all the men in their small group, which included Jerry's brothers, sons, and nephews, set their sights on eating the muffins. Across the room, the Amish women and children were more animated, talking in small groups while the children created their own games with the blocks and magazines provided by the hospital.

Such was the way of the Amish when one of their own needed hospital care. Aaron was mindful of the fact that they did tend to take over the space, but the prevailing attitude was that when someone you knew had to go to the hospital, you went along to provide comfort and support.

As bishop, he was especially obliged to attend these procedures. In his estimation, the head of an Amish church was meant to be a kind but stern father, guiding members to stay close to Gott and keeping the community together.

Sometimes it was a heavy yoke to bear.

Other times, his faith was renewed, his energy stoked so that he felt he could soar like an eagle, as the Bible said in Psalm 103: *"Bless the Lord, O my soul. And forget not all his benefits—Who forgives all your sins and heals all your diseases."*

Closing his eyes for a moment, he extended the Bible verse into a silent prayer for Jerry Kraybill, who needed his heart healed for continued life in this family of folks who loved him. *Our Father in heaven, hear our prayers and bring Jerry through this operation with a heart that beats as good as new. Bless the Lord, O my soul.*

Early in his ministry, when he had felt unqualified to lead folks through the twisted paths of life, Aaron had taken to memorizing sections from the Bible. He had not been a good scholar in the one-room schoolhouse, nor a particularly religious young man, but he had always had a fire in his heart to know Gott.

All the fire without any of the fuel. His selection as a religious leader had been a real kick in the hind quarters, the push he needed to know Gott better. Thus, when duty called, he had begun to educate himself in the ways of Gott, to feed on the Bible so that when he was searching for answers, he had the word of the Lord to fall upon.

He opened his eyes and took another bite as Doug,

Jerry's brother, talked with his son Abe about the need to get more of the corn in before the rains that were predicted next week. It was a busy time of year, with the harvest upon them and wedding season just around the corner. He wondered if he'd make it over to Iddo's in time to help him run the harvester. Not that he regretted his time here at the hospital, staying with Jerry's family at a time when they needed their spiritual leader. It was just that he had other commitments.

Overcommitted.

It was a problem for men in his position: bishops, ministers, and deacons who were called to serve, but received no pay or training. A man in an Amish ministry was expected to take on his leadership duties while still tending to his family and livelihood. Sometimes, it was a quandary how to make all the ends meet. He could only try his best and pray for the rest.

The men's attention shifted as Len and Linda Hostetler came in the door, along with the church deacon, Seth King, who wasted no time asking Netta about her husband's progress.

"They're doing the procedure now," she reported. "We're hoping to get good news soon."

"I see." Seth's beard bobbed as he nodded. A tall man, with a reliable smile and hair the color of summer wheat, Seth had a way of cajoling even the most stoic of church members. "What is this they're putting in? A clock to keep his heart ticking?"

"Something like that," Netta said. "The doctor said it's called a pacemaker. The doctors insert it right under the collarbone, and somehow the pacemaker sends a message to the heart to make it keep beating."

"Is that so?" Seth tipped his straw hat back and wiped a bit of sweat from his brow.

"You'd think they'd put it right into the heart," said Len Hostetler.

"Just what I was thinking," Linda agreed, squinting a bit suspiciously. "Not to meddle or anything, but . . ."

In Aaron's experience, any sentence that started with "Not to meddle" or any such denial was usually followed by the offense it pretended to steer clear of. And since Linda Hostetler was involved, there was no doubt that advice would be dispensed.

He closed his eyes and lowered his chin as Linda presented her case. Did this doctor know what he was doing? Had he done this sort of thing before? Maybe Netta could speak to him and suggest that he place the pacemaker inside Jerry's heart. Maybe there was still time. Linda would go with Netta and talk to the nurse, find the doctor, stop them from making a terrible mistake . . . .

"But Dat's already in surgery," Jerry's son Jacob piped up. "You can't interrupt them now."

Linda extended a hand toward Netta, as if to pull her to her feet. "We can try. Come, Netta. I'll go with you."

Aaron pursed his lips, ready to intervene. It was just like Linda to suggest busting in on a surgery. So dramatic, that one, but lacking in wisdom.

"Nay. I don't think so." Netta declined, reaching forward to give Linda's hand a reassuring squeeze. "Thanks for caring, but I'm convinced that this doctor is a good man who knows his business. I do appreciate your prayers, Linda." Netta's eyes scanned the group, finally landing on Aaron. "All your prayers."

"Yah, we must pray for Jerry," Aaron said, stepping in, "and we know Gott is watching over him." He rose, using the opportunity to engage the group in prayer. "Let us pray . . . ."

With heads bowed, the group settled into a new calm,

beseeching Gott for mercy and the healing of Jerry Kraybill's heart. After all these years, Aaron was no longer nervous about leading prayers. His spiritual duties were a blessing. It was the business end of managing a congregation that tended to weigh heavily upon his shoulders. Especially when some of the plain folk constantly pushed to have their way, arguing for the adoption of technologies or inventions that would benefit their family or business.

As bishop, Aaron didn't decide the rules for his district, but he was the person in charge of deciding which issues would be put to a vote. And year after year, he found that certain folk, like Len and Linda Hostetler, always had a hard opinion on what they wanted done. While he never let them wear down his resolve, their constant pushing made him weary.

After the prayer, the hospital waiting room settled back into casual conversation. Linda Hostetler spoke with the women about the upcoming visit of her sister Sally, who would be arriving later in the week from Erie, Pennsylvania.

Deacon Seth spoke of the adjustments they were making on his small family farm to pass it on to his sons before moving to Indiana. A tall, solid man in his forties, Seth was a hard worker who understood the workings of a farm. Much to Aaron's regret, Seth had made the decision to leave Lancaster County and open a small wheelwright shop out west in an area where land didn't cost so much. It was the problem with Lancaster County these days: too many farmers and new homes, too little land.

"This time next year, I'll be helping my brother Noah bring in the hay on his farm. After that, I hope to set up a small shop for myself. Wherever there's Amish folk, there's buggies with wheels that need fixing."

"We're going to miss you around here, my friend," Aaron said. "When do you expect to leave?"

"I'll stay on at least until November to help the sons with the harvest. After that, I need to get moving before the winter comes," Seth said. "For a long road trip like that, you've got to stay ahead of ice and snow."

"Indeed," Aaron agreed. "Though it's hard to think of winter weather in the height of August heat."

The men nodded, their beards bobbing as they spoke of the harvest and the work to be done this week. As the conversation went on, Aaron thought of Seth's upcoming departure and the need to replace him when he left at the end of the year.

Like most Amish churches, their ministry was made up of a bishop, a few ministers, and one deacon. As bishop, Aaron oversaw their church district and acted as spiritual leader. The ministers, or preachers, were responsible for delivering sermons on church Sundays. Amish ministers preached with a range of styles. Some spoke humbly in earnest tones, while others sought to deliver the word of Gott in bold, heavy-handed ways.

But the deacon, now what was a thankless job. The deacon's tasks were varied and a bit pushy, if you asked Aaron. They included collecting alms from members so that the church could assist those who had high medical bills or financial needs. The deacon was also responsible for warning wayward members who went against the Ordnung in their use of technology or electricity. It took a special man to have the good will to scold members while helping them recognize the importance of the Ordnung, and Seth King fit the bill to a T. Seth had a gift for reaching out to people with a fatherly discipline and a shepherd's skill for pushing the wayward back to the fold.

Who in their community would Gott call to replace their deacon?

For now, the question required prayer.

When a tall, trim beardless man wearing bright blue baggy pants and shirt called for Netta Kraybill from the hallway, everyone stopped speaking and held their breath to hear the surgery results.

"The procedure went well," the doctor announced, scanning the anxious faces of the Amish folks crowded into the room. A grateful sigh washed over the room.

"Thanks be to Gott," Aaron said.

As the doctor advised that only immediate family would be able to see Jerry for the next few hours, Aaron rose and prepared to leave. His work here as a bishop was done. Now, off to be a farmer.

Chapter 8

Grace Sullivan sucked in the sides of her cheeks and folded her arms across her chest, doing her best to keep from crying. Her sister Megan was leaving the Lapp Dairy Farm, heading off to college in a Pennsylvania town called East Stroudsburg. Dad had driven over from Philly to help Megan and her boyfriend, Isaac, make the move into the dorms, and now Grace felt the double impact of having to say goodbye to Dad and to Megan.

Although it was time for them to go, the family seemed to be stalled in an endless loop of goodbyes in the lane outside the farmhouse. Serena chattered on with optimistic platitudes about how much fun her twin sister was going to have away at college. Megan and Dad stood near the open doors of the Jeep, surrounded by the circle of Lapp relatives they'd come to know so well over the past year. Aunt Miriam and Uncle Alvin. Their older cousins, Sam, Essie, and Annie, who had gotten the three Sullivan girls through some rocky times on the farm.

The younger ones, including thirteen-year-old twins Peter and Paul, currently occupied the Jeep, the boys pretending to drive in the front, while Lizzie gave instructions from the back seat and Sarah Rose tried to climb up on the console. Having grown up with horse-drawn buggies for transportation, the Amish kids were fascinated with cars, especially cool cars like the Jeep, that had a removable soft top. When Sully came to visit, the younger kids loved going for a ride in the open air—no matter what the season.

Looking from her father to Megan, Grace swallowed hard over the knot forming in her throat. She loved them both so much! Tears would only upset them, she knew that, but it was hard for her to say goodbye.

Earlier, when Grace had sat next to Dad at dinner, directing him to seconds on the barbecued ribs and laughing at his corny dad jokes, she'd observed him carefully. He missed them—she knew that much from his warm hugs and millions of questions when he came to dinner at the farm each month. Sully missed his girls, all right. But at the same time, he seemed calmer and happier than the days when they'd been struggling together after Mom died.

Serena said he had a girlfriend, but Grace didn't want to ask about that. She just wanted to be sure he was okay, living without them in the city. She noticed that the sides of his hair were definitely graying a bit, but then he still had his hair. And he was smiling more. That was good. He seemed to be okay. But Grace would keep an eye on him.

As the worrier of the family, Grace figured it was her job to watch out for her father and sisters, and right now, concern about Dad was going to have to take a back seat to worries about Megan, who was moving to a strange place full of people she didn't know. Moving into a dorm room she'd never even seen before.

"I don't know how you have the courage to just go blindly like that," Grace had told her sister as she'd helped her pack that afternoon. Megan's twin, Serena, was downstairs chatting with Dad, which gave Grace a chance for some one-on-one time without that twin thing, that unique twin connection that made Grace feel like an outsider. "What if you don't like your room?" Grace asked.

"Every student gets a bed, a dresser, and a desk," Megan said. "It'll be fine."

"And you'll have a roommate . . . a total stranger."

"I talked to Tara a few times, and she's cool," Megan said. "We're both trying out for the soccer team, so there's that. And you know me; I can get along with anyone."

It was true. Of the three sisters, Megan was the most accepting of other people. "Still, I'm going to worry about you," Grace insisted.

"I know." Megan nodded as she stowed her toothbrush and paste in her travel pouch. "You can't help yourself, and I love you just the way you are, Gracie."

The two sisters had hugged, Grace gripping her older sister tight before letting go. Sometimes you had to let go. She'd learned that lesson the hard way when their mom had died more than two years ago.

"I'm going to miss you so much!" Grace whispered.

"Same!" Megan patted her sister's shoulder, and then leaned back. The tips of her short bronze hair framed her face, emphasizing her round brown eyes. "But this is going to be a good thing for all of us. I'm excited about starting college. And before you know it, you'll be in the same boat."

Grace shook her head. "I can't imagine that."

"What do you mean? You're the best student of the three of us."

"I don't know if I'll ever be able to go off on my own. It's too scary, like jumping off a cliff."

"I get that, and I admit, I'm a little nervous," Megan admitted. "But I keep thinking that there'll be hundreds of students on campus who are in the same boat. I'll have a roommate who's got my back. And Isaac will be on campus. And I've got you and Serena and Dad on the bench if I need you." She touched Grace's cheek and playfully pushed back a lock of emerald-green hair. "So I know I'm going to be fine. And so are you."

As they hugged again, Grace wished she shared her sister's courage.

Now, as Megan stowed her backpack in the rear compartment of the Jeep, Grace frowned at the scant possessions she was taking with her. Just two duffel bags, a laptop, and a backpack that had seen Megan through high school.

"You've barely got any stuff," Grace exclaimed. "What about pillows and sheets and towels?" Grace scraped her hair back in mock horror. Mom would never have let Megan go off so ill-prepared.

"Relax, Gracie," Dad said. "We've got it all planned."

"Dad and I are going shopping when we get there," Megan explained. "There are plenty of stores near campus, and that way, I can see exactly what I need in the dorm."

"Ooh, I want to go shopping!" Serena said, dramatically pleading, "Take me with you!"

"Not this time," Megan said. She opened the passenger side door and shooed the kids out. "You ready, Dad? We're supposed to meet Tara in time for dinner."

"I'm on it," Sully said, tapping information into his phone. "Just making a note of the date of Sam and Sadie's wedding. A Wednesday, huh?"

"That's right." Aunt Miriam beamed. "We like weddings midweek so they we're not rushing around preparing or cleaning up on the Sabbath."

Megan stood on the running board and waved. "I've already hugged you all a million times, so I'm just going to say *auf wiedersehen* and duck into the car," she said, throwing in a bit of German, the language close to the Pennsylvania Dutch dialect spoken by their Amish family. "See you all in a few weeks for Sam's wedding!"

Everyone responded with farewells and waves. Grace pushed forward to give her father a hug, and then sank back into the small group as the doors closed and the Jeep started down the lane.

A glum feeling fell over Grace as she watched them go. Everyone around her was headed off—back to the barn or kitchen, ready to tackle Saturday-afternoon chores. Grace knew she should focus on the positive. She liked her life here at the Lapp farm. She was one of the top students in her class at school. And pretty soon she'd be too busy to worry about anything, as she needed to take a job for a few months to get "work credits" toward graduation. Life was good!

But Grace couldn't shake the sadness of saying good-bye. She kept her gaze fixed on the lane until long after the Jeep had disappeared beyond the fence and trees and bushes.

"And there goes our college girl." Serena slung one arm over Grace's shoulders.

"I'm going to miss her," Grace said without looking away from the lane.

"I'll be here for you, Grace." Serena would be staying on at the farm, splitting her time between her boyfriend, Scout, her furniture refinishing business, and community college classes over in Plumdale.

"I know. I just hate when things change." Losing people. Her world shrinking. All the fears that had squeezed her a year ago, all the anxiety that had gripped her, seemed to be knocking on her door once again.

The panic, the fear of being left alone. Though that

hardly seemed rational here, on a farm with nearly a dozen relatives.

Over the past year, Grace had gotten used to living with her Amish relatives. There was a lot of comfort and joy in being part of a large, loving family, even if she did miss having TV and Wi-Fi at home. Not to mention electricity. A blow dryer and curling iron. A microwave in the kitchen. A blender for smoothies. The list was long, but surprisingly, she'd gotten used to those sacrifices, which hardly compared to the benefits.

"I don't mean to sound whiny, but what if Megan's not happy at college? And then there's Dad, still alone in the city." She thought it must be awful for Dad to be all alone in the apartment where she had grown up with her sisters. She vividly remembered gripping the covers tensely as she'd waited for the sound of a key turning in the front lock on those scary nights when Dad had been working and her two older sisters had stayed out past curfew with their friends. "I just thought he might be getting lonely."

"Don't worry about Dad," Serena advised. "He's fine, and you know he wants you to do what's right for you instead of worrying about everyone else. You internalize these things way too much, Gracie. Like you have the weight of the world on your shoulders."

Grace looked away, knowing her sister was right.

She was the worrier of the family, a trait that had made her sick last year . . . .

Those last few months in Philadelphia, she'd suffered horrible periods of panic: long moments when her heart raced and she struggled to breathe and she was sure she was going to die. Serena and Megan helped her through the terrible attacks a few times, rubbing her back and sitting

with her as they talked or watched a sitcom rerun on TV.
For a while, Grace thought she had things under control,
until one of the attacks shut her down when she was alone
at home.

She'd been sure that she was dying. Sure that she had
cancer, the same disease that had killed Mom.

Alone in the dark apartment, she didn't know what to
do, how to save herself. With trembling hands, she picked
up her cell and thought about calling 911, but what would
she say when they asked her to describe the emergency?
What was actually wrong?

She paced the dark apartment, sweat forming on her
upper lip as she gasped for air, sure her heart was going to
burst in her chest. Tomorrow, someone would find her.
She'd be collapsed on the floor and no one would understand what she'd suffered.

When her heart wouldn't stop pounding, she finally
gave in to fear and called her father's cell. "Daddy?" she
croaked in a squeaky voice. "I'm sorry to bother you at
work, but I think I'm dying."

What a relief when Dad told her he was on his way. He
was truly her hero. He'd arrived at the apartment in minutes
and whisked her off to the hospital emergency room. The
whole time, he never chastised her for taking him away
from work or hiding the attacks she'd been having. He
wasn't even mad when the doctor on call told them she
wasn't dying.

"Panic attacks," the doctor said. "The symptoms, which
can be quite severe, are caused by fear or emotional stress."

"You mean I'm not dying?" she asked.

There was sympathy in the young doctor's doleful eyes.
"Not based on these symptoms." He explained that panic
attacks were episodes caused by intense fear. The body lit-
erally tried to shut down.

"But I didn't have anything to be afraid of," she said.

"Something triggered you, and those triggers and hidden fears may take some time to unravel."

Her lower lip curled in as her fear turned to embarrassment. How could all the symptoms have felt so real if there was nothing physically wrong? The emergency room doctor recommended therapy and reassured her that her heart was in good shape.

"That's good news," Dad had said. "You're going to be okay."

Gripping the edge of the ER cot, trying to hold on to a thin thread of "normal," Grace didn't see anything good in the situation.

At first she made Dad keep the hospital visit a secret from her sisters. It was too embarrassing, too overly dramatic to actually think she'd been dying. But in a few days Grace let the truth slip out. She never was good at keeping secrets from people she loved. Megan and Serena were sympathetic, but Grace could see they were off in their own worlds, distracted and fighting their own emotional battles. Even when someone stayed home with her, Grace realized she was alone with her dismal thoughts.

No one had the power to make the attacks stop. Not her sisters, not her father.

All alone in the world.

Soon after the ER visit, Grace felt a panic coming on late one night. She went into the bedroom to wake Megan but couldn't get her to respond. Something was wrong, Grace knew it. She called 911, and Grace summoned paramedics in the nick of time. Megan had overdosed on drugs, but the medics were able to revive her.

Dad was distraught, and the incident was compounded by the fact that Serena was out partying with her friends that night, leaving Grace to deal with it on her own.

It had been the final straw for Sully. Grace's reliable, good-natured dad was stretched too thin, with his job as a cop, his need to keep after three daughters, each of them struggling with serious issues. He'd packed all three of them into the car and brought them out here to live with their Amish relatives.

That had been a year ago, just last summer, but it seemed like a lifetime had passed since then. She'd gone an entire year without an attack. Not that all pressure had dissolved since they'd moved here. Grace knew that everyone had stress. But here, among her large Amish family, Grace always had someone to talk to, someone to help ease her worries before they accelerated into full-fledged panic.

From the very start, Aunt Miriam's smile had been unwavering. She had kissed the girls good night as if they were her own daughters. She had welcomed them into her kitchen and taught them cooking tips. At times, Grace saw shades of her own mother in the way Aunt Miriam celebrated the good things and let the bad things bounce away like summer rain on the pavement. Most of all, Aunt Miriam and Uncle Alvin and the Amish cousins had shown the girls new paths to joy in their lives.

And here on the Lapp farm, Grace was never alone. Her big, Amish family brought her comfort, but she couldn't stay here forever. Next year around this time, she'd be expected to head off to college, down that same road Megan had just traveled.

"I have just the thing to cheer you up," Serena said as they headed back toward the house. "Scout's coming over in a bit and we're going to catch a movie in Plumdale. Want to come along?"

"No, thanks." Grace didn't want to be a fifth wheel.

"Come on, Gracie," Serena prodded.

Just then Lizzie came racing out to them, the strings of

her kapp flying back. "Grace! Mem says come quick if you want a job. She's going into town and she'll take you by the shop her friend Rachel owns. She's sure to hire you."

"Really?" Grace looked down at her torn T-shirt. "I guess I should change."

"What kind of job is it?" Serena asked.

"Rachel owns the Christmas shop," Lizzie reported.

"Oh, definitely change your shirt," Serena said. "Maybe you have something with a little bit of holly? Or a Christmas sweater with Rudolph and a light-up nose?"

Grace rolled her eyes. "Very funny. But I need this job."

"Then go for it," Serena said. "You got this, Gracie."

"Come on, then," Lizzie said. "Annie's harnessing the horse, and you know Mem is almost ready to go."

"Okay." With a deep breath, Grace followed her cousin into the house to change clothes. That was one of the positive points of life at Lapp farm. There was always so much going on, there was no time for a pity party. "Are you coming along into town?" Grace asked.

"Who me?" Lizzie asked. "I'm too young to get a job."

"True, but maybe we can persuade your mom to stop at the ice cream store. I've got some money for cones."

Lizzie grinned, joy flashing in her hazel eyes. "Count me in!"

Chapter 9

"September is upon us!" Collette announced as she pointed her pen up to the calendar that hung on the wall of the bishop's kitchen. "It's time to turn the page!"

"Is it really that exciting?" Tess asked as she spread jam on her toast.

"It's a busy month. There's the harvest. Your grandmother's hip surgery is finally scheduled. And it's the beginning of wedding season."

"A hectic time for Dat," Amy said, "but I love going to weddings. I get to spend the entire day with my friends."

"Well, you'll be happy to know you've got four weddings marked on this calendar for September," said Collette. "You'll be coming to the Lapp farm for the wedding of Sam and Sadie. I've been trying to help Miriam prepare, but she's got it under control, I think."

"Goody." Tess finished the last of her eggs. "I'll spend the day with Suzie and Grace."

"Suzie would like that," Collette said. In the past few weeks she'd noticed daughter Suzie spending more time with Tess, as well as with Miriam's Englisch niece, Grace. All good girls, though the bishop had voiced some concern over his youngest child becoming friends with an outsider.

There was so much pressure on the bishop's family to live a model life.

September would bring other changes in the Troyer house. Tess would be headed back to school for her last year in Joyful River's one-room schoolhouse, and Amy would be needing some serious homemaking lessons or a job in town to keep her occupied without her sister around. Would the bishop still be wanting Collette to come around and work the same hours?

She hoped so.

Just a few weeks with the Troyers and Collette had begun to care for the girls who had been sullen and sassy when she'd started as their housekeeper. Each day in this house she came to see that Gott had a purpose for her here. Maybe not so much to be a friend to the bishop, as she'd hoped, but to prepare these girls to be good Amish women, women with the skill to care for their families and greet each new day with joy and glory to Gott.

It was an important task, one she was grateful to take on. Funny how she'd taken this job on mostly as a means of supporting her family, but in her dealings with Amy and Tess, her involvement here had taken on a new light. Almost like a child's coloring book that started as simple black lines on white paper and now was a burst of vivid colors.

Most surprising to Collette was the realization that no one beyond Miriam and her kin seemed to realize that she was working here. She and the bishop had kept the development to themselves, more out of discretion than secrecy, and had kept their usual social distance at church events. When meeting church members, Aaron traveled to members' homes or scheduled meetings here on the days when she wasn't present. Collette had suspected that word would quickly get out in the small community once someone saw her hanging laundry or riding in the bishop's buggy, but so far they seemed to inhabit a quiet space in which she'd had a chance to fall into the patterns of life in the Troyer house, where the girls seemed to light up a bit when she appeared. Quite a contrast to her other job, where members of the Hostetler family treated her like a plow horse, dismissing small courtesies like her opinion or simple eye contact.

No matter. She gave Len and Linda a solid day's work, then returned home. And their lack of interest made it easy to keep mum about her position here, not wanting to give folk any reason to wag tongues about their bishop employing a younger widow. She figured folks would find out soon enough.

Listening to the girls' conversation as they rinsed and dried dishes at the sink, she smiled. It hadn't taken them long to shed some of their bad habits. When she arrived in the morning they were out of bed, beds made, breakfast finished, and while it was a chore to get them cleaning, both girls were quite curious about the tasty things that could be assembled in the kitchen.

She let the girls finish washing the breakfast dishes and stepped out through the kitchen door to the summer garden. In the past two weeks she'd managed to remove the weeds from the front of the house and plant some colorful chrysanthemums.

Now her focus was on the somewhat neglected vegetable garden. She had re-staked some fallen tomato plants and trained Tess to water the garden so that the soil and leaves wouldn't shrivel in the sun. The cherry tomatoes were sweet as bits of candy, and the heavy pea pods were a velvety rich shade of green. Walking through the garden, she breathed deep the smell of green. Heavenly, she thought. Stepping over the cracked earth under the rambling vines of squash and cucumbers, she summoned Tess.

"Come," she called to the girls through the screen door

on the kitchen. "The soil is dry, and the peas are ready to come in."

Tess was the first one out the door, heading toward the hose. She enjoyed watering the garden and Amy didn't mind picking, but neither girl would consent to digging up weeds.

"I don't like to get dirt under my nails," Amy had said peevishly when Collette had pressed her last week.

"I don't much like it, either, but I hate to lose good plants to weeds. They grow fast and choke the good things out of the soil. Such a shame," Collette had explained, and Amy had swallowed the lesson without comment.

Now Collette motioned Tess toward the spigot before the squash and zucchini got waterlogged. Tess obliged and joined them over by the trellises covered by climbing pea vines.

Within a half hour, the three of them had filled two large baskets.

"We'll do a contest to see who can shell the most peas," Collette suggested. She'd found the sisters to be a bit competitive, not the supportive team she'd expected to find in the bishop's family, but they did love a contest. She carried one of the full baskets over to the back porch and pulled three chairs into the shade.

"What are we going to do with all these peas?" Tess asked, looking down at the two bushel baskets yet to be shelled. There would be more than the family could use in the next week or so.

"Trust me, they won't go to waste. For starters, I'll show you how to cook them into a dinner tonight, and you can put some up in your freezer. We can give some to neighbors and we'll take some to your mammi. You know her surgery is next week."

"I miss her," Amy said. "I thought she'd be done with all that by now."

"That was the plan, but the doctors wanted her swelling to go down before the surgery," Collette said. "But I'm sure Dinah will be glad to see you."

"With a bucket of peas," Amy teased.

"Peas, peas, peas," Tess muttered. "I'm sick of them already."

"Mmm. I remember a winter when peas made me so happy." Collette plunked a row of green orbs into the bowl as she latched on to the memory. "It was during that big snowstorm, when everything was shut down, the roads covered with snow and ice. No way to get to town for days. What was in the cellar? A few onions and a big bag of dried peas. I made them into soup with a bit of bacon."

"Pea soup?" Tess's cute nose wrinkled as she scrunched up her face.

"It was delicious. Warm and hearty. Perfect with a crust of bread."

"I would like peas if they didn't get wrinkled," Amy claimed.

"You would love peas if they provided you the only chance of a hot meal." Collette wanted her point to hit home, but she spoke without rancor or judgment. "This is why, before every meal, we thank Gott for the bounty on our table."

From the tender look in Amy's eyes as she paused from shelling, Collette suspected that the older daughter was considering this carefully.

Tess, not so much. She kept shelling peas with a frown crossing her cute face. "So are we going to make pea soup tonight?"

"Nay. Too hot. Maybe a fresh salad."

"Salads are boring," Tess said.

Grabbing a handful of pea pods from the basket, Collette settled back onto the chair. "I'm hearing a lot about the things you girls don't like. Let's think more positive and talk about things you enjoy. Things that are fun."

The girls exchanged a mild look, but didn't answer immediately.

"Am I hearing crickets sing?" Collette grinned. "Or just silence. You mean to tell me you crabby appletons don't like anything?"

Tess's eyes opened wide, and then she let out a laugh. "A crabby appleton? What's that?"

"Sour like a crab apple." Collette dropped the peas into her lap to reach out and give Tess's arm a light pinch. "Mean like a crab."

Tess squealed. "Like a crab in the ocean! I've seen pictures of the ocean." The girls couldn't help but smile at that.

"I like to hang out with my friends," said Amy. "Dat won't let me go out on weekends, so I only get to see them at church and singings and rumspringa parties."

Hang out. Such an Englisch expression. Maybe Aaron wouldn't be so concerned if Amy didn't talk that way. "You're seventeen?" Collette asked.

"Almost eighteen," Amy answered.

Rumspringa age. Most youth at that age had more social freedom. "Why can't you go with your friends?"

"You know." Amy tossed an empty pea pod away. "We're the bishop's daughters. You're supposed to set a good example when you're the son or daughter of a church leader."

"I understand that," Collette said. "But it's not a sin to have friends."

"Dat wasn't always so strict," Amy said. "When our sister Laura was in rumspringa, she was out with her friends all the time. Mem was a lot more lenient, and Laura didn't cause any trouble. She married Clyde and they opened a shop in Bird-in-Hand, and that was that. They're so happy."

"I wish we could see them more, but the shop keeps

them busy," Tess said. "And the little ones. They have three children now."

"I do remember your sister Laura from a few years back," Collette said. "So, her courtship went well. But nowadays, you can't get out very often."

"Dat doesn't trust us," Amy lamented.

"We didn't do anything wrong. Mose ruined everything for us," said Tess. "He was on rumspringa, going wild, and Dat couldn't stop him. And then he ran away, and—"

"Don't blame Mose," Amy insisted.

"But he broke Dat's heart!" Tess insisted, her eyes glimmering with a fierce intensity.

Amy shook her head resolutely as she reached for more pea pods. "It was Mem's death that broke Dat. That's what changed things. The problems with Mose, all that happened after things fell apart here."

The raw emotion that was suddenly revealed was unusual for a casual conversation, especially one including a stranger to the family. Collette kept her head down, her hands busy as the two sisters discussed their wayward brother, their father's reaction to Mose, and the general discord that had pervaded their home when Mose lived there.

So much pain here. Collette wished she could console the girls, wash away their doubts and worries. If only it were that simple. Despite the fact that they acted a bit younger than their years, they were no longer simple children, and the complexity of emotion and pain this household had endured could not be easily unraveled.

Besides, she wasn't their mem. Just a housekeeper, a woman the girls knew from church, like so many others. One day, they would circle back to the subject of their runaway brother and probably their mother's death, too. For now, Collette thought it best to let the difficult topic pass.

She continued listening and absorbing the situation with the girls' brother, Mose, until the conversation dwindled.

"So what were we talking about before?" Collette said without looking up. "Ah, yes. Things you girls do for fun. Amy likes to be with her friends. How about you, Tess? What brings you joy?"

Tess shrugged. "I like school, I guess. Teacher Julie says I could be a teacher someday if I set my mind to it."

"She's a regular bookworm, this one," Amy said. "She can't get her hands on enough books. That's all she wants for her birthday or Christmas."

"Let *me* talk!" Tess glared at her sister. "I do like books. When I run out of things to read, I'll read my old books over and over again. My books are like old friends."

"It must be nice to have your good friends close by," Collette said, though she thought it might be lonely, too. Too many afternoons she had tugged Tess out of the house to get some fresh air and activity.

"Yah." Tess looked toward her sister. "See? My hobby will keep me out of trouble."

"Do you ever check books out of the library in town?" asked Collette. When Tess shook her head, she went on to explain how they could go over to the little library building in town and sign Tess up for a library card. Amy, too. "And then you can look through the books, find a few that interest you, and if you check them out, you're allowed to bring them home for a few weeks."

"How much does it cost?" Tess asked.

"It's free. A borrowing system. Of course, you need to return the book before it's due, and be careful not to lose it or spill anything on it."

"I would be ever so careful!" Tess insisted.

"Good. We can go to the library sometime, and one of the librarians will help you get set up."

"I'm so excited!" Tess turned to her sister. "I'm getting some new books!"

Amy shook her head, unimpressed.

"Can we go today?" Tess asked. "Please?"

"There's not enough time today, with having to make dinner," Collette said, calculating aloud. "But here's what we can do. If you girls help me put together a dinner, share the dishwashing after you eat with your dat, and be up and ready at a decent time on Friday, I'll take you both over. And maybe stop for ice cream on the way back."

Tess nodded eagerly, and even Amy seemed interested. Collette suspected that Amy had a better chance of running into a friend while out and about in town than penned up here on the farm.

"But why can't we do it tomorrow?" Tess asked.

"Tomorrow's my day to work at the Hostetlers, and I've got to help them get their place ready to host church."

"I wish you could come here every day," said Tess, no longer glum, and no longer expressing disdain for the new housekeeper.

Such a transformation. Collette hoped that it lasted.

Around four p.m., Collette showed them how to make one-pot Amish beef stew with a twist—fresh peas added at the end, so they wouldn't wrinkle. The girls watched as she showed them how to make the cuts to dice an onion. Then Amy sautéed it in butter. "Just keep it heating until the onion starts to look clear and silvery," she said. Next they added the ground beef and spices, following her cues to break the meat into a crumble and cook it until it browned. They added potatoes, beef broth, a bit of tomato sauce, and then simmered it for thirty minutes.

"Now set the lid on and put it aside. When you're about ready to eat, bring it to a simmer again."

"And add the peas," said Amy.

"That's right," Collette said. "Serve it with the coleslaw we made and you have a meal that mostly came from your summer garden. It feels good to live close to the earth, doesn't it?"

"I'll feel good if it tastes good!" Tess said.

"It smells good already. I'm sure my brood at home will be happy to tuck in." Collette found the small casserole dish she'd brought from home and spooned a few heaps into the bottom. Whenever she cooked for the bishop and his family, she made enough to bring home for her family's supper. The bishop didn't mind. Collette always made extra, which saved her from having to cook two dinners that day. "Now look away so you don't see me break the recipe," Collette said as she tossed handfuls of peas in, then covered the dish.

Tess froze with her mouth open. "You're adding the peas now?"

Collette chuckled. "I told you not to watch."

"But they'll get all wrinkled," Tess insisted. "Does Suzie like wrinkled peas?"

In just two weeks, Tess had developed a keen interest in cooking and in Collette's daughter. "Suzie eats what she's given, without a complaint about wrinkled peas."

"Not everyone is as finicky as you, Tess." Amy nodded knowingly.

"I just don't like wrinkled peas," Tess insisted.

"To each his own." Collette set aside the casserole dish and set to tidying up the kitchen. She expected the girls to retreat to their rooms, as usual, but instead they stayed in the kitchen and lent a hand. Probably mesmerized by the cooking aromas, especially the biscuits that she'd quickly dropped onto a baking pan and popped into the oven. The weather was a bit too warm for baking, but she thought the meal should have something to help sop up sauce, and there wasn't a crust of bread in the house.

When the biscuits emerged, golden brown and smelling delicious, she heard the sound of a horse and buggy out on the lane. "You can each have one biscuit before dinner," she told the girls.

"Denki." Amy was immediately upon the cookie sheet, blowing on the corner biscuit so that it would cool.

"See you Friday!" Tess called.

"Friday. Don't forget—twenty minutes on the final ingredients."

Outside, Aaron had stepped out of the buggy and walked around the house so that he could see the front yard. "I just noticed that you fought the weeds and won!" he remarked.

She nodded. It had only taken him a week or so to notice the changes, but then she knew the bishop had many things on his plate.

"And the mums brought back some color to our front yard."

"Aye, and today we picked a good amount of berries and peas from your garden. The cherry tomatoes are sweet as candy."

"It's a good time of year for our gardens."

She placed the warm casserole dish onto the floorboards of the buggy. The bishop looked weary and a bit warm as he pushed back the brim of his straw hat and swiped the sheen from his forehead, but he still maintained a positive attitude. Collette climbed inside. "I'm grateful for the ride," she said, as he took the reins and started the horse moving. "Walking is good exercise, but sometimes at the end of the day, it's a bit much."

His eyes glimmered as he nodded. "Gives me a chance to check in on the girls."

"They're coming along right good," Collette assured him. "How was your day? How's Jerry?" Aaron had mentioned his plans to take Jerry Kraybill into town for his doctor's appointment.

"Good. The doctor says Jerry's pacemaker is working just fine."

"'O, bless the Lord, my soul,'" she said, quoting a psalm of thanks. "We can always be grateful for good news. And your work at Iddo's farm?"

"It was a productive day. Iddo hired one of Ezra King's boys to make the work go faster. A wise move." When Collette commented that he seemed to help Iddo every day, he explained that it was Iddo who was helping him. "Managing the fields has been too much without the help of my wife and son."

She nodded, knowing that Mose's departure was a point of pain and embarrassment for Aaron. A parent couldn't control a teen in the rumspringa years, but at the same time, there was a certain shame in parenting a child who strayed from the plain life. A shame that probably hit harder for a church leader, who was a model for the community. Avoiding that potential sore spot, she asked, "How is Iddo Dienner helping you?"

"We struck an agreement. We help each other when necessary, but mostly he manages my fields and keeps my crops on schedule. Which is a necessity, as I'm called away more often these days in my duties to the ministry."

"That's no surprise," she said. "I can see there's much to do to lead an Amish community, and I don't know the half of it."

"You're a keen observer," he said. "I suspect you know more than most."

She smiled despite her reserve. The thought that he knew that about her warmed her heart. For so many years she had been content to blend into the Amish community, mix with the women, spend time with her family, and obey all the rules.

Circumspect.

That was Collette's one-word description of herself over the past decade. Not your everyday word; she knew that. It meant wary, careful, or on guard, which accurately described Collette's life as a single woman in an Amish community with an absentee husband. Widows were treated with deference, and single women, even the older ones, had a decent chance of finding a husband and blending into the community of Amish families. Not so with an abandoned woman. Throughout those years of missing Jed, Collette could not remarry, as divorce, even for the reason of desertion, was not allowed among the Amish. Hence she'd found herself caught in a social trap. A single mother, she'd needed to earn a wage while trying to raise her two children without their father.

Forbearance; maybe that should have been her word. Hers was a life of restraint and tolerance.

While hard work didn't faze her, the social isolation had worn on her at times. Although no one said the words, the sentiment of some in the community was that there had to be something wrong with a woman who could drive her husband away. Something objectionable or unpleasant. Something ungodly.

They simply didn't know the truth. Perhaps they didn't want to know? Their imaginings were probably much racier than reality, though not nearly as sad. She was staring out at the golden fields leading to the lavender hills when he broke the silence.

"Collette. Here I am puffing on like a bellows and we haven't talked about how the day went for you. I trust the girls stayed in line?"

"It was a fine day. I showed them a few tips in the kitchen, and they should have your dinner ready for you when you get home. A skillet stew. I took your feelings about casseroles to heart."

"It smells delicious!" he exclaimed, nodding at the covered dish at her feet. "Though it's only Yumasetti that makes me wince."

"I remember that. We had some good talks, the three of us, and when I heard how much Tess likes books, I promised to take her to the library." She turned to study his face. "If it's all right with you."

"The library is fine for borrowing books," he said. "Just as long as she doesn't get on those computers. I know our church rules allow Amish folk to use computers if they don't own them, but it's not something I want for my daughters."

"I understand. Books only. Which is the only thing she's interested in right now, Gott bless her."

"And Amy?"

"Older and wiser than her sister, of course. I'd love to see her life filled with more activity. I'm wondering, has she ever gone looking for a job?"

"Nay. When Dorcas passed, Amy was about to finish school. She left to take care of her mother in those last months, and when that was all over . . ." He shook his head. "My mother started taking care of the girls, who both seemed too fragile to do anything beyond the basics. Tess made it to school, and Amy, she didn't do much beyond church and youth events. I guess I should have pushed her to get work, but I didn't know what to do. I was lost myself."

"A hard thing for a family to go through," she said. "We do our best."

He frowned. "So you think Amy should look for a job?"

"I do. And I think I know the perfect place for her to start."

"Well, if you can talk her into it, I'd be most obliged."

She studied his face as he stared off in the distance and sighed. Amy would be thrilled to have a way out of the house, a way to be with Amish youth, a way to socialize.

And you don't know that about your daughter. Collette marveled at the burdens that had distracted the bishop from the needs of his children.

"Raising children has been nothing like I expected. I thought the hard work would be done when they were talking and out of diapers. My mistake. It goes on, and beyond the Bible, I know of no parenting guide."

She chuckled. "They're good girls. Count your blessings. Though they'd both be happier if they stopped trying to outdo each other."

"The competitiveness? Yah! I don't know where that comes from."

They chuckled together as an afternoon breeze sifted in through the buggy flaps and cooled Collette's warm cheeks. Sitting next to Aaron seemed to push her temperature up a bit, but she couldn't let that get in the way of the sweet ease between them.

When he dropped her off outside the Dawdi House, she felt a glow of contentment and promise deep in her heart. Their end-of-day conversations were so comforting and interesting, like a warm meal after days without a crumb. So many folks feared the bishop of their community, sometimes with good reason, as the church leader often had to rule with an iron fist as he laid down the laws of the Ordnung.

But somehow, Aaron didn't inspire fear in Collette's heart. When she answered his questions and he lowered his silver-tipped head to listen, she felt as if she were confiding in a friend she'd known for many years.

A friend that she hoped would be around for a good time to come.

Chapter 10

Miriam paced the shiny tile floor of the large Lancaster Railway Station as she waited for her parents' train to arrive. Sunlight streamed in the three arched windows high overhead, but the heat did nothing to warm the cool air pumped in around her. Aah! Such lovely cold air! It was as if she had crawled inside the refrigerator for a short break from the wilting summer heat that had lasted into September.

"Now arriving on track twelve," came the announcement, "the Pennsylvanian from Pittsburgh, Pennsylvania, track twelve."

Her parents' train.

Shaking off the jitters, she turned to face the entrance to the doorway from which the passengers would emerge. A handful of folks in the cavernous room veered closer, too, and Miriam smiled at a little girl happily brushing past as she skipped by her.

To be young and carefree again, instead of worrying about keeping her mother happy throughout the duration of Lois's visit! For days she'd been worried about making things go smoothly with Mem, and now that the train had arrived, she vowed to put those fears behind her.

Passengers passed through the archway, some striding off and others pausing to greet folks. The little girl squealed with delight as a man emerged from the gate and lifted her into the air.

Smiling at the reunion, Miriam caught sight of her own mother, a grim look on her face as she labored ahead, weighed down by two shopping bags.

"Mem! It's so good to see you." She reached out to hug her mother, but was a bit put off when Lois's strong frame didn't ease into the embrace.

Instead, Lois gave her daughter's back a perfunctory pat and muttered, "Oh, my, there's a lot to hug here. And here I thought you were kidding about needing a diet."

Miriam winced. She regretted mentioning that in her last letter. Her love for food and sweets had thickened her through the waist, a matter that was a challenge and a sore spot at times. Best to let it pass.

"How was your trip?" she asked, leaning back to meet her mother's gaze. "I know you've been traveling all day."

"Fifteen hours from our house to here. Two buses and then we switched to a train in Pittsburgh. At least we could sleep on the bus. After midnight, the driver asked folks to dim the lights. A right kind thing to do."

"I'm so glad you're here," she said, leaning back to meet her mother's gaze. "It's been so long, Mem. Alvin and the children can't wait to see you, and Sam and his bride are grateful that you could make the wedding." She gave Mem's hand a squeeze. "It's been too long!"

"Well, you could have moved to Michigan like your brothers, and you'd be a lot closer."

Miriam smiled, tempted to laugh out loud at the ridiculousness of such an idea. When you marry a man who owns a share in a dairy farm and has spent all his years working the family acres of Gott's good earth, you commit to his way of life. Such a good life she shared with Alvie! Years ago she had tried to explain it all to Mem, but apparently it hadn't sunk in.

"That's a long trip. You must be tuckered out."

"We did catch a few naps along the way, but it's cold in here," her mother said.

"True, but it's such a nice break from the heat outside." Miriam smiled, savoring the familiar contours of her mother's face, plus a few small creases here and there. "I'm trying to soak it up while I can."

"It was cold on the train, too," Lois added. "I told the conductor but there wasn't a thing that could be done about it."

"Did you bring a shawl?"

"That would be foolish, wouldn't it? Who would think to pack warm clothing in this weather?"

Miriam was distracted as she searched the faces of the other emerging passengers. "Where's Dat?"

"He'll be coming up with the luggage. It was too big for the overhead bin, so he had to check it with the porter."

"Does he need help?" Miriam asked. She may have put on a few pounds since she last saw her mother, but she was strong and hardy.

"He'll manage," Lois insisted.

Miriam edged closer to the track entrance, relieved to see a lean Amish man appear, looking strained in his dark jacket and straw hat. Or maybe it was the burden of the fat suitcase he carried.

"Dat!" she called with an excited wave.

A smile brightened David Stuckey's face as he moved in their direction.

"Such a large suitcase!" Miriam exclaimed. "Do you want help with that?"

"I got it just fine." He puffed a bit, then set the suitcase down. "It's got wheels, you know. Glides on the ground, as long as you're pushing it on good, flat ground."

"I see that. Is it new?"

"New for us. We're borrowing it from your brother Junior. He and Birdie got it for their trip out west."

"Very nice," Miriam said. "And how is Junior and his family? His children now have children of their own!"

"Doing fine. Nothing new, but then we see them all the time."

Miriam gestured toward the wide station doors. "If you want to push it over this way, our van is waiting right outside."

"A van?" Lois's brows rose. "I thought Alvin was waiting with the buggy."

"It's a bit too far for the horse," Miriam said. "And this will get us home much faster."

Outside, their driver, Demetri, loaded the suitcase and passengers in with assurance that he would adjust the air conditioning so Lois wouldn't catch a chill. "Everyone buckled up?" he asked, looking in the rearview mirror. "And off we go."

"Essie's working on dinner. She's my oldest, now married to Harlan Yoder." It had been so many years; Miriam wasn't sure if her mother remembered all seven of the Lapp grandchildren. "They live in the Dawdi House, and we often make our dinners together."

"We know. We read your letters," said Lois.

"Then you know that Sarah's girls are with us," Miriam said tentatively. "Well, one of them just went off to college, but she'll be back for the wedding. They're eager to meet you. Especially the youngest, Grace."

"Why would they want to meet us?" Lois asked.

"Mem, you're their grandmother."

Her mother's lips curled down in a frown. "Well, I know that, but Sarah left. What would they want from me?"

Maybe your love and support. Miriam wished she could say the words, but it would be cutting too close to the bone right now.

"You mentioned them in your letters," Dat said. "It's hard to believe Sarah's girls are nearly grown now, eh, Lois?"

"It's odd that they had nowhere else to go." Mem shook her head. "You'd think their Englisch family would offer to take them in. Three Englisch girls on an Amish farm are like a fish out of water."

"It was a bit bumpy at first," Miriam admitted, "but they're family, and they've brought us so much joy."

Lois's only response was a frown, as if she had forgotten the meaning of joy.

"I hope she's making something good. We're pretty hungry after losing most of the food we brought for the trip. Four sandwiches, I packed."

"Oh, dear. You lost your sandwiches?"

"And homemade granola. My stomach has been growling for the last hour."

"We bought fried chicken at the Pittsburgh station," Dat said. "It was right tasty."

Lois folded her arms, looking petulant. "It was a bit greasy for me."

"And we didn't lose our food," Dat said. "I gave it away to a young man who needed it more."

"A robber," Lois said, her voice gritty. "That's what I thought he was."

"What happened?" Miriam's alarm was tempered when she turned back to take in her father in the third-row seat. Despite Mem's annoyance, he was calm and solemn.

"He didn't rob us," he said quietly. He spoke with delicate patience, as if treading around brambles and trying to avoid getting stuck. "He asked for spare change, and I told him I had none. But his sign said he was hungry, and I saw hunger in his face, too. Skin and bones. Now I know you think I've lost my wits, sweetheart, but it seemed to me that if the Savior met a hungry traveler, he'd have given His food away."

Mem was turned toward the window. "I think he'd have had the good sense to hold on to one sandwich."

Miriam stared at her mother, not sure what to make of the cold response. She'd never seen her parents argue, never seen her mother quite so disgruntled. Granted, Lois had always been quick to voice her disapproval, but in the past she had maintained a level mood and had always supported her husband. Now she seemed to have sunk to a new level of discontent.

"You'll feel better when you've had some dinner," Dat said. He leaned back on the seat and stretched his arms out with a sigh. "It will be good to land in your home, daughter."

Miriam nodded, grateful to have the conversation back on sure footing. "I'm glad you're here. Now tell me something good that happened during your trip. You must have seen some interesting sights in half a day's journey."

"I finally laid eyes on one the Great Lakes," Dat said. "We saw Lake Erie! The breeze whipped up the blue waters like Gott had a hand beater. It's one of Gott's wonders, indeed. So big, you can't even see the land on the other side!" he exclaimed.

"What a marvelous sight!" Miriam had seen photographs, but she hadn't yet experienced such a sight.

"And we passed through more cities than I thought possible to visit in a day. Detroit, Toledo, Cleveland, Altoona, and Pittsburgh." Dat counted them off on his fingers as he spoke. "I tell you, I'm feeling like a right seasoned traveler."

"It was nighttime when we passed through Detroit and

Toledo," Mem pointed out. "You can't really see a city in the dark."

"But there were so many lights. Tall buildings like boxes with square windows of light. It was quite a sight." Dad chuckled. "So many lights, I was sure I wouldn't sleep a wink. But soon enough, our bus started to leave the city. The buildings turned to houses, and then they were scattered and it was mostly darkness with tall lampposts along the road."

"So you managed to get some sleep?" Miriam asked.

"Sure did."

"He snored most of the way to Toledo," Mem said, turning back toward Dad.

Miriam saw them exchange a smile, and then the tension was broken, the mood in the van lighter, at last.

Still, Mem's sour mood was a worry.

Watching the passing landscape, green earth and blue sky merging into a blur as she became lost in thought, Miriam wondered if her mother had slipped into a depression of late. Although she'd always been critical of Miriam and Sarah, Lois had generally maintained a calm disposition with the rest of the world.

Maybe she's just tired. After all those hours cooped up on a bus or a train, Miriam knew she'd be weary and cross, too.

On the other hand, Dat had revealed a new level of patience and a sense of wonder about the world around him. Good for him! After years of holding his tongue, he'd found some words to spark joy.

Sitting quietly as Mem fussed about the air conditioning, Miriam hoped that Mem brightened after a nice meal and a good night's sleep. That would do it.

Didn't everything look better in the morning?

Chapter 11

Grace's Amish grandmother was not at all what she'd expected.

The night the Stuckeys arrived, her grandma seemed cranky and tired, quick to bite anyone's head off for comments she didn't like and loathe to express approval of anyone or anything.

At first, Grace just figured that her grandma was tired, but then her grandfather had endured the same long journey, and he was pleasant and friendly that very first night. He thanked Essie for the delicious dinner and laughed along with everyone when Lizzie told how she'd had to chase Daisy the cow off the road that day.

"Good for you," David told Lizzie, looking over the family with pride. "How big you've all grown! We're so happy to see you, all of you. Sam, I'm glad we could make it for your wedding." Grandpa David clapped Sam on the back, but when Grace turned toward their grandmother, she found her chair empty. Lois had gone up to bed even before the strawberry-rhubarb pie had been brought out.

Grace felt deflated, but reminded herself that relationships didn't happen overnight. She sensed that she was going to have to woo her grandmother, like an advertiser going after a client.

Sales had never been her thing, but with three weeks to get to know her grandmother, she had to give it a try.

The next morning, Grace went out of her way to make conversation with her grandmother in the kitchen as she downed her coffee and buttered bread. She followed Lois to the chicken coop, trying to make an impression, though it wasn't easy with Lizzie and Sarah Rose showing their grandmother how they tended the chickens.

After school, instead of settling into her room to do homework, Grace spent an hour or so down at the kitchen table, participating in Lois's sewing circle, where scraps of material were hand-stitched into quilting squares. All female hands pitched in. Lizzie and Essie were always there, and Sadie, Serena, and Suzie joined in when they weren't working. Even Sarah Rose was given a place at the table, where she liked to rearrange straight pins in a cushion that resembled a tomato. Aunt Miriam tended to comment from the other side of the kitchen, where she promised to join in as soon as she was done preparing this or that.

Grace knew that Aunt Miriam disliked sewing. Although Miriam wouldn't say a cross word about anything, Grace had seen that she was all thumbs with a needle and thread. Seams puckered and thread snagged. Miriam even had trouble running a straight seam on the foot-powered sewing machine. Now, as she worked on the same wrinkled square of cloth day after day, Grace was beginning to see Aunt Miriam's point of view. It was fun to gather around the table together, but the work was deadly dull, and Grace felt sure no one would ever use her wrinkled square of cloth in their Amish quilt. But it was a way to talk to her grandmother.

Each day in the sewing circle, Grace asked her grandmother questions about the family. How had Lois met David? Did her parents approve of him? Why had they left

Joyful River for Michigan? What was Aunt Miriam like as a kid? What about Sarah, her mom?

Her grandma gave a few short answers, but mostly she shut Grace down. "I think you'd best pay more attention to your sewing and less attention to the past," Lois would say, nodding at the sewing notions on the table.

"I don't think she likes me," Grace said one night as the girls were getting ready for bed. When Serena and Lizzie looked over at her, she clarified, "Grandma Lois."

Serena's eyes softened with sympathy. "I sense hesitance whenever she looks at me. It's because we're not Amish, I think. We make her kind of nervous."

"Maybe it's my hair and nose ring," Grace said. "Some people get put off."

Lizzie looked from Grace to Serena and shook her head. "Who doesn't like green hair?"

That was Lizzie, always trying to make the people around her feel better. Usually it worked, but this time, Grace wasn't going to be satisfied until she made a real connection with her grandmother.

Over the next few days, Grace kept trying. Each time she went out of her way to try to spark conversation with her grandmother, Mammi Lois seemed sour. Cold and tight as a clam. Far from the stern but kindhearted Mammi Esther, this woman was about as huggable as one of the scarecrows in the cornfields.

Grace suspected that Mammi Lois had secrets, lots of issues stuffed down deep inside her. But that seemed to be the opposite of Amish people, who prided themselves on living simple lives. What sorrows burned in the heart of Lois Stuckey?

Grace could only wonder.

* * *

When Grace made her way down to the kitchen for some milk late one night, she noticed that the front door was open, the glider on the porch singing under the weight of a person.

Probably Serena and Scout, or Sam and Sadie. Recently, Grace had realized that everyone around here from their late teens up had become part of a couple. Weird.

"You're next," Serena said, when Grace pointed it out.

"Meh" was Grace's lukewarm response. She wasn't into dating. Right now, she had things to figure out about herself first.

"Are you a sheep?" her sister had asked. When Grace nodded, Serena rolled her eyes. "Very mature."

Smiling at the memory, Grace now pushed open the screen door to peek outside. "Somebody out here?"

"Just us chickens," came a low male voice.

Grace peered out to find her grandparents sitting on the porch. Jackpot. "What are you guys doing up so late?" Usually her grandparents were the first ones to bed.

"We thought it be a good night to get some fresh air," her grandpa said. "Almost a full moon."

"But it's getting cool." Grandma had a loose blanket over her shoulders, a crocheted quilt from Aunt Miriam's sofa. The air out here was humid and warm as velvet, but Lois seemed to find comfort in snuggling into the throw blanket.

"That is a pretty moon." Grace stepped out and took a seat on one of the metal chairs, all the while staring at the moon. "On nights like this I'm amazed at how bright it can be. A light in the sky."

"One of Gott's gifts," Grandpa said with kindness in his voice. That was his usual demeanor, upbeat and cheerful, a lot like his daughter Miriam. "And what are you doing up, young Grace?"

"I was up doing homework. Came down to get some milk." She tucked her bare legs under her and nestled into the corner of the chair. "But I'd rather hang out with you."

"Up so late with schoolwork?" He shook his head "Whoa, now. That must be quite a lot."

"It is, but I like school." She told them about her assignment on *The Grapes of Wrath.* "It's a story about farmers, but they're very poor and have to leave their home to look for other places to make a living."

"A sad thing," he said. "We've known folks in that situation, haven't we, Lois?"

Grandma nodded curtly. "I haven't read the book."

Grace and her grandfather talked for a bit about the difficulties of farming. Then he stood up and stretched. "Speaking of farming, I promised Alvin I'd help him bring in the hay tomorrow. I'd best be getting to bed . . . ." He turned to Grace, adding, "Though I'd rather hang out with you."

She smiled up at him. "Good night, Grandpa."

He patted her shoulder and went to the door.

"I'll go up, too," Lois said, gathering the blanket around her with one shoulder as she gripped the arm of the chair.

"No, Grandma. Stay with me for a bit. Please? We never get a chance to talk, just the two of us."

Lois sighed, but she remained in the chair. "We can talk. But I'm afraid I can't say the things you want to hear."

"And why is that?" Grace asked. "Why don't you want to talk about my mother?"

"When it comes to the past, it's best to leave old stones unturned."

"That sounds really wise, Grandma, but I don't have a clue what it means."

"You should call me Mammi." Her grandmother's brows lifted in a stern look. "It's easy enough to remember, isn't it?"

"Sorry, Mammi. It's just that it sounds so much like Mommy, which is what we called our mother when we were little kids, and . . ."

The older woman tapped her chest. "And it touches a tender spot in your heart, yah?"

"Exactly."

"I understand. But you should call me Mammi out of respect."

"Of course, Mammi," Grace said. "I'm really glad for this chance to talk. I have so many questions about my mother, but you always change the subject when I ask about her. What's the deal with that?"

Lois's right hand smoothed over the metal armrest of her chair, as if memorizing it. "If you swat a fly enough times, eventually it will find another pie."

"Wait . . . What? Are you comparing me to a fly?"

"That wouldn't be kind."

"But you're implying that I'm bugging you with all these questions."

Her grandmother sighed, those creases appearing on her upper lip. "You never give up. That can be a good quality sometimes. Makes a good housekeeper or a right-good farmer."

"But not what you're looking for in a granddaughter," Grace said bluntly.

"Now, now." Lois leaned forward to pat Grace's hand. "Gott doesn't let us select the qualities we want in our family members. We must appreciate the good and learn to cope with the rest."

"Mammi Lois . . ." Grace let out an exasperated sigh as she looked into the older woman's chocolate eyes. "I wish you'd stop talking in circles and answer my questions."

The older woman leaned back in the chair and tapped two fingers against her chest. "I have a tender spot, too.

Your mother. There are things I don't remember; other times that are too painful to bring up again. I just . . . I can't talk about this."

Crestfallen, Grace fell silent, her jaw dropping as she considered her grandmother's point of view. What terrible things had happened in the past to make her grandmother too wounded to think of her own daughter?

"Isn't there anything you can tell me? Something from when she was a little kid?"

"It was so long ago, and my memory doesn't serve me well." Letting out a heavy sigh, Mammi closed her eyes, retreating like a sleeping owl. All closed down.

Grace was about to give up when Mammi perked up, straightening in her chair. "I can tell you one thing: Sarah was an answer to my prayers. Your mother was the light of my world when she was born." The older woman turned and met Grace's gaze for a moment, before looking away. "There, I said it. I loved her so, my first baby girl."

"Grand—I mean, Mammi, that's so sweet." Grace could imagine a younger version of this woman holding an infant girl in her arms, and for a moment, it felt good to know her mother had been so loved.

"I'd prayed for a girl for years, you see, but Gott had given me only boys. And then, along came Sarah. We named her after Sarah in the Bible. Do you know her story?"

Grace shook her head, not wanting to admit that, aside from a few Christmas stories, she knew very few anecdotes from the Bible.

"Sarah was a good woman who was unable to have children. And then, though Sarah was very old, Gott promised her a child, and made good on his promise." When Grace squinted at her grandmother, Lois added, "Yah, it was a bit different. I wasn't so old, and I had sons already, but the daughter, she was my heart's desire. When she was born, I knew that Gott had answered my prayers."

"So you were happy when my mom was born," Grace said, trying to pin Mammi Lois down. It wasn't often that the woman said something positive.

"I was, indeed. There's something wonderful about having a daughter. It gave me hope that she would be able to carry on in the world when I ran out of steam. I know that may sound silly, but there you have it. David was also bright as a peach, thrilled to have a daughter."

Grace treasured the new warmth in her grandmother's voice, the lift of her spirits. "This is wonderful, Mammi. It's exactly the kind of story I've been searching for. See? You do remember."

"Well," Mammi said, rubbing her hands together, "just a little bit."

"I love that story. I can imagine you and Dawdi holding Mom when she was a little baby. It's so sweet!"

Mammi nodded, though she seemed to melt into the chair a bit, as if telling the story had drained her.

"I know it's late, but tell me more. I want to hear what she was like as a little kid. Was she always so bright and outspoken? Did she like to draw pictures as a kid? I always wondered about that, since she was so artistic."

But Mammi kept her gaze down. "No. I need to go to bed."

"You're tired. I understand. I'm just so excited to be talking about her. We can talk again tomorrow. Maybe you'll remember some other great stories about her childhood."

"No, Grace. No more talking about her." Gripping the arms of the chair, she pushed herself up and scowled down at Grace. "That's the end of it."

"But Mammi, wait—" Grace followed her in through

the door, but her grandmother kept plodding ahead. "Please, don't be mad."

"I'm not mad." She plucked at the edges of the crocheted wool blanket, pulling it tighter over her shoulders. "I just don't like all your questions. Questions falling on my head like fat raindrops. I try to run away, but the rain finds me. And it's you causing me all this grief."

"I just want to know more," Grace said.

"You want too much." At the bottom of the stairs Mammi turned to face Grace. "That will be the end of it, you hear me? The end."

Crestfallen, Grace stood at the bottom of the stairs, not daring to breathe as her grandmother climbed up and out of sight.

The end of it, she'd said. Over before it had even begun.

Grace was taking her last sip of coffee the next morning when Aunt Miriam popped into the kitchen from the yard.

"There you are," Miriam said. She wore her royal blue dress, and a black apron and cape were neatly pinned. This was not Aunt Miriam's usual at-home attire. "I'm heading into town for some errands if you'd like a ride to school."

Like it? Not having to sit on the grunting dinosaur of a bus as it wove through the countryside would be a huge lift in her day. "I'd love that." Grace slipped her backpack over one shoulder and put her cup in the sink. "Do you need help with the buggy?"

"Alvin's got Brownie brushed, harnessed, and all set between the shafts of the buggy." Miriam smiled as she motioned Grace out the door into the sunlight. "I love a productive morning!"

Although Grace was not a morning person, there was

no denying the wonder of the farm on a sunlit day. The sun-warmed grass under foot. The smell of clover and honeysuckle. That bit of cool moisture that still lingered on the leaves of the trees lining the lane.

Brownie nickered impatiently as they approached. "Where's Sarah Rose?" Grace asked as she placed her backpack inside the square, gray buggy. Miriam's youngest child was usually like her shadow around the farm.

"Her grandparents are going to mind her for a bit," Miriam said. "Gives my mem a chance to have some one-on-one time with her."

One-on-one time, Grace thought, a bitter taste on her tongue as Miriam called to Brownie to start them down the lane. "I know I'm not as cute and sweet as Sarah Rose, but I'd like a shot at my grandmother, too. Don't I deserve to get to know her?"

"I heard you talking with her out on the porch last night."

"Not a good conversation," Grace admitted miserably.

"I know. She's a tough nut, my mem."

"Serena thinks it's because we're not Amish. She thinks we make Mammi Lois uncomfortable."

"Your grandmother has had plenty of experience with Englisch folk before. It's got to be more than that."

"I just want to get to know her. I thought she'd want to discuss all her memories of my mother. Why does she always cut me off or run away or change the subject?"

"I'm sure there's a reason," Miriam said. "Maybe it's too painful for her to think of Sarah. After Sarah left Joyful River, Mem seemed to push her out of her mind. Like she'd never existed."

"So, was my mother shunned?"

"Not at all. To be under the ban—or shunned, as you say—you need to be a baptized member of the church.

That's the thinking; once you choose baptism, you join the Amish for life, and commit to following the rules of the gmay, the church."

"And Mom didn't get baptized?"

"She did not. Sarah made friends with some Englisch girls. She had lots of friends, both Englisch and Amish. Everyone liked being with your mem. Anyway, Sarah was going to parties during her rumspringa. Lots of Amish youth drink and go a bit wild during that time. Mostly I think Sarah liked meeting people and exploring new places."

"She always liked to take us places when I was little," Grace said. "All the museums in Washington, D.C. To the beach at Bethany, and there was a winter festival with ice sculptures that she really liked. And here. I remember camping here on the farm, and fishing in the river. And the frogs down by the pond! They were so loud at night, I felt sure they were creeping closer to us, ready to pounce."

Miriam chuckled. "It must have been mating season. They croak for hours, but I'm so used to it I barely hear it now. I'm glad you have fond memories."

"We loved visiting you here. Mom said there was nothing better than a summer day wading in the cool water of Joyful River."

Miriam clapped a hand to her breast. "It does my heart good to hear that."

"She loved you, Aunt Miriam."

"I know that. But now when I think back on those summers when you visited, I recall that my parents stayed away."

"But they had moved to Michigan."

"Not in the early years. There were many times when you visited that my parents lived right here in Joyful River. Of course, I invited everyone over, tried to bring the family together to see Sarah and meet you girls. But Mem and Dat never came. I think it hurt Sarah, but she didn't dwell on it. She wasn't one to hold on to sorrow."

"I don't remember any of that."

"You were so young, how could you? And I don't think your sisters were aware of it, either. Sarah had such a way of moving forward without regret." Miriam called to Brownie as they approached a stop sign, and the horse abruptly halted. They waited as two cars and a yellow school bus drove past.

"That might be my bus," Grace said. "But here I am riding in my own royal carriage instead. Thanks for the lift."

Miriam smiled. "It's a modest buggy, same as other plain folk, but I'm glad you're enjoying the ride. I wanted to do a little something for you after last night. I know how difficult my mem can be, and sometimes disappointment falls heavy on our hearts."

As they passed fields and farmhouses, Grace wondered if she'd expected too much of her grandmother. Had she been imagining a perfect family? An idealized world in which her mother and grandmother had enjoyed a story-book relationship?

She should have known better. Aunt Miriam was right. She should have taken cues from the fact that her grandparents hadn't been around when Grace and her family had visited Joyful River. She should have realized something was up when her grandparents hadn't come around when Mom was dying. "You know what's weird? That Mom's parents weren't there in the end," Grace said. "They didn't visit when she got diagnosed with cancer. They didn't even come to the funeral."

"That's always bothered me." Miriam stared ahead glumly. "Mem blamed it on a number of things. The weather being too bad to travel. The expense of a trip. Dat getting the flu. But really, I have trouble understanding any of those reasons."

"I'm sure she wanted to come." As Grace spoke, an image of her mother in her purple, red and pink turban came to mind. She'd tried to wear a wig after losing her hair to chemo, but found it too itchy and hot. "This suits me to a T," Mom had said, modeling the silky turban for Grace and her sisters. Mom accessorized the turban with a silky purple oversized blouse, cowboy boots, and blue jeans that were fashionably "distressed," with slashes and frays in the fabric.

For a moment, Sarah Sullivan danced through Grace's mind in that brightly hued getup. A rock star in living color.

Grace still missed her like crazy.

Trying to swallow back the knot in her throat before tears welled up in her eyes, Grace realized just how far apart her mother and grandmother had been. "It's probably a good thing Mammi and Dawdi didn't come to see Mom," she said.

Aunt Miriam seemed surprised. "How's that?"

"I don't think they would have understood her. You know, the woman she'd become. I don't think they would have appreciated my mom. And I'm not sure she needed their approval."

"This is true." Miriam nodded. "But I have to say, if something happened to one of my daughters, to Essie or Lizzie or Sarah Rose—or to you or your sisters—I wouldn't be able to stay away. I'd have Brownie hitched to a buggy lickety-split, or I'd ride a bus night and day to get to you."

Now Grace was full-on crying, tears slipping down her cheeks at the thought of Aunt Miriam riding through the night to come to her rescue. She had known this about Aunt Miriam for a while now. She knew she was loved, here in Joyful River. But it meant so much for Aunt Miriam to say the words.

"Oh, my dear!" Miriam gave her arm a squeeze. "We must take care of the ones we love."

Grace nodded, swiping away her tears with the back of one hand. "I know. I love you, Aunt Miriam. And even if she's trying to fend me off, I won't back down. I'm not giving up on Mammi Lois."

"Good for you," Miriam said. "But if she disappoints you, remember that you can always count on me. Gott willing, I'll come to help you."

"Galloping in a buggy, or on a Greyhound bus," Grace added.

Chapter 12

Such a day! Already September, but surely it had to be one of the hottest days of the year. Collette tried to ignore the bead of sweat that dripped down the center of her back as she slathered whitewash onto the fence that ran along one side of Len and Linda Hostetler's lane. It was Thursday, and her part-time employers were beginning to fret over the final tasks to prepare their home to host the gmay—their church gathering—this Sunday.

Eager to pitch in, she'd scrubbed the linoleum floors, washed down the walls, and cleaned the windows until they were as clear as the surface of a still pond. She had made bacon and eggs for Linda and her daughters and her visiting sister, Sally, who was supposed to be "such a big help," but seemed to enjoy being waited on. And once the breakfast dishes were done, Linda had sent Collette out here to whitewash the fence, as it would be the first thing visitors saw when they came up the lane.

"A lot of work to make a fence white," Collette muttered under her breath as she swathed the brush over a wide plank. Who noticed a graying fence when it was surrounded by green grass and tall trees reaching their sturdy limbs toward the heavens?

She paused a moment to lift the hem of the smock she'd

thrown over her dress. Pressing it against the sweaty spots
on her upper lip and neck, she sighed. Not that she felt
sorry for herself. She was just hot, and this was her job. She
was a hired hand here, as Linda had clearly explained to her
sister Sally last Tuesday as the two women sat and hulled
strawberries at the outdoor table while Collette washed
down the walls inside the house—another tedious preparation for hosting church.

"I admit, it's a bit of charity on our part," Linda had confided in her sister. "You know me. I don't need a maud.
But Collette needs to support her daughter, and I've known
her for years."

"A widow?" Sally had asked.

"Recently widowed, but the husband was scattered to
the winds for many years. So . . . *an abandoned wife*."
Linda had said the words as if they had the stink of a pile
of manure, and Sally's murmured sigh indicated her pity for
the lowliest of women.

An abandoned wife. Collette had borne that title for so
long, she'd grown accustomed to it, as if it were an old
nightgown with holes and worn spots that you could navigate with your eyes closed. Patched and worn-out; was that
how most folks thought of her? The notion of being
chucked aside so easily made her heart heavy at times, but
it was the Amish way to blend in with others in the community. And the fact that she went unnoticed made it that
much easier for her to blend into the background, tend to
others, and look after the ones she loved.

A good life, she thought now as she pressed the wide
paintbrush to the weathered wood and gave it a chalky
sheen. Gott had blessed her with a loving son and daughter,
and now with the goodness of the Lapp family, Harlan's
in-laws who had offered her a place to live for as long as
she needed. "Thanks be to Gott," she murmured.

"Collette?" A voice came from the yard. "Collette . . . where did you go?" Linda Hostetler, the boss, stood on the porch, one hand up to shield her eyes from the sun.

"I'm right here, finishing the fence." *Just as you told me to do.*

"There you are! Come make us more lemonade. The pitcher's gone dry, and it's such a hot day. We're going down to the river to cool off, and I thought we'd fill a thermos. What do you think? Doesn't that sound nice?"

"It sounds heavenly." To dip her feet into the cold, clear water, navigating over smooth stones as the current coursed past her bare legs. Collette saw her day quickly improving. "I'll make another batch," she said, setting down her paintbrush and starting across the yard.

"Good. Len will be back any moment, so you'll need to make him some lunch while Sally and I are gone."

It was suddenly clear that Collette was not invited to the river, after all. Of course, she wasn't. She was the maud, the hired hand. And there was plenty to do to get the house ready for hosting church on Sunday.

"We'll also need a dessert for Sunday church. Something cool and refreshing, I think. It's bound to be another hot day. And be sure to fetch the fishing tackle. Sally seems to think she's going to be able to catch us our dinner."

"I know how to find the fish," Sally said as she held the kitchen door open for her sister.

Hands on hips, Linda paused in the doorway. "It's been years since you fished in Joyful River."

"I have my ways," Sally teased, and the sisters laughed.

Heading toward them, Collette noticed the similar features of the sisters. Both women had sharp noses and dark eyes, but the features that were so sharp and cold on Linda were softened on Sally. More kitten than fox.

As Collette approached, Linda gave the screen door a

slight push with one hand, not really holding it open for Collette, but not letting it slam in her face.

And that summarizes my relationship with Linda, Collette thought as she went to the sink to wash her hands.

Once the two women were gone, Collette allowed herself a sip of lemonade before returning to work. On the kitchen counter sat two flats of berries from the market, ready for Linda and her sister to make into a jam after sundown. Surely Collette could use a pint or two of the ruby red strawberries for the Sunday dessert—the strawberry Jell-O mold that had reminded the bishop of earlier times.

That way, she could look forward to seeing Aaron enjoy a serving of it after church. She imagined looking over at him as he ate the ruby-red dessert layered with sweetened cream cheese. He'd be seated among the men, of course, and she'd remove herself from conversation with the women to watch him take a bite. And maybe he'd look up and catch her gaze, and they'd have a moment—a secret exchange—sharing the knowledge that she had made the dessert especially for him.

Wouldn't that warm his heart?

She smiled as she loaded the berries into the colander for rinsing. Although cooking and baking were simple tasks, they could feed a need in a person. The need for comfort. The need for strength. The need to remember a mother's love. For Collette, that was the true joy of cooking: answering a need in someone's heart.

Step by step, she got the recipe started, setting aside the berries until the Jell-O had cooled a bit. Outside, the unpainted corner of the fence barked at her like a hungry dog: *Finish me!* Yah, she'd best get back to it before the stain dried in the can. She pulled on Linda's frumpy paint smock and headed back outside.

Reaching for the low spots on the fence, she felt a crick in her lower back. She'd sleep well tonight. She usually did after Linda put her through the paces during a day of work here. Not that she didn't work hard at the bishop's house, but there the hours of the day flew by because she felt needed. She was teaching Amy and Tess skills that they would use for the rest of their lives and pass on to their children. Here, she was assigned tasks that Linda and her older daughters could easily manage; they simply preferred to pay her to cook and clean. And paint fences.

She was nearing the last slat of unpainted fence when she heard the clatter of a horse's hooves in the distance. The buggy coming down the lane had two men sitting in the front seat—Len Hostetler and Bishop Aaron.

Aaron.

She raised a hand and smiled in greeting, and the men inside the buggy touched the brims of their hats as they passed by. She hadn't expected to see Aaron today, but then she knew he was good friends with Len.

Turning away from the lane, she noticed that paint splattered her hands and wrists, and her skin felt damp and sticky. What a sight she must be! A fat gray cow in this raggedy smock, worn down from the heat of the day. She was glad to be finishing the paint job, at last, but felt a bit annoyed that Aaron had seen her when she was a ball of sweat and grime. Was that vanity? *If so, Gott forgive me, but I want the man to like me.*

She leaned down to put the lid on the can. As she tapped it into place, a pair of men's feet stepped into her view. She straightened in surprise. "Bishop Aaron."

"You've done a good job on that fence. You can see it, bright and clean, from the road."

"Exactly what Linda wanted," she said.

"Len told me to leave you be, but I wanted to say hello and let you know I haven't told him that you've been helping out with the girls. As you said, no need to fuel the rumor mill."

She nodded. "Folks will find out soon enough, but I've kept quiet on it, too." Of course, Miriam and Alvin had nearly made the arrangement, but even bubbly Miriam could keep details under the table when she set her mind to it.

Collette looked over toward the house. "Will you be having some lunch with Len? I'll make sandwiches."

"That would be wonderful," he said.

"Linda and her sister Sally went fishing," she reported.

"We saw them along the road. Gave them a ride to the Joyful River landing near the bridge," he said, backing toward the house. "I hope they catch a whopper. But I'm surprised you didn't go along with them on a hot day like this."

She shrugged. "So much to do back here." She was tempted to enumerate the chores ahead of her, but then realized she would sound like that poor servant girl in the fairy tale, Cinderella. *Poor, poor me.* And pity was not the response she wanted from Aaron Troyer.

"It's a good thing I'm here to put together some lunch for you and Len," she said.

"Indeed. I'm grateful for that. No Yumasetti, I hope."

A laugh slipped out. Yumasetti had become a little joke between them. "Not today," she teased.

He nodded, then went back to join Len on the porch.

Watching him walk across the yard, she realized with a pang that her attachment to him had grown far too strong. It was one thing to favor a man's company, quite another to feel your heartbeat quicken whenever he was near.

This is not good, she thought to herself. She should put the brakes on. Tamp down the emotion. A woman her age couldn't be acting like a teenaged girl on rumspringa, her heart running wild.

But as she headed to the shed, she didn't want to let go of the joy that sparked within her at the thought of Aaron being nearby. Was it so wrong to enjoy that feeling? What was the harm in savoring the sweet emotions that Gott placed in her heart?

After she stowed the paint can and removed the cumbersome smock, it was a relief to wash up and return to that most familiar place, the kitchen. In no time she made BLTs, using bacon left over from breakfast and juicy tomatoes from the garden. Len had already served up the lemonade, so the rest was easy. Without interrupting their conversation, a talk about the upcoming wedding season, she delivered a tray with sandwiches, pickled cucumbers, and celery. Len looked right through her, as if she were a pane of glass, but Aaron met her eyes with a grateful nod.

Oh, those eyes. When Aaron met her gaze, she saw so much in his eyes. Wisdom and compassion, curiosity and humor. Eyes were windows to the soul, as her friend Miriam liked to say. One look from Aaron, and Collette felt comfort and understanding.

She left the tray and went back inside, where there was some sweeping to be done, and that dessert to complete before she finished for the day. The thought of the strawberry Jell-O mold made her smile. It felt like a secret gift to Aaron—their very own secret.

Sunday would be a special day indeed.

Chapter 13

From his place on the porch glider, Aaron looked past his chattering friend to the distant fence, where Collette had toiled, painting in the sun. Must've been hot out there. After her quick retreat to the kitchen to make lunch, Aaron realized his gaffe in asking her why she wasn't down at the river.

She was a hired hand here. The same status she held at his home, though he liked to think that he and the girls treated Collette as a member of the family.

Did they? The fact that he could not answer immediately concerned him. Did they pay her the considerations she deserved? Did they take the blessing of her care for granted?

He had finished his sandwich and was drinking her lemonade, a recipe just sweet and tart enough to be refreshing on a day like this.

Across from him, Len had launched into a conversation that was a bit stilted, as if he was reading from a script. A sermon, though Len was not a minister. Most times, when Len gave a talk this way, it turned out that his wife, Linda, was behind it.

Today, the talk had started with a question about Dorcas, Aaron's dearly departed wife who'd been taken by cancer.

"I understand the waiting process," Len said. "We all

need to grieve and heal when we lose someone we love. We were all at a loss when Dorcas passed. How many years has it been?"

Aaron put his lemonade on the small porch table and pressed back on the glider. "Two years," he said. Nearly three, though sometimes it seemed like another lifetime. He had pushed back many of the bad days, the times when she struggled to find peace and relief from her pain. The final days when she'd been so heavily medicated that he felt her slipping further and further away from him.

Time had allowed him to push the bad times away and remember the good. Their courtship, the two of them young and full of hope and humor. The time he threw dried corn at her window to wake her, only to have it fly in through the screenless opening and scatter in the girls' bunkroom. Their purchase of the little house, and the barn-raising that had drawn Amish carpenters from near and far. He would never forget the joyful sight of the wood framing with dozens of Amish men propped up or dangling from the structure. Men shimmying up from ladders and straddling the bare bones of the roof. How the years had flown by as they worked and lived each day for the glory of Gott! They'd been blessed with four children: one daughter, a son in the middle, and then two more baby girls. His good wife. He missed her, but he understood that Gott had a reason for everything under the sun. His was not to question.

"Have you thought about marrying again?" Len tossed the question off naturally as a farmer spreads seed in his field. So smoothly that Aaron held in his annoyance.

"Not really. For now, I'm making do with the girls. My mother's been a big help."

"Just wondering." Len pushed his straw hat back and rubbed at his brow. "You know, Linda's sister Sally has never married."

"Is that so?" Suddenly, Aaron could see where this was headed.

"Not for lack of Gott's blessings. You've met her. Good with a needle, and right handy in the kitchen. She'll make some lucky fella a fine wife."

Aaron leaned forward, picked up the cup of lemonade, and took a sip. A stall tactic as he considered how to answer without encouraging or insulting Len. He had no doubt that Linda's sister Sally was a good woman, but Aaron was not looking for a wife.

"You must be right thirsty there, Aaron," said Len.

Aaron nodded as he swallowed. "Reckon I am. It's a hot day."

Len leaned back in the wicker chair and smiled. "Don't want you to think I'm pushing you or anything like that."

It sure felt that way, though Aaron kept silent as Len went on.

"It's just that, a man with all your responsibilities could sure use a wife to ease the burden. Truth is, folks kind of expect it of their bishop."

"Is that so?"

"With all the things you need to do, that kind of commitment, you need a good Amish woman by your side, Aaron."

Again, Aaron took a drink, avoiding any form of answer. He was not going to marry again, but he didn't want to argue with his friend. Best to let Len get things out of his system.

Len was happy to talk on. "I don't know what I'd do without Linda to run the house and corral the youngies." He removed his straw hat and fanned himself with it. "Yah, marriage is a blessing. Did I tell you about the time that I got kicked by a horse, and Linda took over the shop for two weeks?"

Aaron nodded, but that didn't forestall Len from

launching into the story of how Linda had saved the harness shop, sold a saddle for a very good price, and stalled business until Len could get back on his feet. Aaron had heard the account a dozen times or more, but he found it comforting to sit back on the glider and let Len's voice fill the summer afternoon.

He didn't mind that Len was trying to fix him up with Linda's sister Sally. It would be easy enough to duck out of that one.

What stuck in his craw was the comment about the church folk. Were people really waiting on Aaron to marry again? As if it were a duty of his role as a bishop?

An Amish bishop. Even now, some twenty years after his life had been turned upside down, it was hard to believe he had been chosen.

Twenty years ago, Aaron had been a happily married farmer when one of the church ministers had passed. At twenty-eight, he'd been a father already—sweet baby Laura—with one on the way, and already he was living a very full and busy life. He hadn't known Jacob Zercher well, but had heard him preach many times. He had a way of speaking in a bold voice with soft edges, reminding members of Gott's commandments while always stressing the golden rule to love your neighbor as yourself.

During the Sunday service, the bishop instructed the congregation to pray that Gott would guide them to a man of solid faith who presided fairly over his household and kept his home in order. "A man's faith, and the way he lives the Amish life in his home, his daily habits, his attitudes—that's what matters," Bishop John assured them. "Don't worry if a candidate isn't good at public speaking or counseling. These things can be learned by a good Amish man."

Sitting on the bench, Aaron thought of Emery Lambright, a good man who owned and managed the Country Diner with his wife, Madge. Emery was an answer to his prayer. Aron would nominate him when the ordination came 'round after the spring communion service.

After church, conversation buzzed with the question of choosing a new bishop.

"Who can replace him?" men asked as they huddled together to talk after church.

Everyone agreed there was no man quite like Jacob Zercher, and that was true. But their church needed a leader, and all the congregation had faith that Gott would lead them to the right choice.

Two weeks later, the gmay reassembled to choose a new minister. Only men could be chosen, but nominations were made by both men and women. Aaron had been through the process before, always refusing to think of the possibility that every baptized Amish man had engrained in his mind.

It could be you. Your life could change today.

On this day, he and Dorcas had talked of other matters during the buggy ride. Finding a painter for his mother's house. How his friend Iddo had helped him fix the winch in the barn. They talked of anything but the upcoming lot.

Once assembled, the members bowed their heads for a silent prayer before ministers went off to a separate room to receive names. And then, one by one, church members filed past the room, stopping for just a moment to whisper the name of a nominee to one of the leaders.

"Emery Lambright," Aaron whispered, and Bishop John nodded sagely, turning to the next person in line.

Aaron returned to a bench among the married men and waited with the rest of the congregation as the ministers tallied the nominations. Any man who received more than three would advance to the final round, a simple process in which each nominee selected a hymnal from a batch prepared by the ministers. Only one hymnal has a slip of paper inside. The man who chose the hymnal with the note would become the next bishop.

At last, Bishop John and the ministers returned with the tally.

"We have four men nominated," the bishop announced.

For the first time during the proceedings, Aaron looked over to find Dorcas in the women's section. Gazing forward, she was sitting at the end of the bench near the aisle, their daughter, Laura, perched in her lap. With a thumb in her mouth, Laura seemed the picture of contentment.

Peace and calm, Aaron thought, trying to relax the muscles in his tense jaw. The peace of a baby.

"Harvey Stoltzfus," the bishop said, his words flickering like fireflies in the still, expectant dusk. "Mervin Lapp. Ezra Lantz." He paused, taking a breath. "And Aaron Troyer."

In that moment, Aaron felt sure his heart stopped beating. He didn't seem to be breathing anymore. And yet, he rose and walked to the front of the room when the bishop called the four men to come forward.

Aaron's body felt numb, but his thoughts reeled as he stood with the other three men, watching Bishop John place four copies of the Amish hymnal, the *Ausbund*, on a table at the front of the room. He wondered who had nominated him. Why had he been chosen? He was young to be a minister, only twenty-eight, but there was no prescribed age. He knew he should feel honored that someone thought he was worthy, a good example of Amish life. And yet, he knew he was far from God-like. No one was perfect. But he didn't fit the role of a minister, did he? He didn't have the charm of their deacon, with his funny jokes. He wasn't warm and big-hearted, the way Jacob Zercher had been.

And he wasn't ready to take on something so big . . . so consuming.

Surely there'd been a mistake for him to even be nominated. He looked to the ministers, but he knew the truth. They had acted in faith. Gott was intervening to choose a new minister. And Gott did not make mistakes.

There was a reading from the Bible, and then the bishop called on everyone to kneel and pray that Gott would intervene in this very important selection. The air was thick with hope and anticipation as everyone in the congregation fell into a steadfast prayer. And then, folks returned to their seats, and the bishop summoned Aaron and the others closer.

"This is as far as we humans can go with the choice," Bishop John said, opening his hands to take in the entire congregation. "The rest, we leave to Gott."

Aaron joined the other men at the table, where each selected a hymnal. The room was silent, but there was a ringing in Aaron's ears as the bishop went first to one man, then the next, searching the hymnals for the piece of paper.

Aaron was third. He held his breath as the bishop opened the book and a flash of white, like a dove peering through leaves, appeared in the book.

The paper.

Like every other baptized man, Aaron knew exactly what the note said. On it was written a line of scripture from Proverbs 16:33: "The lot is cast into the lap; but the whole disposing thereof is of the Lord."

He had been chosen.

He was going to be a minister in the church?

He felt crushed and elated, all in the same moment.

"Aaron"—the bishop's eyes held a somber wisdom—"stand up." Wasting no time, the bishop proceeded to ordain Aaron into the ministry right then and there. It was the way it had been done for generations, the same words used to ask for Gott's blessing and set the new man on track to serve the ministry of faith.

A simple tradition, but one that would change Aaron's life forever.

"You've been very quiet, Aaron," Len said, narrowing his eyes. "Is that a sign that you're thinking on it, or are you ready to take my advice?"

Snapped back to the present moment, Aaron realized that he hadn't been paying attention for some time now, and he wasn't sure quite how to answer. "Hmm. Are those my only two choices?"

Len slapped his thigh and let out a laugh. "You're trying to avoid giving an answer. Am I pushing too far?"

"You know me well, Len." He leaned forward and reached for his glass. "Is there more lemonade?" He wasn't thirsty anymore, but it would be a way to escape the conversation.

"Everyone agrees you need a good Amish wife in your life, and Sally would surely fit the bill."

"Sally seems like a right good woman," Aaron said slowly.

"I know she's a bit old to be single, but it's Gott's will that she hasn't met her match. At least until now."

"Whoa, now. I didn't mean—"

"No one's pushing," Len insisted. "But it'd be a good match, and look at that. Such a perfect opportunity right before our eyes. She'll be staying for a few weeks. Maybe longer if need be. She's got that quilting shop to return to, but she can hire someone to manage the store."

"Let's not put the cart before the horse." Aaron rose and reached for his hat. "Patience is a virtue."

Len smiled. "I guess I'm impatient for your happiness, my friend."

"I appreciate your concern, but a man must manage his own home and hearth, in his own good time." Aaron was aware that he was putting his friend off in the vaguest of terms. Since it seemed to be working, it would spare him having to tell Len, in plain language, to back off.

A creature of habit, Aaron disliked change. Why meddle with a man's routine when it suited him just fine? There were days when he missed Dorcas, but most of the time his head and his days were filled with hard work in the fields and the many meetings and decisions required to shepherd Gott's people in Joyful River. The notion of taking a wife seemed fanciful and selfish. That sort of love was meant for the young, not a forty-eight-year-old man.

"Promise me you'll think on it," Len said.

"I'll do better than that. I'll pray on it," he said, putting on his straw hat to ward off the afternoon sun. "And now, my friend, I've got some fields to tend."

"And I've got to get back to the shop." Len got to his feet. "Want a ride? Your place is on the way."

Normally, Aaron would accept, but today he was eager to escape this conversation. "I'm happy to walk. It's close enough." With a nod and a forced smile, he hightailed it out of there.

Chapter 14

A good Amish wife.

Len said that the bishop needed a good Amish wife in his life. He'd said that everyone in the community seemed to agree. That news had made Collette nearly sing out in joy. She had never expected that kind of support from the church community, but here they were, leading Aaron to get married again.

The prospects made her grin from ear to ear as she gripped the kitchen counter and lifted her eyes to the heavens in thanks.

Until Len had mentioned Sally.

He seemed to think that Sally Renno, Linda's sister, was the perfect match.

Collette released the knife she'd been gripping, placed it on the cutting board, and turned away from the kitchen window in a daze. She'd been cutting the leafy tops off beets, but had frozen when she got a drift of the men's conversation. She couldn't help but overhear. The front porch was but a few yards from the kitchen window, and she'd been intrigued by the good humor and strong persuasion in Len's tone. *What plan was he trying to pitch?* she'd wondered.

A wife for the bishop. A wife who was not Collette.

All the hope and joy drained from her body.

Pacing across the kitchen, she tried to fend off the bitter taste of disappointment. She should have kept preparing the beets and hummed a song to block out their voices. Instead, she'd listened in and now bore the guilt of eavesdropping and learning of the matchmaking that was going on behind her back. And then there was Len Hostetler, pushing the bishop toward Sally. He might as well have driven a pitchfork clear through Collette's own heart!

Not that Linda or Len knew of her feelings toward Aaron. She'd been discreet. So secretive that they didn't even know she'd been working as his housekeeper! Ach, this was a fine web she'd woven herself into.

Peering out the window once again, she saw that the chairs were empty. The bishop had disappeared, and Len was tending his harnessed horse, preparing to depart again. At least she didn't have to face Aaron in her moment of shame. She set to work preparing dinner for the Hostetler family, hoping to have everything in place so that she could leave as soon as the women returned from the river. She couldn't stick around and watch as her employers planned a match between Aaron and Sally. She just couldn't bear it.

"Four fat fish! Would you look at those whoppers!" Len exclaimed as he came upon the women standing at the picnic table covered with newspaper.

"Wait 'til you hear how we caught them," Linda said, her face flushed with excitement and heat.

As Collette cleaned the bass, scraping the blade from tail to head to remove the scales, Linda regaled her with the story of Sally's fine instincts on the river, and their mutual surprise when she hooked a half-dozen fish.

"There were two that had to be thrown back, but the

rest were big enough to make our supper," Linda said. "All because Sally insisted that the bridge wasn't the best spot. We ended up catching these down the river a ways, in the deep water where those sugar maples hang low. Good for you, Sally."

Collette kept her chin down, her eyes on the blade of the fish knife, careful not to make a wrong move. At the moment, she was not about to join in on commending Sally, the woman who'd just swept into town and apparently intended to capture the heart of the bishop.

"That was one of my favorite fishing spots when I was a girl," Sally admitted wistfully. "Those were sweet days, growing up in Joyful River."

As Sally reminisced a bit, Collette started scaling the last fish. Without looking up, she listened for details of Sally's memories that she could find fault with. The typical antics of a naughty or selfish child. But she could find none. Good, kind Sally lacked the cool manipulations that made Linda so difficult to deal with.

Just my luck that the bishop gets matched up with an Amish woman who's caring and ever so pleasant, Collette thought as she removed her apron and turned to Linda.

"There's cold chicken, potato salad, and coleslaw in the fridge, and a bowl of yellow beets and a basket of biscuits right there on the counter." Collette said. "I'm going to leave you to pan-fry the fish. Just dip the fish filets in flour, salt, and pepper to taste, and then sauté them in butter."

"I know how to prepare fish," Linda said.

"I'm sure it will be delicious," Collette said, folding the kitchen apron.

"But where are you going, cutting out early? I thought you were going to set the table?" Linda frowned.

"You might ask one of your girls to do that. I'm not feeling so well. I best get home."

"Oh, dear, you do look a bit ruddy," Sally said, eyeing Collette with concern. "Do you want to sit down? How about some lemonade?"

"No, denki. I'll just be heading home."

"I'll give you a ride." Sally turned to Len. "Can you help me hitch up a buggy?"

"Chester is still harnessed, if you want to take my buggy."

"Sally, no," Linda insisted. "We're about to have dinner, and Collette can find her way home."

"She's right. I don't mind the walk," Collette insisted.

"Not if you're feeling poorly, and on such a hot day," Sally said, patting the shoulder of Collette's dress. A kind, gentle touch. "Besides, a buggy ride will give me a chance to explore the Joyful roads I used to travel as a girl."

"Let Len take her," Linda suggested. "You might not find your way."

"You forget that I spent twenty years here. I know these country roads like the lines in my hands. And Chester is a well-trained mule. He'll serve us well." Sally seemed to straighten and stand tall, as if the prospect of stepping out on her own was an adventure. "I'll be back shortly, but don't wait dinner for me."

Heading out the door, Collette squinted at the lavender and apricot sky as she considered the intriguing twist of events. Here she'd thought she'd be fleeing the villainous Sally, when in fact, it seemed that she was providing the woman a brief chance to escape her family. The offer of a ride deprived Collette of plodding home, feeling more and more sorry for herself each step of the way. Maybe that wasn't such a bad thing.

In the buggy, Sally was all smiles as she took the reins. "Here we go," Sally said, signaling for the mule to move ahead. Despite her enthusiasm, Chester plodded down the lane slowly. "Come on, boy," she cajoled him, to no avail.

At least we'll be safe, Collette thought as they rolled onto the main road at a snail's pace.

"So you live at Alvin and Miriam Lapp's Dairy Farm?" Sally asked, nodding. "I remember where that is. Such a lovely spot."

"I'm lucky enough to be living in the Dawdi House, for the time being," Collette said.

"Alvin's cousin Elsa was a childhood friend," Sally said. "I'm looking forward to seeing some old friends at church on Sunday. I know you've been working hard to prepare for it. My sister gets so caught up in things, sometimes she forgets to be mindful of the people around her. Even during my limited time here, I can see how hard you work, how much you keep Len and Linda's home going smoothly. And such a good cook! They're blessed to have you."

"Denki." For the first time Collette allowed herself to lift her chin and meet Sally Renno's gaze, and it took but a second for the truth to hit her. Linda's sister was not really a pushy, selfish person, not the way Collette had painted her in her mind. Compassion and kindness ran deep as a river in her shiny blue eyes. Turning away, Collette clamped her teeth together, annoyed at herself for judging another woman so harshly.

"Linda told me you were recently widowed," she said. "I'm so sorry for your loss."

Collette turned to stare at the passing cornfield, not sure how to respond. Jed's death was complicated to explain to a stranger. In all honesty, she had to admit that it had been a relief to learn of the passing of the husband who'd left her so many years ago. Not out of anger or resentment at having been abandoned. Mostly there'd been a sense of relief knowing that after years of suffering from tortured thoughts, her husband, Jed, was finally at peace.

"I didn't mean to touch on a tender area," Sally said. "I

have a bad habit of saying the wrong thing. This is why I'm best tucked into the house, just me and my quilting. That way I can't offend anyone."

"You did nothing wrong," Collette reassured her. "I was just thinking that my husband is at peace now, Gott rest his soul."

"And you were blessed with children."

Collette nodded. "A wonderful blessing. My son, Harlan, was married in December, and daughter, Suzie, is sixteen."

"Rumspringa age." Sally smiled. "You must sleep with your eyes open at night."

"I'd be worried if she weren't such a quiet one. Good children, both of them. I thank Gott every day for our little family."

"I hope to have children one day. Linda and I came from a family of twelve children."

"That's quite a brood. Where were you in the lineup?"

"The baby. Oh, how they spoiled me! I think the older siblings carried me around until I was five years old! Showered me with love, they did." Sally shook her head. "And now it's time for me to pass that love onto little ones, which is what I want more than anything in the world!"

"But you need to find a husband first," Collette said.

"There's that pesky problem," Sally agreed, and the two women chuckled together.

Collette found herself warming to this woman despite her reservations.

"I've always wanted to be a wife and mother," admitted Sally. "As a young woman it seemed I had all the time in the world, and I was happy to live with my parents and enjoy the rumspringa years. Then it seemed that I awoke one morning and all the friends of my childhood were married and having children. Somehow, I'd fallen behind!

I began a serious courtship and got engaged with a young man from our church, but as the days went on, I couldn't go through with it. The young man was a stranger, and I found no joy in his presence." Sally let her head loll to one side as she stared at the road ahead. "I suspect he found me to be a bit strange, too. But he's married now, with four children. He found his way, and I remained alone."

"But you still want to marry?"

"More than anything. I accepted that Gott had brought me on a different journey, but I've never stopped praying for love, praying for a husband and family of my own. I was beginning to think it will never happen. But now, I've met someone and . . . I don't want to get too far ahead of myself and trip over my feelings for him. I've been in bad tangles before, but this time seems different. He's a wonderful good man, and, oh, bless my soul . . ." Taking a deep breath, she lifted her eyes to the heavens and smiled. "My heart is bursting, it's so full of hope."

Collette kept her face toward the window as Sally's words burst into flame around her—a wildfire of proclaimed love. How could this be happening? That Gott would send this sweet, lonely woman to fall for the one man who'd awakened love in Collette's heart?

Blinded by a panic, she murmured, "I'm happy for you, Sally."

"I'm so giddy with happiness myself. Sorry if I'm blathering on, but I don't have close friends here, and I have to talk to someone before I shout it from the hilltops." Sally chuckled softly. "Silly I know, but what about you? Have you ever been in love, Collette?"

I am, Collette wanted to say. *I'm in love with the wise, kind, true man that you want to marry.*

Instead, Collette surreptitiously pinched her arm, trying to bring some sense back to her mind. "I did love my husband.

I like to think Gott brought us together to save each other when we were young," she said quietly, jogging her memory back to those old days when they'd rallied together. Their escape from the harsh settlement in New York. The need to make their love sacred with proper vows. The trip to Lancaster County to find jobs and a place to live and a church that would accept them.

"Your husband. Of course, you loved him."

"It was a wonderful thing to have someone I trusted, someone who did his best to take care of me. We tried to take care of each other," she said, "but there came a point when he couldn't be around me or the children anymore. He suffered so." When Sally's brows rose in curiosity, she explained. "Mental illness."

"I'm so sorry," Sally said. "I truly am."

"Gott's will be done," Collette said, and both women sat in silence a moment, knowing that Gott's way was beyond human comprehension.

"There's the road to Lapp Farm," Collette pointed out as Chester approached the turn. "The Dawdi House is down the lane, then to the left. Denki for the ride."

"I'm happy to help. If things work out, if I end up staying here in Joyful River, I'd like to count you as a friend," Sally said. "You've been so kind. I know we just met, but I feel like you understand what I'm going through."

"I think I do," Collette said quietly, then bit her bottom lip to keep from crying as the buggy rolled to a halt in front of her home. She'd been wrong to try and paint Sally as an enemy when they were both searching for the same thing. The love of a good man. "Please, count me among your friends. I'll pray that Gott leads you to the good match and the family you desire. In the end, family really is everything."

"Indeed." Sally looked around and turned toward a trio

of trees beside the Dawdi House. "Do you hear that? The sweetest birdsong. They must be in those trees over there."

Collette smiled, listening to the happy sounds of whistling and chirping. Beyond the fields, the sky was still a bold blue with rows of cotton swab clouds hanging over the western hills. In the beauty of that moment, Collette knew she needed to give up her dreams of Aaron and let the path be clear for Sally. She didn't know exactly how to do that, how to bear it, but it was the right thing to do.

"What kind of birds do you think those are?" Sally asked.

Collette opened the buggy door and paused to listen to the bright, trilling sound. "I'm not a birder, but I'd say they're happy birds."

"Such a positive outlook." Sally nodded as Collette climbed down from the buggy. "I have a feeling that we're going to be very good friends."

Chapter 15

Aaron Troyer smiled despite his reservations.

The clip-clop of Thumper's hooves on the road were like music to his ears, punctuated by the laughter of Collette and Tess over a little joke they'd shared. Friday traffic was a bit thick, September being high season for tourists to pour in on weekends to observe the Pennsylvania Dutch foods and crafts. Somehow, the lineup of cars and buggies didn't bother Aaron today. The afternoon chores in town were usually tedious for Bishop Aaron. Small matters could be time-consuming for a man who had the greater task of leading an entire congregation of believers. But today, riding alongside Collette with daughter Tess in the back, Aaron found that it was actually enjoyable to embark on family errands.

He stole a glance over at Collette, who wore a purple dress that reminded him of an iris in the spring. Collette nodded as Tess chattered from the back. This good woman had been a true gift from Gott. Not only had she brought order to his household, she'd done it in a way that had lifted the girls' spirits and engaged them in the chores they'd sloughed off since their mother's death. These days when Aaron came into the house at the end of a day's work, the girls had prepared a dinner, often with the help of Collette.

The kitchen was sparkling clean, and the rest of the house got its fair share of scrubbing and sweeping. And after supper, his daughters worked together on the cleanup, singing as they washed and dried the dishes.

Like a cool autumn breeze, contentment wafted through their home now, suggesting that each member of the family felt a new sense of purpose and belonging.

All thanks to Collette, Aaron thought.

First they visited the library, where Tess nearly skipped inside the building, eager to return her armful of books and check out a brand-new batch of things to read.

"No computer time," Aaron called after her as she exited the buggy.

"Oh, Dat! I don't care about computers. You know it's books that I love!"

"Should I go in and keep an eye on her?" Collette offered. She'd been the one to suggest the library, the person who'd brought Tess for her first visit and helped her get a library card, with the strict rule that Tess was not to use the computers or other machines at the library. Yah, it was allowed in their congregation, but Aaron didn't want anyone in his family pushing the limits.

"We'll both go," Aaron said, tying the lines to a post in the parking lot of the redbrick building.

Inside, the building held the musty smell of old yellowed paper, not surprising considering the shelves of books that filled the room for as far as the eye could see. Tess quickly deposited her books in the return slot, then disappeared between the stacks under a sign that read FICTION.

Pausing in the aisle, Collette peered after her. "It'll take her ten or twenty minutes to choose. She's a careful one, and besides that, she's already read quite a few books in the last few years, with many passed to her by friends. She's a real bookworm, your Tess."

While Aaron had been aware of his daughter's hobby, he hadn't understood the extent of it, not in the way that Collette had discerned in the month that she'd been working in their home. "Well, now, being here, I see that you've helped her find the mother lode."

Collette's lips pressed together in concern. "I thought it would be all right."

"It's a good thing," he said with a nod of approval. While Collette went off to consult some recipe books—who knew a library held something so practical—Aaron found his way to the rows of cubicles that contained machines for the use of patrons.

Computers.

Aaron neither liked nor disliked the machines themselves. The problem with computers and televisions was that these devices tended to pull folks away from the larger Amish society. On the pro side, he saw the merit of using them for business. For a harness-maker or craft person who needed to take orders from out of town, it was certainly faster than using the mail.

But speed was not something Amish society welcomed or needed.

Thus the use of televisions or computers was not taboo in their district. But ownership of such an item or an electric feed coming into a home—that was forbidden.

An Englisch woman seated at a desk by the entryway looked up when he paused there. "May I help you with something?"

He declined her offer; just looking. That was when he spotted the dark jacket of an Amish fellow seated down the aisle. He walked that way, just curious, and was surprised to find Deacon Seth seated before the screen and keyboard.

"Bishop Aaron." Seth nodded. "Not a place I usually see you."

"My daughter's getting books." Aaron caught a look at the screen, which listed a business for sale, a small shop that resembled Skip Horst's buggy repair business here in Joyful River. Seth had worked for Skip off and on over the years and was now the man to see when you had a problem with a wheel of your buggy. "What's that you're looking at?"

"It's a wainwright shop, for sale in Indiana." Seth explained that his brother had recommended the business as something Seth might purchase once he moved. "It's a tidy-looking shop, that's for sure," Seth said. "But the fella's asking a hefty chunk of money, and I'm not sure I want to go so big. Maybe just a home-repair shop to start me off once I get to Indiana."

Aaron thought Seth wise to start small, though he was impressed by the information he'd gathered through the computer. Quite informative, but still . . . Aaron would stick with his Amish newspapers and magazines. "Whatever you decide, we'll be sorry to see you go," he told the deacon.

"I'll miss you, my friend, but I think this is the right move for me. My life here's been stagnant since Edna passed. I believe Gott has a new path for me, and I'm grateful to pursue it."

Just then Collette appeared down the aisle, signaling that it was time to go. Aaron patted his friend's shoulder and then they were off.

Their next stop was just a few blocks away at the Smitty's Pretzel Factory where Amy was now working. Another arrangement Collette had made that was working out well. Since Amy had started her job there, the sparkle had returned to her eyes. Like a songbird released from her cage, Amy was now all aflutter. Most days Amy made her way home alongside her friends, but today Aaron had arranged to pick her up for a family visit to his mother, Dinah.

What joy he found in the happiness of his daughters! Perhaps he'd been too neglectful, licking his wounds since Mose left. Too angry with his son to recognize the needs of his daughters.

"There they are!" Amy exclaimed to the girls at her side as Aaron prompted Thumper to halt at the edge of the parking lot. He'd pulled up behind the factory, the loading area, where horse-drawn wagons and one van were backed into the bays with wide garage doors.

"Look what Smitty gave me!" Amy held up a bag. "Pretzels for Mammi. The soft kind, that won't hurt her teeth." Standing with her friends and coworkers, Amy seemed so pleased.

"She'll be happy to get them, and happy to see you," Aaron said. As Amy climbed into the buggy, he took note of the other girls. There was Collette's daughter, Suzie— a shy one—and Eve Schmucker, both pretzel girls, and one of Alvin and Miriam Lapp's Englisch nieces, the one with the bright-colored hair. Green hair today. Aaron didn't even try to understand the ways of the Englisch.

So far, Amy's job had brought some peace to the house, as it gave her a chance to spend time with friends and other girls her age. This socialization was appropriate during rumspringa. In fact, most girls her age were courting boys or going out with friends on Saturday nights. But Aaron would not allow that yet.

Turning away, he frowned. He'd been reluctant to let his daughter out of the house after losing Mose so completely. Another example of the way Collette had woven a happy solution through their torn family.

"Are you girls finished with your shift?" Collette asked the other girls, gaze focused on her daughter, Suzie.

"We are, but Grace has to go back to the Christmas store for a bit," Suzie said. "Eve and I are going to get some ice cream while we're waiting."

"All right then," Collette said. "I'll see you at home a bit later."

"Bye, Mem," Suzie called, one hand pressed to her cheek as the other girls smiled and nodded.

Calling to Thumper, Aaron steered the buggy out of the parking lot and onto Joyful River's Main Street, heading toward his mother's house.

"Those pretzels smell so good!" Tess said from the back bench.

"They're still warm," Amy said.

"I wish I could have one."

"They're for Mammi."

"But just one?" Tess lowered her voice. "She'll never know."

"And we have a chicken casserole for her here," Collette said, "so she won't go hungry."

Aaron set his jaw in anticipation of an argument from the back of the buggy. Instead, Amy let out a sigh.

"Okay, just one," Amy said. "Mammi won't miss it."

"Denki!"

"Dat? Collette? Do you want one?" Amy offered.

They declined as the bag rustled behind them.

Aaron smiled and turned to Collette. "How about that?" he said, his voice a low murmur. It was truly a sign of improvement.

Collette nodded and turned toward the side window. She seemed distracted today. A shame, as Aaron was enjoying their family errands with an enthusiasm he hadn't felt in years.

* * *

When they arrived at Dinah's house, the girls fairly flew out of the buggy and into the house to see their grandmother.

"Mind you, your grandmother must stay off her feet," Collette called after them.

"We know!" Amy called back. "We'll make her some tea."

"Bone on bone," Collette confided to Aaron as she lifted the casserole dish from the buggy. "That was how the doctor described the state of her hip. It must be quite painful for her."

Nodding, Aaron tied Thumper to the hitching post and came around the buggy. He'd been aware that Collette had brought the girls here to visit Dinah, though he hadn't expected his mother to open up to an outsider about her medical condition. "My mother doesn't complain much, but her hip's been a bother for years now. It will be good to have the surgery done. Thanks to you, she was finally able to stay off her feet long enough to get the swelling down."

"Just doing my job," Collette said.

And much more, he thought. So much more, though this was not the time for that conversation. Glancing up for a moment, he noted the weathered condition of the house.

"It looks like the trim needs paint before the winter sets in. And the roof seems to be missing a few shingles." He touched his beard, concerned. "I hope it's not leaking already."

"It could use some sprucing up," Collette agreed.

"I'll add it to the list," he said. "Maybe I can get up there next week while she's in the hospital."

Collette turned to him, her brows high, as if she'd witnessed an amazing feat. "You're going to climb the roof?"

"I am."

She snickered.

"I spent a few years on a construction crew as a young man," he said. "I can hold my own with roofing and carpentry."

She paused at the front porch. "I'm sure you can, but there's a time and a place for everything. 'To everything, there is a season,' yah?"

"'And a time for every purpose under heaven,'" he said, finishing the Bible verse. "Do you think I'm too old to go up on a roof?"

"Nay, not at all. It's not that you can't do it. It's that you probably have a hundred other tasks that need doing, and many of them require the touch of you and you alone. There's a large congregation of folk who look to you for advice and guidance, every day. A huge responsibility, I know, but they will come to you and only you for the help they need." She nodded toward the house. "And there's a loving mother who needs care now, and two growing young women who need their father. They need you, and only you, Aaron. So much to do, and you never shirk off a task. But with such a heavy yoke, surely you might hire a crew to do some roof repair and painting?"

"A crew?" The notion seemed indulgent. "It sounds fancy."

"Plenty of plain folk work in construction. Doug Kraybill has a crew that does repairs and renovations. His son Abe works with him now, and I'm sure they'd be happy to help. And my Harlan is good with a hammer and saw. He'll pitch in after work if you need him."

"Amish folk." He nodded as the idea sank in. "Why didn't I think of that?"

"Because you're very busy tending to Gott's work," she said with a teasing smile as he held the front door open for him.

His heart felt light, unburdened, as he followed her into

the house. It felt good to know that Collette had observed his daily commitments, that she seemed to feel the weight of his responsibilities, that she understood and stood beside him to help carry the load.

Just knowing this lifted his heart.

Inside, he was glad to see his mother seated at the kitchen table while Amy poured her a glass of iced tea and Tess brought her bottle of pills over.

"I can't believe you're really getting a new hip next week, Mammi," Tess said.

"Where do they get the hip bone for you?" Amy asked.

"They make it in a factory somewhere," Dinah said, leaning her cane against the table so that she could manage the tea and pills. "It's made of something hard so it lasts."

"It's made of titanium," said Aaron. He'd paid attention when he'd taken his mother to all those doctor's visits. "The doctor said it's very hard, like the blade of a plough."

"Imagine that," Collette said. As she set the casserole dish on the counter and started the fire under the kettle, she seemed quite comfortable in his mother's kitchen.

Oddly, his mother did not seem to mind, but it was surprising. Like most Amish women, Dinah Troyer was the queen of her kitchen. How had it happened that she'd relinquished control to Collette, who'd visited only a few times?

"I'm making you a fresh pitcher of iced tea, and we'll warm the casserole before we go," Collette said as she untangled the strings of a few tea bags. "Are you hungry now, or should I wait?"

"I'm a bit peckish, so might as well start it now," Mem admitted, then turned to Amy. "This pretzel is scrumptious. How's it going at Smitty's factory?"

"It's the best job ever. I get to see my friends nearly every day, and we're allowed to talk while we twist the pretzels,

as long as the work gets done. Smitty—he's the owner—
he tells corny jokes and he loves having people come in and
tour the factory. My friend Suzie says he's a pretty nice
boss, though he seems stricter with the boys who do the
deliveries. But Mammi, it's more fun than I ever thought I
could have."

"Well, that's wonderful good," Dinah said. "As long as
you help Collette and your dat with the chores when you
get home from work."

"She's been a big help in the kitchen," Collette said.
"Both girls are becoming good cooks."

"And we do some farm chores, too," Amy said, glancing over at Aaron. "But lucky for me I have the job to fill
my days."

"Lucky for you," Aaron teased, pleased that she'd found
a niche for herself.

Meanwhile, Tess was setting up a handful of library
books on the kitchen table, arranging them so that Dinah
could see the covers. "I brought you some books to read
while you're recovering. Here's one from that series you
like. The minister with the big dog."

"Preacher Tim," Dinah said with a smile. "Denki for
bringing it."

Pleased, Tess held up a larger book. "And this here's a
birding book."

"Birding . . ." Dinah considered. "I'm no expert."

"I know, but look at the pictures." Tess opened to a
glossy page with a large photo of a yellow finch. "I thought
you might be able to learn some of the birds that come to
your feeder."

"Such vivid pictures!" Dinah nodded. "Makes me feel like
I'm out in Gott's green nature instead of my own kitchen.
Very nice!"

"We'll make you a birder yet," Collette teased. "By next summer, you'll be going on hikes with Birdie Eicher herself."

The girls giggled at that. They'd always had a fascination for the Amish grocer's wife who had a yard full of birdbaths and feeders. Before long, Collette and Dinah were chuckling, too.

Everyone was laughing, except Aaron.

Not that he didn't enjoy the idea of Birdie and his mem traipsing around with binoculars. He was simply miffed at the cohesiveness of this group of women, young and old, in his mother's kitchen. So tightly woven together, it seemed. Helpful and kind. Cheerful and joyous.

No more bickering teenagers. Gone was his sour, over-worked mother.

This was his family now.

All thanks to Collette.

It wasn't just that she'd brought the discipline and order that he'd asked for. She'd breathed new life into his family, sparking joy into every person she touched.

Aaron hadn't seen his own mother in such a peaceful, upbeat mood in years. He'd actually heard her laugh, and her face seemed smoother and pinker, now that the strain of chronic pain had eased from her body. At last, his mother had healed enough to sail through her surgery next week.

Thank you, Gott, for bringing this capable woman into our home, into our lives, he prayed silently as the women chatted on. He hadn't realized how much they'd all needed help, but the Lord had seen their struggles and brought them just what they needed. A good Amish housekeeper.

Chapter 16

Grace pulled sheets of white paper from the box and carefully rolled Christmas ornaments up before packing them into the Christmas shop's white boxes. She was impatient to be done with her shift and late meeting her friends, but there was nothing she could do about it but work her way through. The store owner, Rachel Fisher, had been so nice about asking Grace to stay a bit to help with this customer, a small, angular woman with a perfect bob of gold-tipped hair and a surrounding cloud of sweet perfume. She'd popped into the shop at the last minute and scarfed up dozens of ornaments for some kind of charity function in her town, and Grace knew that a sale that big would be a boost to the small business.

"I do love these little snowman ornaments," Mrs. Mayhew said. "I'm wondering if you might personalize a few for my grandchildren?"

"Happy to do that for you," Rachel said. "How many grandchildren?"

"Five."

Rachel shot an apologetic look to Grace. "Have you wrapped any snowmen yet?"

Grace sucked in a breath. "I think there are two in here." She stopped wrapping and went back to search a packed box for the ornaments. "Here were go." Grace handed over the ornaments, and Rachel got to work with her special gold pen.

"Thank you," said Mrs. Mayhew. "I'm thrilled to have officially begun my Christmas shopping!" She clapped her hands, giddy with excitement.

Grace smiled. The woman's last-minute appearance in the shop had been a pain in the neck, but at least she was upbeat and pleasant. Most people in the Christmas shop were pretty nice. That was the thing about Christmas: even on a warm September evening when you wanted to get home after a day of school and work, thoughts of Christmas eased the stress. In her short time working here, Grace had learned that snowflakes, puffy fake snow, holly, glitter, and shiny glass ornaments could be quite therapeutic.

With the purchases finally wrapped and paid for, Mrs. Mayhew thanked them profusely and sighed over her stack of boxes. "I'm afraid I'm going to need some help getting these out to the car."

"Of course," Grace said, lifting the heavy stack of three fat boxes.

"Wonderful! I knew your little Christmas elf would help me out."

Christmas elf? Are you kidding me? Grace stuck her tongue out, knowing that the stack of boxes would hide her face from view. She definitely should have changed her hair from green to pink or blue before starting this job. When she'd applied at the shop to get the work credits she needed to graduate from high school, she hadn't expected anyone to make the elf connection, but this was the second time she'd been hit with it.

Mrs. Mayhew hitched her purse over one shoulder and took the two smaller boxes, chattering on as Rachel held the shop door open for the two of them. Grace was not surprised to see that Mrs. Mayhew owned a cream puff of a car—a white Mercedes that sparkled in the late-afternoon sun. After Grace helped place the boxes so that they wouldn't roll around in the trunk, Mrs. Mayhew held out a rolled up ten-dollar bill.

A tip! "Thanks!"

"Please, spend it on something worthwhile," she said, pressing the bill into Grace's hand.

"Definitely. I'm saving up for college next year."

"Good on you!" The older woman seemed to be so pleased, Grace felt a new warmth in her heart. This was the sort of things normal grandmothers did. Not chasing you out of the kitchen and refusing to talk about memories.

After Mrs. Mayhew drove off, Grace went back to help Rachel close up the shop, but the exchange with the older woman lingered in her mind. *Why can't I have a grandmother who thinks of me at Christmastime? A grandma who wants to spend time with me and hear about my day?* No, things had not been going well with her visiting grandmother, her last tie to Mom's childhood. Grace worried that she'd ruined things by pressing Mammi with so many questions.

She let out a sigh and finished straightening up the boxes and packing paper. Enough with feeling sorry for herself. She was on a campaign to make Mammi Lois like her, and she tried some little joke or favor each day. As Aunt Miriam always said, easy does it!

As soon as the shop closed, Grace hurried over to the back of the pretzel factory, where she'd planned to meet Suzie and Eve. A truck was parked at the loading dock, where a few young men hauled supplies into the building.

No sign of her friends, but then again, she was at least twenty minutes late.

Anxiety squeezed her at the thought of heading home on

her own. There was still plenty of daylight and she knew the way, but it was the aloneness that scared her.

She moved closer to the back of the factory, approaching the little covered area where employees left their scooters. There were only a handful of scooters left, but she saw that a Schmucker scooter was there, parked right beside Suzie's.

"Still here," she whispered with a sigh of relief.

Just then a worker walked by, a tall Amish boy with blond hair. He was pulling a dolly of boxes.

"Hey, you work here?" she asked.

He nodded and paused as she stepped closer. He was thin as a beanpole, but his shiny gold hair was really something special. If Grace had hair that color, she wouldn't dye it so often.

"Have you seen my friends hanging around? They work here, making the pretzels. We were supposed to meet, but I got held up."

He gave her a second look, his eyes opening wider. "Ach. You're the girl with the green hair."

"That's me," she said. "Grace."

"Your friends were here with ice cream cones. The Schmucker girl, and the one with the scar face, right?"

His words were like a punch in the stomach. "She's got blue eyes and a great smile, and yeah, she was injured in an accident, but you don't have to be a knucklehead about it."

"Knucklehead?" He seemed wounded. "I was just trying to—"

"I don't want to hear your excuses. Can you just tell me where they went?"

"What's her name?" When she scowled, he added, "So I don't have to mention the scar again."

Grace wasn't sure she wanted to tell him. She didn't trust him not to mock Suzie right to her face. But then again, if he knew her name, he wouldn't have to be a jerk.

"Her name is Suzie Yoder. *Suzie*. And if you ever, ever call her scar face again, you're going to regret it, buddy."

"I never called anyone that!"

She held her hand up to stop him. "And what's your name?"

His eyes were steely with impatience. "Josiah."

"Josiah, where did my friends Suzie and Eve go?"

He let out a huff of breath. "Inside. They went to see the boss. Smitty and his wife are still in the office."

She pointed to a walkway. "That door there?"

He nodded, and she strode off. It didn't take her long to locate her friends in the building and explain that she'd been stuck at work.

"We figured that was what happened," Eve said as they headed back out through the loading dock.

Grace was relieved to see that the truck was gone. Good. The employees had probably cleared out for the day. But as the girls retrieved their scooters and walked them down the ramp, someone called after them.

"So long, girls!"

As if on cue, the three girls paused and turned to face Josiah, who stood on the platform with a broom. "See you tomorrow, Suzie." Okay, he did have a nice smile, but Grace still didn't trust him.

The three girls said goodbye. As Suzie and Eve turned away, Grace noted the shock and delight on their faces.

"I will always treasure this moment," Suzie whispered.

"Oh my friends, did you hear that?" Eve reached over and jiggled Suzie's arm. "Josiah Graber just said goodbye to us, and he knows your name. He knows who you are!"

"So what if he knows my name?" Suzie's astonishment belied her dismissive tone. "I'm sure he knows lots of girls."

"What does it matter?" Grace asked. "He's just a guy on the loading dock, right?"

"He's very popular," Suzie said.

"Every girl our age likes him," Eve said. "But Suzie has a special crush on him."

"I don't," Suzie insisted. But even the hand held up to her scarred cheek couldn't hide the enormous smile that lit her face.

Grace wanted to groan, but she kept quiet and pushed her scooter along, hoping that this Josiah kid didn't turn out to be a jerk.

Halfway home, they passed the road leading to Eve's house. "See you tomorrow," Eve called, slowing her scooter to make the turn down the gravel road.

The other girls called their goodbyes as they sailed past her. There was still plenty of light, but the clouds formed layers in the sky, bursting with orange and lavender and rosy hues. Grace glided downhill, enjoying the ride. It wouldn't be long until rain or darkness or snow would force them to get a ride home in a buggy or hired car.

They chatted as they pushed their way up the rise of a hill, then rested their feet on the scooter as they soared down. Grace loved the feeling of flying, the wind in her hair. She felt free from the burdens of school and work, free from stress and fear.

A car slowed, came up the hill, and passed them. Down below, an Amish buggy was pulled over to the side of the road, stopped there.

Suzie lifted one hand to point. "Who's that?"

Grace shook her head. She didn't recognize buggies or horses the way Amish people did. They all looked alike to her. "Maybe they have a flat tire," she said.

"You mean a broken wheel," Suzie called as they rolled closer.

Both girls applied their brakes to slow down and circle safely around the buggy, which sat in part of one lane of the road. The right wheels rested on the gravel shoulder, which dipped down precariously, though, at the moment, the buggy remained on solid ground.

"Nay," Suzie said, inspecting the buggy. "The back wheels seem okay." Her eyes opened wider as she looked up at the buggy with caution. "Someone's inside. But the mule! Look! It's Sunny, one of the Lapp mules. The buggy belongs to your uncle and aunt." Suzie doubled back, edging closer to the front compartment of the buggy with caution. "Hallo?" she called.

Grace came around behind her, curious to see who was inside. An older Amish woman sat frozen, her face stiff and agitated beneath her black bonnet.

It was her grandmother, alone in the buggy. Grace's heart dropped at the sorrowful sight. From close up, Grace could see that her cheeks were damp with tears, her eyes wild with confusion.

"Mammi Lois, what's wrong?" Grace asked, climbing onto the running board so that they were face-to-face. "Did something happen?"

Slowly the older woman turned, her dark eyes searching Grace's face. "Oh, my girl!" Lois exclaimed, lifting her arms in the air as she caught sight of Grace. "I'm so glad it's you. I need to get home, and I seem to have lost my way."

"You mean, back to Lapp Farm," Suzie said.

"No, not that." She waved Suzie off as if she were an annoying insect. "Back home to our farm." Lois turned back to Grace. "Thank goodness you're here, Sarah. You know the way."

Sarah? Grace touched her hair, wondering if she really looked that similar to her mother.

Behind her, Suzie seemed confused. "Why is she calling you that?"

"It's my mother's name," Grace muttered before turning back to her grandmother. "I do know the way home. We can get you there."

"Good. You're in the nick of time. I need to get my dinner going for the family." Lois scooted over and held the reins out to Grace. "Here you go, Sarah. Come along now."

"Just a second," Grace said. "We're going to put our scooters in the back." She turned down and motioned Suzie toward the rear of the buggy. "She wants me to drive her home. I mean, I know the way, but I'm terrible with horses. Can you get us home?"

"I'm not sure." Suzie winced. "I've practiced with Harlan once or twice, but that's with Beebee, and she's a sweet mule. It's always Harlan or Mem who drives the buggy."

"But you know how," Grace said.

Suzie shot a worried look at the mule, then nodded resolutely. "Sunny will get us there. Come. Put your scooter in the back. But sit up front with me, so you can keep her calm. She seems to trust you."

Grace nodded. "She trusts me because she thinks I'm her daughter," she said quietly as they lifted their scooters into the rear of the buggy. The bittersweet realization endeared the older woman even as it saddened Grace.

"Do you think she'll be okay?" Suzie asked, her brows creased in worry. "I can't imagine what happened to her."

"We need to get her home," Grace said. "Aunt Miriam will know what to do once we're there."

It was a tight squeeze, three on the bench with Mammi sandwiched in the middle, but they made it work. At first

Grace worried that Suzie might not be able to handle the mule, but once the girl called out "Sunny!" with such authority that the mule began to trot, she was able to breathe again.

"So, Mammi . . ." Grace took her grandmother's hand and rubbed her arm reassuringly. She was glad to see that she'd calmed down, and the evidence of her tears had been wiped away. "Where were you going, all alone in the buggy?"

"I had errands. This and that. Always so much to do. But then on the way home, I just had a moment when . . ." She shook her head, her mouth puckering. "A bad moment. Nothing looked right anymore. I was looking for the turnoff to home. I was sure it was down this way, but suddenly every tree and field began to look the same. I just . . . I knew something was wrong and . . ."

"It's okay." Grace rubbed her arm, trying to soothe her. "You're safe now."

"Denki for helping me, Sarah." Mammi gave Grace's hand a squeeze. "I don't know what I would have done if you hadn't come along just then."

Grace felt a swell of love for her grandmother. Even if Mammi didn't realize who she was, it felt good to be needed, good to be loved.

"We'll be home soon, thanks to Suzie, our excellent horsewoman," Grace said.

Suzie flashed her a nervous smile, but quickly turned her gaze back to the road.

"Everything is going to be fine," Grace said softly, and was rewarded when her grandmother closed her eyes and let her head relax against Grace's shoulder.

Chapter 17

Miriam pressed her palm against a loaf of whole grain bread, testing the temperature. Still too warm to slice, though it would be ready when she put the rest of the dinner on the table. Two loaves of bread—probably the last of the baking that she'd have time to do before the wedding. On Monday the wedding wagons would arrive complete with half a dozen stoves and ovens, sinks with hot and cold running water, dishes, and silverware. The church bench wagon would be sent over, too, and a dozen other details would need to fall into place. So much to do, but many hands made lighter work. They'd assembled a crew of family and friends to attend to the food, set up, and clean up. Sam and Sadie had chosen their wedding attendants, as well as many cousins and friends chosen to serve the wedding dinner.

Oh, dear Lord, I know You'll get us through this wedding so that Sam and Sadie can take their sacred vows in Your love. It would be nice if everything went smoothly, but if there were a few wrinkles along the way, they'd survive. Challenges were the crooked stepping stones that made the journey more interesting.

Checking the wall clock, she realized suppertime was fast approaching. Usually, at this point in the day, the twins were stomping their boots in the entryway, leaning into the kitchen to ask about dinner. The teenagers were often already in the kitchen, snitching at a platter while Miriam advised them to have an apple or a carrot. But aside from Sarah Rose playing with her doll in the next room while Lizzie read her a story, the house was quiet. Not even Mem and Dat stopping in for a glass of tea.

Where was everyone?

Miriam finished tearing spinach into the big salad bowl and wiped her hands on her cooking apron as she pushed out the back door and went 'round to the front porch. Over by the barn, she saw the twins scurrying around Comet, trying to get the horse to remain steady between the shafts of the buggy, while Alvin and Sam gave instructions. Squinting, she saw that her father was there, too, his gray head slumped over in concern.

Why were the men hitching up a buggy this late in the day?

Just then, a buggy turned down the lane, heading toward their house. A visitor? Strange, but it sure looked like their mule Sunny pulling it along.

Indeed, it was. So it was one of their buggies that had been out and about, though Miriam didn't know of anyone taking a trip into town, aside from the children on scooters.

The mule trotted forward and bellowed, that odd mule sound that started as a whinny and ended in the hee-haw of a donkey.

That got everyone's attention. The men stopped what they were doing, having noticed the buggy. Peter and Paul came running across the paddock, as if they were stable attendants. Alvin, David, and Sam weren't far behind.

A runaway buggy? No, the driver seemed to have it under control. There were three in the front. Grace, and the small figure in the black bonnet looked like Miriam's mother. And the driver? Oh, Miriam needed to get her eyes checked. A young Amish girl, that was for sure.

Lizzie came up beside Miriam on the porch. "Is that Suzie?" she asked. "I didn't know she could drive a buggy."

"She can now," Miriam said, recognizing Suzie Yoder managing the reins. Miriam knew that Suzie and Grace had worked in town this afternoon. What were the three of them doing off in a buggy?

"Halloo!" Pete called as he raced toward the buggy. "You made it back!"

"Stay out of the way now," Alvin called to the boys as the rig kept moving toward the house.

Suzie kept the mule on track, slowing his pace only slightly before stopping by the front of the farmhouse. At that point, the buggy was fairly surrounded by the ebullient family, everyone eager to know what had happened.

"Is everyone all right?" Alvin asked, peering into the front seat.

"We're fine," Grace said, "thanks to Suzie's awesome driving."

"I had to drive," Suzie explained. "We were on our way home from work when we found Mammi Lois and the buggy on the side of the road."

Everyone watched in silence as Grace climbed out of her side of the buggy and turned to lend her grandmother a hand. "We're home, Mammi. Safe and sound."

"That's good," Lois said, taking Grace's assistance and climbing down to the ground.

It seemed that a connection had developed between the two of them. That was good, but Miriam sensed that something about her mother was a bit off.

"We were just hitching up a buggy to go and find you, Mammi," Paul said. "Everyone was getting worried."

"Oh. My." Lois's eyes were dark with confusion as she looked around.

Her husband was instantly by her side. "It's all right, Lois," he said, gently taking her arm.

"Come." Miriam beckoned. "Let's sit down on the porch and you can tell us your story. Sounds like someone had an adventure, but we're glad to have you home."

Lois straightened her black bonnet—the hat women wore when going out in public—and looked up at the farmhouse. "Well, you're wrong. This isn't home."

This confirmed that something was wrong. Miriam stepped forward. "You're at Lapp Farms, Mem. Our home. Visiting for Sam's wedding."

Lois stared off for a second, then frowned. "Well, sure. I knew that."

Suddenly, everyone seemed to be talking at once. Grace said something about how she and Suzie had been on their way home from town when they'd come upon the buggy sitting on the side of the road. Suzie talked about taking the reins and getting the buggy rolling, despite her lack of experience. The boys complimented her on a job well done.

"You gave us a scare, Lois," Dat said. "But everything's fine now."

Miriam took her by the other arm, and together she and her father walked Lois up the stairs. "We didn't know you'd gone off alone in the buggy until Annie mentioned it," David said patiently.

"Annie hitched up a buggy and let you go without—" Miriam looked around for her teenaged daughter, but Alvin quickly caught her attention.

"It's not her fault. Annie's off in the barn, feeling bad right now," Alvin said. "She didn't know it would be a problem. Just following her grandmother's instructions."

Miriam nodded, beginning to understand the situation. "Poor thing. She must feel terrible."

"I'll go talk to her," Sam offered. "And we'll get these horses unhitched from the buggies." He climbed into the buggy that had sat idle in the yard and directed Sunny back to the barn.

As the mule clip-clopped away Miriam nodded, grateful for the maturity of her oldest son, glad he would continue working the farm after his marriage to Sadie. When she continued guiding her mother along, holding tight as they climbed the porch steps, she felt her hands sink deep into the cloth of Mem's sleeve. Such a thin, bony arm. When had her mother gotten so slight? So feeble?

"You were gone awhile, do you know that, Lois?" David asked his wife. "We were hitching up another horse to go look for you."

"A search party!" Paul said, a little too eagerly. "Everyone was worried."

So that had been the harried task of the men. A search party. Miriam shook her head slightly as they led Mem to a chair on the porch. Miriam thanked Gott that she hadn't known about the potential crisis until it had been averted.

"I was just down the road," Lois insisted. "Don't know why anyone would get bent out of shape about that."

"We talked about this, Lois," Dat said quietly. "I thought we agreed you wouldn't be taking a buggy out on your own." When Mem didn't respond, Dat looked toward Miriam. "She gets turned around sometimes."

Miriam nodded sympathetically as the reality of her mother's mental lapse sunk in. So this wasn't the first time.

"I get confused, that's all it is," Lois said sharply.

"It's okay, Mammi," Grace said, taking a seat on the glider beside her grandmother. "Everything's fine now."

"Thanks to this one," Lois said, patting Grace's arm.

The warmth between them lifted Miriam's heart. After all of Grace's attempts to get Lois to recognize her, she had suddenly broken through. At least something good had come from this situation.

"I lost my way a bit." Mem actually smiled as she lifted her head. "Then Sarah and her friend came along on their scooters and straightened everything out."

Miriam exchanged a concerned look with her father at the mention of her lost sister. Dat gave a sad shrug, and Miriam moved past it for now. "Well, everything turned out just fine, and you're back in time for supper. Children, you best go inside and wash up. Let Mammi sit here a bit and settle in. Suzie, do you want to join us? We're having tator-tot casserole."

"Denki, but I'll be getting home. Mem will be expecting me."

As the children went into the house, Miriam stepped toward the girl to thank her. She put a reassuring arm over her shoulders and leaned close to whisper her thanks in Suzie's ear. "It sounds like you saved the day."

Suzie gave a pleased nod, but answered, "It was Grace, really. She stayed calm and knew what to do."

"You girls did the right thing." Miriam patted Suzie's shoulder, noticing that, for once, she wasn't shielding her cheek with one hand. That was progress.

Turning back to the porch, Miriam was confronted by her father, who motioned her a few steps away from Lois. "I was going to mention this, but didn't think it would be a problem during our visit."

"She's had episodes like this before?" Miriam kept her voice low, not wanting to disturb her mother.

"A few times. She just gets confused . . . loses track of where she is or where she's going." David rubbed his temple, just above one wispy white eyebrow. "At first, I prayed it was a one-time thing, a bad day, but then when it happened again, we went to see a doctor. He ruled out stroke or anything with her heart. It's more a matter of memory loss."

"Oh, my goodness. She's always been sharp as a tack."

"In more ways than one." David winked. "I know she's always been a bit hard on you, and this seems to make her worse. Bit of a grouch, sometimes."

Miriam gazed across the porch at her mother's petite form, which seemed to shrink beside Grace. "It must be frightening for her, to feel confused and lost." Her heart ached for this woman who had raised her, taught her to cook, clean, and manage a house. She thought of the many cures advertised in her favorite Amish magazine. Pills that offered restful sleep, a boost to the immune system, and mental clarity. Friends had tried different things, but no one she knew had ever found an outright cure for their ailments. "We'll take care of her as best we can. Did the doctor have any suggestions? Any medications that might help?"

"Nothing unusual. Plenty of sleep, vitamins, activity, and a good diet. Good to keep the mind busy. The doctor thought she might stay sharp through puzzles and crosswords, but you know your mother. She never was one for reading or word games."

"No, but she does like to keep busy." Glancing at her mother, Miriam considered the busy days ahead. "I'll make sure she has tasks to do for the wedding. And as soon as that's squared away, we'll break out the jigsaw puzzles. I *love* a good puzzle!"

"Are you talking about me over there?" Lois demanded.

"Mem, we were just saying that we can set up puzzles and games after the wedding," Miriam said, pulling a chair over so that she was sitting opposite her mother.

"The wedding!" Lois pressed her palms to her cheeks. "That's what my errand was about. I went off to the fabric store to get a sampler pattern. It's to be my wedding gift. But I couldn't find the store." Lois seemed to have snapped back to herself, brighter now, as if the light had returned to her eyes.

"Mem, I would have taken you to the store," Miriam said.

"After spending most of my life in this town, I didn't think I'd have a problem getting around. But things change. The town has changed, and so have I." Lois looked up at Miriam. "Besides, you're so busy, hands full with children and housekeeping and whatnot."

"I would have found the time for you, Mem," Miriam said, her voice cracking with emotion. For the first time in many years, she felt as if her mother actually saw the person she was. It was a rare moment, one to savor. "We'll find a way to get you to the fabric store. But you'll need to work quickly to finish a sampler so fast."

"I'm quick with a needle," Lois said. She turned to Grace. "You know, granddaughter, I might teach you a thing or two, if you have patience."

Grace nodded. "I'd like that."

"And Lois, just so you know, this one here is named Grace," Dat said, with a nod at Grace.

Lois puckered her mouth and turned to Grace. "I knew that."

Miriam rose, knowing it was time to get the dinner on the table. "You called her Sarah, Mem."

"Did I?" Lois turned to Grace and squinted. "It's no wonder, considering how she looks just like her mother."

Grace's mouth curved in a hint of a smile. "I do have green hair, you know."

"Yah, but everything else reminds me of Sarah," Lois insisted. "Those eyes, and that upturned nose." She nodded sagely at Grace. "You're the spitting image of her. I admit, that upset me a bit when we first got here, but you're really growing on me."

"Same!" Grace said, patting her grandmother's arm.

Seeing the two of them, snuggling on the glider, Miriam smiled. You never knew what surprises the day might bring, bad and good. She could only trust Gott to hold this beloved family in His hands and continue to bless them with His love.

Chapter 18

On Sunday morning, Collette kept quiet in the back of the buggy as Harlan drove the little family to the Hostetlers for church. Most church days she looked forward to seeing friends, praying with the community, and listening to the preachers' sermons on faith and love. Church was the thing that brought Amish folk together, the glue that made them a community.

But today, she worried that her disappointment and sorrows might show through. Much as she wanted to see her friends, it would be a strain, keeping emotions cool and under the skin when she saw their bishop courting another woman.

She smoothed the purple fabric of her good dress over her knees, a nervous gesture that sometimes soothed her. How could she hide that her heart was aching? On Friday, when the bishop had gone along on the family errands, she had relished the moments when the family had joined together, laughing or discussing an important matter. The daughters were pursuing things that made them happy, while learning how important it was to be loving members of their family. At the end of their visit with Dinah, Aaron's mother had whispered to her that she'd done wonders with the family. "Even him!" she'd exclaimed, referring to Aaron.

Collette had laughed the comment off, pretending it to be a joke. If Collette had any influence on Aaron, it was merely as a housekeeper, a nanny for his grown-up children. She'd been the dutiful servant, and he appreciated her as such.

But oh, those moments when he had seemed so delighted with her, pleased with his family. She'd allowed herself to pretend that he truly loved her. Just for a few fleeting moments.

As Harlan and Essie talked amiably in the front of the buggy, it dawned on Collette that soon the young couple would be riding to church separately, one day, Gott willing, with a buggy full of children of their own. Time changed with each season, and soon Collette and Suzie would need to find a place of their own so that Harlan's family could expand. These would all be good changes, though Collette couldn't deny the twinge of bittersweet that accompanied the growth of her children. Like autumn leaves, they developed their own bursts of color and light, only to fall away from her at the end of the season.

Harlan had moved on, though Suzie was still within reach. Collette leaned over toward daughter Suzie and squeezed her hand in encouragement when she shared a funny story about how the boss had made all the girls at the pretzel factory laugh.

"Smitty takes the cake for his jokes, but this week you proved yourself to be quite responsible," Collette said. "Miriam says you saved the day when you drove the buggy home. And without any real lessons, too."

Suzie shrugged. "It wasn't so hard. You think I've been daydreaming in the back here, all these years, but I've been watching you, Harlan."

Everyone chuckled.

"Well, let me know when you want some real lessons,"

Harlan said. "A woman needs to know how to get around in a buggy."

Collette nodded, heeding another sign that her children were growing older. Had Harlan just called Suzie a woman? Indeed. She reached over and pulled Suzie's cupped hand from her cheek, where it sat covering the slight scar. Leaning close, she kissed her daughter's cheek.

"Does it hurt?" she whispered.

Suzie shook her head and turned away to look at the passing fields.

Collette let the matter drop. How her heart ached to ease the girl's insecurities! But Collette knew that there came a time in a girl's life when the last thing she wanted to hear was advice from her mem.

For the rest of the ride, she listened to Harlan and Essie talk amicably in the front seat. A happy young couple. One of the bright spots in Collette's world.

Once they turned down the Hostetlers' lane, the fence was white against the green grass and bushes. Too white. Too fancy. Like one of those Englisch restaurants in town with porch pillars and picket fences. Collette frowned, annoyed at herself for being so critical. Every Amish family put in a lot of work to prepare their home for hosting church. It was wrong to be sour on Linda and Len when Collette didn't even have a home that would accommodate the congregation.

As they waited in a line of unloading buggies, Collette closed her eyes and braced herself to step out of the buggy and greet the other women in their church group. Most church days she looked forward to the music and sermons, the time of reflection and prayer, and the gathering that followed. Food and conversation, sharing stories and visiting friends' worlds for a bit. She vowed not to let her heartache taint the day. Well, at least she would try her best.

Harlan stopped the mule and everyone disembarked, ready to separate into their various groups sorted by age and gender. It was one of the prescribed routines of the worship service, a gathering that brought the community together every other week for worship and socializing. Climbing down from the buggy, Collette was glad to see her friend Alice Yutzy walk by carrying a Tupperware container.

"Women in the kitchen," Alice said, nodding at a whiteboard sign with directions. "That's us. And Suzie, you're in the buggy garage. Leah and Glory are already headed over there."

Answering with a smile, Suzie turned and hurried off to join her friends.

A teenaged boy, one of the teens acting as a hostler for the day, spoke with Harlan and climbed into the buggy to park it. Harlan headed off to join the men in the barn, while Essie went off to the living space of the house to gather with the young married women, many of them toting infants.

Walking along the path to the kitchen alongside Alice, Collette clung to Gott's message: "Let not your heart be troubled." Today, she would walk in faith with her community.

The sermon preached by Lee Fisher that day resonated with Collette. "The Bible in Matthew 7:1 tells us, 'Judge not, or you too will be judged.' Now you might think that you're good and kind to everyone you know. But oh, boy, there's bound to be someone who crosses you now and again. You think someone is stingy or cold. Even the way they look at you makes you suspect that they're up to no good. You're sure they have ill motives," Preacher Fisher said, his calm demeanor matching his smooth voice.

"But you are judging them, thinking that you know

what's going on inside here," he explained, tapping the side of his head with one finger. "You think that person is cold, but maybe their mind is taken up worrying about someone in the family—a sick parent or child."

Collette pictured Sally, the way her face had softened when she'd talked about her fading dream to have a family. Before that moment, Collette had resented the quiltmaker from another town. At first she'd judged Sally to be a minor inconvenience—one more person to take care of in the Hostetler household. And then, when she'd heard of the matchmaking plan between Sally and the bishop, Collette had resented Sally's very presence.

How easy it had been to judge Sally, to think of her as a bad person who'd swooped in like a hungry crow landing on a picnic spread. The nerve of this woman, coming to Joyful River and getting in the way of Collette's plans.

But then during the buggy ride, when Sally confided the spark of attraction and the dream of marriage and a family, it became clear that Sally wasn't a bad person at all, but a woman hoping to fall in love and build a life with a good and kind man.

As the preacher spoke of the downfall of judging others, Collette let her eyes scan the churchgoers in front of her, rows of prayer kapps and shoulders rising above benches in the Hostetler home. The windows had been opened wide, allowing fresh air to waft in from the sunny September morning. Not so easy to identify someone from the back, but she managed to find Sally seated next to Linda, who could be identified by the vibrant purple color of her dress. A new dress. Linda loved new things, but Sally appreciated old gems. She had been delighted to go through the rag bag at Linda's house and extract bits of cloth to piece into her quilts.

A good woman, that Sally. Unlike Collette, she hadn't

experienced the joys of marriage and motherhood. Was this Sally's chance to live the life she'd only dreamed of? Blessings that Collette had known. Much as it pained Collette, it seemed that this was a match made in heaven . . . Gott's plan.

Oh, dear Lord, give me the wisdom to know Your will. And the strength to respect it, she prayed as the song leader started the congregation in a hymn.

After church, Miriam greeted folks quietly as she found her way to her good friends. Miriam Lapp always managed to shine a positive light on things, and her younger sister-in-law Greta Lapp had a smile for everyone, despite her league of young ones who sometimes set Collette's head spinning. Greta patted the back of the baby sleeping on her shoulder as she spoke with Rose Graber, who was also cooing to an infant in her arms. Rose was a decade younger than Collette, though they often shared stories of rearing boys when Rose lamented the antics of her ten-year-old son, Ezra.

"How's the dear little one today?" Collette asked, taking a seat on the bench next to Rose.

"Sweet as pie!" Rose said. "Hazel was fussing and crying through the night. Teething, I think. But we're feeling happy now, aren't we?"

The baby opened her mouth wide in a gummy smile that warmed Collette's heart. "So cute!"

"Do you mind taking her for a bit?" Rose asked. "I need to help my grandparents get set up with sandwiches. Dawdi's not so steady on his feet these days."

"I'd be delighted." With the baby quickly whisked into Collette's arms, she felt joy fill the hole in her heart that she knew to be loneliness. This was love, staring into the sparkling eyes of a baby who needed to be held and comforted and cajoled. Pure love.

Collette was so smitten she wasn't tracking the conversation between Miriam and Greta. She only joined in for a moment when Miriam made a point to compliment Suzie on driving home the stranded buggy with Lois inside.

"I do believe your Suzie helped save the day," Miriam said cheerfully.

"I'm glad she could help. She's a good girl."

"Time to start the driving lessons, I think," Greta teased. "I'm so glad mine are still younger. Lloyd doesn't have the patience for those things, so I'll be the one giving the lessons when the time comes."

"I'm hoping her brother, Harlan, can ride with her a bit," Collette said, her gaze on the drooling baby. In truth, she sensed that Suzie was hesitant to drive after last year's buggy accident. It was something that needed to be smoothed out when everyone in the family wasn't so busy going in their separate directions.

She didn't even notice when Linda Hostetler, their host for today, stopped by and took a seat.

"Did you get food yet?" Linda asked.

"Don't worry," Greta said. "We'll get there. We're just waiting for the line to go down."

"And don't forget the dessert table. Sally made a shoofly pie, if you've got a hankering for something sweet today."

"Wonderful good," Miriam said. "You must be so happy to have your sister here with you after so long."

"I am," Linda said. "And Gott willing, she'll be staying on permanently if all goes well with a bit of matchmaking."

"A match?" Greta blinked and leaned closer to hear the news. "Who's the lucky man?"

Collette caught herself staring, dumbfounded, and quickly swiveled away, cuddling the baby close. She had to avert her face, afraid her stormy emotions might break through.

"I wouldn't want to gossip. Let's just say he's a widower we all are well acquainted with, and though it's hard to read any man, it seems that he's interested."

"A widower . . . Are you talking about Bishop Aaron?" asked Miriam.

Collette heard the surprise in Miriam's voice, which brought her a new shade of humiliation. Miriam was the only person who understood Collette's feelings for Aaron, and now, Miriam would want to know why Collette had failed to engage him.

"You got that on the first guess, Miriam," Linda said. "Honestly, I think it's high time the man took another wife. We all know he grieved for his departed wife for a long time."

"Dorcas was a good woman," Miriam said. "Gott rest her soul."

"Sally's timing may be just right to save that man and his girls. I know Dinah has been helping out, but I cringe to think of a household without a woman running it," Linda continued.

But I've been working with them, Collette wanted to say, *and they're doing well. The girls are learning and thriving in the kitchen and in the garden. They did lack a woman's touch, but now they have it, and their home is a happy home.*

"And you know that my Len and Aaron have long been good friends," Linda went on. "Wouldn't that be convenient if it all worked out?"

"You'd have your sister close by all the time," Greta said encouragingly.

"Indeed." Linda arose and clasped her hands together. "Such a blessing. I pray that Gott will keep Sally with us for years to come. Now don't forget to try a piece of Sally's pie."

With that, Linda was off, leaving Collette feeling as

deflated as a party balloon that had lost its air. Greta arose and said something about getting food, but Collette's attention was diverted as little Hazel, who'd been fussing a bit, broke into a full-bellied wail. Teething.

Collette pressed the baby to her chest and patted her back. "I know the feeling, I do. The pain makes you want to cry out loud." As she spoke, she spotted a red rubber gel ring perched on the top of Rose's open bag. Grabbing the toy, she strode away from the benches, away from curious churchgoers and observant eyes who might wonder why she was on the verge of crying like the baby in her arms.

"It's not what he's *doing,*" she told Hazel. "It's not that he's socializing with the Hostetlers and Sally, that he's falling in with them and enjoying their company. It's what he's *not* doing that hurts me."

When she reached the fence that she'd whitewashed, she shifted the baby in her arms and plied her mouth with the chewy toy. Hazel's eyes opened wide as she bit in.

"That's it, sweetie." She continued to walk along the boundary, determined to be clear of listening ears from the congregation. The baby was still whimpering, but the motion of walking seemed to be calming her.

"So should I be upset that he doesn't speak for me? When Len told him about the match, he didn't say that he was interested in someone else." There'd been no mention of her, no mention of another woman in his life, a woman he enjoyed spending time with and maybe, maybe hoped to pursue a deeper relationship with.

A woman who might one day want to share his home, sit with him to watch sunsets on the porch. He would be the head of the house, the protector and breadwinner, and she would manage his home and cook and clean for him.

And love him.

"Love is a gift and a burden," she said quietly, observing

the heft and the sweet scent of the baby in her arms. "Love comes unbidden, and when you realize you can't use it, there's no sending it on its way."

Little Hazel nibbled on intently, but she tipped her head up to stare at Collette.

"I know what you're thinking. A woman shouldn't be falling in love with a man who hasn't even courted her, but this is different. We've gotten to know each other well. I'd even say we're friends."

Hazel winced and let out a squeal. It was as good a response as any.

"Collette!"

The sound of Miriam's holler made her turn around and face her approaching friend.

"There you are," Miriam said. "I looked over and you were suddenly gone."

"Hazel was fussing, so I took her for a walk."

"Perfect timing, as I figured you were eager to escape Linda's bit of chatter." Miriam tilted her head to one side. "I was surprised to hear about Linda's sister."

"I admit, I'd gotten wind of the match." Collette kissed the top of Hazel's downy head. "Have you met Sally? She's smart and pretty easy on the eyes and she's never been married. She'd make the perfect Amish wife for a man like our bishop."

Miriam stepped closer and slipped an arm around Collette's shoulders. "Except that I think his heart belongs to another fine Amish woman, who's also pretty easy on the eyes."

Collette looked away and let out a sigh. "A woman who was abandoned by her husband comes with a taint of misfortune."

"Don't even say that," Miriam insisted. "Right now, I'd

say your worst misfortune is in crossing paths with the likes of Linda Hostetler."

"You have a point there. But Linda will be Linda. And I can't blame her for the path my life has taken."

"Though you must admit, she's thrown a few obstacles in your way," Miriam pointed out.

"Indeed. But when Gott sends us a tornado, we don't ask questions. We get out of the way."

The two women chuckled softly, and Miriam patted her friend's shoulder. "Have you given up completely? I mean, on love?" She swiveled Collette and the baby around so that they were facing the church crowd. There, on the benches in the shade of the barn, sat the group of men, their beards wagging as they talked. "On him?"

She meant Aaron; Collette knew that. Funny how friends could sometimes speak to each other in a language all their own. Collette understood the question, but she didn't know the answer.

"It's hard to give up on a man when your heart yearns for him," she said quietly. "But Sally is a kind and good woman who's never been blessed with a husband. Never blessed by a man's love." She shook her head, sorrow weighing heavy on her soul. "I'm afraid Gott has other intentions for him." When she blinked, tears formed in her eyes, and she had to look away.

"My wise friend," Miriam said gently. "You're right. We can never know Gott's plan for any of us. But Sally is here for a reason. And so are you."

"I wish I knew . . ." Collette began.

Miriam nodded. "We can't know the future, but you can act. You have a choice in matters you can control."

It seemed that there were few matters in which she had a choice. The amount of pepper in a stew. The day of the week to do laundry. Even her own children were beyond asking her advice. And the most important thing—the love of a certain man—that was well out of her reach. "And the things that are beyond my control?"

"I pray for the grace to accept them."

Collette nodded. She was no stranger to prayer.

"But don't give up," Miriam said. "I've no doubt that Sally Renno is a good woman. But so are you, and you know Aaron well. You've had a special relationship with our bishop. All of those times he visited you in the rehab center and when you were recovering at Len and Linda's. He enjoys your company; I can see that. A wise man. He knows where to go for interesting conversation."

"And quiet," Collette said thoughtfully. "He's a man who understands that people can come together in the quiet spaces of a conversation."

"The quiet spaces . . ." Miriam nodded. "You know I love chatting with Alvin, but it's often the easy silence, those quiet moments that wrap around us like a quilt and draw us together."

"Our men are different when they're not running with the pack." Collette glanced toward the menfolk near the barn. She quickly spotted him—that bold brow and blue eyes always caught her attention—and then looked down at the baby girl in her arms. "You know, Aaron's different when other folks aren't around, when it's just the two of us. Not so stern. He's listens to what I have to say. Listens more than any man I've ever known, and he cares. I know that he cares about me and every member of our church. He's more than just a rule keeper and a leader. He tends to the folk as a shepherd tends his flock, trying to keep everyone together, keep us safe."

"Gott has blessed you and Aaron with a special bond. Most folks don't know that, but I've seen the two of you together. I don't know what the future might bring, but Gott doesn't make mistakes."

Collette held on to those words as she and Miriam returned to their friends and rejoined the conversation. Something in the air had changed; a cool but damp breeze lifted napkins and paper plates from the bench tables. Rain was coming. Collette could feel it deep in her bones.

Rose thanked her for looking after little Hazel, admitting that it was nice to have a break.

"And I enjoy having a babe in my arms, just like the old days," Collette admitted. That smooth skin, those round eyes. The feel of a warm bundle of life in her arms, a heartbeat near hers, a little life reliant on her. Those were the joys of motherhood. So far behind her, though she had hope that Harlan and Essie might make her a grandmother in the next year or so.

Collette enjoyed a sandwich with her friends, and then the women ventured over to sample the desserts. When Collette saw that the bishop was in line ahead of them for dessert, along with Deacon Seth, she was glad for the cover of her surrounding friends.

Thinking fast, she called to Rose, who gladly rewarded her by passing Hazel into her arms once again. Somehow, with a baby snuggled in the crook of her neck, Collette felt needed and invisible to the nearby men.

At the front of the line, Collette took a small slice of shoofly pie and moved aside with her friends. The sugary pie filling wasn't her favorite, but she thought it would be nice to compliment Sally next time she saw her. As the other women ate, she set her slice aside and watched Aaron and Seth, enjoying the fact that she could partially hide behind the infant on her shoulder.

The bishop was eating from his plate, and he seemed

pleased. "This is one of my all-time favorites," he commented to the men around him.

So he liked the pie?

Collette squinted for a better look and saw the pop of color on his plate. Red. It was her strawberry Jell-O dessert. The one he'd loved as a child.

Her heart ached as she thought of all her best intentions, the love she'd poured into that dish when she'd made it. Maybe it was silly, but the dessert had seemed to connect her to Aaron in a special way.

In that second his head turned and his gaze caught hers.

He knew she'd made it. He remembered their exchange. And he seemed to be reaching out to her. *I see you,* his gaze said.

She watched him, wanting more of a message, but someone in the group moved in the way and the connection was lost.

She could only listen as Aaron commented again on the tastiness of the dessert, and a few of the men murmured their agreement.

"Well, you can thank my sister Sally," came Linda's response, and now Collette could see the woman's head bobbing from behind the dessert table. "It's good, yah? Sally and I got the flat of berries from Eicher's Amish Market, fresh as can be."

Deacon Seth held up a spoonful of the ruby-red dessert, his eyes twinkling with delight. "If your Sally can do this with a flat of berries, she must be handy in the kitchen."

"Oh, she is!" Linda assured the men with a wave of one hand.

And that was how Linda Hostetler gave her sister Sally credit for the strawberry dessert that Collette had made. It wasn't a lie, just an odd twist of words. But it was enough to make Collette feel defeated. In a race against Sally, Collette was going to come in second.

Chapter 19

Such a comforting Sunday night rain, Miriam thought, staring out the kitchen window at the silver drops slanting across the window. The dinner and dishes were done, and the long list of wedding chores would begin tomorrow morning. For now, she had a moment to linger and enjoy the wriggling silver drops on the glass. Gott willing, the rain would help pack down the gravel and dust, water the grasses and trees, and prepare the property for Wednesday's wedding crowd. Nothing brought a fresh, clean scent to the farm like a crisp fall rain.

Tomorrow, the real challenges would begin with the arrival of the wedding trailer and the team of cooks. The men would erect a tent and set up porta-potties, and areas would be designated for guest horses and buggy parking. Oh, and the signs? Miriam needed to make sure they set up signs directing folks, gifts, and horses to the proper areas. With hundreds of guests attending, they would need some direction.

Behind her, on the other side of the kitchen, Lizzie sat reading a storybook to Sarah Grace, who must have been too tired to fidget as she sat with her chin resting on the table. Mem sat in the padded chair near them, her fingers moving deftly as she guided the needle in and out, in and out. The sampler was taking shape beautifully, and the project seemed to have given Mem a boost in energy.

The incident with Lois stranded in the buggy had been an eye-opener for Miriam. It seemed as if overnight the small but mighty mother who had raised her with a stern gaze and high expectations had shrunk to a softer, oft-confused old woman. Although Miriam knew this was Gott's plan, the natural progression of aging and growing old, she was struggling to accept the changes. Change could be so difficult! Despite her mother's occasional and tender child-like moments, Miriam felt a sickening guilt lacing through her. Over what? She wasn't sure.

As Miriam gazed out the window, she saw a floating light from the distance, coming from the Dawdi House. A lantern. Someone was coming.

She placed the kitchen towel on its rack and went to the mudroom, where the rain tapped out a steady beat on the thin roof. Stepping out, she saw Essie running through the rain, hugging something to her chest. "Essie? Come in, come in," she called, ushering her daughter into the outer room.

"I was trying to run ahead of the rain," Essie said, giving her head a shake and wiping her feet on the concrete floor.

"Do you want a cup of tea?" Miriam offered, entering the kitchen.

"Nay, denki." Essie crossed to the table and plopped down into a chair while holding on to her bundle. "I'm afraid I have a problem."

Miriam put the kettle down and snapped to attention. "Lizzie, take Sarah Rose upstairs. You can finish reading her book up in your room, then get ready for bed."

"Yes, Mem." Lizzie's eyes were round with curiosity, but she resisted and took her sister upstairs.

Essie straightened and started to unfold her bundle,

which Miriam now saw was made of cloth. "It's such a small problem, really," Essie said. "A good problem. But somehow, I just want to laugh and cry about it at the same time, and I—I don't know how to fix it. And I know you can't fix it, either, Mem."

"Essie, daughter." Miriam sat beside her and touched her shoulder. The sight of her eldest daughter in such distress tugged at her heart strings. She couldn't remember seeing Essie in such a state of high emotion. "What is it? I can't fix everything, but we can certainly put our heads together and try to come up with something."

"It's this dress I sewed for Sam and Sadie's wedding. I—I followed the usual pattern when I sewed it last month and . . . and it fit me just fine. But now . . ." Tears welled in Essie's eyes as she unfolded the pretty forest green dress and held the bodice up to her shoulders. "It doesn't fit me anymore!" she sobbed.

"Oh, dear." Miriam's mouth tensed. She'd never known Essie to be so emotional about an ill-fitting dress. "Well, we'll have to make some alterations."

"But you're all thumbs with a needle and thread. You know it's true."

"True, but I can assist." Indeed, sewing was Miriam's weakest skill.

"And I can follow a pattern just fine, but this . . ." Essie shook her head as tears ran down her cheeks. "It's just too small now. I can't get the hooks to fasten. And there's no time to sew a new dress, with the wedding just days away and so many other things to do."

Over in the corner, Mem looked up from her embroidery, watching intently. Were her squinting eyes a sign of disapproval? Miriam wasn't ready to handle that right now.

"Essie, honey, I know I'm not good with sewing skills,

but we'll figure this out." Miriam smoothed the fabric of the dress over her daughter's thigh. "You say it's too small now?"

Essie nodded, swiping a tear from one cheek.

Tucking the dress around her daughter, Miriam noticed that the bodice didn't seem to fit over Essie's bosom. Or the rounded mound of her belly.

Her belly?

Oh, wondrous Father in heaven!

Now it was Miriam's turn to mist over. "Oh, my dear girl! You're having a child!" She embraced her daughter in a joyous hug. She should have realized it sooner! Of course the dress didn't fit! "I'm so happy for you and Harlan," Miriam whispered.

When Miriam leaned back, Essie was smiling—a huge grin that belied the tears in her eyes. "It's a blessing, I know," Essie said. "And we're so happy and grateful to Gott."

"Well, that's good news!" Lois said, nodding in approval.

"I know it is, Mammi," said Essie. "Harlan and I are both over the moon with joy. I don't know why I'm so upset about this dress, but here I am, all broken up about it. I cry at the smallest thing these days."

"It's no wonder, being in your condition." Lois placed her embroidery on the table and pushed out of the chair. "Let me see this dress. Stand up, now."

Miriam watched as her mother held the dress up to Essie, squinting as she calculated.

"And where is it tight?" Lois asked.

"The bodice. All through here," Essie said, pointing to parts of the dress.

"Do you have extra fabric?" Lois asked. "Because if you do, if there's half a yard, I can alter the dress to fit you."

"Could you?" Essie asked hopefully. "Oh, Mammi Lois,

that would be wonderful. I have some leftover fabric. I feel so stupid for not ordering a bigger pattern when I made the dress. I don't know what I was thinking."

"No matter. We'll open up the seams here and here, and put in an extra panel on each side." The older woman nodded. "It will look like a normal dress when I'm done, and it shouldn't take me too long."

"Denki for saving my dress!" Essie bent over her petite grandmother and planted a kiss on her cheek. "You're the best, Mammi. I'll run home and get the fabric right now."

"Nay, stay and have some hot cocoa with me," Lois said. "It's late and we don't take up a major task on the Sabbath. Tomorrow is soon enough to start real work on the alteration." She folded the dress and placed it over the back of a chair. "Sit now, and tell me about this husband of yours. What did you say his name was?"

"Harlan," Essie said. "I'm Mrs. Harlan Yoder now. You've met him a few times."

Lois picked up her embroidery and sat at the table, next to Essie. "And what does this husband of yours do?"

"He's a right good carpenter . . . ."

As Miriam made a pot of hot cocoa, Essie answered her grandmother's questions, filling her in on the recent details of her life and marriage. Lois had been away so many years, in some ways, it was as if she were meeting her grandchildren for the first time. Since Grace had brought Mem home last week, Miriam had noticed the older woman making more of an effort to pay attention to her grandchildren, telling them stories and dispensing advice. Now a sense of comfort lifted Miriam's heart as she stirred the milk and listened to the conversation. In the future, Miriam couldn't let so much time pass before the family saw her parents again.

After a half hour of cocoa and conversation, Essie returned home and Miriam gathered the pot and mugs in the sink and added a dollop of soap to the water.

"Denki for offering to alter Essie's dress," she said. "I don't have the time or skill to do it myself. But I've haven't seen her in such a rattled state since she was a child." She smiled. "Now having a child of her own. Gott is good."

"She reminded me of myself, when I was pregnant with my first. Your brother Andrew. Your father and I were about Essie's age, children ourselves. Oh, but we thought we knew what was what. We were living with my parents, but I wanted to cook his dinner myself every night. Drove my mem batty, I think. But I parsed out our separate meals and did my cooking until the day came when I was feeling poorly. I fell asleep and left a casserole in the oven until it burned to a black crisp. Dat teased that I'd nearly burned the house down. I cried and cried over my mistake. My failure."

"And Dat? Was he upset with you?"

"Not at all, especially after my mem served him up her chicken stew. Anyway, turns out I was feeling poorly because I was expecting. Only, I wasn't quite as wise as Essie and I didn't even know it at the time." Lois shook her head, her fingers deftly moving the needle. "I was a ball of emotion, though."

"And months later, Andrew was born."

"And our family was started."

"That's a sweet story," Miriam said. "Funny, too. You should share more of your stories, Mem. Sometimes we can learn from other people's experiences."

"I would tell you more if I remembered. Sometimes things come back to me, but most times, it's a bit fuzzy."

"Well, if something pops into your mind, I'm happy to hear it." Miriam turned to her mother as she dried a mug.

"I hope this doesn't put you behind on your sampler. It's coming along nicely."

"My sampler can wait. Even though it's a gift, I can give it to the happy couple a few days after the wedding. Essie's deadline is more crucial."

"It is, and it's so important to her to be there to support her brother at his wedding. Denki, Mem. You know I would have tried to alter the dress myself, but I don't know my way around a needle and thread."

"And you're hosting a wedding in this house in a few short days," Lois said. "I'd say you have your hands full, daughter."

Indeed. It would be a busy week for Miriam, but she hadn't expected her mother to be so considerate. It was as if Mem was suddenly seeing things she'd been blind to for most of her life. It brought to mind the popular hymn, "Amazing Grace."

As Miriam folded the towel, she hummed it, thinking of the words. *"I once was lost, but now am found. Was blind but now I see."*

How lovely that Gott might open a person's eyes to new truths. Why, just a few minutes ago, standing here in this kitchen, Miriam's eyes had opened wide enough to see that her daughter was expecting a child. And now, she also knew that her mother had once been a headstrong, tearful newlywed, similar to Essie.

That night, on her way up to bed, Miriam heard the sound of a voice coming down the hall. Someone was singing. Pausing at the top of the stairs, she listened quietly to her mother's voice, small and cheery as a child as she joyously sang a later stanza from "Amazing Grace." "'Tis grace that brought me safe thus far. And grace will lead me home."

How precious that Mem remembered some things so well. With hope in her heart, Miriam tiptoed off to bed.

Chapter 20

"Look at that! The wedding wagon is here," Collette said as Harlan steered their buggy to the side of the road to allow the wagon to pass down the lane at Lapp Farm. After a rainy night of feeling glum, it was a bright Monday morning and the sight of the shiny white truck pulling the modern trailer lifted Collette's spirits with the thought of this week's wedding. Nothing warmed the heart like Gott's blessing of two people in love, a man and a woman starting their life together.

Collette looked on longingly as the cook wagon passed by. "I wish I could be around to help Miriam today," she said. She had volunteered to help serve and help with dishes during the wedding, but how she'd love to spend today in the shiny mobile kitchen! There'd be half a dozen women there, chatting and joking as they chopped onions and celery and bread to prepare the traditional roasht served at the wedding. The teamwork would surely take her mind off the ache in her heart.

"Why don't you take some time from work?" Harlan asked. "I'm sure the bishop or Linda Hostetler could spare you."

"Nay. Dinah's having her surgery today, and the family

needs me. It's more than work, Harlan. It's about making a commitment to folks and keeping it."

He shot her a curious look. "So serious for a Monday morning."

"I'm a serious person," she said with a stern smile. "Now, off to the bishop's house. I need to get the girls to the hospital so they can visit their grandmother when she gets out of surgery."

"Beebee!" Harlan called to his mule. "Let's go!"

When Collette arrived at the Troyer home, she was surprised to see that Amy and Tess were up, dressed, and ready to go.

"I've been up for hours!" Tess said. "I wanted to go with Dat to check Mammi into the hospital, but he said that plans had been made, and he didn't want to upset the apple cart."

"So instead, she woke me up," Amy said. "And we made these blueberry muffins to bring. We followed the recipe from Mem's collection. Measured carefully, the way you showed us." She lifted the cloth from the basket to reveal a mound of golden muffins.

"They look perfect! I knew something smelled wonderful sweet when I came in the door." Collette was pleased by their effort, pleased by their thoughtfulness. It seemed that they might have actually been listening some of the times when she'd had talks with the girls about pitching in to help others in the community.

"Do you want one?" Tess asked. "Amy and I had one for breakfast."

"Along with some fresh berries," Amy said.

"Our ride's on its way, so I'll wait until we get to the hospital. But I'm proud of you girls. Good job."

Both girls smiled, glowing in the compliment. She wished Aaron could see them now, so eager for his love and approval. From outside came the sound of gravel crunching under tires. "That'll be our hired car. Off we go. And don't forget the muffins!"

During the ride to the hospital, the girls chatted amiably— far different from the way they'd been when Collette had first arrived. Now that Dinah had finally had her hip replacement surgery, Collette wondered about her attachment to the Troyer girls. Dinah would be back on her feet in a month or two. Most likely the woman would continue to keep house for her son and granddaughters.

Collette would be out of a job and pushed out of the girls' lives.

The thought of leaving these girls made her heart ache, but perhaps that was Gott's will. All for the best. It would spare her having to see Aaron courting another woman.

A good chunk of the hospital waiting room was occupied by Amish folk who'd come to see after Dinah Troyer. Aaron was seated next to the deacon, Seth King, a colorful painting of a sun setting over farmland hung over their heads.

"How's Mammi?" Tess asked, going directly to her father.

"Still in surgery," Aaron said, his eyes opening wide when Amy offered him a muffin. "You baked these on your own?" he asked.

"They were done before I arrived," Collette reported.

"And we cleaned the kitchen," Tess said. "Which is definitely the worst part."

"Delicious," Seth said, turning to Aaron. "Aren't you the lucky man to have two bakers in your home!"

"Indeed, Gott has blessed me with these daughters," Aaron said.

There was a glow of satisfaction in the girls' eyes as they moved about, offering muffins throughout the waiting room. Collette drew in a breath, pleased that things were on the mend between Aaron and his daughters.

Collette took a seat among the older women, Dinah's friends, who were talking about surgeries they'd had or needed. Cataracts. Hip and knee replacements. Cancer treatments. Collette knew that being in the hospital spurred that sort of talk, but she'd had quite enough of it last year when she'd spent months in rehabilitation for a broken femur suffered in a buggy accident. *Dear Gott, thank You for healing me and giving me back a full life,* she prayed as the women chatted on. It had been a difficult episode, but it had brought Aaron into her life. As a friend, she reminded herself through a veil of disappointment. Just a friend.

Madge and Emery Lambright arrived with large thermoses of coffee, which they set up so that everyone in the waiting room could serve themselves. "Such a nice thing to do," Collette said, though Madge insisted it was not a problem at all. As owners of the Country Diner in town, they had access to such supplies for catering events.

After pouring a cup of coffee for herself—and one for Tess, who saw coffee as part of the grown-up world—Collette followed Tess over toward the bishop, where they took two empty seats.

"When will they be done?" Tess asked.

"When they're done," Aaron said.

"I'm just so nervous. I want everything to be fine," Tess said, cradling her paper cup.

Collette patted her arm.

Len Hostetler came in and joined Aaron, and Linda and Sally weren't far behind.

"We brought cookies," Sally said. "Snickerdoodles from the Amish bakery in town."

Well, at least this time Linda wasn't trying to pass it off as Sally's home baking. Maybe it was petty to stew over that, but that incident with the strawberry dessert had gotten under Collette's skin.

"We were talking about you on the way over," Linda said, nodding at the bishop. "Not gossip, mind you, but an idea we had. Go on and tell him, Sally."

"It was just a thought." Sally perched in a seat across from the bishop so that she was eye to eye with him. "Knowing that your mem is laid up with this operation, we couldn't imagine how you were making do at home without her. So since I'm here, I thought I might come by a few days a week and help with the cooking and cleaning. I'd be happy to do it."

"But we have Collette," Tess blurted out.

"Collette?" Linda's lips pursed, giving her face that pointed snout look of a fox. "What's Collette got to do with it?"

Collette couldn't find the words; it seemed unfair that she needed to explain, as if defending herself. She looked to Aaron, who touched his beard, obviously preparing a careful answer.

"She comes to our house three days a week." Tess lifted her chin as she spoke, as if staking her claim. "She cleans and stuff, but mostly she's teaching us how to cook and tend to the garden and take care of the house."

"She's a right good teacher," Amy said. "And a wonderful good cook."

"Well, doesn't that take the cake," Linda said, shooting a peeved look to her sister. "And here I thought you worked for me."

"I come to you Tuesday and Thursday," Collette said in a measured voice. "That leaves other days to help the Troyers."

"Well, no matter. Though I'm surprised that you didn't say anything, Aaron."

Aaron turned his head slowly to take in the listeners. He was not a man who enjoyed sharing details of his personal life, especially in a public forum. "It was an arrangement between Collette and me, a job that needed to be done, and she does it well. All the same, there are some matters a man keeps to himself."

Collette's eyes burned at his words. Everything he said was true, and yet . . .

A job? It was another reminder of the professional scope and breadth of their relationship.

Suddenly, she felt weepy. Such a strange emotion—and at a terrible time! She rose and turned away as Len suggested that his wife was overstepping bounds.

"Sally and I are just trying to help." Linda's voice traveled after Collette. "And I don't see why Sally can't go over and help out on Tuesdays and Thursdays. She's able-bodied and you need the help, Aaron."

Not wanting to hear anymore, Collette made her way past the waiting people and into the hallway, where a bank of windows overlooking the parking lot offered a bit of escape from the drama behind her. Drawing in a deep breath, she focused on the trees below, a few of them bearing a flourish of red and gold, early signs of fall. The sight of the trees was calming, but she feared that her sorrows would come rushing back if she returned to the waiting room.

The whole thing was an embarrassment. To have feelings come flooding in while she was out in public! It just wouldn't do for a woman her age to flout the emotions of a teen in rumspringa! Maybe her response surprised her because she thought she had accepted the fact that she was just a housekeeper. She had thought it would be possible to sweep her feelings for Aaron under a rug and let them stay put.

But now she saw that the lumpy rug was going to trip her up.

She pressed the back of one hand to her cheek, which seemed warm. Not from sickness, but from tamped-up emotion. She couldn't go back into that room.

"Do you see our horse and buggy down there?" asked Madge Lambright, coming up behind her.

"Can't see the buggy parking from here," Collette answered, "but I'm sure your rig is fine."

"We're heading out," Madge said. "We're going to leave the thermoses, but we'll be back later to pick them up and bring food." She turned toward the doorway. "I just need to extract my husband."

Collette nodded as an idea popped into her head. "Would you mind giving me a ride back to town? I could walk to the bishop's house from there. I figure it might be best to get back and get working on a dinner for the family."

"We'd be happy to have you along for the ride," Madge said.

"Denki for the offer. Let me just tell the bishop I'm going." Collette smoothed down the skirt of her dress, preparing to go to the bishop and make her excuses. She hadn't realized that her shadow, Tess, had been sitting near the doorway with a book in hand.

"Collette, you can't go home now," Tess said. "Mammi will want to see you after the surgery."

"With so many friends here, I'm sure she'll make do without me," Collette said.

"But you should stay." Tess looked toward the waiting room. "Stay with me, please? Or else I'll go with you. I don't want to spend the whole day here. I can come back later, when Mammi is awake."

"You should stay with your father," she told the girl. "When Amish folk go to the hospital, their family and friends stay nearby. It's what we do." It was a tradition Collette usually enjoyed, knowing that friends and family had gathered to show their love for an ailing member of the community. "You need to stay."

"But you're leaving," Tess pointed out.

"I'm the hired maud." The words spilled out before Collette could check them. "You know I'm fond of your grandmother, but my purpose is to keep you fed and keep the household running smoothly." *That is all,* she thought. *I need to learn that it's a job, nothing more.*

"But Collette . . ." Tess said quietly, taking her hand. "We need you here."

Collette took in a breath. How to escape this terrible feeling? She was steeling herself and preparing to be firm with the girl when a woman in teal-green hospital scrubs and surgical hat strolled down the corridor. A doctor.

"I'm looking for Aaron Troyer," she announced at the door to the waiting room.

"That's my father!" Tess offered, brightening before the woman with short-cropped blond curls. "He's over here."

Collette followed to hear the news: "Your mother did just great," the doctor announced. "Mrs. Troyer has a brand-new hip, and we're hoping she'll be able to try it out in the next twenty-four hours. She's in recovery right now, but when she wakes up, they'll move her to a room."

"When can we see her?" Aaron asked.

"I'd say it'll be an hour or so."

The waiting room filled with animated conversation, everyone overjoyed at the good news. It was enough to lift Collette from her tearful mood. She quickly told the Lambrights that she would be staying, and then was swept into the planning for visits to Dinah's room that afternoon. Although visitors were limited to three at a time, most

Amish friends stayed on, passing the time with conversation and snacks folks had brought along to share.

Aaron was the first to visit, along with Deacon Seth and Esther Lapp, Dinah's good friend. They stayed for a few minutes, and then it was Collette's turn to pop in with Amy and Tess.

"You look bright as a new penny," Collette said, surprised to see Dinah sitting up in bed and finishing a container of Jell-O.

"I feel like I just had a short nap," Dinah said. "Though they say I might not feel so spry when the pain medication wears off."

"But the doctor said that everything went well," Amy said.

"I was so worried," Tess said, getting close enough to pat her grandmother's shoulder. "But you're going to be just fine."

"Don't you worry," Dinah reassured the girls. "It takes more than a cranky hip to wear out an old plough horse like me."

"You're not a horse, Mammi!" Amy insisted, and the girls chuckled.

"The doctor said I'm starting physical therapy tomorrow. I should be walking with my new hip in no time."

"Back to your old routine, Mammi," Tess said.

Collette nodded. "I'm sure you'll be glad to get back to tending to Aaron and the girls."

"These two?" Dinah squinted at the girls. "I'd say you've done a much better job of getting these girls to pitch in and help with the cooking."

"We baked fresh blueberry muffins this morning," Tess said. "All on our own."

"We shouldn't have left them in the waiting room," Amy said. "Maybe Mammi would like one."

"There'll be plenty of goodies in here for me," Dinah

said. "But that's a wonderful good thing, you girls learning to bake and keep house. I think I enjoy you a might more when I'm not being the cook and cleaner in your house." She turned to Collette. "I hope you'll stay on."

"I don't think Aaron will want that," Collette said, shaking her head.

"He'll come around," Dinah said confidently. "Dear Collette, you're the best thing to happen in that house since my son married Dorcas, Gott rest her soul. Countless times I tried to get Aaron to hire a maud, but he refused. Didn't want a stranger in the house. But bringing you in, that was a smart move. He got to know you through church, and it's clear that he knows and trusts you well."

That much was true. Collette simply wasn't sure if she had the mettle to continue her housekeeping chores in the bishop's house without becoming hopelessly attached, falling for Aaron while he gave his heart to another. "We get along well, and he's easy to work for."

"Then it's settled. I'll be sure he keeps you on. I don't always have sway with my son, you know." Dinah pointed to her bandaged hip. "But with this, my old bones, he was forced to make a move. And it's no surprise that he likes having you there."

"We all like having you with us, Collette," Amy insisted. "Please, promise that you'll stay."

"Forever and ever," Tess added.

"It's nice to be wanted, but forever is a long time," Collette said, moved by their tender request. It would satisfy her heart's desire to be a full-time housekeeper for the Troyers and it was nice to know the women in the family appreciated her. "I'd be happy to stay on for the time being, but I have my own daughter to look after. And we must remember, your father is the head of the household. We must respect his wishes."

"I suspect he can be swayed." Dinah gave a wink.

"Maybe not. It seems someone's offered to replace me. Someone he may . . . favor."

"You mean Sally Renno?" Tess scrunched her face until her freckled nose was wrinkled. "That will never work."

"I heard that she offered to help out, but we don't even know her," Amy insisted.

"I've spent some time with Sally, and she's a right kind woman," Collette said. "Mind you, everyone should be treated with respect and love."

"Yah, of course," Amy said, her blue eyes flashing with remorse. "I meant no disrespect."

Ignoring the plastic clip on one finger, Dinah pressed her hands together in prayer position and brought them to her lips. Situated on a pillow in the hospital bed, she looked downright cozy and alert, not what Collette would expect after a surgery. "It's time I talked to him. A mother can be persuasive in these things."

"Would you do that, Mammi?" Amy asked. "Please, please, please. He listens to you."

"That might not be such a good idea," Collette said. Knowing the strong will of Amish men, Collette could imagine a variety of ill-fated scenarios.

"But it's perfect!" Tess insisted. "Mammi will smooth everything out."

"I'll talk to him," Dinah said. "For now, we'll leave it in Gott's hands, with a little nudge from me."

Chapter 21

Aaron was just about to doze off in the chair when his mother spoke to him from her hospital bed.

"You can go now, son. I'm all set here, and visiting hours are going to end soon. Go home. I'll see you tomorrow at the care facility."

"Are you sure?" He rose from the chair and went to her bedside. It had been a long day, and the notion of heading home held great appeal. Still, he didn't want to leave her alone if she needed anything. "I can stay for a bit longer."

"Go home. The girls already got a ride with Alice Yutzy. Her daughter is friends with Amy, you know. And Collette will be back in a moment with my ice cream, and then you can give her a ride."

"Ice cream?" The treat was one of his mother's favorites.

"They sell it in the cafeteria." Dinah put aside the book she'd been reading and smiled. "I'm getting a dinner tray soon, and I hear there might be some ice cream on that, too. A double whammy."

"A good day for you," he agreed.

"But before you go, there's something important I want you to know. Once I'm recovered and finished with rehab, I don't think it wise for me to return to housekeeping for you."

"You don't?"

"I don't feel quite up to it." She smiled, and he noticed that the strands of gray at her temples were now turned to solid silver. Mem was getting older, as was every person on earth.

"You're tired now, but you'll feel differently when you get back on your feet," Aaron assured her. "The doctor says the new hip is going to improve your range of movement. You'll be walking without pain, Mem."

"I thank Gott for that, but it doesn't change my plans. This time on my own has made me rethink what's best for everyone. I've enjoyed my granddaughters' visits far more than I expected. I don't miss the nagging I had to do when I was housekeeping for you. They're good girls, but they still need guidance. You all need help in the house, but I'm not fit to do it." She clasped her hand around his wrist to be sure she had his attention. "You need to have a housekeeper in your home, for good. Make it a long-term commitment."

"But Mem, I don't think . . ." Thoughts of Collette came rushing in, but he couldn't go there. It was wonderful to have her in their home, but she had her own family to tend to. Besides, he'd only asked her in as a temporary substitute for Dinah.

"Folks in our church are bending over backward to help you, Aaron. When people offer to help, you need to accept that help."

Was she talking about Sally Renno? Aaron didn't think it would be a good idea to have her come into their home. She was a good woman, no doubt, but a stranger to his girls. Not to mention the strings attached if he opened the door to her. "Mem, I don't think it's wise. You don't understand—"

"Are you too proud to admit that you need help?"

He bristled. Pride was a sin that led man away from Gott. "That's not it."

"You're worried about what people will say?" Her brows rose. "This is not fodder for gossip, Aaron. Not when you're answering a need. And if you can't admit you need help, then do it for your girls. I can't return to the housekeeping schedule I was keeping, and your girls need to keep improving their kitchen skills."

He nodded. That much was true.

"So you'll do it?" Dinah asked. "You'll have a housekeeper so that I can simply be a grandmother?"

With a sigh, he agreed. "I'll do it."

"Wonderful good." She leaned back and settled her head into the pillow. "I'll rest so much easier knowing you and the girls will be well taken care of."

"Well, at least one of us will be resting easy," he teased her.

"Something keeping you up at night?"

"Just my schedule. A very full plate. Iddo is under the weather, so I've promised to work at his place and bring the rest of the hay in this week. Also there's a wainwright reunion starting Thursday that Seth needs some assistance on. Oh, and that wedding Wednesday."

"Sam Lapp and Sadie Beiler," Dinah said. "I'm sorry to miss it. Though weddings are fun for old-timers like me. You have serious responsibilities to conduct those sacred vows."

He nodded, feeling the weight of those responsibilities, along with his commitments to his parishioners, to his friends, to his neighbors. Sometimes it seemed that everyone needed something from him. At the end of the day, he often felt amazed that there was still the light of the Holy Spirit glimmering in his weary body.

"Go home, son," Dinah said. "Rest up for your busy week."

He leaned over the bed and kissed her on the forehead. "Denki for the advice, Mem. I admit, it strained my ears to hear it. Few folks have the wits to advise a bishop."

She chuckled. "You're never too old or too important to take advice from your mother."

He knew this to be true. Every church leader and bishop was merely a humble believer in the eyes of the Almighty.

After Aaron retrieved his horse and buggy from the stable of a friend near the hospital, he headed back to pick up Collette.

"Such a long trip for you, Thumper," he said aloud, as if the horse could hear him. "Next time, I'll hire a car." Thumper was a reliable horse, but he knew better than to push the old boy past what he could endure.

As Thumper's hooves clip-clopped on the road, Aaron couldn't get his mind off the visitor, Sally Renno. Every instinct in his body told him it would be wrong to bring her into his home, but he'd promised his mother, hadn't he?

He wished that Linda's sister had never made that offer. Aaron knew that folks meant well, but he wished they would stop intruding in his family's life. Things were going smoothly with the girls and Collette. Why not leave them be?

He'd resisted pressure from Linda and Len. But now, his mother was insisting that he hire Sally Renno. He didn't like the feeling of inviting a stranger into his home. It had been different with Collette. He'd come to know her well over the past year, especially after the accident when she'd been laid up and unable to walk or venture outdoors without a wheelchair. Initially he'd scheduled regular visits to minister to her, making sure she knew she had the support of her church community.

Over time, he'd come to look forward to those visits. Time spent with Collette had been like a reunion with an old friend. She listened as well as she shared. Somehow, she understood that balance in a friendship: giving and receiving in the moments of lively conversation and silence. Their relationship had set down new roots when he'd hired her to help out during Mem's recuperation. There were a hundred ways that she made his daily life easier. Was it any wonder that he thought of her fondly, the treasured time that they spent together? In his busy life, his work of counseling and consoling church members while trying to keep his own farm afloat, Collette had found a place for herself. Her voice, her opinion, her presence. Collette belonged in his home now, just as much as the ticking of the mantel clock or the beating of his own heart. He would never find the same peace with any other woman in his home.

The weight of his mother's demand added to the weariness weighing him down as he pulled up in front of the hospital entrance where Collette was waiting. She seemed small and vulnerable, waiting there alone. Beautiful in the way she held her head up and shifted from foot to foot to ward off the growing cold. Resourceful. No matter the obstacles, she never gave up.

Prompted by a deeper instinct, he exited the buggy, came around, and helped her climb in. Her hand was cool to the touch, and yet it ignited a warmth that surprised him.

"Denki," she said.

Once he was back in his seat, she offered him half of the buggy blanket. Abandoning caution, he accepted, and suddenly their hands touched again. And then they were sharing the blanket, his legs just inches from hers, the warmth of their bodies melding under the plaid wool weave.

Aaron stared ahead, trying to ignore the feelings that he knew should not transpire between a bishop and a woman in his employ.

"Here we go," he said, his voice suddenly rusty. "The end of a long day."

"You must be tired, getting Dinah to the hospital before dawn."

"And you, too. It's been a long day for both of us, but I'm relieved the surgery went well."

"Dinah will be up and about in no time," she said.

"Gott willing." He swallowed, considering what to do. He hated to ruin the warm, close moment between them, but the truth needed to come to light. "She's let me know that after her recovery, she won't be coming to keep house for me anymore."

"Is that so?"

"She wants to spend her time being a grandmother. Not to mention the quilting bees she enjoys so much." He didn't dare look at Collette, not now. "But she made me promise to have a housekeeper, for the sake of the girls. She wants me to hire Sally Renno. You know her, Linda Hostetler's sister."

"I do know Sally. She's a good woman."

"She is, but . . . I hardly know her."

For a long moment, the only sound was the burr of a truck engine behind them and the tapping of his horse's hooves on the pavement.

"And you say Dinah suggested you hire Sally?"

"She did." He gave a sigh. "Actually, she insisted. She went on a bit about how it's too much to handle major housekeeping at her age. I do understand, but I'm conflicted about her advice. Hiring Sally seems like the wrong move, but I'm backed into a corner. A man must respect and honor his mother. Not that I must follow every bit of advice she gives, though, in this situation, it does affect her."

Collette's lips were pursed, as if considering this complex situation. "Seems you are facing a dilemma."

"It's a pickle, all right. If it were simply a matter of refusing Sally's offer, I could buffer the situation by explaining to Len. But now, with my mother so deeply involved"—he shook his head—"I don't see an easy way out."

An easy silence settled between them as the buggy moved on. Considering various approaches, Aaron realized that no one else was in a position to understand his situation the way that Collette did. She knew the girls well. She understood the workings of his household. She seemed to know when to support his ministering to others and when to remove herself and allow the privacy a minister needed. And when it came to his mother, there was a female bond between Dinah and Collette that allowed them to speak in the language of women, a code that Aaron was sure mortal men would never completely understand.

"What would you do in my situation?" he asked.

"I couldn't say. Seems that whatever you do, it's going to ruffle someone's feathers. But then again, the easy decision is not always the best, is it?"

He nodded. "Wise words."

"I do have a question, though. If you hire Sally as a housekeeper, will you be dismissing me?"

Despite the calm in her tone, the question set him on edge, like a clanging triangle at the back door. Let Collette go? He couldn't imagine going on without her! "Nay. We wouldn't want that to happen," he said. "The girls would never forgive me, and I . . . no telling how I'd manage to keep things together without you at this point. You're family now, Collette. That is, if you want to keep coming to us three days a week. I figured I'd hire Sally on for Tuesdays and Thursdays, and even that seems like an intrusion. But it's my problem to solve. For now, I guess I should have started by asking you if you want to stay on with us?"

When he turned to her, her gaze was lowered, her expression as stiff as a stone. "Do you want to? I know you have a daughter at home still, and many family commitments. Are you able to stay on?"

She drew in a breath and lifted her head. "I would like to stay on. Suzie is a good girl, kept busy by her job at the pretzel factory. It's not a problem for me to be off at work during the week."

"I'm grateful for that." A surprising sense of relief welled up inside him. "We've come to need you, Collette." As soon as he said it, he realized the attachment that his words revealed. It was not the sort of thing he said lightly, but it was all true when it came to Collette. And oddly enough, it didn't create awkwardness when he shared it with her. She was indeed part of the family.

And she was going to stay on.

With that part resolved, the Sally Renno dilemma was sure to work itself out. It bothered him that his mother was interfering in his affairs at this point in his life. He was a grown man, far too old to be worrying about small social things. But no matter his age, a man had to respect his parents.

It wasn't like Dinah to insinuate herself in his decisions, but then he reasoned that the stress of the operation had been weighing on her heavily. What could he do to ease her mind? Maybe he could hire Sally part-time. Maybe he could convince Dinah that they didn't need Sally's help. At least the important matter—holding on to Collette— was resolved. And if Dinah questioned him about keeping Collette, he'd step up and defend her. She was a good Amish woman, hardworking and kind and sharp as a tack. Right now, driving home beside her, sharing a blanket, he realized she was probably his closest friend in the world.

All thanks to Gott.

Chapter 22

"Hey there," Grace said, approaching the loading dock of the pretzel factory where Suzie stood, leaning on her scooter and talking to the Amish guy with the golden hair. As Josiah Graber had been the buzz of conversation among Suzie and her friends since she'd spoken with him last week, Grace wasn't exactly surprised. But there was no mistaking the chemistry between the two teens.

Romance was definitely in the air.

Josiah kept on talking—something about his bazillion brothers—and Suzie smiled as Grace walked past to retrieve her scooter. Grace didn't want to pull Suzie away from the guy, but it was Monday evening, and Grace needed to get home and finish off two school assignments for tomorrow. "You ready?" she asked Suzie.

Suzie nodded as Josiah scrambled toward the scooters and bikes. "Josiah is walking with us for part of the way," she announced.

Walking? That would take forever. Grace leaned closer to Suzie and lowered her voice. "Listen, I can go ahead on my own, and you two can walk together."

"No!" Suzie gasped. "I can't be alone with him. Not yet. If someone sees the two of us, word will get out and it'll ruin things. Please, Grace, stay with me," she said, looking over her shoulder to make sure Josiah wasn't listening.

"Fine." Grace glanced over at Josiah. "But can't we ride?"

"It's too hard to talk while we're riding," Suzie said.

"Come on, girls," Josiah called to them. "I can show you a shortcut out of town. There's a walking path by the river, but it's too bumpy to ride."

"Okay," Grace agreed. "We'll take the scenic route."

As they walked to the bridge at the edge of town, Grace kept to herself as the others talked. Josiah seemed interested in what Suzie had to say, and he cracked a few corny jokes to keep things light. Grace was beginning to think that she had judged him a little too harshly.

When they reached the big stone bridge, they stopped to peer down into the gushing waters of Joyful River.

"This part of the river moves fast," Grace said. There was a September wind that whipped up occasionally, lifting a cold mist up to them, and for a moment Grace closed her eyes and basked in the refreshing sensation.

"The mist," Josiah said. "See? Grace likes it."

"It feels nice," Suzie said.

"My mammi, my grandmother, she calls it one of Gott's blessings."

"That's so nice," Suzie said.

"Mammi Mary also believes it will cure a fever, but this I don't think is true."

They chuckled and headed on, rolling their scooters down the footpath from the street to an embankment that ran low along Joyful River. It was a new route for Grace, and she let the others talk as she took in the water, which stretched wide in spots, narrowed in others, ran smooth as a mirror, and then swirled into rapids over rocks and boulders.

"I heard a story about you girls," Josiah said. "I heard that an old woman got stranded in a buggy last week, and you came along and saved her," he said, his gaze fixed on Suzie. "Is it true?"

"We did come upon Grace's mammi in the buggy," Suzie said. "But we didn't really save her. I mean, she wasn't in danger."

"But she definitely needed help," Grace said. "You're too modest, Suzie. It was you, taking the reins and managing the buggy that got us all safely home. Even though you don't have a lot of experience driving a buggy. It was your first time, right?"

"First time?" Josiah's face was lit with enthusiasm. "That's quite a good deed. Sounds like you really did save the day. Someone should write your story for that Amish magazine."

"That would be cool," Grace agreed. "You're a hero, Suzie."

"Nay," Suzie said, pressing her hand to her cheek. "I'm just a plain girl."

Just a plain girl, flirting with a plain boy, Grace thought.

"Are you going to the wedding this week?" he asked. "Sam Lapp and Sadie Beiler?"

Grace nodded, but she noticed Josiah intently focused on Suzie for her answer.

"I am," Suzie said. "My brother, Harlan, is married to Sam's sister, so we're family. We live in the Dawdi House at the Lapp farm."

"Is that so?" Josiah asked. "Well, now I know where to find you. In case *I* need rescuing sometime."

Suzie and Josiah chuckled, and even Grace had to smile. These two.

"I'm going, too. My parents know everyone from church."

"That's how it goes with church folk," Suzie said. "Everyone knows everyone."

Grace had figured that much out in her year here in Joyful River. Amish people formed attachments to each other through their church gatherings, socializing with the same group of people every two weeks. And if they met someone outside the congregation, they often were able to make connections through a brother, cousin, or friend. It was a never-ending network, as integrated as a patchwork quilt.

As they talked on about the wedding, Grace realized she was looking forward to it, too. Megan would be coming home from college for the event, and Dad would drive over from Philly so that their family would be together for the day.

Her Englisch family.

Sometimes she missed the life she used to have in the city. Always, always there was the memory of the way their family had been pulled together by Mom's love, work, and skillful negotiation. Back then, they'd worked as a family, a wonky but loving team. But after Mom died, the good times had been scarce. It seemed that she'd spent all her time squabbling with her sisters and trying to deal with feeling alone in a city of countless strangers.

And now, after a year in Joyful River, Grace and her sisters had been absorbed into the big, good-natured Lapp family. Looking back, Grace was kind of surprised that Aunt Miriam and Uncle Alvin had been willing to put up with three Englisch girls with attitude.

"They're family," Aunt Miriam had told her children. And that had explained it all.

Looking back, Grace realized that coming here had probably been the best thing that had ever happened to the Sullivan sisters. All three of them were on a better path now.

Mom would be happy to know we're here, she thought as she pushed her scooter on the path alongside the river. She liked to think of her mother watching her and her sisters, looking down from heaven, as if she were sitting in the skybox of a baseball stadium.

"This is where the path merges onto the road," Josiah said as he led them up the embankment.

"Nice shortcut," Suzie said. "I'm glad you showed it to us."

"I like it," Josiah agreed. "It's good to be near the water, under the trees. Nature is good."

"Sure is," Grace agreed, though she didn't think either of them heard her, as they seemed to be lost in a gooey-eyed gazing match.

They walked their scooters along the road for a bit, and then Josiah said goodbye and headed off.

"Well, that went well." Grace stepped one foot on her scooter and coasted ahead.

"Wait!" Suzie scootered alongside her. "Do you really think so?"

"Absolutely. He's so into you."

"He's into me," Suzie repeated, as if in a daze. "Oh, Grace, I can barely believe it. I've never had a boyfriend before."

"Well, it looks like you've got your first." They were coming to the crest of a hill, and Grace pulled both feet up and put one foot near the brake, just in case.

"I'm so happy," Suzie said. Then, as if announcing it to the hills and valleys, she called, "I'm soooo happy!"

Soaring and smiling, they scootered the rest of the way home, only slowing when they turned off the road to the lane leading to Lapp Farm. It was moving toward sunset. These were long days for Grace when she went from school to work. But with jam-packed days, she found she had less time for stress. As the property and outbuildings came into view, Grace noticed the new vehicles parked beyond the main house. The girls hopped off their scooters and rested them against one of the picnic tables on the lawn as they took in the sight.

"The cook wagon is here, and look! They've set up two tents," Grace said as she stepped onto the seat and sat on the tabletop. "Wedding prep."

"It's going to be a wonderful wedding," Suzie said. "I'll bet Sadie is so happy. To be a bride and an Amish wife is every girl's dream."

Not my dream, Grace thought. Sure, it would be great to fall in love and all. But that was just one of the bazillion things she wanted to happen in her life.

"You know, after the accident, I mean, when this happened to me, I was sure that no boy would ever look at me." Suzie stared straight ahead, her eyes shiny with tears. "I really like Josiah, but I'm so afraid I'll mess everything up."

"Aw, Suzie, no you won't. He seems to really like you. And I'm impressed at how relaxed you seem around him. You step up and speak your mind, which is what a decent guy wants from a woman."

"He does?" Suzie pressed a hand to her cheek. "I didn't know that. There's so much to learn. Will you help me, please?"

"You're doing great on your own," Grace said. "And I'm

not a good person to give advice. I don't have a boyfriend right now. Maybe you should talk to Essie, or what about Serena? She's got good instincts when it comes to guys."

Suzie shook her head. "You're my friend. And actually, I was hoping you could help me with this." She moved her hand to reveal the mark on her face. "Someone told me there's a way to fix it. That maybe a doctor could smooth it out?"

Grace's mouth dropped open. "Oh. You mean plastic surgery?"

"If that would fix my face, yes. Can you help me get it done?"

The thought of her friend getting surgery made Grace anxious. "I could research it, but, it's not a simple thing. It'll be expensive, and you don't have medical insurance."

"How much?" Suzie asked. "I get to keep part of the money I make each month. I could use that."

Grace shrugged. "It would be hundreds, maybe thousands. You'd have to find a doctor, and get permission from your mother, since you're not eighteen."

Suzie's lips pursed. "I don't want my mother to know. At least, not yet. This has to be our secret until I've got it all figured out."

"I won't tell a soul," Grace promised. "But you need to know, surgery is a bigger deal than you might think. Besides the cost, there'll be some pain. And really, Suzie, your scar is barely noticeable."

Suzie let out a disgusted breath. "I hate it."

"I know you do, but the people who love you don't see it at all." She put a hand on Suzie's shoulder and gently moved Suzie's hand from her face. "Now that I'm really looking, I'm pretty sure it's faded a lot over the last year. It's definitely not as red as it used to be. I can barely see it."

"It's still ugly."

"Suzie, come on. Don't be so down on yourself. Everyone has something about themselves that they don't like. Big ears or a big bottom. Freckles or thin hair."

"This is different. It came from an accident."

Grace hunched forward over her knees and started to roll up her jeans. "Take a look at this."

Suzie turned to her with a look of curiosity as Grace pulled her pant leg up, revealing a pink, two-inch scar on her knee. "This came from an accident, too. I fell off my bike when I was five. Mom said it probably should have been stitched, but that never happened."

"Does it still hurt?" Suzie's pout softened a bit when she saw the scar.

"No, but it was painful at the time." Grace remembered crying when it happened, when Mom rinsed the cut and wiped the dirt. Even walking had been painful while the cut healed. She'd been a little kid at the time, but some of the trauma had stuck with her. She wondered if that was true with Suzie. Maybe the trauma of the accident was the thing that really bothered her, and the scar was just a physical sign.

"You're lucky to have your scar on your knee, where no one can see it," Suzie said.

"That's true." Grace pulled her pant leg down and hopped off the table. "I'd better get going or I'll be late for dinner. But we'll talk about this more, and I'll do some research."

"Denki for helping me, Grace." Suzie grabbed her scooter and pushed off toward the Dawdi House. "You're a good friend," she called.

Watching her go, Grace hoped that was true.

Inside, the kitchen was uncharacteristically quiet for this

time of day—the predinner hour. There was only Mammi Lois, seated by the warm stove, bent over some sewing work.

"Where is everyone?" Grace asked.

"Out and about. Some are setting up inside the tent. Some are in the cook wagon, setting to work. There's two hundred pounds of chicken to be roasted for the main wedding dish. Always a big job."

"Wow." Grace removed her jacket and hung it on a hook by the door. "So no dinner tonight?"

"There's a tator casserole in the oven, ready when the timer goes off. But your sister Serena said it's a YOYO night."

"Yoyo?" Grace asked.

"It stands for You're On Your Own. Get it?" Her grandmother chuckled. *"Y-O-Y-O."*

Grace let out a sigh as she poured herself a glass of milk. "That sounds like Serena." She looked over at the sewing work on the table—an Amish dress in a pretty lavender color. Mammi was probing a sharp metal tool into the seam, ripping one bit of thread with each jab. "What's that you're working on?"

"It's Essie's dress for the wedding." Mammi checked to make sure they were alone, and then added, "Seems there's a baby on the way, Gott willing, and Essie needs her dress altered."

Grace blinked as she swallowed the milk. "Essie's pregnant?"

"Hush now. We don't talk about these things."

Grace sat down at the table, trying to wrap her mind around this development. Essie had still been a teen when she'd married last year, and now she was going to be a mother at age twenty.

"I know this is the Amish way, to marry young and have kids right away. But . . . wow."

"Wow is right." Mammi nodded. "It's good news."

"But Essie's still so young. She was a teenage bride, you know. I can't imagine any of that happening to me, being a mother in a few years."

"Hm. Many years ago your mother said the very same thing," Mammi Lois said.

"Wait. What? She did?"

"*'I'm never going to be a teenage bride.'* That's what she told me. I thought she would come around. She didn't have to marry right away, but I figured she'd settle down and get baptized. Find the joy in living plain. But I was wrong."

"She left."

Mammi nodded. "She went to the city. She'd already been dressing Englisch, like a city girl." Lois lifted her head and shot a look at Grace. "She dressed a lot like you. Blue jeans! Like an Englisch farmer. And I told her that." She shook her head. "We argued about her path in life. I just wanted her to do the right thing and be a good Amish woman. But she had her hopes set on other things. Seeing the rest of the world. Exploring, she said. I thought that she'd get it out of her system after a few weeks, but that didn't happen."

It was one of those dilemmas without a clear right or wrong. Grace could understand her mother's need to move out and explore, but at the same time, she felt for her grandmother. "You must have missed her terribly."

"I did. She broke my heart. Sarah was the duckling that fell out of line and got lost in the rushes."

"It must have been hard on both of you." Grace could imagine her mother arguing with Lois. Those teen arguments that could be so cutting and frank. In the end, Sarah had made the choice that was right for her, but it came with the terrible consequences of hurting her Amish family.

"It's all part of rumspringa, I guess. You're supposed to let your child go a bit wild, figuring they'll come back to the roost. That's what I expected of Sarah, and I waited days, and weeks, and then months." She winced over her task of seam-ripping. "The waiting was so hard. When she came back at last, she was a different person. Married to an Englisch fellow."

"My dad, Sully."

"Once I heard she had married an outsider, I knew our Sarah was gone." Lois's mouth puckered, but she kept on attacking the seam.

The work seemed to be a salve for many wounds. Or at least a distraction. Grace wanted to tell Mammi that her daughter hadn't completely disappeared all those years ago. Sarah had still been there, the same stubborn streak, the same laugh beneath her jeans and tie-dyed shirts. But it seemed wrong to reopen old wounds, especially since death had taken Sarah forever.

Instead, Grace commented on the pretty color of Essie's dress. She asked Mammi how she'd learned to sew. When the timer dinged, she got up and removed the casserole from the oven. And when Peter, Paul, and Lizzie came bounding into the house, Grace helped them dish up plates of the steaming casserole—ground beef with tator tots on top. She served Annie and made a bowl for Sarah Rose, blowing on a steaming mound until it cooled down enough for the little girl.

Later, as she was doing dishes with Lizzie and Annie, she thought about why it had taken her so long to feel at home here. She'd been stuck on the fact that she wasn't Amish, but Aunt Miriam had always made it clear that

Grace and her sisters were part of the family. *Freundshaft* was the Amish word for family.

All these months, Grace had been waiting to become part of the family. As if she needed to be let in. Now, pitching in to help with the dishes, she realized she'd had it all wrong.

She'd been family all along.

Chapter 23

Before Wednesday dawned, Collette was up and doing her share to keep the meal preparation going in the cook wagon. Several folks—church members, friends, and family of the bride and groom—worked steadily at their various tasks. With its multiple sinks, ovens, and stoves, the trailer was a beehive of activity, and the hum of conversation and laughter brought her joy as she joined the busy fray.

The master recipe for the traditional Amish main dish, the roasht, was tacked up on the trailer's little bulletin board, and workers occasionally checked it to make sure their team was preparing enough ingredients. Collette always marveled at the magnitude of it! Thirty chickens, fifty-six eggs, twenty-eight crocks of bread crumbs, eight pounds of butter . . .

Their main cook, Madge Lambright, had been here with her helpers all day yesterday, roasting the thirty chickens that would go into the popular dish. Today, Collette was on the veggie team, and she happily spent the morning slicing and chopping celery, which was a major ingredient of roasht, as well as the creamed celery side dish for the wedding meal. Across the trailer at another counter, Rose Graber and Alice Yutzy were chopping fat heads of cabbage for cabbage slaw, and somewhere outside on a folding table, ladies were cutting bread into cubes for the stuffing.

Of course, no pot or tub could be large enough to make the roasht in one batch. But every stovetop in the wagon was currently occupied by women sautéeing celery, chicken gizzards, hearts, and liver in butter. Once cooled this would provide much of the flavoring for the bread stuffing, which would be tossed with salt and pepper, beaten eggs, and bits of roasted chicken, then baked for an hour or two.

The work, the company, the chatter all combined to make Collette smile as her worries about Aaron and Sally faded. Hard work was an important spoke in the wheel of Amish life, and Collette knew that it was good for a healthy outlook and disposition. Few things lifted the spirits like a job well done!

As the morning wore on, the chopping was done and the large pans of chicken and stuffing had been slid into ovens to bake. Collette and others cleaned up their stations, knowing that there'd be plenty more cleanup to come before the day was through. Madge delegated folks to various tasks, some to finish preparing the coleslaw and creamed celery.

"We'll need someone to check on the desserts and make sure they're all set out," Madge said.

Collette and Rose volunteered for the assignment and, armed with serving utensils for the cakes and pies, they headed out of the wedding wagon. On the way to the wedding tent, they passed guests who were streaming in from the main road. It was clear that the ceremony, held in the buggy garage, had ended, and the wedding supper and games would begin soon.

"They've got a right good setup for a wedding here," Rose said. "But why didn't the bride's family host?"

"You know Sadie's parents couldn't shut down the orchard this time of year." Collette didn't know the Beilers well, but Miriam had confided in their difficulty at the orchard. "It's harvest time, and they couldn't host a wedding with all the picking going on there."

Friends greeted them as they headed to the tent, everyone in a jovial mood, but there was no time to pause and chat. There were pies and cookies and cakes to attend to.

When a horse-drawn buggy came down the lane and moved past the parking area, and pulled up close to the house, many people paused to observe.

"That'll be the bride and groom," Rose said, grabbing Collette's arm in excitement as the young couple emerged from the buggy. "Oh, I love that shade of green Sadie chose for her dress! And don't they look happy together?"

"Very happy," Collette agreed. She didn't know Sadie well, but she knew Sam to be hardworking and kind, and she was happy for the girl who, today, had married into the wonderful Alvin Lapp family. Last year when Collette's son, Harlan, had married the Lapps' oldest daughter, Essie, Collette had found that the family's love and support had extended to her and to Harlan's sister, Suzie. Their love was a gift beyond measure.

"Weddings are such a blessing," Rose said as the women continued on their way. "Sometimes, when I'm drifting off to sleep, I think about the day I married Ray. It was October twentieth, cooler than today, and . . ."

Rose was talking, but her words seemed to float off on the breeze as Collette noticed Aaron walking up the lane from the line of buggies where boys were taking vehicles off to park while they tended the horses and mules.

He was alone. She suspected that Tess and Amy would be arriving with friends. The slight breeze tousled his silvered hair back, away from his prominent cheekbones. His skin was tanned, probably from all those extra days spent in the sun, harvesting at Iddo Dienner's farm. She sensed a certain serenity in his eyes—or was he just tired? She had developed a knack for recognizing both states of mind, though not from this far away.

He glanced up from the path and there was shift in his face. A tension, and then the forced calm of a minister.

"Good morning," he said, nodding at Rose and her. "We've got a nice breeze blowing today."

Collette and Rose greeted him, though the words seemed meaningless in Collette's mind. She could only feel his presence, like a warming fire on a cold day. And then he passed and was behind them.

Oh, that man!

Sometimes it was a thrill and a heartbreak to be near him—two very different emotions all at the same time, much like the alternate layers of a cake. Being next to him in the buggy, sitting in the glow of his warmth under the blanket. Their legs had touched a few times, just briefly, and the sensation had stolen her breath away.

The way he confided in her, sharing his worries and hopes—the calm conversations with Aaron made her feel elevated, as if the two of them were the only ones left on Gott's earth, talking things out, searching for solutions.

It was no surprise that she'd fallen in love with him.

She'd known it for some time now, though it wasn't a sentiment she wanted to acknowledge. She knew that love was the thing that bonded humankind, and there were so many kinds of love in the world, like a mother's love for her child, and the love shared by good friends. But the love that swelled in her heart for Aaron was different. More intimate. Romantic, and yet grounded in the fabric of everyday life as she participated in his home life. Working beside him, she was becoming her best self.

She wanted to think that she was indeed becoming like family to Aaron and the girls. Hadn't he told her that earlier this week?

"You're family now, Collette," he'd told her in the privacy of the buggy ride.

"We've come to need you," he'd said.

She believed that was true, but she also wanted to think that she would eventually be welcome in the home as more than a loving maud. And so far, Aaron hadn't given a strong indication that he was willing to cross that line into new territory.

As they were about to reach the tent, Collette spotted her daughter over on the lawn, where a dozen or so young people were hanging out. She held up a finger to Rose and stopped to watch.

Wooden boxes had been set up to play cornhole, and Suzie was engaged in a round of the game with her friends Grace and Tess. No doubt Tess was thrilled to be included in with the slightly older girls. Collette would get an earful later. After Suzie took a throw, missing the box completely, a thin, blond Amish boy came over to her and said something that made them both laugh. He reached for the beanbag in her hand, and there was a brief, playful tug-of-war. Then he moved close to her, leaning in behind her to guide her hand in an expert throw. Suzie's face was aglow, her smile all-consuming as she enjoyed the flirtation.

A bold flirtation, Collette thought, unnerved at the boy's attention to her daughter.

Her shy, sweet daughter.

Collette stared blatantly, wondering why Suzie didn't turn away or call out to her friends. Wasn't she frightened or at least annoyed by the boy?

Just then, Suzie and the boy tossed the last beanbag together, and Suzie scampered ahead to retrieve the bags, laughing all the way.

Collette took a breath as the truth sank in. Her daughter was no longer a shrinking violet. She was a young woman who was enjoying the company of a young man.

Rose glanced over to see what Collette was watching. "Oh, that's your Suzie. She seems to be having a good time."

"She does," Collette agreed, before snapping back to the task at hand. "Now . . . let's get these desserts set up."

Inside the tent, rows of guest tables were covered with plastic tablecloths in a pretty shade of lavender that matched the attendants' dresses, and the tables were set with flatware and plates, ready for the first seating of guests. Over in the corner, the L-shaped table known as the eck had been set up beautifully with white linens and an emerald-green drape that Collette suspected would match Sadie's pretty wedding dress. Platters and Tupperware containers covered the outer part of the table, but in the center, in front of the spot where the bride and groom would sit, sat a heavenly white layer cake.

"Look at the wedding cake!" Rose cooed. The three white-frosted layers were shaped like a heart and trimmed in lavender with "Sam and Sadie Lapp" written in swirly letters on top of the cake. "It's gorgeous!"

"And I'll bet it tastes delicious, too," Sadie added. "Delilah has outdone herself." Their town baker, Delilah Esh, had the knack for making cakes that looked magnificent and tasted good, too.

"This cake is surely our centerpiece," Rose said, opening up a bin of white frosted cookies. "We'll start with the cake in the center and arrange the sweet treats fanning around it."

"With a side cake on each end," Collette said, lifting a white sheet cake and carrying it to the outer ends of the eck.

Collette and Rose worked efficiently, trying to display the goodies to best advantage while the wedding tent began to fill up with guests and young people who had volunteered to work as servers. The bride and groom's families were seated, as well as the ministers and the bridal attendants. When Sam and Sadie took their place at the eck, they both noticed the beautiful wedding cake, and made a point of thanking Rose and Collette for helping with their special day.

"We're so happy for you!" Rose told them, then turned to Collette. "We'd best skedaddle back to the cook wagon."

Collette nodded. Plates of steaming food were being served, and while the atmosphere was delightful, there were plenty more tasks that needed to be done behind the scenes.

She and Rose ducked out of the tent and scurried off like two schoolgirls escaping their chores.

"I do love weddings," Rose said, "but I must admit, it's so much more fun to be working behind the scenes than serving every minister and grandmother in the gmay."

"I'm always happiest with my hands tied up in work," Collette agreed. The chopping and dishwashing gave her a chance to lose herself in the company of other women. Joyfully she submerged herself in the work of serving and cleanup. This was the life she'd been born to. She enjoyed making others comfortable, bringing them a moment of happiness, even if it was as fleeting as the sighting of a butterfly.

The day passed quickly, a tumble of events that kept Collette and dozens of others on their toes. The work was constant, and by midafternoon Collette's feet ached. But their labor was all in the name of a joyous occasion, and Collette cherished being a member of Team Wedding.

Her work did not go unnoticed. At one point Alice Yutzy approached her to ask for help at the reunion the deacon was hosting. "It's a paying job for Thursday and Friday, a small amount of cooking and serving. He's expecting Amish wheelwrights from as far away as Indiana."

"I'd like to help, but I need to clean for the Hostetlers tomorrow, and then the bishop's house on Friday."

"No worries. I'm asking around, putting together a crew of gals."

"Be sure to ask me next time," Collette said, glad to be asked.

After the second meal, Collette wove through the more casual groupings of tables and benches, picking up paper cups and plates that were used and abandoned. She chatted with some of the women, trying to maintain a safe distance from the bishop and other men. Still, she couldn't help but notice Linda pressuring sister Sally to swoop by the men's table with her and chat with the bishop.

That Linda! She always seemed to be pushing her sister on Aaron. First she had pushed her to be a maud for him, next she would probably push Sally to claim him as a husband.

The resentment that ran cold in Collette's veins made her shiver for a moment, and she reminded herself that Linda and Len Hostetler had offered her shelter when she needed it, allowing her to stay in their one-story house while she was recuperating and unable to climb stairs. There was goodness in all people. She needed to remember that.

While Linda remained in place, speaking with the bishop, Sally went around the table and paused to speak with Deacon Seth. They talked quietly and casually, both of them looking off in another direction. Sally listened intently as he spoke, and then nodded.

Turning away to wipe down a bench, Collette thought that Sally did not seem happy today. It dawned on her that Sally was caught in the middle of her sister's matchmaking. Collette felt a twinge of sympathy for Sally Renno. No one liked being pushed around.

She picked up some cups, sticky from lemonade, and sat down on a bench to reach a toppled cup on the ground. When she looked up, Sally was gesturing for her sister to come away with her, and the two women headed off toward the main house.

Collette straightened and glanced across the tent. Aaron sat with his good friends, Deacon Seth, Len Hostetler, and Jerry Kraybill. Their beards wagged as they spoke, and Collette wondered what men spoke of when they didn't have housekeeping, cooking, and child-rearing in common. She was about to turn away when the bishop turned his head and latched his gaze on to hers.

Aaron . . . Her pulse beat like a powerful bird as they locked eyes.

Despite the folks gathered 'round, he seemed to see only her.

Why can't you speak what's in your heart, tell our friends and community of the bond between us. The love between us?

Although she only asked the question with her eyes, he clearly didn't read it well. He turned to Deacon Seth and made a comment, which was followed by nods of approval. Lost in the company of men, he was.

Why did she even try to win him over?

He was a bad habit, like a sweet tooth or a streak of vanity. She needed willpower and determination to kick that habit and start on a new path. A life without heartbreak and mooning over a man.

She *needed* stability. Oh, but she *wanted* Aaron Troyer.

Chapter 24

The sun had not yet risen when Aaron's alarm clock clattered by his bedside Thursday morning. He threw back the quilt and pushed in the small toggle on the clock to stop the noise as his feet swung down to the cold floor at the side of the bed.

The room was dark and chilly, too early for sunlight to seep in around the window shade.

"I'm more tired now than when I went to bed last night," he muttered, raking back his hair. The many events and commitments of the past few days had drained him. Yesterday's wedding had consumed the entire day. Every other day this week, Iddo's fields had soaked up endless hours. There was more work to be done to bring in the rest of the soybeans, and since Iddo had missed the wedding, Aaron feared that his health hadn't much improved. There'd been an afternoon helping Seth clean up the field behind his home shop in anticipation of the group of men coming for the reunion. And now, he needed to get over to Seth's place and help him put up a tent before visitors arrived for the reunion.

He turned on the battery lantern and dressed quietly in its harsh light. Today was Collette's day off, so at least he wouldn't be missing anything, spending the day working first with Seth and then Iddo. He'd found himself looking forward to the three days that she came here each week, sometimes changing his schedule so that he could spend more time here at the house, enjoying a casual conversation with her.

He wished she was coming today so that he could talk to her again about the Sally situation. Last time he was visiting Len, on Tuesday, he'd offered to employ Sally at the house on Tuesdays and Thursdays. A contract, plain and simple. But to hear folks talk about it yesterday at the wedding, you'd think he proposed marriage.

It was terrible, the way things got blown out of proportion when folks got hold of a bit of information.

Feeling like a bear plucked from hibernation, he passed through the kitchen, pulled on his jacket, and headed toward the barn. Seth had promised to have a thermos of coffee ready for his volunteers.

It was cold enough to see his breath in the barn. Thumper nickered, looking more spry than Aaron felt. The horse waited quietly in place until Aaron ordered him to back up. Dutifully, the horse stepped back between the shafts, which Aaron lifted high and then inserted into the harness loops.

Attaching the shafts, Aaron felt himself slipping into a grim pool of self-pity. Here he was hitching up a horse on a cold morning with no prospect of seeing Collette all day. Why was that making him feel deflated, like a balloon losing air?

Were these new signs of weakness within? He pressed one hand to his forehead, checking for fever. His skin was cold and dry, normal, but he felt off-balance.

In the years since he had lost Dorcas, he had kept his emotions on solid ground, solid as a rock. He couldn't go weak now.

He climbed into the buggy and called to his horse. "Thumper, giddyap!"

As the buggy rolled forward, he prayed. *Dear Gott, please grant me strength. Please grant me stamina to help my friends and community during this busy time. Please keep my head clear of emotion, free from the taint of gossip. I pray that our church folk might live in Your truth.*

Rolling along past the orange and yellow foliage of the country road, he knew Gott heard his prayers. And that was enough.

Over at Seth's place, there was time for a quick swallow of coffee while Seth and Aaron waited for the tent to arrive. Seth brought out two paper cups of coffee, and the two men leaned against the post-and-rail fence.

"Ray Graber's bringing the tent, and I've lined up some young men to help, too. They may not know what's what, but they'll have the muscle we need."

"Glad to hear it," Aaron said. "I'm about worn-down from bringing in Iddo's bean crop this week."

"Sorry to hear he's feeling poorly," Seth said. "Is it a flu bug?"

"Not sure. I'm headed over to his place after we're done here." Aaron sipped the warm, dark coffee, savoring the strong brew as he surveyed the lot beside the shop. "We did a good job clearing the weeds and thistle, didn't we? The tent should fit nicely in that spot."

Seth nodded. "I'm happy with the way it's working out. Everything should be in place when the first visitors show up around noon. Emery Lambright is delivering fried chicken from the Home Diner, and Smitty is sending a boy out with pretzels. Yesterday I picked up some of Delilah's pies and cookies from the Amish Bakery, so we're in for a right good meal."

"Fried chicken and pie?" Aaron shook his head, considering Seth's tall, lean frame. "I don't know where you put it, my friend."

"I find if you keep moving, it can't catch up with you." Seth patted his flat belly and both men chuckled.

"It's good to see you laugh," Seth said. "You've been dragging your heels lately. Stretched too thin?"

"Maybe." Aaron frowned. "And I may have gotten myself into a pickle." He explained that he had asked Sally Renno to come work as a part-time housekeeper, though he now regretted the move. "Folks are taking it all wrong. She doesn't even start until next week, but I heard a bit of a buzz going on yesterday at the wedding."

"Mmm." Seth pressed his lips together. "A bit of matchmaking going on between you and Sally?"

"If Linda Hostetler has anything to say about it, she'll have us wed before the end of the month, I think."

"It's natural for Linda to fend for her sister, but Sally is a grown woman, and you're a man who knows his own mind, I'd say."

"I should have been more careful." Aaron shook his head. "I was asking for help with the housekeeping, plain and simple. Somehow, folks are thinking that constitutes a proposal for courtship. Not my intention at all."

"These things spin out of control sometimes," Seth agreed. "We preach about gossip at church, probably three, four times a year. Folks take it seriously for a while, but over time they slide. I think some folks find it hard to separate friendly conversation from talk that spreads stories about others. False stories. But once the tongue wagging starts, it can spread like wildfire."

"Gossip is a sin, plain and simple," Aaron said.

"Worth reminding our members," Seth agreed. "In the meantime, I'm glad to know the situation. Linda and Sally will be here around noon to help with the lunch."

"How did you happen to pick them?" Aaron asked incredulously.

"They're part of a group assembled by Alice Yutzy," Seth answered. "When it comes to feeding a group of men, you need to have women in charge."

"Indeed," Aaron agreed. "We would all go hungry without them."

"Do you want me to speak to Sally or Linda?" Seth asked. "I could approach the topic, explain your dilemma."

Aaron raked his hair back with one hand, groaning. "Kind of you to offer, Seth, but a man needs to put his own affairs in order. Though I'm not sure that a discussion with Sally and Linda would solve anything right now."

"True. Sometimes, these things just need to weather the seasons." Seth clapped him on the shoulder. "I'll leave that up to you. And I guess if Sally can't win you over, there must be someone very special who's caught your eye."

Aaron turned to stare at the red and gold flames of foliage, wondering if Seth knew about Collette. How could he know? He felt embarrassed to admit his feelings, but he and Seth were always frank with each other. "There is someone. Dear to my heart, I admit."

"That's good," Seth said. "Do you think you'll marry?"

"Nay. That can't happen."

"And why not?"

"Oh, I'm too old, and my church duties take up most of my time. No woman would want to play second fiddle to that. And also, I've a reputation to maintain. Trying to model a good and moral life."

"You won't tarnish your reputation by getting married," Seth pointed out.

"It's not as simple as that. The whole of it is that I can't marry."

"You can't? Or you won't?" Seth asked.

"Both." Growing uncomfortable with the direction of the conversation, Aaron wondered what was holding up the tent wagon.

"That's quite a statement. If I pour you another cup of coffee, will you explain more?" Seth asked.

Aaron was saved by the sight of Ray Graber's wagon clambering down the road. "Look at that. The workers are here," he said. The wagon was followed by a buggy loaded with young men. He recognized a few of the faces—Jacob Kraybill and Micah Brubaker—former friends and acquaintances of his son, Mose.

Young, strong workers.

Finishing his coffee, Aaron breathed a sigh of relief. He would be happy to instruct these young men on the best way to construct a tent, as he'd done it dozens of times. But today, the heavy lifting would go to the young. After that, he'd be sure to make his exit, ahead of the arrival of the womenfolk.

Best to avoid more questions from Seth, and best not to fuel the flames of gossip by spending time around the likes of Sally Renno.

Chapter 25

Guilt ate away at Grace as she pushed her scooter alongside Suzie and Josiah. How did she get herself into this mess? She wanted to be a good friend to Suzie, she really did, but she didn't think that trying to lend some moral support would entangle her in a plan that seemed fraught with problems.

Steeling herself, she plodded along the road, the cool autumn breeze blowing her hair back.

This walk had become their after-work ritual. Each day, the three of them walked together out of town until Josiah turned off the road to his house, and then she and Suzie scootered home. Suzie was totally crushing on Josiah, and he seemed to like her, too. Grace didn't mind being the fifth wheel. Not at all.

The problem was Suzie's new obsession, a plot in which Grace was an accessory.

Plastic surgery.

Grace didn't like anything about it. She hated hospitals, and after the treatments her mother had gone through, doctors made her nervous. The idea of Suzie going through surgery just to smooth out the slight scar on her face frightened Grace.

But Suzie was determined. She'd pushed Grace to find

a doctor and do a little research. And now, Suzie was talking about surgery as if it was definitely going to happen the minute she turned eighteen, the age of consent. She wanted Grace to help her set it up without even telling her mother. Which made Grace uneasy. Grace worried that the girl wouldn't be making an informed choice. And it would be awful to go through surgery without the love and support of family. Grace kept trying to argue her way out of the situation, but Suzie wasn't budging.

Now, as they were walking on the path by the river, Suzie was spilling the beans to Josiah.

"So my exciting news is that Grace found a clinic in Plumdale that does plastic surgery," Suzie told Josiah.

He squinted. "What's that?"

"As soon as I turn eighteen, they'll fix the scar on my face. At least make it so it won't stand out."

"Let me see." He walked ahead of her, touched her chin with his fingertips, and moved her head from side to side. "Actually, I don't think it's that noticeable."

"Thank you," Grace said. "I agree with Josiah. You can barely see it, Suzie."

"You guys are my friends," Suzie insisted. "You're just being nice to me."

"We are your friends, but we're telling you the truth," Grace said. "When I look at you, I don't notice the mark on your face."

"But strangers do. They stare. I hate it when people stare at me."

"Did you ever think maybe they're watching because they like the way you look?" asked Josiah.

Coming from an Amish guy, Grace figured that was about as romantic a comment as you could get. Suzie seemed to agree.

"That's nice of you to say," Suzie said. "But I hate this

scar. I'll do anything to get it fixed. I've got some money saved. If it's five hundred dollars, I can almost pay for it myself."

"That's the minimum," Grace said. "The woman at the Plumdale clinic said it would cost between five hundred and three thousand."

Josiah gave a whistle. "Three thousand dollars! That's a lot of pretzels to sell."

"It won't be that much," Suzie said, looking down at the ground. "And it'll be worth it. I'm going to give them a deposit next time I can get a ride to Plumdale. My life will be perfect if they can make this scar go away."

"No one has a perfect life," Grace said.

"Everybody has something they don't like about themselves," Josiah said. "We're not supposed to question the way Gott made us, but we all have qualities we don't like. Growing up with lots of brothers and sisters, I got used to being teased. Siblings have a way of figuring out your soft spot and taking a poke at it."

"What did they do to you?" Suzie asked. "I've got only one brother, and most of the time he's nice to me."

"You're lucky. My brothers and sisters called me Scarecrow. I didn't like that at all." He frowned. "I've always been a skinny one, and in my family, everyone liked to throw around nicknames. They didn't think twice about it, but I have to admit, it hurt."

"Did you make them stop it?" Suzie asked.

"Nay. If they knew I was upset, that would have egged them on even more. So I pretended I didn't care. That made it hurt a little less, I guess."

Grace swallowed hard, feeling sorry for him. "It's a form of bullying," she said.

"Maybe," Josiah said. "But truth is, every child in my family got a nickname. My sister was Dolly. My younger brother got called Shorty, 'cause he was the littlest one. That seems ridiculous now. Once he turned fourteen, he grew taller than me."

"And they still call him Shorty?" Suzie asked.

"We do, at home." Josiah picked up a stone and expertly skipped it over the water. "Lucky for me, the nicknames didn't carry over to school. I'd hate for the likes of those guys at the pretzel factory to be calling me Scarecrow."

"You don't look anything like a Scarecrow," Suzie said sincerely. "Shorty isn't the only one who grew out of his name."

He gave a shrug and tossed another stone over the surface of the river. "I guess."

Bending down to find a smooth, flat stone, Grace acknowledged that she had underestimated Josiah when she'd first met him. He really was a decent guy, and Suzie seemed to realize that. She just wished Suzie would back off on the idea of surgery.

Grace and Suzie arrived home as the cleanup was in progress in the fields and house at the Lapp farm. When she'd left for school that morning, Grace had been sorry to miss the whole operation. She'd participated in it last year after Essie and Harlan's wedding, and despite all the work, it had been fun when everyone pitched in together to pack up the rented trailer and church benches, take down the tent, and restore the house and buggy barn.

But as a college-bound high school senior, she had to keep her school attendance up, and after school, Rachel needed her at the shop, so she'd been gone from the Lapp farm all day. *Part of the double life I lead,* she thought. *My weird life as a city kid living on an Amish farm.*

Over in the distance there was activity by the doors of

the buggy barn, where Sam, Uncle Alvin, and helpers were moving some farm implements and buggies back into the space that had been used for the wedding. Lizzie and Sarah Jane were playing by the swing in the tall oak tree, and Suzie wheeled her scooter over to chat with Lizzie.

"I'm just going to put my scooter away," Grace said. She wheeled it toward the storage shed, slowing down when a sharp feeling pierced her chest. Suddenly, it was hard to breathe.

Oh, no, please no! Not a panic attack.

It had been months since she'd suffered an attack, but she recognized the cold, sharp claws of panic. Her heartbeat was thudding rapidly, and her throat seemed tight.

Her hands gripped the scooter tightly as she made a point of taking slow, deep breaths. She closed her eyes and tried to concentrate on her happy place—a time and place that gave her peace.

Christmas morning, she thought. Gathered around the colorful, glittering tree, she had sat on the floor in her pjs with Mom and Dad, Serena and Meg. They took turns unwrapping gifts, and then ate cinnamon buns with hot chocolate.

Eyes closed, she tried to go there and relax. She concentrated, but the scene didn't feel right. That life was too far away from her now. She needed a new source of comfort.

This farm. The dinner table, with everyone gathered around it. Everyone went silent for the prayer, and then the twins told boisterous stories of their antics, while the family passed around large bowls of chicken and stuffing, mashed potatoes, peas, and corn. Her married cousins were at the table, joining in with their spouses. Uncle Alvin kept a quiet watch over the family while Aunt Miriam asked questions to check in with each child.

Another deep breath, and she could feel her heartbeat

slow as the image began to calm her. A moment later, she was calm enough to walk her scooter over to the shed and put it away. When she emerged from the shed, she nearly ran into Aunt Miriam, who was on her way back from the buggy barn.

"Oh, my goodness, Grace, you look pale as a sheet. Are you all right?"

"I just . . . there's something you should know. Actually . . ." She glanced over at Suzie, who was telling a story to Lizzie and Sarah Rose, though the younger girl was more focused on fanning Suzie with a bundle of lemon-yellow leaves she'd collected. "The thing is, it's really Suzie who needs to tell her mother, but I'm kind of involved, and I don't feel right about it, and I don't know what to do."

"I can see that you're troubled." Miriam put a hand on Grace's shoulder. "Come into the kitchen. We just put all the furniture back in place. Come, we'll talk." That was one of the amazing things about Aunt Miriam. There could be a million things going on and a dozen people in the room, but if you needed her attention, she had the ability to give you one hundred percent.

Inside the house, Grace hung her backpack on one of the pegs in the laundry room and then poured herself a glass of milk.

"Look at this." Aunt Miriam sat down beside her at the table and opened a plastic bin. "Leftover cookies." She took a snickerdoodle and pushed the bin toward Grace. "Leftovers are one of the perks of hosting a wedding. So tell me what's going on with Suzie."

Grace chose an iced lemon bar for herself, but she didn't feel like she could enjoy it until she explained the situation. She told her aunt the truth, starting with Suzie's self-consciousness about her scar, and finishing with her guilt over helping her friend do something that might be dangerous.

"Suzie seems determined to get the surgery. She can barely stop talking about it and she's going to put a deposit down at the clinic soon. I want her to be happy with herself, and I hate to disappoint her, but I can't do this."

"Oh, dear." Miriam pressed a hand to her mouth as she chewed, her eyes round with concern. "I don't know anything about plastic surgery, but I do know that we need the support of our family to get through these major obstacles in our lives."

Family support sounded so comforting, and it was not what Grace had expected. "So Suzie won't get in trouble if she tells her mother?"

"Collette will be concerned, but there won't be a punishment. Not for a young woman Suzie's age." Miriam pushed up from the table. "I'm going to ask Suzie to come in here, and we'll talk about this. We can help her share it with her mother." She touched Grace's shoulder. "Don't you worry about this. We'll work it all out."

Grace felt her shoulders relax as she watched her aunt go. At least she wasn't alone in this anymore. As she took a bite of the lemon bar, her grandmother walked in.

"Mammi, come sit with me. Do you want a cookie?"

"No goodies for me. Don't want to ruin my supper." Lois took a seat at the table.

Since the day she and Suzie had found Lois in the stranded buggy, Grace had felt accepted by her Amish grandmother. "How was your day?"

"Busy. After you left for school, a big truck came to haul away the wedding wagon. Your dawdi and I took our coffee and went out back. Stood at the fence to watch them back that truck in and hook the trailer up, quick as a jackrabbit. I didn't even need my shawl. Then, after breakfast, they took the tent down. Now that took longer. I sat in a rocker on the porch, with a blanket over my shoulders. David wore his coat. I would have brought my needlework out, but it was too chilly. Your fingers stiffen up in cold like that."

"Wow. You had a full day."

"We did, indeed. The bench wagon had to be loaded up, too. Not to mention all the folks bustling around, picking up and moving things back into place. When they came in the house to move furniture, I warned one young man not to carry me away! I belong here."

Grace chuckled at the image of her grandmother standing her ground. "I'm glad they didn't take you away, Mammi."

"Me too!"

They both looked over at the door as Aunt Miriam came in, trailed by Suzie, Lizzie, and Sarah Rose.

"Have a seat, Suzie," Miriam said. "Do you want a glass of milk? We have some delicious cookies left over from the wedding."

"Cookies!" Lizzie reached toward the table as if mesmerized by the sweets.

"You girls may have one," Miriam said. "Mind you, just one." She served milk, got everyone else settled, and took a seat. "Now. What's this I hear about you getting plastic surgery, Suzie?"

"That's my plan." Suzie shot a look of annoyance at Grace. "It was supposed to be a secret."

Grace shrugged. "I'm worried about you. Surgery is serious."

"And necessary." Suzie pressed her knuckles to her face. "This thing has to go. It's so ugly, and if a doctor can remove it, I'll pay anything."

Miriam nodded. "I'm sorry you were injured in the buggy accident. But really, the scar is but a small part of your face now. No one really notices."

"I notice," Suzie said. "And it's embarrassing. It's depressing. For a long time I didn't want to leave my room, afraid people would see it."

Lizzie and Sarah Rose watched quietly, and Sarah Rose slid from the bench and stood beside Suzie to take her hand. "It's all right," she cooed.

Suzie gave her a sad smile.

"You know, there are things you can do to make a scar better," Mammi Lois said. "Do you have aloe vera in the house, Miriam?"

"I'm not sure. We've used it for sunburns."

"Aloe vera is very good." Mammi went on. "Also rose hip oil or shea butter. Have you tried those?"

"Nay." Suzie frowned. "Where do you find them?"

"I see them advertised in my Amish magazines all the time."

"Maybe you can try one of these remedies?" Miriam said hopefully.

"That's a good idea," Grace agreed. The remedies had to be cheaper than surgery. Safer, too.

"I don't want to waste time trying things that might not work," Suzie said.

"Wait. I've got it." Mammi gave Suzie a stern look. "Apple cider vinegar. Miriam, do you have that in your pantry?"

"I think I do." Miriam got up and searched the cabinets for the special vinegar.

"You're amazing, Mammi. How do you know all these treatments?" Grace asked.

"My Amish magazines, and I raised six children who had their share of bumps and cuts."

"Here it is!" Miriam held the glass bottle high. It was half-full of amber liquid.

"Good," Mammi said. "Now mix some with water. One part cider vinegar, four parts water."

Curiosity filled the kitchen as Aunt Miriam blended the concoction together. Grace liked the immediacy of a solution. Even if it didn't work, she figured it was worth a try.

"Now dab it on your scar," Mammi ordered.

Suzie seemed reluctant, until Lizzie offered to help.

"Can I dab it on?" Lizzie asked. "I'll be very gentle."

Miriam handed her a clean kitchen towel, which she dipped into the liquid and delicately pressed onto Suzie's scar. "Okay, then." Lizzie squinted as she leaned close to Suzie and pressed the edge of the towel against the scar. "Is that okay?" Lizzie asked. "It doesn't hurt, does it?"

"It feels fine," Suzie said.

"That should make the redness go down," Mammi advised. "Now you can buy vitamin E capsules at the store and you cut them open and put the oil right on your scar. It's very soothing, and if you massage it in, it will make the scar smaller."

"So many good ideas, Mem," Miriam said. "And your mother might know more cures, Suzie. Before you decide on surgery, you need to talk to her about the whole matter."

All eyes were on Suzie, whose lips were puckered in a sour expression. "I'll tell her. But she probably won't understand."

"You'd be surprised," Miriam said. At that moment, Miriam caught Grace's gaze, and she nodded. "I know what we'll do. I'll write a note inviting your mem over for dinner. We have so many leftovers from the wedding. Grace can take the note over and put it on the door, so you can stay here. We might be able to whip up one or two more scar treatments before supper."

"I'll help with the treatments," Lizzie volunteered. She loved most any activities that got her involved with the older girls. It seemed Lizzie didn't have many friends among the other twelve-year-olds at school. Grace suspected she was a bit too scholarly, and maybe a little more mature than her peers.

"I'm happy to run the note to the Dawdi House," Grace said. "And that means you can stay for dinner, Suzie." All the girls seemed pleased with the development, including Sarah Rose, who had squeezed her way onto the bench beside Suzie so that she could see the healing power of vinegar up close.

"Okay, let's see our progress," Mammi said, motioning to Lizzie. The cloth was removed, and everyone studied Suzie's cheek.

"It's not as red, I think," Mammi Lois said.

Miriam looked up from the note she was writing and nodded. "More of a soft pink."

"Much better," Lizzie agreed.

Grace got up and headed out the door with the note, leaving them to chat about other cures. She already felt freer as she jogged to the Dawdi House. It was a relief to have the weight of Suzie's surgery off her shoulders. When she returned, Serena had joined the group, providing a bottle of aloe vera that she used for sunburns.

"You can gently rub it in," Serena said. "Massage is supposed to be good for circulation. Over time, it can reduce a scar."

Suzie closed her eyes as Lizzie pressed gently, treating the task as if it were a delicate surgery. "Is it getting better?" asked Suzie. When no one answered, she opened her eyes. "Is it worse?"

"It takes time," Serena said. "You can keep the aloe, if you want. Rub a little bit in every night, before bed. Over time, you should see an improvement."

"It's all a step in the right direction," Miriam said, tying on an apron. "Now let's get organized. We need to get the table set, and heat up some of the leftovers. I've got the oven on for the roasht and we'll put the creamed celery on the stove."

"I'll set the table," Lizzie offered as the group began to disperse.

"I'll help you," Suzie offered. "We need to remember to add a place for Mem and me."

"Grace?" Mammi Lois dropped a hand on Grace's shoulder. Her other hand held her shawl tightly together in an odd way. "Come. I have something to show you."

Grace followed her grandmother out to the back porch, where the older woman sat on the glider and patted the spot beside her. As Grace took a seat, Lois shifted her shawl a bit and removed a book from under it. "I sneaked this down from upstairs. I thought if the others saw me giving you a gift, they might get jealous."

"A gift for me?" Grace faced her grandmother, hoping that the older woman could feel the love inside her. "That's so nice, but you didn't need to do that."

"I did." She took the book and pressed it into Grace's hands. "This should be yours. It belonged to your mother when she was your age, my Sarah."

Grace's mouth opened in surprise as she turned the small, black leather-bound book in her hands. The book was titled *Die Bibel.* She leafed through it but saw that it wasn't written in English. "Is it German?"

"Yah. Amish church is in German, and Amish children are given German bibles. But see here?" Lois flipped through the book until she found a page with some lines highlighted in yellow marker. "Your mother marked this. I would never write in a book, but then Sarah didn't mind the rules the way most do."

Grace smiled. "Mom was definitely a rebel."

"I thought you might like to have it, to see the passages that interested her, the things she cared about."

"That's so cool! It's a wonderful gift." Grace stared down at the highlighted passage. It was marked lines one through eight, but she couldn't make sense of it. "Can you help me translate?"

"Me, I'm not so good with that sort of thing. But maybe Lizzie can help you? She likes her books."

"I'll ask her. It could be a project for us to do together. And if we get stuck, I can always look at Google Translate when I get online at school." Smoothing her hand over a page, Grace noticed something written in the bottom margin. "What's this? She wrote: *The Byrds' song— "Turn! Turn! Turn!" To everything there is a season.* She looked up at her grandmother. "Do you know what that means?"

Lois shrugged. "Birds sing, but I never heard a bird sing a Bible verse." She laughed, and Grace giggled along with her as she looked back down at the book. To think she was holding her mother's book in her hands made her feel happy and hopeful that it might be a window to the woman who was gone from her life too soon.

"Mammi, this is wonderful. Really. To have something that my mother owned, something she wrote her thoughts in . . . I'm really touched."

Lois gave a sage nod. "Good. Then the book is in the right hands now."

"Thank you." Grace hugged the Bible to her chest. The heft of the book was reassuring. "Denki. This means a lot to me."

At last, a connection to her mother.

Chapter 26

The dark-haired receptionist at the rehab center on Friday was not someone Collette recognized from her own stay at this facility last year. Nevertheless, Collette glanced at the girl's name tag and peeled open the lid of the Tupperware container she'd brought from home.

"I'm here to visit Dinah Troyer in 144," Collette said. "Would you like a snickerdoodle cookie? They're homemade."

"Thanks!" The young woman pushed her glasses onto the top of her head and took a cookie. "You just need to sign into the book."

"Very good." Collette signed her name, grateful that Essie had found time to bake the cookies for the staff. While Collette had mixed feelings about visiting the same facility that she'd been stuck in many months ago after the buggy accident, she'd always been grateful for the kind help of the staff. She made her way down the hall, recalling the times when she'd paced these corridors using a walker.

Dinah's room was simple, with a hospital bed, room around the bed for medical monitors and equipment, a closet, and a single visitor's chair. A small space, though the double windows allowed a view of neighboring fields, now shorn to cold stubble, and the purple hills beyond.

"I'm so glad to see you," Dinah greeted Collette as she

paused in the doorway, not wanting to interrupt the medical professionals who tended Dinah like bees to a hive. "Please, come in," Dinah insisted.

"We're just taking Mrs. Troyer's vitals," the nurse explained.

"And everything's working fine," Dinah said. "The reason they're keeping me here is because I'm a fall risk and I live alone. Isn't that right, Nurse?"

"That's right. The doctor doesn't want you home alone until you're steady on your feet, Mrs. Troyer. Unless you can get twenty-four-hour care at home. But most folks can't afford it."

"It's too expensive." Dinah waved her hand, as if dismissing the idea. "And so, here I am."

"But you're doing well," Collette reminded her. "We must be grateful for that."

"I thank Gott every day. But still, I'm working on getting home," Dinah said.

"You've been a trooper in PT," the aide said. "Your physical therapist said you get a gold star for effort."

"I don't need a gold star," Dinah said. "Just a way to get back home."

"Well, keep up the good work," the nurse said, wheeling away the blood pressure monitor, stopping only to accept a cookie from the bin Collette was passing around.

Cookie in hand, the aide reminded Dinah to press her call button if she needed anything, and then departed.

"You've got a nice room," Collette said, recalling the relative quiet of the facility.

"It's fine. I've made a cozy nest here with things to occupy me. I've got books to read, homemade jam from Esther Lapp's granddaughter, and plenty of yarn. I'm knitting Aaron a scarf for Christmas." She held up a work-in-progress, a pretty patch of knitting in a fiber that varied from navy blue to periwinkle to white.

"That's lovely yarn," Collette said. "It will bring out the blue in his eyes."

Dinah nodded. "He got his father's eyes." Her fingers worked the knitting needles and yarn methodically as she spoke. "It's good that you came today. Esther Lapp visited yesterday. Gave me the update on the wedding. Sounds like a good time was had by all! But I heard that my son caused quite a stir with this Sally Renno, asking her to be his housekeeper."

"For two days a week," Collette said. "She'll be filling in when I'm not there."

"I can't believe he asked her out of the blue like that. What was he thinking?"

Collette turned away to put the lid on the cookie bin, hoping to hide her own frustration and disappointment with Aaron. "From what he told me, he thought you wanted him to hire Sally."

"I wanted no such thing! What gave him that idea?"

"I don't know, but it seems the damage is done for now. Sally will start work on Tuesday, at the same time that I'll be over at the Hostetlers' place cleaning up after her." Collette forced a wry smile. It would have been comical if the situation didn't make her want to cry.

"Esther said it was the talk of the wedding. That Linda even hinted that Aaron and Sally might wed."

"I don't know if it was the talk of the wedding. It was Sam and Sadie's day, after all," Collette said, trying to veer Dinah away from what might be considered gossip.

"Married!" Dinah put her knitting aside. "As if a man Aaron's age would jump into such a thing."

Collette gave a sad sigh. "We know he's not one to jump into anything."

"Don't you worry." Dinah reached over and patted Collette's hand. "My son may be slow to make a move, but you can be sure that when he does, it's been well thought out."

Collette wasn't so sure. "I'm not so sure that anything will actually happen between us. We've become good friends, but . . ." She gave a shrug, feeling awkward. "I don't know that he feels anything more."

"Of course, he does." Dinah lifted her chin, her eyes shiny and solemn now. "I see you with Aaron, and I recognize all the signs. The knowing smiles. The silent looks. You two are of the same mind. I think that sometimes you even finish each other's sentences."

Dinah's frank remark hit Collette hard. It wasn't the sort of thing folks discussed among casual acquaintances. "I do enjoy his company," Collette admitted.

"I've noticed. Watching you two, it's clear that Gott has a plan. You and my son are on a path together."

Collette shook her head. "I'm not sure he's aware that he's walking a path with me. Despite our friendship, when we're around other people, he's so . . . so distant."

"This is what I worry about," Dinah said. "He needs to step up and be a man."

"Dinah, please, don't say such a thing." Collette couldn't bear to hear Aaron demeaned. "He's a strong man, shouldering so many burdens and leading our community in faith. I see the way he steps up for others, every single day."

"Then why isn't he stepping up for you?" Dinah persisted.

"I don't understand his hesitance, but I don't think it's fear." How could Collette explain to Aaron's mother that the situation was wrought with complexity, all the twists and turns of public expectations and human emotion. No one expected Aaron to be matched with a woman like Collette, a woman with the taint of abandonment in her past. And now there was public pressure for him to court Sally, whom most considered to be a suitable match.

"We probably shouldn't be talking of this," Collette said. "Aaron wouldn't like it."

"I'm too old and cranky to worry about that at this point. I'm turning eighty-eight soon, my hip aches, and my toddler grandson over in Bird-in-Hand walks faster than I do. But those are all things I can cope with. What I can't manage is my grown son, the bishop."

Collette tilted her head to one side. "Now think about it, Dinah. Have you known an Amish man who allows himself to be managed by a woman?"

Dinah chuckled. "When you put it that way, I don't believe I have. But Aaron has become impossible for me to understand. What's going on in that man's head that makes him so aloof at times?"

"That I don't know," Collette said. "But lately, he's definitely burning the candle at both ends. I've barely seen him in the past week. He's been managing Iddo's harvest while the man is ill, on top of his church commitments. And today he's at the wainwright reunion, helping Seth." Collette was relieved that she'd been unable to help out with the food service there. With the buzz about Aaron and Sally going on, Collette couldn't bear to be in another public place with the two of them.

"The day of my surgery, I could tell he was stressed." Dinah pointed a finger to her eyes. "I saw that. He bears a heavy load on his shoulders."

"He does." Collette let out a heavy sigh. "But when I see him in his home, he seems to find a way to relax." Collette shared the easy way they moved about in his house. They both knew their roles and responsibilities, as if they'd been together for years. At the end of most days, when he gave her a ride home, their conversation flowed naturally. "We make plans together, laugh together, share updates on Amy and Tess, and even my daughter, Suzie." She pressed a hand to her cheek and closed her eyes. "Though Aaron hasn't yet heard about Suzie's latest shenanigan."

"She's in rumspringa?" Dinah's eyes opened wide for a moment. "Maybe you shouldn't tell him."

"My girl is pushing the limits, even for a rumspringa youth. She wants to get plastic surgery."

"Plastic what?"

"She wants a doctor to do an operation to smooth over the scar on her face."

"What is this scar? I don't recall seeing it."

"It happened in the buggy accident last year." Collette explained that Suzie's injury had healed just fine, but she remained self-conscious about the mark on her cheek. "At first I told her that no one noticed it. Lately, I've tried to let it go, thinking that she'd get over it. She has many friends among her coworkers at the pretzel factory, but it must be hard to feel that this mark is making her unattractive, especially during the rumspringa years."

"Ach. You do have your hands full. Are you going to tell Aaron about it?"

"I don't intend to." Collette hugged herself, shuddering at the thought. "Our church leaders will never need to hear of the surgery, because I'm going to talk Suzie out of it."

"I wish you luck on that," Dinah said. "And I hope she's not as stubborn as most teens."

"My Suzie's a quiet one." It was true, though Collette had recently discovered the mettle within her daughter. Defiance. Not wanting Dinah to see her concern, Collette started folding the throw blanket that had become twisted at the foot of the hospital bed. "She's a good girl."

"All youngie in rumspringa have good in them," said Dinah. "It's our place as elders to guide them, for sure, but I've found that if we fasten the harness too tightly, they break loose and run wild."

The comment made Collette pause in folding the blanket. "Are you thinking of Mose?"

Dinah folded her hands under her chin with a sigh. "Has Aaron told you about him?"

"The girls mention him sometimes. They miss him. They worry about him when they can't sleep at night."

"It's a sad situation. No one to blame, really. As bishop, Aaron expects his family to live to a higher standard, to model Amish values and Christian faith. The girls tried. We all did. But Mose lost faith when his mother died. He was angry with the world, and when Aaron tried to talk to him about it, you'd think someone had poured kerosene on a fire."

Collette gave a sympathetic nod. "Sometimes it's hardest to reach the person you love most." She had learned that during her marriage to Jed.

"There was drinking, which I know a lot of men partake in. But with Mose, it was too much. He pulled other Amish youth into the mischief. Threw big parties with his Englisch friends." She frowned. "A terrible situation. Count your blessings that your son walked the straight and narrow in his rumspringa."

"I'm grateful for that," Collette agreed. "Do you think Mose will ever come home?"

Dinah pulled the bed sheet up to her chin and sighed. "I pray that day will come. I miss him."

Collette sensed that Aaron missed Mose, too, though he never spoke of him. For all the things she understood about Aaron, there seemed to be many mysteries compacted deep in his personality. For all the simplicities of living a plain Amish life, there were just as many complexities beneath the surface. The mysteries of Aaron Troyer might take a lifetime to unravel, but, given the chance, she would gladly spend a lifetime on that journey.

Chapter 27

In a rare moment of quiet near the swirling whirlpools of the river on a lazy Saturday, Aaron settled into the lawn chair perched on a sandy bank of Joyful River and closed his eyes to the warm September sunshine. Seth had ended his reunion yesterday and seen off his out-of-town wheel-wrights this morning so they could travel home before the Sabbath. In a fit of cleverness, Seth had asked for Aaron's help this afternoon, only to reveal that he needed help choosing a good spot on the river for an afternoon of fishing.

With a million tasks on his plate, Aaron had scowled at his friend. "With Iddo's crops, and my mother still recovering, and folks from the gmay to visit, I can't be spending an afternoon doing nothing."

"But this is an important job," Seth had insisted. "I need a fishing companion, and you need a mindless task for an hour or two."

Face-to-face, the two men stared sternly and then burst out laughing.

"You're right," Aaron admitted. After this busy week, an afternoon on the river near Gott's good land was just what he needed. So much hectic activity could make a man lose sight of the things that mattered. You couldn't see the forest for the trees. And he needed the grace and wisdom to see it all: forest and trees, wood, leaves and pine needles, too.

So now, while Seth explored downriver for a better spot, Aaron sat contentedly with his fishing rod, watching the bobber as the events of the last week washed through his mind like the moving river. His mother, the wedding, the Sally situation, the gossip. Events like these usually didn't weigh on his mind. His mother would be fine. The gossip would blow over.

But he couldn't shake the tightness in his throat when he thought of the situation in his home. Sally would be starting work on Tuesday, but he flat-out didn't want her there.

He wanted Collette to tend his home, greet him in the mornings, talk with him about everything from the price of soybeans at market to the colors of the sunset.

Collette belonged there, and this week, he had made some foolish moves that threatened to push her away. Much as he hated to admit it, he had made some mistakes this week.

It pained him to think about it, so he focused on the leaves of a red maple that were reflected like fire on the surface of the water. Scarlet flames, shimmering on the shadowed river. Gott's creation was brilliant and mesmerizing.

He closed his eyes and slept.

It was a wonderful, smooth interlude. How long he slept, he couldn't be sure, but when the sounds of birds and the breeze shimmering through leafy branches tipped him back into consciousness, he found his friend sitting at his side. The afternoon seemed cooler, and the sun had shifted so that the trees on the riverbank formed a wall of shadow over much of the water. Noticing that the line had gone slack, he reeled in his bobber and saw that the line was tangled. Leaving it for later, he put down the rod.

"Looks like an afternoon of fishing was just what you needed," Seth said.

"Sounds about right. It was a busy week, but that happens sometimes, especially during wedding season." As bishop, Aaron was not only a spiritual leader, but also the person in charge of important events such as baptisms, weddings, and funerals. At times the commitment kept him hopping from one thing to another. "How did your reunion go?" Aaron asked.

"Good. I got an invitation to work for a buggy repair shop in Indiana, once I get there. But mostly, folks wanted to talk about the use of steel wheels. Two men, Old Order Mennonites from Iowa, were interested in the cost of rubber-rimmed tractor wheels. Their community leaders allow only steel wheels on tractors, but they're considering making a change."

"You had visitors from as far away as Iowa? That's quite a distance."

"I think they were also stopping in Ohio for a wedding. But steel wheels were the hot topic."

Both men knew the history of steel wheels in Lancaster County. Originally, the Amish allowed only steel wheels on their buggies, though the steel created a distinctive grinding noise and caused ruts in the road beds.

"I'm glad our gmay allowed rubber rims on our buggy wheels long ago," said Aaron. "The rubber rims have calmed the ire of many an Englisch neighbor. I don't blame them. The steel was noisy on the pavement, and over time, the roads got damaged."

"That's true. Steel wheels are rough on asphalt," Seth agreed. "Anyway, that was the big excitement of the reunion. Along with delight over Delilah's pies."

"A productive gathering, then."

"Yah. Denki for your help setting things up. I'm afraid I pulled you in during a busy time."

"I'm glad to help."

"You help everyone, Aaron. All the time. That's why I'm worried about you. You take care of Iddo's fields, spend entire days baptizing or marrying folks in the gmay. You're always taking care of others, but who takes care of you?"

Aaron brushed some dirt from the arm of his chair. "I make do."

"That's why we need to talk."

Relief washed over Aaron as he looked to the deacon. Aside from Collette, there seemed to be no one he could completely confide in.

Seth continued. "As ministers, we don't open up to everyone. And I have something to confess. This business with Sally Renno has struck me in two ways. First, I'd like to pursue Sally if you're truly not interested."

"What?" Aaron squinted at his friend. "That's fine by me. I told you I had no plans to court her."

"I heard that, but I wanted to be sure, because she's a wonderful woman. Funny and bright and very considerate. She has a good heart."

"I never doubted her character," Aaron said. "And I wish you both well. But you know me well, Seth. I'm beyond that. I'm too old to marry."

"Too old . . ." Seth stroked his beard. "You know, I never read that rule in the Bible, or heard it mentioned in the Ordnung."

"It's not from the Bible. It's my own conclusion."

"You're saying that a man becomes too old to remarry in our faith?"

"Nay, not as a rule of the Ordnung. It's simply the best path for me. I was into my forties when Dorcas passed away. Far beyond courtship age, and I'd enjoyed decades of a good marriage. We had a full life together. It was enough."

"So, help me understand," Seth said. "You decided to sacrifice your life as a man after she died?"

It sounded self-important, even indulgent when Seth put it that way, but there was a grain of truth to it. When Dorcas died, something broke inside him. Women talked about broken hearts, while men pointed to loneliness or a numbness in their soul when they lost someone. Depression was what the doctors called it. But Aaron knew himself to be broken, like the snapped blade of a plough or a crack in the glass of a window.

When Dorcas had died, he could feel the break deep inside. The anguish tormented him late at night as he lay in bed staring at the dark ceiling. It was as if he could run his fingers over the jagged edge, a reminder of his loss, a pronouncement of his solitary status in the world.

A broken man.

Half of a married couple.

"It's hard to put to words," Aaron said, "but I know Gott does not make mistakes. Dorcas died for a reason. I'll never understand His ways. But it was Gott's will that I continue my life without a wife."

"For a time, yes. A time to grieve her. But Gott spared you, Aaron. He means for you to live."

Aaron let out a sigh, turning away. This was too hard to explain.

The deacon squinted as he pinched his beard. "Forgive me, but I'm struggling to understand, Aaron. In the Bible, Gott lays out a plan for men to find a companion in life. A man must 'hold fast to his wife and they shall become one flesh.' Gott tells us to find a companion. This is one of the good things in life."

Aaron cocked his head to one side. "I had a wonderful

wife, gone too soon. So now, here I sit . . . here we both sit, two old, widowed men making our way through life without a wife by our side."

"Old men?" Seth chuckled. "You can speak for yourself on that. But yah, sadly we both lost our wives too soon. I lived in grief, as I know you did. I saw Edna everywhere, every day when I took a meal in her kitchen or fed the chickens or passed the empty flower beds beside the house. My children tried to help me, tried to get me to move to Indiana with them. Our church came to accept me as the widowed deacon, and I got my fair share of boxes of cookies and crocks of casseroles. I didn't want anything to change, but at the same time I knew I was living as if my life had ended along with Edna's."

Lifting his rod, Seth worked at untangling the line. "And then one day, everything changed. I fed Edna's chickens and made coffee in her kitchen and started to clear out a kitchen drawer. That was when I found an envelope with my name on it, in Edna's writing." He shook his head. "It woke me up from my sleepy half life."

"Was it a letter left by Edna?" Aaron asked.

Seth shook his head. "There was only a slip of paper inside. On it was written: *'The lot is cast into the lap; but the whole disposing thereof is of the Lord.'*"

Aaron was well familiar with the verse from Proverbs, which was written on the slip of paper placed in a hymnbook when ministers were selected. "It was the lot you drew the day you became a minister. Edna saved it for you?"

"She did. Maybe she thought we would recollect or pray about it one day, when we were old and gray. Instead, I found it that day, and I have to say, it gave me a jolt. Brought me back to the day I drew the lot."

Aaron remembered it well. "I was the bishop who ordained

you that day. Such a moment, when you're chosen. You know Gott is at work, changing your life."

Seth nodded. "I admit, there was some fear. It was like stepping out on a frozen pond in spring, not sure if the ice would hold."

"To be chosen by Gott to serve," Aaron said, recalling his own experience, "that moment changes a man's life forever."

"Nothing was ever the same. I was aware that I had to live a good Amish life as an example to the parish. My family felt the same pressure. And I knew Gott had chosen me for a reason. Gott was changing my heart and soul in a way that I didn't understand. And every day, I tried to open my eyes to the journey."

Aaron nodded. His experience had been similar, having drawn the lot. "What did it mean to you, finding the slip of paper years later?"

"It reminded me that Gott is at work in our hearts and souls every day. You don't have to be chosen as a minister. It's the path we're on, and Gott is with us for every step. The true blessing is in knowing He's there."

Aaron squeezed the arms of the lawn chair, considering the last time he'd sensed the presence of Gott in his life. "I'm a man of faith," he said. "I'll admit, I can't recall a recent moment of inspiration. But isn't that the point? That we have faith, steady and true?"

"Faith is a must," Seth agreed. "But I wanted to share that moment to show you that change can be good. Gott brings us change. Whether or not we're open to it is another issue."

"And what am I supposed to change?" Aaron asked, hearing grumpiness in his own voice.

"I recommend you alter your self-inflicted rule about marriage. Married life is Gott's plan for us, Aaron. A man is meant to share his life with a woman. Gott created Eve for Adam. We humans are social creatures." His eyes squinted as he observed Aaron. "But you have chosen to go it alone?"

"It seems to make the most sense at this point in my life. It's easiest to model good behavior when I don't have a wife to worry about. Gott knows, I've not set a good example with the raising of my son."

"Mose? What does he have to do with this?"

"He's been a bad example. A bishop's son who left the faith, refused baptism." Aaron stared down at the running waters of the river, his face warm with humiliation. "It's been an embarrassment."

"Mmm. I understand your disappointment that he left."

"To be honest, it was almost a relief when he ran off. At least it put an end to everyone watching his bad behavior here. Luring Amish youth out to parties, and all the drinking. Bad enough that he brought shame on our family, but to pull other young Amish boys down with him . . . I couldn't forgive him for hurting others in his path."

"I'm sorry, Aaron. We can't control our children, and yet, we suffer shame at their actions."

Shame . . . that had been so much of it. The anger that had consumed Aaron at the realization that his son had ruined the good moral example he had always tried to set.

"But this wasn't your sin, Aaron. Much as we want our children to follow the path of our Savior, we can't make that choice for them."

"I know this."

"But you seem to be making yourself suffer for it."

Aaron shrugged. "Old habits die hard."

"But habits can be changed. We can have a change of heart." Seth swept a hand over the panorama of colorful trees, water, and plants at the riverbank. "Our Gott who created all this beauty can move mountains in our lives."

"I don't need a mountain moved," Aaron admitted.

"Just a stubborn heart," Seth said, and both men chuckled. "I understand. I was there, too. Stuck in the muck, as I like to say."

"Well. I'll pray that we both get our boots out of the mud," Aaron said, only half teasing.

"Gott willing. And I'll pray for you. Gott opens our eyes to new people and new possibilities. That's my hope for you. When Gott works at changing your heart and soul, I pray that you will be open to that change."

Aaron nodded. "Denki. I'm grateful for our recent talks. You have a way with persuasion. One of the things that makes you a fine deacon. Even when we don't agree, I enjoy meeting you halfway."

"That's all a man can ask." Seth gazed up to the blue sky dotted by slow-moving clouds. "The sun's shifted. We'll need to head home soon."

"No fish today," Aaron said. "Though with our rods here on the ground, it's no wonder the fish stayed pretty safe."

Chapter 28

It was Sunday evening, a lazy time on the day of rest, and Miriam moved through the living room eyeing the female members of her brood with deep affection. How lovely to have the girls and women gathered together while the men tended to the milking!

Dinner had been a simple fare—sandwiches and a beef barley soup that took the edge off the chill in the air. By Amish tradition, Sunday suppers were easy affairs, since no one wanted to work on the Sabbath. Miriam had once told Alvin she was grateful to Gott for giving mothers off on Sunday, and somehow it had become an inside joke in the family, that Sunday was her day.

Puzzle pieces—five hundred of them!—were spread out inside the box and on the edge of the table. Annie worked on the blue sky while Serena tried to piece together the purple and white ice of a mountain glacier. Sarah Jane kneeled on the bench and scrutinized puzzle pieces.

"Here's a blue one!" she said, handing it to Annie, who thanked her.

"Do you want to help me with the glacier?" Serena asked.

"I like the flowers," Sarah Jane said.

"You can do the grass with the flowers," Annie said. "Just start collecting all the pieces that show a hint of flower. We'll help you put them together."

"Flower, flower, flower," Sarah Jane said, staring intently at the loose pieces.

Miriam smiled, pleased by their teamwork. Little Sarah Jane loved to be included in activities with the older children.

Miriam glanced over on the couch, where her team of scholars combed through the Bible that had once belonged to Miriam's sister, Sarah. Lizzie had taken to helping Grace translate from German to English, and Grace had figured out that she could get the full passage by looking up the specific book and line in an English Bible she had gotten from the library.

Today they were talking about a passage from First Corinthians. Not being a Bible expert, Miriam didn't always know what quote came from where, but this particular passage had always been dear to her heart, as it addressed the power of love.

"Did you see what she wrote in the margins?" Grace asked. "'Faith, hope and love.'"

Lizzie nodded. "And she underlined the word *love* three times."

"That's because the passage says that love is the most important thing in the world," said Grace. "See here? It says even if you have all the knowledge in the world and can move mountains with your faith, without love, none of those things matter."

"'The greatest of these is love,'" Lizzie said, pointing to the page in the Bible. "Your mother picked out some beautiful passages."

"She did." Grace smiled as she smoothed down the page of the open Bible. "It's just so cool reading the pages she marked, learning what was important to her. Mammi says she got the Bible when she was around my age. It makes me happy to relate to my mom in a brand-new way."

It was a lovely moment. Miriam was tempted to join the girls on the couch, but she paused behind the upholstered chair where her mother sat. It was time to let Grace go unbridled, time to let her make her own connections to Sarah.

Right now, the best Miriam could do was to let the girls explore Gott's good book, and thank Gott for the memory of Sarah that she now saw in Grace's expression. How she'd missed free-spirited Sarah after she left home! Her older sister had a knack for making a game of chores, and there'd been many a time when they'd made each other laugh for the silliest reason.

With a happy sigh, Miriam squeezed the top of the upholstered chair where her mother hummed as she stitched. Glasses perched on her nose, Lois worked slowly but steadily, inserting a needle in the cloth made taut by a wooden ring.

"Mam, that's turning out so nicely," Miriam said, admiring the stitchwork. "Looks like you're almost done."

"Almost." Her mother glanced up at her. "One day this week, I need a trip to town to find a frame for the sampler. That will complete the gift."

"I'll take you in tomorrow, if you don't mind stopping at the dry goods store," Miriam said. "I know Sadie and Sam will love your gift. It's so personal, from your loving hands."

"You know I enjoy my needlework." Lois smiled as she moved the needle deftly. "I'm glad your father and I made it here for the wedding. I don't enjoy the travel, but it's been wonderful to acquaint with family again."

"And we've loved having you and Dat here," Miriam said.

The other girls chimed in, showering Lois with sweet words about the joy of having her here in Joyful River. Miriam watched as her mother seemed to puff up a bit, as if breathing in the love in the room. How nice it was, having Mem here. Hard to believe that only weeks ago she had dreaded her parents' arrival, fearful of being scalded by her mother's disapproval. What had happened to change that? Perhaps it was Mem's getting on in years that had changed Miriam's view of her. Or maybe it was Mem slowing down that had made her appreciative of her daughter. Either way, it was a blessing to feel her mother's love and approval. It would be hard to say goodbye to her parents come October.

"I'm glad the wedding turned out well," Mem said. "Seems like everyone had a good time at the supper. I did notice one thing: Your bishop is a good-looking fella. It's a wonder he hasn't found a bride."

Miriam smiled. Mem noticed the most surprising things. "He's widowed, but I think he's met his match."

"But not married yet?"

"He hasn't proposed yet."

"Men can be so slow to make a move," said Lois. "If I hadn't stood up for your father way back when, I wouldn't be sitting here today."

"Mem, really?" Miriam wasn't sure if her mother was joking.

"I'm sure of it. You see, in our church we had a frolic for young folks in the spring that was intended to raise money for the church charity fund. Sort of an auction. Each teenaged girl—single girls, of course—would pack a picnic basket, and those lunches would be auctioned off to the young men. According to the tradition, when a fella chose a girl's hamper, she joined him for the picnic lunch."

"So there was a bit of matchmaking going on," Miriam said.

"Just a bit," Lois said. "Folks thought of it as a church social."

"That sounds like a blast," said Serena.

"Wait. I want to hear all of this," Grace said, rising from the sofa.

"Me, too," Lizzie agreed. Both girls settled on the braided rug near Lois's feet to listen.

"No one was supposed to know what girl went with what basket," Lois continued. "It was all supposed to be a happy surprise. But I never liked surprises. So I told David that my hamper would be the one with the flower on it. I cut a pink rose from the garden and brought it along with a right good lunch. Thought I was so smart! I figured David would know it was mine for sure."

"Did your trick work?" asked Annie.

"Not so good. When it came time to put the hampers on the table, my rose was browning and drooping. I was ready to cast it off. Meanwhile, Gladys Huyard's basket had a handful of daisies sprouting from the handle. She wove them in just right. It was like a springtime garden."

"Oh, no!" Lizzie exclaimed. "So, did Dawdi pick Gladys's basket?"

Lois set her teeth. "I didn't give him a chance. Your grandfather had been courting me for a few months at that point. I fancied him, and I wasn't about to let him slip away to the likes of Gladys Huyard. So when David said he wanted the basket with the daisies and everyone looked back to the table, my basket had the sagging rose and some torn daisies on it. And Glady's was left with torn green stalks."

Laughter rippled through the room.

"Mammi, did you take the flowers from her hamper?" asked Lizzie.

Lois nodded. "Ripped them right off, and I didn't regret it. I knew he was the fella for me, and no bunch of daisies was going to stand in my way."

Miriam shook her head. "Mem, that sounds just like you." She'd never heard the anecdote before, but it seemed true to Lois's personality. "If I ask Dat, will he remember it the same way?"

"Oh, I'm sure he'll have a different story to tell. Memory is a funny thing. Folks recall things differently."

"True," Miriam agreed, glad to see her mother so animated over the memory.

"I think it's a great story," Grace said. "You fought for the man you loved."

"More like I stood up to the daisies," Lois admitted.

"Was Gladys mad at you?" asked Serena.

"Well, she wasn't happy at all to have lost her chance at a picnic lunch with David. He was a handsome man, and lots of fun to be around. Can't say that I blame her. But I made it up to her. I did drop by Glady's house with a bouquet of roses that week. She accepted my apologies, and ended up being a newehocker in our wedding, so there's that."

"So you became her friend," Miriam observed. "That makes it a happy ending, Mem."

"Yah," her mother agreed. "In the end, it all worked out fine."

Miriam squeezed her mother's shoulder affectionately, trying to memorize the details of the moment so that she could cherish it forever. What had Mem said about looking back? Memory was a funny thing. Folks stretched and condensed their recollection to make it to their liking. But for Miriam, this moment was just right.

Sometimes, it was the quiet, unexpected moments that made life so sweet. Looking from one face to another, she captured the details in her mind, hoping to remember this evening forever and for always.

Chapter 29

When Collette arrived at the bishop's house Monday morning, she was surprised to see that he had already departed.

"He's off at Iddo's fields again," Tess said glumly as she packed items into a cooler for her lunch. There was a sandwich, celery sticks, and a container of yogurt from a six-pack, which Collette had convinced their father to add to the family's shopping list, much to the girls' delight. "He took off for Sunday, of course, but every other day, he's back to Iddo's. You'd think they'd run out of beans to harvest."

"Thank goodness for the Sabbath." Collette smiled, amused by Tess's attitude and pleased by the orderly state of the house. "Looks like someone's been keeping house here. Are you and Amy pitching in?"

"We are." Tess beamed, her round face rosy with pleasure. "I decided that clean is better than messy."

"Good for you," Collette said, tying on an apron.

"And Amy has figured out that Dat lets her see her friends more if the chores are done around here."

"Mmm. Smart girls, both of you. Where is Amy?"

"Already on her way to town. She's been getting a ride

with her friend, Lucy Fisher. Only, I think the real reason she likes going with them is on account of Lucy's older brother Fred."

"I see." Collette handed Tess an apple for her lunch. "You're an encyclopedia of information today."

"I would *love* to be an encyclopedia," Tess said ardently. "Imagine, knowing every fact that exists in Gott's creation."

Collette chuckled. "I believe only Gott knows that." She went off to find a bucket and mop on the covered porch near the washing machine. When she returned, Tess was on her way out the back door. "Have a good day at school."

"I will!" Tess promised.

The day went quickly, with Collette trying to make sure everything was in good, clean order so that Sally wouldn't have to work too hard when she started her job tomorrow morning. Toward the middle of the afternoon, the house and garden were in good enough shape that she was able to start the dinner meal. Spotting ground beef and a full side of bacon in the fridge, she decided to put together a meat loaf. Her secret touches were crushed butter crackers in the mix, as well as a few strips of bacon layered under the tomato sauce. She was shaping the loaf when the screen door creaked open.

"Collette." Aaron's smile chased some of the weariness from his eyes. "It's a good day when you're here preparing a meal."

"Just pulling together what I found in the fridge." She noticed that he looked tired, his skin a bit ashen, his eyelids drooping, but she didn't address it. If his job as a bishop had him pulled in many directions to keep the flock together, blessed be the shepherd.

She felt a twinge of compassion for him, knowing his desire to serve Gott and their community. Knowing the overall mission, she had to recognize that her concerns that he didn't defend her in public or acknowledge their relationship in public seemed peevish at times.

"I have a young person coming for a discussion," he said, pouring two tumblers of water from the pitcher in the refrigerator. "Leah Yutzy. We'll talk out on the back porch."

"Very good," she said, thinking that this probably meant wedding vows ahead for Alice Yutzy's daughter. When a young person approached the bishop, it was usually to initiate the classes that prepared them for baptism. And generally, the thing that pushed most young Amish folk to join the church was the desire to be married. Collette would keep the meeting in confidence, but she was happy for little things like this. And wouldn't Alice be overjoyed.

Collette finished preparing the meat loaf and was shredding cabbage for coleslaw when the young woman arrived. Collette kept to herself in the kitchen, melting butter for a quick batch of cocoa cookies as Leah and the bishop talked outside. Over the weeks, Collette had seen more than a dozen visitors come and go to consult their bishop. She liked to be able to offer cookies or a slice of pie, but overall she knew the bishop and his visitor needed privacy.

When the girls came home, she popped the meat loaf into the preheated oven and gave instructions for baking time and preparation of buttered noodles.

"We've got it covered," Amy assured her.

When Collette climbed into Aaron's buggy for the trip home, she could see his exhaustion. "You're tired," she said. "I can walk. There's still a good amount of sunlight."

He called to Thumper to get the old horse moving. "After you've worked a full day? I won't allow you to walk home," he insisted.

"Well, I appreciate the ride," she said.

Her thoughts wandered to Sally, who would be his maud tomorrow. Would he give her a ride home, too? Not that it was really necessary, as Len and Linda's property was just down the road. Still, it bothered her to think of Sally riding beside Aaron, close enough to feel the heat of his body inside the small chamber of the buggy. It disturbed her even more to think of Sally in his house, moving through this kitchen and sitting room, chatting in that charming, personal manner she possessed.

Abruptly she turned toward the window, as if the sudden gesture could toss the jealousy out of her. It was wrong to think ill of another person, especially a woman as sweet and kind as Sally Renno.

"How are the soybeans coming in at Iddo's place?" she asked.

"You read my mind," he said. "I was just thinking that I need to get there early again tomorrow. It's best to start cutting when humidity is high in the early morning."

She nodded as he went on about the problems and concerns farmers had during the bean harvest. She listened intently, hanging on his every word. Who knew that soybeans could be so captivating? That was the thing about caring so deeply for a man. His concerns became your own.

Despite Collette's discomfort at leaving the Troyer house for Sally to clean, Tuesday rushed by in service at the Hostetlers. Under Linda's leadership, the day was chockful of chores that included canning the last big batch of garden tomatoes. At least Linda pitched in and insisted that her daughters June and Dotty help, too.

When Collette arrived at the Troyer house Wednesday morning, she saw that Aaron's hat was removed from the hook, his boots gone from the back porch. She had missed the bishop once again.

As she entered the kitchen, the smell of burnt grease seemed to have taken over the room. But there were no pans on the stove. Only Tess was there, spreading Amish peanut butter on a slice of bread. "Did someone burn breakfast?" Collette asked.

"It's from yesterday. Sally left bacon in the fry pan and it started a fire."

"Good gracious! Is everyone all right?"

"Everyone survived. The bacon didn't make it," Tess said glumly.

Despite the heavy odor, Collette couldn't help but chuckle.

"It's not funny. We were supposed to have BLTs, so we were stuck with tomato sandwiches instead."

"That sounds delicious. You had some beauties growing in the garden."

"You should have seen the mess. The bacon was like burnt twigs in the skillet, and there was grease everywhere. Guess who got to clean it up?"

"You and Amy?"

Nodding, Tess wrapped her sandwich in waxed paper and put it into the small cooler. "We were a little peeved that she left us with all that work. Dat was so upset, he didn't eat dinner at all. He didn't even come to the table to sit with us. He told us to eat, that he had to finish up some work in his office."

"Sounds like you had quite an evening."

"You should have seen the flames! Sally put the bacon on, but then went off to do some sewing and got distracted. We're lucky the house didn't burn down. Please don't let her come here again."

"It's not my choice."

"But you can talk Dat into anything. I've seen you."

"Well, not anything." Collette turned away to hide a smile as she tied on the kitchen apron.

"Look, Sally's nice enough. But she's not you."

Collette sucked in a breath, warmed by Tess's comment. She had come to love Aaron's daughters, and it touched her to know that the feeling was mutual. She turned to Tess, not sure what to say. "Denki for saying that. You know I enjoy helping out here. I've grown attached to you and Amy, and . . . no matter what happens, you can always count on me. Come to me with whatever you need."

Tess nodded. "I kinda knew that."

"Good. Now, off to school with you. I need to get started cleaning this kitchen."

Mr. Clean came through for her as she scrubbed the kitchen stove, wall, and counters. The lemony scent gave her a boost, and before she knew it, the room was restored to cheerful, clean order.

With that task finished, she proceeded upstairs to make sure the bedrooms were tidy before thinking about a dinner plan. The girls had made their beds, quite a contrast to their habits back in the summer. Peering into the bishop's room, she was surprised to see the quilt missing from his bed. A crocheted throw blanket from downstairs had been folded atop the sheet, which was stretched to cover the pillows. But where was the quilt?

She went downstairs but found nothing hanging by the washing machine. Opening the side door, she went to the back porch and found it hanging on the line in the backyard. It was dry to the touch, though she suspected that it had been too damp to put back on the bed before Sally left yesterday.

This must have been the sewing project Tess had mentioned, the job that had kept her so distracted that she had failed to realize the bacon was burning.

Collette didn't know what had possessed Sally to take on the task, but she had to admit, the quilt looked brand-new. The pale background that had grayed with use had been cleaned to a lovely shade of cream, and the design had been restored so beautifully!

Sally must have spent all day mending it.

Now a complete wreath of flowers encircled each set of lovebirds situated with a shared heart above them. The missing tulips had been replaced with cloth that matched. The seams that had been pulling loose had been mended. Lovingly mended.

This was Sally's doing, her area of skill. After all, the woman owned a quilt shop. Such a kind gesture, and yet, it seemed a breach of privacy for her to touch something so intimate as the quilt on Aaron's bed.

Observing the pattern of lovebirds and hearts, Collette was reminded of the purity of real love, the earnest love that two people shared under a quilt like this. Surely this had been the wedding quilt given to Aaron and Dorcas when they wed all those years ago.

Sally had no right to it.

Neither did Collette.

And yet, Collette stepped forward. Throwing caution to the wind, she allowed herself to lean forward, bury her face in the quilt, and inhale.

The scents of lavender and citrus soap filled her head with thoughts of springtime and flowers. She pressed closer, took another breath, and squeezed her eyes shut as a sob emerged from her throat.

She couldn't do this.

She could not be a maud in the home of a man who did not share her love. A kind man of faith who had become a close friend to her, but not in the ways that she wanted. The ways she needed.

Turning away from the quilt on the clothesline, she faced the house. She'd come to know every inch, cleaning the place, and she'd enjoyed countless conversations there with Aaron and the girls. She'd formed an attachment to this family, and that was the problem. Her hopes and dreams of having a true place in this home were nothing but dust in the wind, quickly scattered to the hills.

Looking up at the house, the truth became clear. She couldn't spend another day working here. Her work days had become too heartbreaking to bear.

Finish your work and leave, she thought, gently pulling the quilt from the line and carrying it inside.

Tamp down the ache inside. Ignore your quivering hands. Just finish the job and go. She carried the quilt upstairs and spread it over the bishop's bed, adjusting it so that the two sides hung evenly.

How pretty. Crisp and clean and made whole again by another woman.

She went to Aaron's office to write the note, a painful process, but necessary. She folded the paper in half and wrote his name on the outside. Just as she was about to prop it on the kitchen table, she realized the girls would see it first.

Best not to tempt them.

She carried the note upstairs and propped it on the night-stand beside Aaron's bed. Then, her hand smoothed over the time-worn banister, and she breathed the clean, lemony scent of the bishop's kitchen one last time. When the screen door closed quietly behind her, she realized that no one was there to hear it.

The walk home was a good distance—probably three miles or more—but it gave her time to cry out her sorrows and think through a plan. She would keep her job at the Hostetlers. Miserable though that would be, watching Sally court the bishop, she could not afford to give up the one means of support she had left.

And now that she had free time on her hands, she knew just the woman who needed her. Dinah Troyer was eager to return to her home, and Collette could make that happen as long as Dinah agreed to let Suzie and her move in during the recuperation. Dinah's care would fill Collette's days and nights—keep her mind off Aaron—and the move would finally give Harlan and Essie a chance to live as man and wife.

Though the news was still a secret, Harlan had confided that they were expecting a little one. "A buppa!" She let him know that she was thrilled, but didn't mention that she had already guessed as much. Seeing the way Essie's dress had been altered for Sam and Sadie's wedding, Collette had known that motherhood was approaching for her daughter-in-law.

Now, the possibility of leaving the young married couple on their own in the little Dawdi House was another silver lining in Collette's situation. Bolstered by hope, she continued down the road with a plan falling into place.

With a few hours left in the afternoon, Collette didn't waste a single minute. She called a car to take her to the rehab center, where she paid Dinah a visit. Dinah was in the physical therapy center, where Collette recalled exercising on the stationary bike and learning to move with a walker.

"Oh, hello!" Dinah waved to her from a wheelchair. "We're just finishing up here. I climbed that little staircase today. Up and down!"

"I remember that," Collette said, glancing at the three wooden steps. "We used to call it the staircase to nowhere."

The therapist chuckled at that. "Some things never change." She pushed Dinah over to Collette. "Would you like to take Ms. Dinah back to her room?"

As she wheeled Dinah back to her room, Collette felt awkward as a newborn colt. Never one to rock the boat, she hated making changes. But this was the best way forward, she was convinced of it.

Back in the privacy of Dinah's room, she proposed her plan.

"You mean you're taking me home?" Dinah pressed a palm to her chest, as if the news astounded her. "Gott bless you!"

"But you'll have to put up with Suzie and me, so we can be there 'round the clock."

"I'm happy to have you. Plenty of room for all, and it will be good to have a young person in the house. It might lure Tess to come visit me more often."

Collette and Dinah met with the doctor to arrange for discharge on Friday. Collette was told she would need to follow a care plan for Dinah, who would have therapists visit her home three times a week.

"Easy as pie," Dinah assured her.

Collette smiled, a bit surprised that her sudden change of plans was actually going to transpire.

That afternoon, when Suzie arrived home at the Dawdi House, Collette wasted no time sharing her new plan for the future.

"For the next few weeks, Dinah Troyer, the bishop's mother, needs full-time help at home," Collette explained to her daughter. "You and I are going to move into her house, so that we can help her 'round the clock until she can manage on her own."

"We can't leave here!" Suzie exclaimed. "What about Grace and the Lapps? They're family now. And my friends at the pretzel factory?"

"Suzie, Dinah's house is right here in Joyful River. You'll be able to see most everybody at work and church, just as usual," Collette assured her. "But you'll need to ask Smitty to give you Tuesdays and Thursdays off. Those will be the days when you'll stay with Dinah while I go work at the Hostetlers. I can't afford to lose that job, so I'll need your help on this for the next few weeks."

Suzie's blue eyes opened wide as she seemed to process the details. "But I can work the other days? And Saturday?"

"As long as you can tend to Dinah on Tuesdays and Thursdays."

Suzie looked down at her hands. "I can do that. But Mem, why do we have to move out of the Dawdi House and leave Lapp Farm? I'll miss Grace and all the Lapp children so much."

"The Dawdi House was never meant to be our forever home. It was an act of generosity from the Lapps when I needed a home without stairs. Mammi Esther was so kind to make the offer."

"But I love living there."

"I know you do, but things have changed. Harlan and Essie are married now, and they should have their own home. And we need to move on. Not to stay with Dinah Troyer forever, but it's a good thing for now."

Suzie's lower lip emerged in that near-tearful expression Collette knew well. "This is terrible news. I'll never get over leaving the Dawdi House. Never."

"Oh, my dear one, I know change is hard." This daughter was so dramatic, so tender in the heart. At times Collette worried that Suzie would crumble under real world problems. But then, other times, she admired her daughter for letting loose her emotions, the way a stampeding horse released its energy and then settled into a steady trot. Maybe it was best to let the energy out; wasn't that one of the functions of rumspringa? Collette knew from personal experience that swallowing back and tamping down emotions often made them brew into a tempest that festered in the heart.

Leaving you stuck with a storm in your heart, while Linda's visiting sister was courting the man you love.

Collette put an arm around her daughter's shoulders and pulled her close. "I know you'll miss living right down the lane from the Lapp farm. It's been wonderful having Miriam and Alvin close by. Do you remember how Miriam used to bring us dinner every night after the accident?"

Suzie nodded, swiping at her tears with the back of one hand.

"It may feel scary now, but you'll find that there are some new adventures in store for you at Dinah's house." Hearing the words come from her own mouth, Collette realized that she, too, was ready for a new adventure.

"I hope so." Suzie sniffed. "Just as long as I can keep working at the pretzel factory."

Collette nodded, pleased that Suzie had formed an attachment to her friends at work, even if that included a young man. It was time for Suzie to spread her wings, time for Collette to let her chick roam from the nest. "Before I forget, there's one more thing I've decided. For every day that you spend caring for Dinah, I will give you a day's pay for you to use for your surgery fund."

Suzie's hand flew to her cheek. "You're going to let me have the surgery?"

"As long as you delay it for a few months, until after Dinah has recovered and we're on our own again. Then you'll need to talk to the bishop and make sure the church will allow it. Then we'll have to meet with the doctor together. And you'll need to use your savings to pay for half of the cost." Collette thought that the idea of using her own savings might deter her, but she'd been wrong.

"Mem, that's awesome!" Suzie flung herself into her mother's arms, leaving Collette to wonder how a single day could contain "terrible" and "awesome" news, all within an hour's time.

Collette hugged her daughter, treasuring the closeness in this moment. As a parent, Collette knew she had made mistakes while bringing up her children. She was far from perfect, but it was good to know that love could overcome all shortcomings. Together she and Suzie would be turning over a new page, and she was ever so grateful for the path Gott had shown her.

Chapter 30

Over at Iddo's farm, Aaron felt sorry for missing the day's work with his good friend and farming partner. There'd been a death in a neighboring district. Joshua Lambright, ninety-three years old. Aaron didn't know the deceased, but he'd been the grandfather of church member Emery Lambright, and Madge had invited him over to spend some time consoling and comforting her husband, Emery.

Now, at the Dienner farmhouse, Aaron followed Jolene into the kitchen, where heat emanated from the oven and savory smells filled the air. He greeted Iddo and Jolene's oldest daughter, Heidi, who was trying to teach her little one how to frost cookies without licking all the frosting. He apologized to Iddo's wife, explaining what had held him up.

"These things happen," Jolene said as she removed the lid from a pot on the stove and stirred the mouthwatering, steaming stew. "Iddo's out there now. I guess he got some work done. He came in for lunch, then said he was heading back to the barn."

"Denki. I'll go find him." The wind picked up as he made his way out back. A gust whisked over a nearby field, making waves in the stubble. One of the large barn doors had been rolled open, but something was making a banging noise. A small door, banging open in the wind. He moved quickly, stepping into the barn and pulling the door closed, lest the wind yank it off its hinges. Latching the door shut, he gave a second for his eyes to adjust to the shadowed barn.

He passed two small pens, empty and swept clean. A winch hung down from the hayloft, but the barn was eerily quiet. "Iddo?" he called. "Where are you?" No answer came from the quiet space, and the only movement was the dust glittering in a shaft of sunlight crossing the shadows. The smells of cut hay and manure were usually comforting in their familiarity, but today, nothing sat well with Aaron. Something was wrong. It nagged him like a burr in his shoe.

He scanned the stables, the hayloft overhead. Looking past pillars and posts to the array of shovels and rakes, something caught his eye.

A lump of cloth on a bale of hay. Nay, a man. Iddo was collapsed on the bale, hugging one arm. His eyes were squeezed shut, his face pale and damp with sweat.

"Iddo, my friend. Are you all right?" Aaron tried to keep the distress from his voice, not wanting to further alarm his friend.

"Aaron . . . ah, is it time to bring in the beans again?" He let out a huff of breath. "I've been trying to get up, but every time I try, I fall back again. There's something wrong with me. Help me up."

"No, Iddo." Stepping closer, Aaron bent down over Iddo's crumpled form. "Stay there."

"But the beans . . . The weather is changing, and I'll lose the crop. I need to—"

"It'll be fine, Iddo. You need to take care and rest now. Keep breathing." Aaron saw that the man's face was strained and beaded with perspiration. "Are you in pain?"

Iddo grunted and clutched his chest. "My shoulder. That's where it started, but now, the pain's spreading across my chest. Throbbing. I thought it was a strained muscle but . . . aah!" He writhed in pain, and Aaron knew there was not a moment to lose.

"All right, my friend. Now I need to get you up." He helped the moaning man to his feet and tucked an arm around him. "Can you walk? I'll help you. One foot at a time," Aaron said firmly, forcing himself to stay calm, afraid to think too much. "There you go." Iddo leaned into him heavily, but managed to take a few steps. "There you go. Keep walking. Good."

They had made it out of the barn and halfway to the house when Iddo's legs gave out and he fell against Aaron. "Okay, I got you." Aaron gripped his friend around the torso so that he could get him to the farmhouse, his legs dragging gently in the dirt. Once they reached the back porch, Aaron laid him gently on the worn wood, calling for Iddo's wife.

"Jolene!" he shouted. "Jolene! Come quick!" Noticing the bell mounted by the door, he rushed over and pulled the string. The clapper hit the cast iron with a loud clang, over and over. The call sounded loudly, then was carried off on the wind as he rang relentlessly.

The back door was flung open, and Jolene rushed out. "Oh, Iddo!" She fell to her knees beside her husband, cradling his face in her hands.

"I found him in the barn. Might be a heart attack or stroke. Where's your phone shanty?"

Jolene pointed toward the neighbor's house. "Near the road. We share it with the Fishers."

"I'm going to call an ambulance," Aaron said, as Heidi and the little girl came out the door.

"Keep ringing the bell," he told Heidi, then ran down toward the road.

He was running, the phone shanty in sight, when someone came hurrying down the driveway.

"I'm Kristen, from next door. What's going on?" the woman asked breathlessly.

He explained quickly, and she accompanied him to the shanty to make sure the call went through. As they were making the call, a horse and buggy turned down the driveway, responding to the bell, and neighbors from the other side came hurrying down the road to assist.

Everyone huddled around Iddo, trying to assist, but not quite sure what to do. A blanket was brought out to keep him warm, and Kristen said it was good that he remained conscious. Aaron stepped toward the back of the group and prayed.

The ambulance arrived within minutes, and the paramedic checked Iddo's vital signs. The two young men who'd been traveling down the road, Jacob and Ephraim Kraybill, helped lift Iddo onto the stretcher. And then he was loaded into the ambulance and taken away.

"I'm not allowed to ride with him in the ambulance," Jolene said, her hands quivering as she watched the vehicle move down the lane to the rural road. "I had to send him off all alone." Her voice broke on a sob, and her daughter went to her and slipped an arm around her shoulder.

"I'll give you a ride to the hospital," the neighbor offered. From the shape of her kapp and the floral print of her dress, she was probably a Mennonite. The realization only occurred to Aaron now, as the chaos of the emergency waned. Kristen scanned the group to include everyone. "I've got a minivan, so I can take anyone who wants to go."

"We'd appreciate that," said Heidi. "See, Mem? Dat won't be alone for long."

"I'd like to go, too," Aaron said. He knew his place was at the hospital with Iddo, despite all the things that needed to get done here, and quickly.

As Heidi and Jolene went into the house to grab a few things, Aaron turned to the young Kraybill men. "We'll need a crew of men to gather here tomorrow to bring in the last of the soybeans. Do you know how to reach Deacon Seth? He should be at Skip's Buggy Repair Shop. If you get word to him, he'll know how to organize it. And it's important to get the word out about Iddo. Folks will want to lend their support."

"We know Skip's shop," Ephraim offered. He was a young man, early twenties. Aaron had married him to his bride just last year. "We'll ride into town and let the deacon know."

"Denki for your help," Aaron said. "It was good of you to answer the bell."

The young men climbed into the buggy and headed off.

Kristin brought her van around, and soon they were loaded in and buckled, Aaron in the front seat, and Jolene in the back with her daughter and granddaughter. There was even a car seat for the little girl.

"I do a lot of driving for my church," Kristen explained, "as well as my own grandchildren. I mind them three days a week, while their mother works."

"Your daughter's a nurse, isn't she?" Heidi asked.

"She is. Jenny's a pediatric nurse at a hospital in Lancaster. And I worked as a nurse until I retired a few years ago."

"Like mother, like daughter," Jolene said. "As a nurse, what do you think happened to Iddo?"

"It's hard to say from what I witnessed," Kristen said, looking into the rearview mirror. "It might be heart related. Or it could be a stroke. But he's in good hands now."

As the women talked about medical possibilities, Aaron leaned back in the seat and took a deep breath, and tried to slow the adrenaline reaction in his own body. From the moment he'd found Iddo, everything had been on alert, heightened senses, racing heartbeat.

Now, in the calm after the storm, he could see the situation clearly, as if watching from above like a hovering bird.

Iddo had been moving about the farm, and then something had brought him down. A heart attack? A stroke? Whatever the source, it had struck him down.

And just like that, his life had changed in a moment.

It spoke to the power of Gott to change a man's life. Changes that could happen in any person's life. What was it that Seth had said? Gott was changing his heart and soul in a way he didn't understand.

Miracles and tragedies defied explanation . . . and human understanding.

As the van moved toward the hospital, he prayed to Gott to ease Iddo's suffering and put him on the path to recovery. He knew that Gott chose when to take a man to heaven, and yet he wasn't ready to lose Iddo so soon. Aaron wondered if things might have gone differently. If he had arrived at Iddo's farm earlier, would it have changed the outcome?

He would never know.

All he could do now was pray.

When they reached the hospital, the news wasn't good. The nurse at the emergency room ushered Jolene and Heidi into a small private room to meet with a doctor, and Jolene requested that Aaron come along. "He's our bishop," she explained.

The young doctor had short shaved black hair and a face of dark whiskers, but his eyes were bright and sharp. "I'm afraid that Mr. Dienner suffered a heart attack while en route in the ambulance," he said. "The good news is that our paramedic was able to revive him. He did chest compressions for one minute, and then did a cardioversion. That's when we use an electric device to restart the heart. They brought him back to consciousness quickly."

A miracle, Aaron thought. That electricity could restart a human heart.

"Then he's okay?" Jolene asked. "Can we see him?"

"Not just yet. He's upstairs, being prepped for surgery. His X-rays show two blockages in major arteries. We need to insert a stent, which is a tube that will expand the artery that's blocked with cholesterol. Time is of the essence."

"Oh, dear Iddo." Jolene's eyes filled with tears again.

"He hasn't been feeling well for a few days now," Aaron told the doctor.

"I should have pushed him to see a doctor," Jolene said tearfully as she pressed her fists to her chin. "All week he's been telling me his heart hurt, but I thought he was joking. He started saying that when the girls got married and moved off." She sniffed, swiping a tear from one eye. "I didn't know his heart was failing!"

"Your husband is lucky to have gotten here when he did," the doctor went on. He explained that Iddo's cholesterol was high, and that in the future a low-fat, heart-healthy diet and exercise would be essential to Iddo's good health.

"Is he conscious?" Aaron asked. "Can he speak?"

"When he came in, he was lucid enough to let us know

he'd had scrapple and eggs for lunch." The doctor smiled. "That led us to understand that his diet isn't exactly low in fat. But now, with the medication he's been given, he's not conversing. We call it a twilight sleep."

Jolene was anxious to see her husband, but she understood the need to wait. The doctor left her with some paperwork to fill out and a promise that he and his team were going to take good care of her husband.

Over the next few hours, they learned that there'd been some complications—an irregular heartbeat—and they'd needed to delay the procedure. As other friends and family members arrived in the hospital waiting room, Aaron alternately consoled Jolene, and then paced the halls, praying.

Through it all, he kept returning to Aaron's revelation.

Gott is changing my heart and soul in a way I don't understand.

Aaron believed that Gott had brought him to this day to change his own life. Life could end or change in a heartbeat. As the waiting wore on, he ticked through the changes to be made in his life.

He would need to delegate some of the duties of church leadership to other ministers. He'd been wrong to hold every task for himself, and the pull on his time was running him ragged.

He would try to reach out to Mose and make amends. Whether or not Mose chose to be baptized in the faith, he was Aaron's son, and it was wrong as a father to withhold love as a form of punishment.

And Collette . . . How to begin with her?

He would admit to her and to the gmay that he cared deeply for this woman. More than once, Linda and Len had mentioned that Collette's past as an abandoned woman might make her a less than desirable match for a church leader. Aaron acknowledged that others might think the same way, but he knew the truth. The love that Collette had brought into his home was pure and blessed with Gott's goodness. And the love he felt for her had grown steadily since the day he'd first visited her after her accident. He'd been a fool not to see that he'd been quietly courting her for the past year.

He would ask Collette to marry him, and pray that she would have him.

Tuning out the conversation of the waiting room, Aaron paced to the window to stare at the nightscape lit here and there by the circles of streetlights. Gott was changing his heart and soul, and now, it was time for Aaron to follow the light of truth and make those changes in his life.

It was after two a.m. when the doctor came in with the good news.

They had finally been able to do the procedure on Iddo, and things were looking good.

"Thanks be to Gott," Aaron said, smiling at the faces in the small group huddled around the doctor. Jolene went around hugging everyone, thanking them for their love and support.

"When can I see my husband?" she asked the doctor.

"Tomorrow morning, after he's had a good night's rest." The doctor smiled, his dark eyes warming to the group. "You've been a very supportive group of family and friends, but I think everyone here can use some sleep."

"Amen to that!" Preacher Lee said in his booming baritone voice.

Folks were all smiles as they gathered up cups and snack

wrappers and prepared to head home. Iddo's neighbor Kristen had stayed through the night, and now she was corralling her group toward the elevators so that she could get them all safely home. Noticing Heidi's weariness, Aaron picked up her sleeping child from a waiting room chair and carried the girl in his arms. The heft of her small body and the whisper of her breath reminded him of the years when his children had been toddlers, a memory that warmed his heart.

Aaron dozed off during the ride home in the van. When he arrived home, the house was quiet and still, though he could smell and see that Collette had been here. The house smelled of lemon instead of grease, and the kitchen had been scrubbed clean, ridding all traces of Sally's cooking fiasco. His girls had managed to have dinner and still leave the kitchen tidy—a huge improvement over a few months ago.

Upstairs, the refurbished quilt had been replaced on his bed. A welcoming sight.

He removed his clothes, hung them on hooks, and put on a nightshirt. As he moved the lantern to the nightstand, he saw a note propped there. Hmm.

Sitting on the bed, he unfolded the paper and saw that it was from Collette. He scanned it quickly until his gaze stuck on the line: "*I can't work for you anymore.*"

He raked his hair back in concern. What was happening?

"*Please forgive me. I can't explain all the reasons, but I can't work for you anymore.*"

It seemed so final. The note was short, but it convinced him that he had hurt her in some way.

She's leaving me, leaving before I had a chance to tell her how I feel about her.

He sat back on the bed, pillows propped behind him as

he stared up at the ceiling. As if he would find a road map there to navigate out of this dead end. He had awakened to the fact that he needed Collette in his life, but the epiphany had come too late.

He put out the lantern beside the bed and lost himself in the darkness.

An already long night loomed ahead without end.

Chapter 31

Thursday morning, Harlan pulled the buggy to the side of the road and let Collette out near the Hostetlers' place. The sky was still a smudge of gray and there was a chill in the air, but Collette didn't mind the short walk up the lane to their sprawling one-story house. Absorbed in thoughts of bringing Dinah home and moving herself and Suzie into the older woman's house, Collette didn't notice the man coming up the lane toward her until he was upon her.

"Good morning," Len said, touching his hat. In the other hand, he held a small cooler containing his lunch.

"Hello, Len." It was unusual for Len to head into town on foot. "You're heading into the shop early today."

"I'm just heading over to Iddo Dienner's place. You heard Iddo had a heart attack?"

"Goodness, no!" Collette exclaimed.

"Deacon Seth asked a bunch of us over to bring the beans in since Iddo will be in the hospital awhile."

Collette stopped walking. "Is Iddo all right?"

"I wish I could say better." Len was uncharacteristically somber, the corners of his mouth turned down. "He's been in the hospital overnight. The bishop found him sick in the barn late yesterday."

Oh, dear Gott, it sounded serious. Iddo had been feeling

poorly for a week now. She knew that because Aaron had been spending time at the man's farm, trying to keep the crops coming in. "Is there something I can do to help?" she asked. "Will you ask Jolene if I can drop by with a casserole tomorrow?"

He nodded. "If I see her, I'll ask her what she needs."

She nodded, and then watched as he walked off into the gathering light. She prayed that Iddo regained his strength and good health. She also prayed for Aaron, that Gott would grant him the wisdom to guide the folks who needed help. And the energy, too! Oh, how he would need stamina now, and the last few times she'd seen him, he'd been downright weary.

As she approached the house, she reconsidered the question she'd asked Len. How could she help?

Of course she could drop a covered dish off for the Dienners. She assumed that Aaron would be back at the hospital today and every day, and that would certainly put the girls on duty at home. Not that they hadn't learned how to put together a dinner, but Tess also had school, and Amy her job. They needed a maud this week, more than ever.

And she had walked out on them.

At the time, it had seemed like the right thing to do . . . the only thing to do. But now, the winds had shifted. She paused as her hand closed on the knob to Linda's kitchen door. She could hear Linda inside, arguing with one of her daughters. Right now, she wanted nothing more than to leave here and go to help the Troyers, but that was not an option.

She let out a heavy sigh and went into the house. Linda stood at the kitchen sink rinsing a coffee mug, while her daughter picked at half a grapefruit with a pointed spoon. Collette hung her sweater and bonnet on a hook, unnoticed as mother and daughter talked.

"If I was going to get a job," June said, jabbing at the fruit, "which I don't want to do, it wouldn't be at the pretzel factory."

"Lots of girls work there," Linda insisted. "You'd be with your friends nearly every day."

"I don't want to go to work," she whined. "Why can't I just help out around here? You always say housework is every woman's number one task."

Linda turned to scowl at her daughter and noticed that Collette had arrived. "Good, you're here. You can finish these dishes." She wiped her hands on a towel as Collette tied on a kitchen apron and moved to the sink. "I've got to get together something to bring to the hospital for those waiting on Iddo. Poor man. What do you think is quicker, cookies or muffins?"

"Cookies," Collette said as she plunged her hands into the warm, soapy water. She knew a quick recipe for peanut butter cookies that could be done in thirty minutes, but baking was the least of her worries. "I was so sorry to hear of Iddo. I pray he's improved."

"It was sad news," Linda agreed. "And there's laundry to do, so you'd best get on that this morning. I know it's not laundry day, but it never ends with this houseful."

"How about if I help with the laundry instead of standing on my feet in a factory all day?" June asked.

"Smitty is expecting you to start today, June, and that's that," Linda insisted.

Collette kept her chin tipped down, staring out the back window as her hands worked, methodically washing a bowl. Her heart ached with worry and her mind was still reeling from the news about Iddo.

"Mem, please don't make me go to work today," June pleaded.

Linda smoothed back the sides of her hair in frustration.

"I've got enough to do without you giving me a fuss. Now, finish your breakfast. And Collette, as soon as you're done with the breakfast dishes, you need to start with those cookies. Sally and I want to get to the hospital so we can catch the bishop there."

For Collette, the thought of baking cookies and starting up the washing machine was a burden piled onto an already heavy stack. "I heard the bishop was with Iddo's wife at the hospital for most of the night," she said. "They'll need more than cookies. Maybe we should make a casserole for Iddo's family? And Sally can do the same for the bishop. Isn't she cleaning his home today? If you really want to help, it's in the doing of daily chores. That will ease his load far more than bringing him cookies and muffins."

"I wouldn't intrude that way," Linda said.

"But Sally could help him and the girls—"

"I'm not working for the bishop anymore," Sally said from the doorway, where she had a thimble on one finger and a spool of thread in one hand. "I know, I didn't last long in his employ."

"One day on the job is shameful," Linda said, then pursed her lips in a sour expression.

"One day on the job and I knew I was in the wrong place." Linda's retort didn't penetrate Sally's calm; her eyes remained serene as a colorful sunset. "Linda, you know that I'm not as tidy as you are, and I'm not that good in the kitchen after cooking for one all these years."

"You could learn," Linda insisted, sweeping a hand to take in everyone in the kitchen. "Nobody around here is even trying, but you can learn a skill. You girls need to get out and try it."

"Sister, I'm not a girl anymore," Sally said quietly. "I need to be using the skills Gott gave me—sewing and mending quilts."

You go, Sally, Collette wanted to say. She was glad Sally was standing up for herself, though she sensed that this dispute was about more than skills. It was more likely that Linda was disappointed with her daughter and sister for not landing husbands on her time frame.

"Enough of this conversation." Linda took her shawl from its hook. "I'm going to the phone shanty to call a car to pick us up in an hour. We'll drop June at the pretzel factory, then go on to the hospital in Plumdale, where we will deliver our cookies and console the bishop."

Both Sally and June objected, but Collette stayed out of the fray as she rinsed the last of the dishes and dried her hands. Her thoughts swirled around the people in need, blocking out the noise around her. She would cook for Iddo's family, who would need sustenance during this difficult time. The Troyers, too. Two casseroles, a simple chicken and rice. It was a favorite at the Troyer house, a dish Collette had adopted after Tess had dug the recipe card out of Dorcas's collection and shared it with Collette. She'd make enough to feed Suzie and Dinah, too.

And then she would tend to the bishop's house, and offer help at the Dienners. Harlan could get time off from work if the Dienners needed more help with the harvest.

So much to do.

So many things to set aright.

I need to go to him.

He needs me now, more than ever.

Her hurt feelings, the ways she'd been wronged and neglected, his lack of romantic interest in her—all those things now paled in comparison to the fact that this good, kind man needed help right now.

"I need to go," she said. Her tone was soft, but something about her resolve silenced the others.

"What are you talking about?" Linda asked, pausing at the door.

"I'm sorry, but they need me. June, you can take your time with breakfast. You may not have to go work at the pretzel factory, after all," Collette said.

"Really?" June stabbed the pointed spoon into the grapefruit section and gave her mother a mincing look. "See, Mem. Collette understands."

Linda folded her arms, standing her ground. "I don't think Collette understands at all."

"June, if you'd rather work as a maud, you can tidy up and wash floors around here." Collette saw Linda's jaw drop, her mouth open in shock. "And occasionally, that'll include the laundry, some cooking and painting, too."

"Wait, what?" June's head swiveled from her mother to Collette. "What do you mean?"

"I'm saying you can do my job here." Collette untied the kitchen apron and removed it.

"You want me to clean *this* house?" June pushed her bowl away and scooted back from the table. "I can't possibly do all that work!"

"One task at a time." Collette folded up the apron and handed it to June. "If you take things bit by bit, eventually all your chores will get done."

June stared at the apron as if it were a barn mouse and then turned to her mother. "Mem? Do I have to work here?"

"Collette?" Linda seemed off-balance. "Where are you going?"

"I've taken on the care of Dinah Troyer, and for now, that's a full-time commitment." Collette stood tall and confident, suddenly realizing how often she had cowered inside when facing the likes of Linda Hostetler. "I was hoping to keep working for you, too, Linda, but now that the bishop is going to need more help, that won't be possible."

"Now hold on, Collette. You don't want to do anything rash," Linda insisted.

"I've given this plenty of thought." Collette dropped the apron on the kitchen counter and went to the door. "'To everything there is a season,' and this is the time for me to go where I'm needed." She took her black bonnet and cardigan from the hook, then turned back for one last look. Linda stared, open-mouthed, and June watched with eyes round as quarters. Only Sally seemed to understand. Sally, who knew how it felt to be under Linda's thumb, nodded with a hopeful glimmer in her eyes.

"Goodbye." It felt good to walk out the door and step into the cool breeze. It felt even better knowing that she would never be a servant in that house again. She walked briskly down the lane, chasing off two blue jays that had taken over a bird feeder from the finches clustered in a nearby bush. At the ripe old age of thirty-nine, Collette Yoder was standing on her own two feet.

Chapter 32

"Are you sure you don't want some breakfast?" Tess asked, her head tilted and her eyes wide as she stared at him. "I make some awesome scrambled eggs now. Collette taught me her secret."

Aaron appreciated the offer. The past hour in the kitchen with his two youngest daughters passing through had taught him yet another lesson. He needed to spend more time with his girls. They had taken on their new responsibilities with grace and enthusiasm, and the concern they had expressed for their father genuinely moved him. "Awesome eggs sound delicious, but I'm not hungry."

"You should eat something. You don't look so good, Dat."

He could only imagine how scary he looked, hunched over his coffee mug with bloodshot eyes. He straightened in the kitchen chair. "I'm going to be fine, Tess. It's Iddo I'm worried about."

"I'll pray for him, Dat. It must have been awful to find your friend that way, so sick."

"It was," he admitted, acknowledging her concern.

"But you sounded the alarm and got help. You always know to do the right thing, Dat. How do you know that?" Her question was so earnest, so loving, that he would have reached out and hugged her had she been a few years younger.

"I trust in Gott, and pray that He'll guide my actions," he said. It was a true answer, though he suspected she'd be disappointed that it held no quick tips for life.

But when she looked up from the sandwich she was cutting, she smiled. "You're a good church leader. You help so many people, all the time."

"I try." Tess's considerate compliment showed that she'd grown aware of the world around her in the past few months. Amy, too, had shown her concern before she'd been picked up for work earlier that morning. She'd given him a hug and asked about Iddo and offered to make a dish to bring over later.

This adult behavior from his two daughters had taken him by surprise, though he would have known better if he'd been paying attention. This was Collette's influence, days and hours of conversation and instruction and care during which she'd passed not only skills to his daughters, but also lessons in love and community.

All because of Collette.

It struck him that his daughters were going to be quite upset with him when they learned that Collette wouldn't be around anymore. Especially when he admitted that it was his fault.

That he'd thought himself beyond marriage, despite Gott's plan.

That he'd filled his life with church commitments to avoid facing his feelings for Collette.

That he'd enjoyed her companionship without admitting his feelings for her.

Last night, after Iddo's close call, Aaron had seen a clear path. He needed Collette in his life. Their happy life together seemed inevitable—a blessing. But he'd blown it.

Visiting hours at the hospital didn't begin until mid-morning, and so he was stuck with his wary thoughts. Long after Tess left for school, Aaron sat at the kitchen table, his coffee grown cold as he tried to think of ways to win Collette back.

If only he could talk to her, learn the reasons why she'd had to leave.

But he wasn't sure she would meet with him, and he didn't want to push her. He'd be no man at all if he bullied her to come back. Was that how she saw him? He hoped not. He didn't think so. But he'd been so mindless of their growing relationship, he suspected he'd gotten quite a few things wrong.

He abandoned the kitchen and stepped out onto the back porch. The wind was up. The deep blue sky was dotted with magnificently fat clouds that chased past the horizon and over the barn at a good speed. The sight of the fields and surrounding hills had brought him comfort in all seasons, but today, even the wind shimmering through the fiery red leaves of the maples did little to ease his heartache.

Ignoring the chill wind that rippled the sleeves of his shirt, he started walking to the barn. Might as well check on the animals one last time before calling the car.

A bird's cry from above him made him look up. Two large black crows sailed on the wind high overhead, their broad wings spread wide as they circled over the house, the paddock, the barn. A couple of crows. He had read in an Audubon book that crows mate for life. Watching the birds float against the clouded sky, he thought what a beautiful thing Gott had created, that two birds, or two people could find each other and share a lifetime.

He headed toward the paddock, where his horse was waiting since he'd been turned out in the early morning. Thumper came right to him when he called, and Aaron took a moment to stroke his neck. "You're a good horse," he said. "Strong and obedient. But today's trip is too far for you. You get the day off."

The horse nudged him with his mouth, and Aaron laughed. "No carrots with me now, boy."

Turning away, Aaron paused to take it all in: wind and sky, birds and horse, trees and grassland, hills and fields. What a blessed life he lived here on Gott's good earth. He was grateful, but he ached to share it with the good Amish woman who had filled the empty spaces in his heart.

"Aaron?"

The call came from the distance, a woman's voice carried on the wind. He turned toward the main road and saw her walking toward him, the breeze toying with the hem of her dress and threatening the black bonnet she held on with one hand.

For a moment, he was sure it was a daydream, a brief flash of the way he wished things were. But when another wind gust tugged at her apron, he realized his eyes were not lying.

Collette was here.

He strode toward her, quickening his pace until he was running, as if being pushed by the wind. As he got closer to her he saw the reserve in her manner. She wasn't smiling. She might be angry with him. But the fact that she was here, the sight of Collette walking down the lane in her purple dress, filled him with joy that surpassed any worries.

"Collette!" He smiled and slowed his pace as he finally reached her. "I'm glad to see you. Very glad." He stopped walking suddenly, realizing that she might be here with bad news. Good grief! He must sound like a boy in rumspringa. "You heard about Iddo?"

"I came as soon as I heard. Len was heading over to the Dienner farm to help haul the beans in." She grasped her dress to protect it from a sudden gust, and the sight of her looking vulnerable in the wind made him long to bring her inside to a protected place. "How is Iddo?"

"He turned a corner early this morning. The doctor expects a full recovery, with some adjustments to diet and exercise."

"I'm relieved to hear it. I—I heard that you found him. That must have been hard for you. I was upset when I walked out yesterday, but . . . well, I couldn't stay away if you needed me. I figured you'd want someone to talk to."

Tell her you've never been so happy to see anyone in your life. Tell her! But he could only grumble, "I do."

"Well, here I am." She spoke with her chin lowered, eyes on the ground. "I'll go on inside and start cleaning. Maybe prepare some dishes you and the girls can just heat up if you're pressed for time."

She started past him, but he reached out and cuffed her wrist gently. "Collette, denki for coming back. Denki for caring."

She kept her head down, her eyes hidden by the top of her bonnet, though he could see her lips pursed tightly together.

"Listen, I don't know your reasons for leaving, exactly, but I do know that I've wronged you, and I'm sorry that I've been such a fool. Every hour, every day I've spent with you has given me comfort and joy, and I want to think it's been the same for you."

"I felt that I'd found a second home with you." She dared to look up. Her eyes seemed wary but shiny with tears. "But I couldn't continue to stay on as your maud. I need more, Aaron."

"And I want to give you more. I've been caught up in a trap of my own making, thinking I couldn't ever marry again. My mistake, my sin even. A mixture of pride and stubbornness and faulty logic. Whatever the reason, I was wrong, holding myself back from marriage. I enjoyed your companionship but held myself back from you. You, who have shown my daughters the path to womanhood. You've brought love back into our home. You've shown me ways to be a better man."

"You've always been a good man." Tears streaked down her cheeks, unabated. "But with your eyes on the folks in the gmay, so many who need your advice and counseling and help, you've lost sight of the ones who love you most." She pressed a hand to her throat. "That includes me."

She loved him. She had just said the words.

For a moment, the man who was able to preach the word of Gott and converse with his parishioners was so overwhelmed with relief, he was at a loss for words. But he couldn't let this moment slip. He had to speak his heart and mind, once and for all.

"I'm sorry for the mistakes I've made. Sorry that I hurt you. I was moving like a horse with blinders on, trotting straight ahead."

"And now . . . the blinders are gone?" she asked.

"I have a new view of the world around me. Clear as a blue sky. And I see a love that's bold and bright as the sun." The words were uncharacteristically joyful for him, but why not? Why not celebrate Gott's love when he'd been blessed to find it?

He stepped in front of her so that they were face-to-face, toe to toe. From such a close proximity he saw tiny flecks of gold in her brown eyes, and he felt the warmth of her body as he placed his hands on her shoulders and pulled her into his arms. "I love you, Collette. You've opened my heart and transformed my home. And I thank Gott for bringing you into my life."

Her face reflected her wonder and a hint of joy. "And I love you." She shook her head, sniffing back tears. "I'd given up on you. I thought you'd never come around."

"But here I am." He lowered his face to hers. "And here I'll stay. I love you, Collette. Over the past year, I've fallen in love with you." Her face filled his vision as he soaked up her response, her relief, comfort, and joy. When he touched his lips to hers, his senses surged, as if the plants and creatures around them became greener, swifter, more fertile.

He lost himself for a moment as the kiss deepened, and his thoughts were of her—only of her. Her scent, her warmth, the days and nights that they would be together. When she ended the kiss, he opened his eyes and straightened.

"Aaron, you're the bishop," she whispered shyly. "Someone from the road might see."

He straightened, taking in the light in her eyes. "See a man kissing his bride-to-be?"

"Bride?" Her eyes were suddenly round as quarters.

"If you're willing." Willing? Had he really fumbled that word? He didn't mean it to sound like a contract. His confidence flagging, he pulled her close and breathed in the scent of her shampoo, captivated by the feel of her in his arms. Here was a woman whose heart brimmed over with devotion to Gott and love. A woman who needed to serve others, just as he did. He believed that Gott had brought them together, like the two crows that now perched on the gutter of his roof.

"Marry me, Collette. Marry me and let's spend our days bringing each other comfort and joy. You know we're good partners. I will always have my commitments as bishop, but there are other ministers in our fold to help ease the burden. I'll learn to balance my family life and my commitment to the church."

As he spoke, her gaze was fiercely upon him, as if she needed to interpret his every word. How could he convince her? Did she have doubts? He could only repeat the proposal, over and again, and pray that she would say yes. "Marry me, Collette. Marry me and be my wife."

Chapter 33

Collette could barely hear his proposal over the excited roar of the pulse in her ears.

He loved her.

She had begun to think she'd never hear the words, but today, it was as if the sun had broken through the clouds to shine on Aaron and her. Her heart beat like the wings of a joyful dove.

He wanted to marry her, to be man and wife in a union blessed by Gott.

And he was looking to her for an answer, but she didn't know how to tell him that the reality wasn't quite as simple as he made it sound. She had to speak the truth, but with his gaze holding hers, she didn't want to end the sweet moment.

Just then a gust struck. Dust rose around them on the gravel driveway as the wind whipped at their clothes. Collette held tight to Aaron, pressing her face against his chest, her cheek to the worn cotton of his shirt. She didn't want anyone passing by to see them. Aaron had to be a model of the community. But their love was no sin, and the temptation to stay wrapped in his arms was hard to resist. For the first time in decades, she felt loved and protected, safe and secure.

She knew Aaron would take care of her, but she needed to watch out for him, as well.

When the wind settled, she lifted her head but kept her palms firmly planted on his chest, not wanting their intimate embrace to end. "Is this too soon to talk of marriage?" she asked. "I want nothing more than to be your wife, but what will people think?"

"We will tell them that Bishop Aaron is marrying Collette Yoder, and we'll arrange the vows as soon as possible to silence the naysayers. It's a second marriage of two widowed people, so we don't need to wait. A small gathering is traditional."

"As long as we protect your good name," she said. "I don't want to provide grist for the gossip mill."

"Gossip is a sin," he said. "Folks will come around. In my experience, women enjoy a good love story."

She took a deep breath, her heart filling with love and joy and something fresh and new: hope.

"Come," he said, taking her by the hand. "Let's get inside, out of this wind, and we'll figure out our next step."

Hand in hand they walked to the house—a path Collette had walked dozens of times before, but today, everything was transformed by the knowledge that he loved her. Her heart felt free and light as a sparrow.

Inside the kitchen, she hung her black bonnet on a hook and tied on an apron. "Do you want coffee?" she offered.

"No." He held up his hands. "One more cup and I'll be on my way to an ulcer. I've been up most of the night, trying to figure out a way to make things right with you."

The thought of him losing sleep over her made her go soft inside. "I never intended to upset you when I gave up the job here. But right now you need some bread to soak up that coffee. Or French toast?"

"Bread is fine."

She quickly sliced a few pieces from the loaf she'd baked Monday, then set it out with the butter dish.

"Look at you," he said, picking up a slice. "Not two minutes in this kitchen and already you're feeding me and starting chores."

"Like any good Amish woman." She smiled as she wiped crumbs from the counter. Her work was a labor of love, but still it felt good to be recognized. "I think best when my hands are in motion."

"It's a good thing, since you're usually moving, serving folks and helping out at church gatherings and weddings and here in our house." He buttered a slice of bread. "Can you tell me all the reasons you were leaving?"

"Well, as I said, I couldn't go on as your maud. Not that I mind the work. It was just too hard to be around you, feeling the way I do."

"Please forgive an old fool for being caught up in his ways." He gave a weary smile, then bit into the bread.

"Hardly a fool," she said. Despite her frustration with him, her love and admiration had never wavered. But she wanted to tell him her reasons. Honesty was important in a relationship. "And then when Sally came along and you hired her, I didn't know what to think."

"Another mistake of mine," he admitted.

"Which wouldn't have been so bothersome if she wasn't so sweet and kind. Every time jealousy reared its head, it was melted away by that woman's warmth." It was too raw in her heart to discuss, but someday, in years to come, Collette would tell Aaron about the quilt, discovering that the intimate bedding had been tended and restored by another woman. She wasn't sure he would understand how that incident had prompted her to leave; she didn't completely understand it yet herself. Maybe someday . . .

"Sally seems like a fine person," he said. "But not the person I want in my home. It's you, Collette. Only you."

His words made her glow inside. She paused to smile at him across the kitchen table, then turned away to remove a slab of bacon from the freezer. Giddy with love, she felt as if she were floating around the kitchen, keeping busy lest this wonderful joy faded. Later she'd bake a loaf of bacon cheese bread, which could work as a meal or a snack for Aaron and the girls. From the pantry she extracted an armful of ingredients to make dough. Then she went back for a tin of long-grain rice and two pints of chicken broth. She'd make two chicken and rice casseroles, one to send over to Jolene.

"What are you cooking up this early in the morning?" he asked.

"Just planning meals for later. I won't be here very often for the next few weeks because I've taken another job." When he glanced up in surprise, she added, "Taking care of your mother. I'm going to spring Dinah from the rehab center tomorrow, and Suzie and I will move into her house so that she has twenty-four-hour care."

"You're an angel in disguise. Mem has been longing to get home."

"I'm happy to take care of her, but she's giving me so much in return. By giving Suzie and me a place to live, she's allowing me to leave my job at the Hostetlers. And it'll give Harlan and Essie the privacy they deserve." She stopped talking a moment to measure out the flour, sugar, yeast, and salt called for in her bread dough recipe. There. "I'm turning over a new leaf. It's a fresh start for me, something I didn't see coming until yesterday."

He finished the last crust of bread and brought the empty plate to the sink. "We never know when Gott has a surprise coming down the pike for us."

"We never know," she agreed.

He stood beside her at the kitchen counter, watching as she measured milk and water into a pot. When she reached around him for the butter, he placed a hand behind her back and leaned down to kiss her cheek. The touch of his lips sent little starbursts of sensation skittering through her body. Oh, she was going to enjoy being his wife!

"I'd love to stay and talk as you bake up a storm," he said. "But I need to get to the hospital to check on Iddo."

"Off you go. We'll talk more later. When you return, you'll have your choice of dinners."

"That sounds delicious. And I hope you'll still be here this afternoon? I'd like to tell the girls about our marriage plan right away. They're going to be thrilled."

"Suzie, too. She's always longed for a sister, and now she'll have two live-in sisters!"

Within days of Aaron's proposal, it seemed that everyone in the Amish community knew of their upcoming marriage. Whenever Collette shopped in a store or walked through town, she exchanged smiles and greetings with more folks than she could name. For once, Collette was glad to be the subject of folks' conversation.

Their wedding date was set for the first week of December, with the small ceremony and supper to be held at Alvin and Miriam Lapp's farm. Miriam and Alvin had insisted that they should host. "After the last two weddings we've done, your small group will be easy as pie!" Miriam had said.

Aaron had explained that it would have been too hectic to schedule their vows during the traditional wedding season, when he was marrying two to three couples some weeks. Wedding season was a busy time for every Amish bishop, and since they'd need to invite a bishop from a neighboring congregation to administer their sacred vows, December was the time for them.

"I would marry you tomorrow," Collette said, "but we older folks will have to wait until the end of the season." Their plans were unlikely to be disrupted by winter weather, as the small wedding did not require guests to travel from far away.

Also, December would give Aaron some time to try to reach his son, Mose, in the hopes that he might return for the wedding. "I've sent a message through his friends, and asked that he return to us, even if just for a visit," Aaron told Collette. "I can accept it if he wants to live with the Englisch, but I will always love my son."

Collette prayed that Gott might reunite father and son so that their hearts could be healed.

Smitty's wife, Iris, congratulated Collette one morning when she dropped Suzie off at the pretzel factory. Another day when Collette stopped in at the Country Diner to pick up a chicken dinner for Dinah, Madge Lambright emerged from the kitchen to give her a big hug and wish the very best for Aaron and her.

"I can't imagine what it's like to be marrying a bishop," Madge said.

"He's like any other Amish man, only with different responsibilities."

"Still, he makes the important rules. I would live in fear of crossing him." Madge's harsh words were softened by her warm smile. Collette sensed that she meant well. "Are you nervous?" Madge asked.

"Not at all." Collette laughed softly. "I'm so happy, I feel like I'm walking on clouds in the sky."

"Good for you. Happiness is good for the soul," Madge agreed.

Collette nodded, grateful that her life had been touched by love.

The children had taken the news well, too. Tess and Amy were thrilled, and at times they seemed proud that they were the ones who'd driven their father to bring Collette into their home. Laura had seemed pleased on the phone, and she made a point of traveling to Joyful River one Saturday so that Collette could have a chance to get to know Laura, Clyde, and their three children.

Collette counted it a blessing that, after the wedding, Suzie and Tess would be sharing a room in Aaron's house. Or rather, "Our House," as Aaron kept correcting Collette to call it. Suzie had always longed for more siblings, and Tess, with her introverted and bookish personality, would surely benefit from having a girl like Suzie draw her into the social world of Amish youth.

Harlan and Essie were happy for Collette, and after her matchmaking efforts, Miriam was over the moon at the upcoming wedding vows. And Dinah, whose brusque manner had made Collette cautious at first, was thrilled at the news.

It was hard to believe that Collette's once-shy daughter now enjoyed a social life at the pretzel factory and even a boyfriend. Suzie had blossomed in the past few months, thanks be to Gott. While she was still a bit immature on some matters, like the scar on her face, Collette had witnessed many other developments that indicated her daughter was on the right path.

Collette and Suzie had made a quick adjustment to their new residence in Dinah's house. It was so pleasant to have private space in their bedrooms, along with shared common areas with the charming older woman who reigned in the kitchen and dining room, giving them new recipes, gardening tips, and telling them what was what.

"Mammi Dinah is like the grandmother I never had," Suzie observed one sunny day as she and Collette stood together in the yard, pinning damp laundry onto the lines. "Sometimes she mothers me, and other times she gives orders. That's how my friends' grandmothers act."

"You know, Dinah *will* be your grandmother, Suzie," Collette explained. "After the wedding, we'll truly be family."

Smiling, Suzie shook out a pillowcase from the laundry basket and pinned it onto the line. "I never thought I'd get a grandmother when I was a teen," she said. "It's truly a gift from Gott."

"It is." Overcome with joy, Collette let a damp dress drop back into the basket and stood tall to hug her daughter. "I'm so grateful that Gott has restored our family," she said on a contented sigh.

Suzie squeezed her tight, rubbing one shoulder. "It's so wonderful to see you happy, Mem. I'm glad you fell in love with Bishop Aaron."

Collette felt her skin flush to hear her daughter speak that way. So frank, but she spoke the truth. "I've been blessed, for sure."

"You know, he used to scare me, but now that I've talked to him more, I see that he means well. He's got a really good heart." Suzie turned away to clip a towel onto the line. "Did he tell you we talked about my plastic surgery?"

"What?" Collette's heart dropped. Suzie had promised to delay that conversation, though she probably hadn't realized that it might taint the way the bishop felt about Collette. "Suzie, we agreed not to bring that up until things settled down."

"I know, but I was here with Dinah last week when the

bishop came over with Tess, and we got to talking." She shrugged. "One thing led to another."

"Where was I? What day was this?"

"I don't know what day, but you were over cleaning at the bishop's house."

"And what did Aaron say? I mean, about the surgery?" Collette was almost afraid to ask, worried that he might think her daughter was overstepping bounds and bringing shame to the family.

"He was really kind about it. He said that since I wasn't baptized yet, an operation wouldn't be a big issue. But he was worried that I might regret it later. He likened it to getting a tattoo, which some Amish youth do during rumspringa. He said that it seems exciting and new when they get it, but later, it brings them shame and sorrow."

Collette nodded. "These are wise words."

"And then he said the sweetest thing." Suzie hung a washcloth and smiled. "He said Gott had made me just right, inside and out, and he didn't understand why I'd want to change that."

Collette let the words sink in for a moment as the sheets flapped in the breeze. "This is true, Suzie."

"When I said that my scar is ugly, he told me it was a sign of my journey. That I'm still a beautiful creation in the eyes of Gott."

"You are, daughter."

"So that was that." Suzie seemed to shrug it off as she reached into the basket again. "My friends keep trying to talk me out of the surgery, and Josiah thinks I'm pretty as I am. So I'm not going to do it."

"Oh, Suzie, I'm so glad!"

"I knew you'd be happy. But thanks, Mem. Denki for letting me make my own choice."

Collette nodded, recalling how she'd wanted to forbid

the surgery. She'd been accustomed to laying down the rules for her youngest child. But Dinah had advised her to allow Suzie her freedom, and thank the Lord, it had worked out well.

That evening, when Aaron stopped in to check on his mother, Collette pulled him outside for a private talk. "Let's go in here," she said, tugging open the garage door and stepping into the musty shadows. The space, which had once housed a buggy, was clear but for shelves of crates and boxes that lined the wall.

When Aaron tried to close the door behind him, there was a cracking sound and the lower edge of the door dragged on the jamb. "Looks like a hinge just broke," he said, lifting the door slightly. "One of many things to be fixed at this house."

"It is in disrepair," Collette agreed. "But it's home to Dinah."

"And her independence is important to her." Aaron switched his focus to Collette, squeezing her shoulder and letting his thumb trace the line of her jaw. "I can't thank you enough for staying here so that she can be back home."

"I've learned that Gott made me a helper. This is what I do best," she said. "But I wanted to talk about Suzie. Why didn't you tell me she asked you about the plastic surgery?"

His brows rose as he considered the question. "I didn't think it was 'a big deal,' as the youngies say. It wasn't hard to talk her out of it."

"Oh, Aaron." She sighed. "I had pushed it out of my mind, but I couldn't stop worrying about it. Suzie clung to the idea like a dog with a bone. I was afraid she would run off and do something dangerous. I have to admit, I was also afraid that you would feel the need to push us away if the surgery defied church rules. It's really a vanity, and the Bible tells us not to value the flesh."

His blue eyes were full of light, thoughtful, concerned. "We could discuss the rules of the Ordnung," he said, putting his hands on her shoulders, "but dear Collette, it hurts me that you think I would cut you and Suzie off so readily."

Tears filled her eyes as she looked up at him. "I love you so much, Aaron. I don't want to lose you."

"You will never lose my love. Never." He swept her off her feet, and she felt light and delicate and cherished in his arms. In that moment, she knew with confidence that they would always be together. Together in love.

Chapter 34

Sunny the mule gave his distinctive bray as he pulled the Lapp buggy down the road. Miriam leaned toward the open window to call to him. "Don't worry! We'll get you back home to your sweet Annie soon!" She turned to Collette to explain: "Sunny follows her everywhere. Annie has always been good with animals, but these two have a special bond. The other day, at suppertime, Sunny came right up on the back porch and tried to follow Annie in the door! It was quite a commotion when Sunny made it into the mudroom but didn't know where to go from there!"

The two women laughed together as their buggy rolled along. They had just left the general store in town, where they had found disposable tablecloths, napkins, and plates in emerald and gold, perfect for the Christmas theme of Collette and Aaron's wedding.

"I think Sunny's a smart one," Collette said. "He got right close to the kitchen, where the carrots are stored."

They chuckled again, and Miriam settled back in the seat with a cozy feeling of contentment. She was grateful that Gott had brought this good woman into her life, and pleased as punch that the bishop had finally realized Collette was the woman he should spend the rest of his life with. She had never seen Collette so happy. What a joy it had been, planning the small wedding with Collette! Her friend insisted on keeping it simple, but there was so much fun in attending to the small details like Collette's bridal dress and assembling the ingredients for a delicious meal. So often in life, there was joy to be had in the planning.

They passed a small house with half of its roof shingles removed, revealing a scrappy gray material. A handful of Amish men clung to the house like giant ants; they hung from ladders, crawled along the roof, and hoisted supplies up on a pulley. "Someone's getting a new roof," Miriam said. "Good timing. Better check for leaks and seal things up right tight and cozy before winter's cold comes along."

"Aaron had Doug Kraybill's crew come out and patch Dinah's roof last week," Collette said. "Her house is getting in shape, but I wish she'd move in with us after the wedding. She's a joy to have around."

"You keep working on her," Miriam advised. "How can she resist the love of family?"

Collette nodded. "Did your parents get off safely on their trip back to Michigan?"

"They did." Miriam sighed, surprised that she truly missed having her parents around now. She shared that the visit had helped everyone re-establish relations. All the children had enjoyed the chance to get to know their grandparents once again. "Dat is no stranger to life on a farm, and he proved to be a big help and a good companion for Alvie and Sam. And Mem was a huge help with some sewing projects, which I'm simply not cut out for."

"We all have our strengths and weaknesses," Collette said.

"That's so true. I think Mem felt good to be needed again, and the more sewing and embroidery she did, the sharper her mind seemed to get. I hope she keeps up with her crafts at home. And the young folks—they really make a person live in the here and now."

"No kidding. After years of ease, my Suzie seems to come home with new challenges every day now," Collette admitted. "I'm blessed that Aaron has more patience with her than I do."

Miriam nodded. "Every mother loses her marbles with her own at times." She pulled the reins and applied the brake as they approached a stop sign, where they waited for a white delivery truck to pass by. "One more stop for us," Miriam said. "If I turn on Foxhole Road, it'll take us to Netta Kraybill's place. I thought we would order the chickens for the wedding supper from her."

"Good idea," Collette agreed. "I've heard that the chickens she raises are delicious."

"Very tasty," Miriam agreed, then bit her bottom lip as she made the turn. She didn't want to say too much; she wouldn't lie, but she didn't want to admit there was a hidden motive in making the visit to Netta's place. There was a surprise waiting, one that would take some navigation. Miriam believed Collette would greet the matter with her usual kind heart.

At the home of Jerry and Netta Kraybill, Miriam parked the buggy in front of the house and led Collette around to the side door, where a hand-painted sign read: FREE RANGE CHICKENS. NO SUNDAY SALES. She was about to knock on the side door when she saw a few people out in the yard, huddled around the fencing near the chicken coop. Netta seemed to be giving instructions to three young men, who were trying to anchor a sagging post.

Miriam gave a wave. "We've come to order some chickens."

"Be right there," Netta called before she continued speaking with the young men.

When Collette caught up, Miriam explained that the fenced-off area had been built so the chickens could roam free without getting attacked by predators.

"And that chicken coop looks to be in good shape," Collette said. "I'd say Netta's chickens are living a good life."

Netta joined them, ruddy-cheeked and smiling. "We're in the middle of fixing the fence. Do you want to come inside? I've got coffee on the stove."

"We won't hold you up. We just wanted to order some chickens for the wedding in December," Collette said. "We're thinking ten birds, unless yours are large."

"I'll put you in the book for ten, and I'll give you the friends and family discount, too. We're happy to see the bishop finally getting married, and to a right good woman."

"Denki," Collette said, then turned to Miriam. "I guess that's all for now. Should we head out?"

"One more thing." From the corner of her eye, Miriam saw one of the young men approach them. The ridge of his brow and those dark blue eyes were just as distinctive as his father's features. She had never met him formally, but she easily recognized him. "Those are Netta's sons Ephraim and Jacob over there working on the fence. But this young man," she said, clapping a hand on his shoulder, "this young man is someone you need to talk with."

Collette's eyes opened wide as she turned to study the young man. She seemed confused for a moment, then, she gasped in surprise. "I'd know those blue eyes anywhere. You're Mose, Aaron's son."

Netta nodded sternly as she stared at Mose. "He's been here with us for about a week now, and a right good worker. I don't mind him staying on, just as long as he sets things aright with his father." She folded her arms. "I'll leave you folks to straighten that out." Leaving Mose staring awkwardly at the ground, she turned and returned to the fence.

"Mose," Collette began tentatively, "I'm glad to see you back. I don't know if you got the news, but I'm Collette Yoder. I'm going to marry your father in a few weeks."

"I heard." His gaze remained focused on the dirt at their feet. "Jacob's my friend. He reached out to me awhile back. Told me that my father had been asking for me to come home."

"Your father would love to see you, Mose. He'd want nothing more than to have you come home."

"I'm not sure that house is my home anymore." When he looked up, Mose's blue eyes were icy with disdain.

In that look, Miriam saw the pain and confusion that boy must have suffered in the past few years. Her heart ached to reassure him, but she knew she was an outsider in this conversation.

"Listen, I know I'm a stranger to you," Collette said. "But I've gotten to know your sisters, and I hope that you'll give me a chance. The door is open for you, Mose. Your father wants to put the disagreements and anger between you two in the past. Can't you come home and give it a try?"

"You don't understand." He stabbed at a stone in the dirt with the toe of his boot. "You didn't know our mem. You can't take her place just because you move in and clean the house."

"I spoke with your mother a few times at church," she said. "She was a right good woman, but nay, I didn't know her well. Tell me about her."

He held his boot still, surprised by the question. "Are you just trying to get me to talk?"

"I truly want to know," Collette said. "Your father and I are going to be married, Mose. That's a bond between Aaron and me that I cherish. But our marriage was never meant to be a continuation of his life with your mother. I learned early on that there'd be only trouble if I tried to linger in her shadow."

"How's that different from taking her place?"

"I'm not here to fill Dorcas's shoes, which would be impossible by the way. Everything I hear about her says that she was a gracious woman, probably more patient than me, and certainly a better singer."

"Probably," he said, stabbing at the stone with his toe. "So then, why are you here?"

"Because Gott, in His wondrous blessings, has brought me together with your father, and for that, I am happy and ever grateful. Gott doesn't make mistakes, Mose, so I know I'm in the right place at the right time. I believe Gott brought you back here for a reason, too. I'm lacking in His wisdom, so I don't know exactly what that reason is. But something tells me the Almighty has called you to make peace with your father."

Mose lifted his gaze slowly. "Maybe."

"Our door is open for you, always," Collette said firmly. "Please, come by. It would mean the world to your father. He has so much to discuss with you."

"You make it sound so simple, but it's not." Now there was regret in Mose's eyes. "We had some bad blood between us. I'm not proud of the things I did, but he has a standard that no human person could ever reach." He shook his head. "I can't stand to disappoint him again."

"Please," Collette said, touching his arm. "Please promise me that you'll think about it. At least visit with your father. I'm sure it would do both of you worlds of good."

He let out a heavy sigh. "I'll think on it, but don't tell my dat I'm here. The last thing I need is him coming after me."

"He wouldn't do you any harm," Collette insisted.

"Promise me you won't tell him I'm here."

Collette shot a questioning look at Miriam, who shrugged. What choice did she have if she wanted to maintain Mose's trust? "I won't tell him for now. But after we're married, there'll be no secrets."

"Whatever." He nodded toward the fence. "I need to get back to work."

He headed over toward the chicken coop, leaving Collette and Miriam to watch.

"I pray that he finds his way home," Miriam said. "You know, Mose used to be friends with my Sam, part of his buddy group at one time. He's a good fellow. He just took a wrong turn on the road, but that doesn't mean he won't find his way back."

"I pray you're right," Collette said.

Moments later, as Netta walked them to their buggy, Miriam waited until Collette climbed inside, then spoke quietly to Netta. "When you deliver the chickens to the Troyer house, make sure you send Mose to make the delivery."

Netta smiled. "Why, Miriam Lapp, I do believe you're trying to bring this family together."

"Trying," Miriam admitted. "But I'm powerless to work a miracle. Pray that Gott will bless their reunion."

Netta nodded. "Thy will be done."

Chapter 35

As November rolled by, the days grew colder and frost painted the ground and rooftops at night. The change of season made Collette happy, as it brought them closer to December, the month of their wedding.

Thanksgiving was celebrated by having their families joined together at the Troyer farm. Suzie, Tess, Amy, and Laura helped Collette prepare the delicious meal, while Harlan and Clyde chopped a good amount of wood for the fire. Essie baked two scrumptious pies—shoofly and strawberry rhubarb—that didn't last long. Laura and Clyde's little ones brought a special joy to the celebration, and Collette relished the notion that, a few months from now, there'd be another grandchild in the house. Throughout the day, Miriam watched the road, hoping to see young Mose walking up the lane to his home. When he didn't arrive, she prayed that he remained safe, and that he would come to visit his father soon.

With less than two weeks left until the wedding, Collette began to move a few things from Dinah's place to Aaron's home. Her sewing machine, a rocking chair that Harlan had built for her, and some boxes of winter items, such as scarves, mittens, and boots.

"Your rocker fits perfectly in this corner," Dinah commented one afternoon when they were knitting together over hot mugs of tea in Aaron's living room. Although Dinah was now mobile and independent, most days she accompanied Collette to the Troyer house to help with the cooking and keep Collette company. "It won't take much for you and Suzie to settle in here now."

"I'm looking forward to it," Collette said. "Though I wish you'd come with us. Why don't you? We'd love to have you here, under this roof with us."

"I'm fine puttering around on my own."

"But you know Aaron worries about you all alone." Collette leaned closer to Dinah, hoping her eyes reflected her concern. "I worry, too."

"You know what they say about too many women in the house. A kitchen is only big enough for one woman."

It was a familiar discussion. Collette and Aaron had tried to woo Dinah to come live with them, but the older woman resisted giving up her independence. Collette understood Dinah's stance, but she would miss Dinah's daily company.

When they'd finished their tea, Dinah went into Aaron's office to nap on the daybed they'd added for her. With a hearty beef barley soup on the stove and bread dough rising, Collette set to work cleaning the shelves of the pantry, which showed serious signs of gunk, crumbs, and neglect. She was elbow deep in a bucket of soapy water when there was a knock on the back door.

She looked up from the bucket, wringing out her rag and peering toward the back windows. Who was that? Could it be Mose, returning home?

Quick as a bunny she dropped the rag on the counter, wiped her hands on her kitchen apron, and hurried to the door.

But it wasn't the prodigal son. Smiling on the other side of the window was Sally Renno.

"Sally!" Collette beckoned her inside. "Come in! I was surprised to find you standing there."

"I hope it's not rude to drop in, but I wanted to see you before I left town. My time here is coming to an end, and I have much to thank you for."

"Oh, please, sit down." Collette's nerves fluttered like butterflies, as she hadn't really talked to Sally since her engagement to Aaron. She offered Sally tea, and put the kettle on to boil. "I'm sorry to hear you're going. I know Linda was hoping you would stay. Heading back to Erie?"

"Back north to Erie." Sally took a seat at the kitchen table and let her shawl drop to the back of the chair. "But I won't be staying there long. I'm going to close up my shop and pack everything up."

"Really?" Collette was surprised. "No more quilting?"

"Oh, I'll always be a quilter. But I'm taking my craft on the road." Sally chuckled. "My sister is a bit annoyed with me, but I'm moving to Indiana. Can you believe it? Me, the mousiest woman on earth, and I'm packing up my things and following a man to Indiana."

"Oh." Collette blinked. "Oh, my. That's quite a change." She dropped two tea bags in cups and sat down opposite Sally. "I think you need to tell me the whole story."

"I think I do. It begins with the bishop, your beau."

Collette felt her face heat up. "I never intended to steal him from you."

"He was never mine. You see, my sister wanted me to marry the bishop. It was a matter of convenience for Linda. It would have kept me near her, and it would have made for very social dinners, since Len and Aaron are already good friends."

Collette rose to answer the whistling kettle. "And didn't you tell me you were interested in him?"

"I was." Sally smoothed her fingertips over the edge of the table. "I thought I was He's a wonderful man, but really, I think I was in love with the notion of love. There was no spark between us."

"No spark," Collette repeated, placing the steaming mug in front of Sally.

"Now I know he was probably already in love with you. So I backed away, and I told my sister that I was done with matchmaking. Enough was enough. I gave up on love. Linda kept pushing, but the funniest thing happened. After I gave up on finding love, it found me." Sally dunked the tea bag a few times. "One day while Linda was talking with the bishop, I started talking to Seth. You know, the deacon?"

"Seth King?"

"He's such a kind man. So funny and fun to be with. Well, he's funny to me. He always makes me laugh. He has this wonderful gift for conversation. He can talk to anyone and make them feel good about themselves."

"That's a good description of Deacon Seth," Collette said.

"Just talking about him makes my heart swell with love." Sally pressed a hand to one cheek, chuckling. "I know I sound like a teen on rumspringa, but I've never felt this way. We started writing each other in secret. Actually, we're still exchanging secret letters. My sister knows how I feel about Seth, but she's against the match. Seth is moving to Indiana soon, and he wants me to come along. We'll be in separate quarters, of course. At least until we're married."

"So he's your betrothed?"

Sally nodded. "We're going to get married, no matter what Linda says. She wants me parked here in Joyful River, so we can live close to each other."

"Maybe Seth can stay?" Collette suggested.

"He would probably do that for me, but the truth of the matter is that I'd be happy to marry him in Indiana. I don't need to be living in my sister's shadow. In fact, I think it would be better for me to have some distance from Linda. And it's so exciting for Seth and me to be blazing a new trail. He has a lifetime of memories here—good memories—but a new town will make it easier for him to make a fresh start."

Collette put her mug on the table and shook her head. "Sally, I am so very happy for you."

"And I'm grateful to you. That day in the kitchen, you showed me that it's possible to stand up to my sister. You taught me that a woman has to follow her instincts, listen to her heart. I'm most grateful."

Collette reached across the table and squeezed Sally's hand. "To tell the truth, I was only learning that lesson myself."

"Well, then, it was a lesson learned by both of us."

"So." Collette patted Sally's hand. "You are quite serious about this. Gott has led you to Seth King . . . ."

"And I would follow him to the moon and back!" Sally said, gesturing dramatically toward the window, leading both women to chuckle.

"I'm so happy for you and Seth. And that's quite a story. It's a lesson for us all, that we might find love when we least expect it. I'm grateful that you've shared it with me. And a bit shocked that I inspired you."

Sally nodded. "You know, the best quilts tell a little story, and one day I'll make a quilt called Indiana. It will be about finding love, striking out on your own, and following your heart."

"What a beautiful quilt that will be." Sally's tale of love warmed Collette's heart.

"Mmm. And speaking of beautiful quilts." Sally stood and put her empty mug beside the sink. "I almost forgot your gift. I'll be right back." She went out the back door, prompting Collette to lean up against the window to see outside. Sally reached into the buggy that was parked outside. When she stepped away from the buggy, her arms were wrapped around a large, white mound.

"Good grief!" Collette said, leaning out the door. "This looks like a large gift."

Sally laughed, holding the bulky item against her chest. "You could say that it's large enough for two. You and Aaron!" She stepped into the kitchen and looked around. "Shall I spread it on the table?"

That was the moment Collette realized it was a quilt. "Oh, no! I wouldn't want to get anything sticky on it. Come." She motioned Sally into the living room. "We'll open it on the sofa."

The backing was a creamy white, but when Sally unfolded it, vibrant, warm colors swarmed in large intersecting rings. Lavender, emerald, purple, grass green, and turquoise formed blazes of color in the wide circles sewn against the creamy background.

"Oh, Sally, I love it!" Collette pressed her palms to her cheeks in a moment of sheer joy. "It's so hopeful and balanced. Such a beautiful contrast between light and dark. And I love the colors. That lavender. You must have squeezed it from a lilac tree!"

"That was the idea," Sally said, smiling. "And do you know this pattern? It's called a double wedding ring quilt, which I thought would be perfect for a wedding gift. I started working on it the minute I heard you two were engaged to be married."

"It's so beautiful!"

"That's because it's your story," Sally said with a twinkle in her eyes.

"It's a reflection of the skill and love of the quiltmaker," Collette said. "I can't thank you enough."

Sally smoothed her fingertips over one of the colorful ring appliqués on the quilt. "My joy comes from knowing my quilts have a good purpose."

"We'll treasure it, always." Collette spread her arms wide and the two women embraced. It reassured Collette to know that they had both struggled but found their way to love. "Gott bless you, Sally. Best wishes to you and Seth in Indiana."

A new start in Indiana, and a new start here at home. So much hope and love! Collette thanked Gott for the blue skies ahead.

It was a Saturday afternoon, just four days until the wedding, and with Aaron out helping Seth pack up for his move, the girls and women had taken over the house for a sewing bee.

Tess had proven herself to be a whiz with scissors and pinking shears, pinning and cutting out patterns and then trimming the loose threads along finished seams. Amy knew how to run her mother's sewing machine, working the treadle steadily to give it power. Suzie had proven to be a quick learner with needle and thread, which left her to work with Dinah and Collette to hem all four new dresses that would be worn by family at the wedding.

With Collette's lavender wedding dress complete, and

the girls' dresses done except for hemming and trimming, Amy had decided it was time to try them on.

"Would you look at that," Dinah said as the girls paraded out of the study in a lovely flow of emerald-green fabric. "Our three girls have turned into three women."

"I know!" Tess exclaimed, smoothing the fabric over her hips. "I think this is the first dress I've ever had with darts in the bodice!"

"The dresses are so pretty," Suzie said, twirling to watch the dress skirt swirl around her legs. "Aren't they beautiful, Mem?"

"You girls are the ones who are beautiful," Collette said. "Gott's creations." It was not lost on her that her daughter's hands were at her side instead of covering the scar on her face. Although she'd noticed that Suzie was still self-conscious at times, she had become more comfortable in public.

"You can thank Amy for cranking away at that sewing machine for days on end," Dinah said.

"And Tess did most of the cutting," Amy said, going to the front window to check her faded reflection in the glass.

"It was teamwork," Tess said. "And now we just have to get these hemmed."

"That shouldn't take us long," Dinah said, threading a needle with dark green thread.

"Someone's coming." Amy stood staring out the window. "A buggy with two men, but not Dat."

Suzie and Tess joined her at the window. "Whose horse it that?" asked Tess.

"I think it's the Kraybills' chestnut mare," said Amy. "Isn't that Jacob Kraybill?"

Collette stuck her threaded needle into the pin cushion and joined the girls at the window. "Jacob must be here to deliver the chickens for the wedding supper," she said. "And the other fella is—"

"Mose!" Tess exclaimed, running from the window to the front door. "Mose is here!"

Amy pressed her hand to her mouth in amazement as she leaned closer to the window to double-check. "It's our brother," she explained to Suzie, then turned and followed her sister out the door.

What a sight the two of them were—barefoot teens wearing crisp new dresses, hopping and hobbling over the frozen stones in the path. Shrieking from the December cold, discomfort and glee at the sight of their brother. Hugging him and poking at him and tugging him toward the house.

Suzie slid an arm around Collette's waist. "Look! They're so happy to see him."

"They are, indeed." It looked as if Mose's sisters would be more successful at getting Mose home than Collette had been, as he and Jacob were now following the girls into the house, their arms full of bundles wrapped in butcher paper.

"We have ten chickens for roasting," Jacob announced as he came in the door.

"Good," Collette said, trying not to reveal the excited thumping in her chest. "I've made room in the refrigerator to store them. Mose, it's good to see you."

He nodded. "I'm just making a delivery."

"Don't say that!" Tess gave him a playful shove. "You act like you don't care about us at all."

"I do care," Mose said. "You know I do."

"Well, for me you're a few months too late," Dinah said from the chair in the corner. "I could have used your help after my surgery."

Mose removed his hat and leaned down to give his

grandmother a kiss on the cheek. "Sorry about that, Mammi. Next time you need me, let me know and I'll be there."

"I'll hold you to it," she said sternly.

Collette led the way into the kitchen, where the chickens were tucked into the open spot in the fridge. "I'm sorry you missed your father, Mose. He's been out at a meeting, but he'll be home soon."

Mose shrugged. "It's fine." He glanced over at his sisters. "Mostly, I wanted to see these two."

"Of course, you did," Tess said, "but you're not off the hook yet. You have to see Dat. You two need to make up."

Mose let out a sigh. "That's not why I'm here."

"Stay for dinner," Amy said. "Can he stay, Collette?" When Collette nodded, Amy went on. "We're having chicken and rice casserole, from Mem's recipe. You can't say no to that."

"I need to get back with Jacob," Mose said.

Jacob turned back and squinted at him. "No, you don't. I've got to get home to Henny, but why don't you stay? I'm sure the bishop can give you a ride back to my parents' place later."

"We could do that," Collette offered. "Susie and I are taking Dinah back home after supper. You could come with us."

The tension was obvious in Mose's strained smile, but he relented. "All right. I'll stay. But just for supper."

"Yay!" Tess took his hands and tugged him into the living room. "We have to get out of these dresses and finish sewing them, but we want to hear everything."

"All about your adventures," Amy said. "Where did you go, anyway?"

"Over toward Philadelphia," he said. "Though there's not much to tell. Not for your ears."

"Don't be a stick in the mud!" Tess insisted as the group disappeared back into the living room.

Watching them go, Collette thanked Gott for keeping her nerves steady. Mose was back, and she didn't fear that the world was caving in. His presence wasn't threatening her happiness with Aaron. Granted, Aaron might greet the young man with anxiety, but for Collette, she felt a strong sense that the family could be mended. Bridges could be rebuilt. One block at a time.

Some thirty minutes later, she was about to pop a tray of biscuits into the oven when she heard Aaron's buggy come around the house to the barn. She knew it would take him awhile to unhitch the buggy and give Thumper a good brushing, so she took her coat from the hook and set out to greet him.

As she crossed the yard, she watched him at work, speaking to the horse as he moved with strength and purpose. Such a strong, yet kind man. And handsome, too, with those thoughtful blue eyes and broad shoulders that made her feel sheltered and loved in his arms. She thanked Gott every day for bringing him into her life.

"Aaron," she called as the gravel road crunched under her shoes. "I want you know that we have a visitor. Mose is here."

He didn't miss a step in leading Thumper away from the shafts of the buggy, but he didn't take his gaze from her face. "Mose? Here right now?"

"In the living room." She moved forward and reached for the horse. "Go. Talk to him. I'll put Thumper away for you."

"I don't know if I can." He pressed a fist to his mouth and turned away. "I've rehearsed this a million times, but there are so many ways it could go sideways. I want him to know I love him. That he'll always be welcome here, a part of our family. But at the same time, there are rules I can't bend, principles I need to uphold. I'm a father, but also the leader of our church. I need to serve Gott before all else."

"I understand that now, Dat."

Both Collette and Aaron spun around and looked to the other side of the horse. Mose stood there, a tall dark figure against the pewter sky.

"I wasn't eavesdropping," he said. "I came out to see if you needed help with the buggy and the milking."

"But you heard," Aaron said.

"I heard."

"It's good to see you, son." Aaron's expression softened, a tenderness in his eyes. "You were missed around here."

"I missed this place. Spent many nights homesick for the family. I didn't realize how easy I had it here until I left. But it's good that I went away. I was so angry with you," Mose admitted. "So angry with Gott."

Tears filled Collette's eyes at the knowledge of the pain both men had suffered.

Aaron nodded, his eyes bright with sympathy. "You're human. We both are human beings, with flaws and weaknesses. And we both lost someone we loved dearly." He glanced down. "I confess, I made many mistakes. There were things I didn't handle well. I mistook grief for weakness, which put an impossible pressure on you and your sisters. I'm sorry, son."

"I'm sorry, too. If I stay in Joyful River, you can be sure I won't be bringing shame to the family anymore. I've put those things behind me."

Aaron touched his beard, studying his son. "'When I was a child, I spoke as a child, I understood as a child, I thought as a child. But when I became a man . . .'"

"'I put away childish things,'" Mose finished. "I know that's from the Bible."

"First Corinthians." Aaron stepped closer to Mose, lifting his arms. "Welcome home, son."

When Mose stepped into his father's arms and the two men embraced, Collette let out the breath that she'd been holding, pent up inside her. Here was the beginning of a new relationship, father and son finding their way, one day at a time.

Epilogue

"The bride wore purple."

Lizzie said the sentence aloud as she wrote it on a piece of paper with Grace looking over her shoulder.

"Do you think Mammi Lois will want to know the details of the wedding?" Grace asked. "I mean, Collette is family, but she doesn't know Mammi Lois well."

"Everyone loves a wedding," Lizzie insisted.

Collette smiled, knowing that was true. She gave Lizzie a few more details and watched as the young girl penned full sentences in excellent handwriting.

> *Collette said she chose the color because it reminded her of the first crocuses that popped out of the ground in springtime, a shade so pretty she looked forward to wearing it to church in the future. Her dress was new, sewn with help from her daughter, Suzie, Aaron's mother, Dinah, and daughters Amy and Tess. Truly a family affair. The purple dress was accompanied by a white cape and apron, and new black shoes that laced up to the ankle.*

The bride's attendants wore emerald green, in keeping with the Christmas theme celebrating our Savior's birth. Many people pitched in to make the day a special occasion for Bishop Aaron Troyer and Collette Yoder. A beautiful sheet cake celebrating the bride and groom was provided by Delilah Esh from the Amish Bakery. Some seventy guests attended. It was a small wedding by Amish standards, but not unusual when the bride and groom are widowed.

"How's that for now?" Lizzie asked, glancing up. "I can add more after the wedding supper."

"Wonderful. You're a right good writer, Lizzie," Collette said. "You should think about writing a monthly page for one of the Amish magazines."

"I would love that," Lizzie exclaimed. "But writing a letter to Mammi Lois is a good start."

Collette thanked Lizzie and Grace, who had both volunteered to work as servers come mealtime. She helped Miriam slice some bread that had cooled overnight, and then went out to the main room, where the furniture had been cleared out and replaced by benches for the ceremony.

"There's the bride," called Harlan, who was hammering some nails in to repair a wooden church bench. Although Collette didn't enjoy being the center of attention, today she felt comfortable in that role because of Aaron. She knew they had been brought together by Gott—perhaps with a few nudges from Miriam—and on this special day, she possessed the courage to stand before Gott and her family and vow to love this man now and forever.

They talked briefly about the day ahead and Harlan and Essie's future at the Dawdi House. "It seems empty without you and Suzie," Harlan said.

"Oh, you teaser." She patted his shoulder. "It's perfect for two. Even better for three or four," she said, alluding to Essie's pregnancy. "It's a wonderful place for you to start your family and save for a house of your own."

"Well, since you and Suzie aren't coming back, I reckon we're stuck there, just Essie and me." He smiled up at her. "We're in a mighty good place."

"We're both blessed by Gott," she told her son. As he returned to his work, she glanced across the room and spotted Aaron speaking to Bishop Steve Hershberger, who'd come from the nearby Plumdale church district to conduct the wedding.

The groom wore a black suit and crisp white shirt with a black bow tie. With his wide-brimmed black hat and his broad shoulders, Aaron stood tall and calm. His appearance was handsome and striking as ever, but now, knowing him as she did, she realized he was much more attractive because of the beauty within.

The ceremony started around nine, giving folks time to take care of their usual morning chores: milking cows, tending chickens, and tidying the house after breakfast. When Collette saw the familiar faces of family and close friends, she knew she was surrounded by love. Voices lifted in song to praise Gott in hymn after hymn. As was customary, the bishop took Collette and Aaron into the kitchen to speak with them privately while folks kept singing.

"Gott's message to you is to love one another," Bishop Steve told them. He spoke to them of patience and kindness, love and mercy—all the many virtues they would need to make their journey as a married couple, united by Gott. The notion of such a life together brought tears to Collette's eyes, but she felt comforted when Aaron took her hand and laced his finger through hers.

After the private talk, they returned to the larger room with the guests, where the bishop delivered a sermon. Again, the bishop spoke of the power of Gott's love, which could be multiplied like the many loaves of bread Jesus produced in a miracle to feed a crowd of people.

The message hit home for Collette, as she knew that it was Gott's love that had brought her here. The years of being a single parent, working at any job she could find, then keeping house in her few spare minutes—those difficult times had taken on deeper meaning now that she realized that it was Gott's love for her children that had kept her moving forward. And then, that terrible accident that had taken her off her feet for months. What had seemed like the great tragedy of her life had in fact brought Aaron to her side, consoling her, encouraging her, and sometimes, just sharing an afternoon with her.

Somehow, he'd known what she needed.

Sitting at Aaron's side, Collette said a silent prayer of thanks and praise that Gott had led her to this good man. In the time since they'd announced their vows, her love for him had only grown as she had a chance to see him as a father to his son, a peacemaker, a counselor of men, an advisor of women. His choices were thoughtful, his loyalty to her ardent.

This fervor, this was a love that would last all the days of their lives.

Sitting inches away from him now, Collette felt the warm glow that hummed in her veins whenever he was near. Oh, what good times they would have together! Theirs would be a house of love and laughter, a home open to family, friends, and anyone in need.

After the ceremony, Collette could barely stand to watch as the volunteers rearranged the church benches to form seats and tables for the meal. "You know, we could help," she called to Annie and Sam Lapp. "Aaron . . ." She touched her husband's arm. (*Husband! Oh, the thrill of it!*) "Aaron, help me move these benches out."

"No!" Annie and Sam Lapp called out in unison.

"The bride doesn't move benches," Annie said with an amused grin. She'd always been tall with a coltish grace. Seeing the way she could lift a bench, Collette realized the young woman was strong, too. "Go on now, and talk with your wedding guests," Annie insisted.

Collette turned to Aaron with a bemused expression, and he laughed out loud. "Dear Collette, I know you love to serve others, but today, you have a different job. You're the bride."

She felt trembly inside at the realization that he was right.

As the guests headed over to the buggy garage for the meal, Collette and Aaron were surrounded by their family. Lauren and Clyde were there with their three little ones, and more than once Collette succumbed to the temptation to sweep their middle child, Lovina, off her feet and carry her on one hip. With her wispy blond hair and blue eyes, Lovina resembled a miniature angel, and Collette had won her over with cookies during their last visit.

Harlan was there, his arm around Essie's shoulders as they congratulated Aaron and welcomed him to their family. Suzie was sandwiched between her two new sisters, Amy and Tess, and together the three young women hounded Mose, whose presence at the wedding seemed a miracle to Collette.

"What a nice Sunday church outfit you have," Tess said, drawing attention to Mose. "Where did you get such a fine jacket, young man?"

"Um, Walmart?" he said, squinting at her.

"Don't tease Mose," Suzie said. "I'm glad you're here. Now the whole family can be together."

"I'm glad, too," Amy agreed. "We missed you, big brother."

"Time for a hug," Tess announced as the three girls closed in on Mose to squeeze him in a group hug.

Aaron and Harlan chuckled at their antics.

"Hey!" Mose cried through his laughter. "Give the prodigal son a little space. In case you haven't noticed, I'm a grown man now. Not a rag doll to hug all day."

"You'll always be my big brother," Tess said, patting him on the back.

He rolled his eyes, but tolerated her act of affection.

"Tess is right," Aaron said, taking in all family members with a sweeping glance. "No matter what, we will always be family."

"Our family," Collette agreed. Carried on a wave of joy, Collette couldn't help but rise up on her toes and kiss his cheek. This was just the beginning of their road together. No one knew where that path would lead, but oh, with Aaron by her side, she would enjoy the journey.